About the Author

... ly a French/Engli... ...d careers to con... ...appy demands of m... ... much a people person, and always interested in ...ionships, she finds the world of romance fiction a ...ling one and the challenge of creating her own cast ...haracters very addictive.

...A® Award-winner **Anne McAllister** was born in ...fornia and spent formative summer holidays on a ...ll ranch in Colorado, where she developed her idea ...he perfect hero', as well as a weakness for dark-...ed, handsome lone-wolf type guys. She found one ...e university library and they've now been sharing ...oily ever afters' for over thirty years.

...ntelle Shaw enjoyed a happy childhood making ...ries in her head. Always an avid reader, Chantelle ...covered Mills & Boon as a teenager and during the ...mes when her children refused to sleep, she would pace the floor with a baby in one hand and a book in ...er! Twenty years later she decided to write one ...own. Writing takes up most of Chantelle's spare ...t she also enjoys gardening and walking. She ...does...t find domestic chores so pleasurable!

000003054164

The Gorgeous Greeks

COLLECTION

Gorgeous Greeks: A Greek Affair

EMMA DARCY

ANNE McALLISTER

CHANTELLE SHAW

MIX
Paper from
responsible sources
FSC
FSC C007454

This book is produced from independently certified FSC™ paper
to ensure responsible forest management.

For more information visit: www.harpercollins.co.uk/green

Printed and bound in Spain
by CPI, Barcelona

MILLS & BOON

First Published in Great Britain 2020
By Mills & Boon, an imprint of HarperCollins*Publishers*
1 London Bridge Street, London, SE1 9GF

GORGEOUS GREEKS: A GREEK AFFAIR
© 2020 Harlequin Books S.A.

An Offer She Can't Refuse © 2012 Emma Darcy
Breaking the Greek's Rules © 2012 Barbara Schenck
The Greek's Acquisition © 2012 Chantelle Shaw

ISBN: 978-0-263-28174-3

AN OFFER SHE CAN'T REFUSE

EMMA DARCY

CHAPTER ONE

'It's like a great big sail, Mama,' Theo said in awe, staring up at the most famous building in Dubai—Burj Al Arab, the only seven-star hotel in the world.

Tina Savalas smiled at her beautiful five-year-old son. 'Yes, it's meant to look like that.'

Built on a man-made island surrounded by the sea, the huge white glittering structure had all the glorious elegance of a sail billowed by the wind. Tina was looking forward to seeing as much of its interior as she could. Her sister, Cassandra, had declared it absolutely fabulous, a must-see on their two-day stopover before flying on to Athens.

Actually staying in the hotel was way too expensive—thousands of dollars a night—which was fine for the super-rich to whom the cost was totally irrelevant. People like Theo's father. No doubt *he* had occupied one of the luxury suites with butler on his way back to Greece from Australia, having put his *charming episode* with her behind him.

Tina shut down on the bitter thought. Being left pregnant by Ari Zavros was her own stupid fault. She'd been a completely blind naive fool to have believed he was as much in love with her as she was with him. Sheer fantasy land. Besides, how could she regret having Theo? He was the most adorable little boy, and from time to time, knowing Ari was missing out on his son gave her considerable secret satisfaction.

Their taxi stopped at the checkpoint gates which prevented anyone but paying guests from proceeding to the hotel. Her mother produced the necessary paperwork, showing confirmation that they had booked for the early afternoon tea session. Even that was costing them one hundred and seventy dollars each, but they had decided it was a once-in-a-lifetime experience they should indulge in.

The security man waved them on and the taxi drove slowly over the bridge which led to the hotel entrance, allowing them time to take in the whole amazing setting.

'Look, Mama, a camel!' Theo cried, delighted at recognising the animal standing on a side lawn.

'Yes, but not a real one, Theo. It's a statue.'

'Can I sit on it?'

'We'll ask if you can, but later, when we're leaving.'

'And take a photo of me on it so I can show my friends,' he pressed eagerly.

'I'm sure we'll have plenty of great photos to show from this trip,' Tina assured him.

They alighted from the taxi and were welcomed into the grand lobby of the hotel which was so incredibly opulent, photographs couldn't possibly capture all of its utter magnificence. They simply stood and stared upwards at the huge gold columns supporting the first few tiers of inner balconies of too many floors to count, the rows of their scalloped ceilings graduating from midnight-blue to aqua and green and gold at the top with lots of little spotlights embedded in them, twinkling like stars.

When they finally lowered their heads, right in front of them and dividing two sets of escalators, was a wonderful cascade of dancing fountains, each level repeating the same range of colours in the tower of ceilings. The escalators were flanked by side-walls which were gigantic aquariums where hosts of gorgeous tropical fish darted and glided around the underwater rocks and foliage.

'Oh, look at the fish, Mama!' Theo cried, instantly entranced by them.

'This truly is amazing,' Tina's mother murmured in awe. 'Your father always liked the architecture of the old world. He thought nothing could beat the palaces and the cathedrals that were built in the past, but this is absolutely splendid in its own way. I wish he was here to see it.'

He had died a year ago and her mother still wore black in mourning. Tina missed him, too. Despite his disappointment in her—getting pregnant to a man who was not interested in partnering her for life—he had given her the support she'd needed and been a marvellous grandfather to Theo, proud that she'd named her son after him.

It was a terrible shame that he hadn't lived long enough to see Cassandra married. Her older sister had done everything right; made a success of her modelling career without the slightest taint of scandal in her private life, fell in love with a Greek photographer—the *right* nationality—who wanted their wedding to take place on Santorini, the most romantic Greek island of all. He would have been bursting with pride, walking Cassandra down the aisle next week, his *good* girl.

But at least the *bad* girl had given him the pleasure of having a little boy in the family. Having only two daughters and no son had been another disappointment to her father. Tina told herself she had made up for her *mistake* with Theo. And she'd been on hand to take over the management of his restaurant, doing everything *his* way when he'd become too ill to do it all himself. He'd called her a *good girl* then.

Yet while Tina thought she had redeemed herself in her father's eyes, she didn't feel good inside. Not since Ari Zavros had taken all that she was and walked away from her as though she was nothing. The sense of being totally crushed had never gone away. Theo held her together. He made life worth living. And there were things to enjoy, like this hotel with all its splendours.

There was another glorious fountain at the top of the escalator. They were escorted down a corridor to the elevator which would whiz them up to the SkyView Bar on the twenty-seventh floor. They walked over a large circle of mosaic tiles, a blazing sun at its centre, over a carpet shaped like a fish in red and gold. Her mother pointed out vases of tightly clustered red roses, dozens of them in each perfect pompom-like arrangement. The doors of the elevator were patterned in blue and gold—everything unbelievably rich.

On arriving in the shimmering gold lobby of the bar, they were welcomed again and escorted into the dining area where the decor was a stunning blue and green, the ceiling designed like waves with white crests. They were seated in comfortable armchairs at a table by a window which gave a fantastic view of the city of Dubai and the man-made island of Palm Jumeirah where the very wealthy owned mansions with sand and sea frontage.

A whole world away from her life in every sense, Tina thought, but she was having a little taste of it today, smiling at the waiter who handed them a menu listing dozens of varieties of tea from which they could choose, as many different ones as they liked to try throughout the afternoon. He poured them glasses of champagne to go with their first course which was a mix of fresh berries with cream. Tina didn't know how she was going to get through all the marvellous food listed—probably not—but she was determined on enjoying all she could.

Her mother was smiling.

Theo was wide-eyed at the view.

This was a good day.

Ari Zavros was bored. It had been a mistake to invite Felicity Fullbright on this trip to Dubai with him, though it had certainly proved he couldn't bear to have her as a full-time partner. She had a habit of notching up experiences as though she had a bucket list that had to be filled. Like having to do afternoon tea at the Burj Al Arab hotel.

'I've done afternoon tea at The Ritz and The Dorchester in London, at the Waldorf Astoria in New York, and at The Empress on Vancouver Island. I can't miss out on this one, Ari,' she had insisted. 'The sheikhs are mostly educated in England, aren't they? They probably do it better than the English.'

No relaxing in between his business talks on the Palm Jumeirah development. They had to visit the indoor ski slope, Atlantis underwater, and of course the gold souks where she had clearly expected him to buy her whatever she fancied. She was not content with just his company and he was sick to death of hers.

The only bright side of Felicity Fullbright was she did shut up in bed where she used her mouth in many pleasurable ways. Which had swayed him into asking her to accompany him on this trip. However, the hope that she might be compatible with him on other grounds was now comprehensively smashed. The good did not balance out the bad and he'd be glad to be rid of her tomorrow.

Once they flew into Athens he would pack her off back to London. No way was he going to invite her to his cousin's wedding on Santorini. His father could rant and rave as much as he liked about its being time for Ari to shed his bachelor life. Marriage to the Fullbright heiress was not going to happen.

There had to be someone somewhere he could tolerate as his wife. He just had to keep looking and assessing whether a marriage would work well enough. His father was right. It *was* time to start his own family. He did want children, always enjoying the time he spent with his nephews. However, finding the right woman to partner him in parenthood was not proving easy.

Being head over heels in love like his cousin, George, was not a requirement. In fact, having been scorched by totally mindless passion in his youth, Ari had never wanted to feel so *possessed* by a woman again. He had a cast-iron shield up against being sucked into any blindly driven emotional involvement. A relationship either satisfied him on enough levels to be happily viable or it didn't—a matter of completely rational judgement.

His *dissatisfaction* with Felicity was growing by the minute. Right now she was testing his patience, taking millions of photographs of the inside of the hotel. It wasn't enough to simply look and enjoy, share the visual pleasure of it with him. Using the camera to the nth degree was more important, taking pictures that she would sift through endlessly and discard most of them. Another habit he hated. He liked to live in the moment.

Finally, *finally,* they got in the elevator and within minutes were being led to their window table in the SkyView Bar. But did Felicity sit down and enjoy the view? No, the situation wasn't perfect for her.

'Ari, I don't like this table,' she whispered, grasping his arm to stop him from sitting down.

'What's wrong with it?' he asked tersely, barely containing his exasperation with her constant self-centred demands.

She nodded and rolled her eyes, indicating the next

table along. 'I don't want to be next to a child. He'll probably play up and spoil our time here.'

Ari looked at the small family group that Felicity didn't like. A young boy—five or six years old—stood at the window, staring down at the wave-shaped Jumeirah Beach Hotel. Seated beside the child on one side was a very handsome woman—marvellous facial bones like Sophia Loren's—dark wavy hair unashamedly going grey, probably the boy's grandmother. On the other side with her back turned to him was another woman, black hair cropped short in a modern style, undoubtedly younger, a slimmer figure, and almost certainly the boy's mother.

'He won't spoil the food or the tea, Felicity, and if you haven't noticed, all the other tables are taken.'

They'd been late arriving, even later because of feeding her camera in the lobby. Having to wait for Felicity to be satisfied with whatever she wanted was testing his temper to an almost intolerable level.

She placed a pleading hand on his arm, her big blue eyes promising a reward if he indulged her. 'But I'm sure if you ask, something better could be arranged.'

'I won't put other people out,' he said, giving her a hard, quelling look. 'Just sit down, Felicity. Enjoy being here.'

She pouted, sighed, flicked her long blonde hair over her shoulder in annoyance, and finally sat.

The waiter poured them champagne, handed them menus, chatted briefly about what was on offer, then quickly left them before Felicity could kick up another fuss which would put him in a difficult position.

'Why do they have all those chairs on the beach set out in rows, Yiayia?'

The boy's voice was high and clear and carried, bringing an instant grimace to Felicity's pouty mouth. Ari recognised the accent as Australian, yet the boy had used the Greek word for grandmother, arousing his curiosity.

'The beach belongs to the hotel, Theo, and the chairs are set out for the guests so they will be comfortable,' the older woman answered, her English thick with a Greek accent.

'They don't do that at Bondi,' the boy remarked.

'No. That's because Bondi is a public beach for anyone to use and set up however they like on the sand.'

The boy turned to her, frowning at the explanation. 'Do you mean I couldn't go to that beach down there, Yiayia?'

He was a fine-looking boy, very pleasing features and fairish hair. Oddly enough he reminded Ari of himself as a child.

'Not unless you were staying in the hotel, Theo,' his grandmother replied.

'Then I think Bondi is better,' the boy said conclusively, turning back to the view.

An egalitarian Australian even at this tender age, Ari thought, remembering his own experiences of the people's attitudes in that country.

Felicity huffed and whined, 'We're going to have to listen to his prattle all afternoon. I don't know why people bring children to places like this. They should be left with nannies.'

'Don't you like children, Felicity?' Ari enquired, hoping she would say no, which would comprehensively wipe out any argument his father might give him over his rejection of this marital candidate.

'In their place,' she snapped back at him.

Out of sight, out of mind, was what she meant.

'I think family is important,' he drawled. 'And I have no objection to any family spending time together, any-where.'

Which shut her up, temporarily.

This was going to be a *long* afternoon.

Tina felt the nape of her neck prickling at the sound of the man's voice coming from the table next to theirs. The deep mellifluous tone was an electric reminder of another voice that had seduced her into believing all the sweet things it had said to her, believing they had meant she was more special than any other woman in the world.

It couldn't be Ari, could it?

She was torn by the temptation to look.

Which was utterly, utterly stupid, letting thoughts of him take over her mind when she should be enjoying this wonderfully decadent afternoon tea.

Ari Zavros was out of her life. Well and truly out of . Six years ago he'd made the parting from her abso-tely decisive, no coming back to Australia, no inter-t in some future contact. She had been relegated to *ond memory,* and she certainly didn't want *the fond *mory* revived here and now, if by some rotten coin-ence it was Ari sitting behind her.

It wouldn't be him, anyway.

The odds against it were astronomical.

All the same, it was better not to look, better to keep her back turned to the man behind her. If it was Ari, if he caught her looking and recognised her...it was a stomach-curdling thought. No way was she prepared for a face-to-face meeting with him, especially not with her mother and Theo looking on, becoming involved.

This couldn't happen.

It wouldn't happen.

Her imagination was making mountains out of no more than a tone of voice. Ridiculous! The man was with a woman. She'd heard the plummy English voice complaining about Theo's presence—a really petty complaint because Theo was always well-behaved. She shouldn't waste any attention on them. Her mind fiercely dictated ignoring the couple and concentrating on the pleasure of being here.

She leaned forward, picked up her cup and sipped the wonderfully fragrant *Jasmin Pearls*. They had already eaten a marvellous slice of Beef Wellington served warm with a beetroot puree. On their table now was a stand shaped like the Burj, its four tiers presenting a yummy selection of food on colourful glass plates.

At the top were small sandwiches made with different types of bread—egg, smoked salmon, cream cheese with sun-dried tomatoes, cucumber and cream cheese. Other tiers offered seafood vol-au-vents with prawns, choux pastry chicken with seeded mustard, a beef sandwich, and basil, tomato and bocconcini cheese on squid ink bread. It was impossible to eat everything. Predictably,

Theo zeroed in on the chicken, her mother anything with cheese, and the seafood she loved was all hers.

A waiter came around with a tray offering replenishments but they shook their heads, knowing there was so much more to taste—fruit cake, scones with and without raisins and an assortment of spreads; strawberry and rose petal jam, clotted cream, a strawberry mousse and tangy passionfruit.

Tina refused to let the reminder of Ari Zavros ruin her appetite. There wasn't much conversation going on at the table behind her anyway. Mostly it was the woman talking, carrying on in a snobby way, comparing this afternoon tea to others she'd had in famous hotels. Only the occasional murmur of reply came from the man.

'I'm so glad we stopped in Dubai,' her mother remarked, gazing at the view. 'There's so much amazing, creative architecture in this city. That hotel shaped like a wave just below us, the stunning buildings we passed on the way here. And to think it's all happened in the space of what…thirty years?'

'Something like that,' Tina murmured.

'It shows what can be done in these modern times.'

'With the money to do it,' Tina dryly reminded her.

'Well, at least they have the money. They're not bankrupting the country like the aristocrats did in Europe for their grand palaces in the old days. And all this has to be a drawcard for tourists, bringing money into the country.'

'True.' Tina smiled. 'I'm glad we came here, too. It certainly is amazing.'

Her mother leaned forward and whispered, 'Seated at the next table is an incredibly handsome man. I think he must be a movie star. Take a look, Tina, and see if you recognise him.'

Her stomach instantly cramped. Ari Zavros was an incredibly handsome man. Her mother nodded encouragingly, expecting her to glance around. Hadn't she already decided it couldn't—wouldn't—be him? One quick look would clear this silly fear. *Just do it. Get it over with.*

One quick look…

The shock of seeing the man she'd never expected to see again hit her so hard she barely found wits enough to give her mother a reply.

'I've never seen him in a movie.'

And thank God the turning of her head towards him hadn't caught his attention!

Ari!—still a beautiful lion of a man with his thick mane of wavy honey-brown hair streaked through with golden strands, silky smooth olive skin, his strongly masculine face softened by a beautifully sculptured full-lipped mouth, and made compelling by thickly lashed amber eyes—eyes that Theo had inherited, and thank God her mother hadn't noticed that likeness!

'Well, he must be *someone,*' her mother said in bemusement. 'One of the beautiful people.'

'Don't keep staring at him, Mama,' Tina hissed, everything within her recoiling from any connection with him.

Her mother was totally unabashed. 'I'm just returning the curiosity. He keeps looking at us.'

Why??? screamed through Tina's mind.

Panicky thoughts followed.

Had the Australian accent reminded him of the three months he'd spent there?

He could not have identified her, not from a back view. Her hair had been long and curly when he'd known her.

Did he see a similarity to himself in Theo?

But surely he wouldn't be making a blood connection to himself personally, unless he was in the habit of leaving love-children around the world.

Tina pulled herself up on that dark thought. He had used condoms with her. It was unlikely he would think his safe sex had ever been unsafe. Whatever had drawn his interest…it presented a very real problem to her.

Since he and his companion had arrived late at this afternoon tea, it was almost inevitable that she and Theo and her mother would leave before them and they would have to pass his table on their way out. If he looked straight at her, face-to-face…

He might not remember her. It had been six years ago. She looked different with her hair short. And he'd surely had many women pass through his life in the meantime. But if he did recognise her and stopped her from making a quick escape, forcing a re-acquaintance, introductions…her mind reeled away from all the painful complications that might follow.

She did not want Ari Zavros directly touching her life again. That decision had been made before her pregnancy had to be revealed to her parents. It would have been unbearable to have him questioning an unwelcome paternity or sharing responsibility for Theo on some dutiful basis—constantly in and out of her life, always making her feel bad for having loved him so blindly.

It had been a wretched business, standing firm

against her father's questioning, refusing to track down a man who didn't want her any more, insisting that her child would be better off without any interference from him. Whether that decision had been right or wrong she had never regretted it.

Even recently when Theo had asked why he didn't have a father like his kindergarten friends, she had felt no guilt at telling him that some children only had mothers and that was the way it was for them. She was convinced that Ari could only be a horribly disruptive influence in their lives if, given the chance, he decided to be in them at all.

She didn't want to give him the chance.

It had taken so much determination and hard work to establish the life she and Theo now had, it was imperative to hold onto the status quo. This terrible trick of fate—putting Ari and herself in the same place at the same time with Theo and her mother present—could mess up their lives so badly.

A confrontation *had* to be avoided.

Tina pushed back the sickening waves of panic and fiercely told herself this shouldn't be too difficult. Ari had company. Surely it would be unreasonable of him to leave his tete-a-tete with one woman to re-connect with another. Besides, he might not recognise her anyway. If he did, if he tried to engage her in some awful memory-lane chat, she had to ensure that her mother had already taken herself and Theo out of this possible scenario.

She could manage that.

She had to.

CHAPTER TWO

THE rest of afternoon tea took on a nightmarish quality for Tina. It was difficult to focus on the delicacies they were served, even more difficult to appreciate the marvellous range of tastes. Her mind was in a hopelessly scattered state. She felt like Alice in Wonderland at the mad hatter's tea party, with the red queen about to pounce and cut off her head.

Her mother demolished the fig tart and green-tea macaroon. Theo gobbled up the white chocolate cake. She forced herself to eat a caramel slice. They were then presented with another plate of wicked temptations: a strawberry dipped in white chocolate and decorated with a gold leaf, a meringue lemon tart, a passionfruit ball with an oozing liquid centre…more, more, more, and she had to pretend to enjoy it all while her stomach was in knots over Ari's presence behind her.

She smiled at Theo. She smiled at her mother. Her face ached with the effort to keep smiling. She silently cursed Ari Zavros for spoiling what should have been a special experience. The fear that he could spoil a lot more kept jogging through her mind. Finally her mother called enough and suggested they return to the grand lobby and take another leisurely look at everything before leaving.

'Yes, I want to see the fish again, Yiayia,' Theo agreed enthusiastically. 'And sit on the camel.'

Tina knew this was the moment when she had to take control. Every nerve in her body twanged at the vital importance of it. She had already planned what to say. It had to come out naturally, sound sensible. She forced her voice to deliver what was needed.

'I think a toilet visit first might be a good idea. Will you take Theo, Mama? I want to get a few photographs from different windows up here. I'll meet you at the elevator.'

'Of course I'll take him. Come, Theo.'

She stood up and took his hand and they went off happily together. Mission accomplished, Tina thought on a huge wave of relief. Now, if she could get past Ari without him taking any notice of her she was home free. If the worst happened and he chose to intercept her departure, she could deal with the situation on her own.

Having slung her travel bag over her shoulder, she picked up her camera, stood at the window, clicked off a few shots of the view, then, with her heart hammering, she turned, meaning to walk as quickly as she could past the danger table.

Ari Zavros was looking straight at her. She saw the jolt of recognition in his face, felt a jolt of shock run right through her, rooting her feet to the floor, leaving her standing like a mesmerised rabbit caught in headlights.

'Christina…' He spoke her name in a tone of pleasurable surprise, rising from his chair, obviously intent on renewing his *fond memory* of her.

No chance of escape from it. Her feet weren't receiving any messages from her brain which was totally jammed with all the misery this man had given her.

He excused himself from his companion who turned in her chair to give Tina a miffed look—long, silky, blonde hair, big blue eyes, peaches and cream complexion, definitely one of the beautiful people. Another *fond memory* for him, or something more serious this time?

It didn't matter. The only thing that mattered was getting this totally unwelcome encounter over and done with. Ari was approaching her, hands outstretched in charming appeal, his mouth tilting in a wry little smile.

'You've cut your beautiful hair,' he said as though that was a wicked shame.

Never mind the shame he'd left her in.

Her tongue leapt into life. 'I like it better short,' she said tersely, hating the reminder of how he'd enjoyed playing with the long curly tresses, winding it around his fingers, stroking it, kissing it, smelling it.

'What are you doing in Dubai?' he asked, his amber eyes twinkling with interest.

'Having a look at it. Why are you here?' she returned.

He shrugged. 'Business.'

'Mixed with pleasure,' she said dryly, with a nod at the blonde. 'Please…don't let me keep you from her, Ari. After all this time, what is there to say?'

'Only that it feels good to see you again. Even with

your cropped hair,' he replied with one of his megawatt smiles which had once melted her knees.

They stiffened in sheer rebellion. How dared he flirt with her when he was obviously connected to another woman? How dared he flirt with her at all when he'd used her up and left her behind him?

And she hated him saying it felt good to see her again when it made her feel so bad. He had no idea of what he'd done to her and she hated him for that, too. She wanted to smack that smile off his face, wanted to smack him down for having the arrogance to even approach her again with his smarmy charm, but the more dignified course, the *safer* course was simply to dismiss him.

'I'm a different person now to the one you knew,' she said oddly. 'If you'll excuse me, I'm with my mother who'll be waiting for me to catch up with her.'

Her feet obeyed the command to side-step, get moving To her intense frustration, Ari shot out a hand, clutching her arm, halting a swift escape from him. She glared at him, resentment burning deep from the touch of his fingers on her skin, from the power he still had to affect her physically. He was so close she could smell the cologne he used. It made her head swim with memories she didn't want to have.

The amber eyes quizzed hers, as though he didn't understand her cutting him off so abruptly. He wanted to know more. Never mind what she wanted.

'Your mother. And the boy...' he said slowly, obviously considering her family group and what it might mean. 'You're married now? He is your son?'

Tina seethed. That, of course, would be so nice and neat, dismissing the intimacy they had shared as nothing important in her life, just as it hadn't been important to him.

She should say *yes*, have done with it. Let him think she was married and there was no possible place for him in her life. He would shut the door on his *charming episode* with her and let her go. She would be free of him forever.

Do it, do it! her mind screamed.

But her heart was being ripped apart by a violent tumult of emotions.

Another voice in her head was yelling *smack him with the truth!*

This man was Theo's father. She could not bring herself to palm his fatherhood off on anyone else. *He* ought to be faced with it. A savage recklessness streaked through her, obliterating any caring over what might happen next.

'I'm not married,' she slung at him. 'And yes, Theo is my son.'

He frowned.

Single motherhood did not sit so well with him. She was free but not free, tied to a child.

No ties for Ari Zavros.

That thought enraged Tina further. She fired bitter truth straight at him.

'He's also your son.'

It stunned him.

Totally stunned him.

No seductive smile.

No twinkly interest.

Blank shock.

With a sense of fiercely primitive satisfaction, Tina got her feet moving and strode past him, heading for the elevator where she hoped her mother and Theo would be waiting for her. She didn't think Ari would follow her. Not only had she cut his feet out from under him, but he was with another woman and it was highly unlikely that he'd want to face her with the complication of an illegitimate son.

Though a fast getaway from this hotel was definitely needed. No loitering in the lobby. She'd tell her mother she didn't feel well—too much rich food. It was true enough anyway. Her stomach was churning and she felt like throwing up.

She shouldn't have told Ari he was Theo's father. She hadn't counted on how much he could still get to her—his eyes, his touch, the whole insidious charisma of his close presence. Hopefully telling his wouldn't make any difference. For a start, he wouldn't want to believe her. Men like him usually denied paternity claims. Not that she would ever make any official claim on him. All the same, it had been stupid of her to throw the truth in his face and give herself this panic attack, stupid and reckless to have opened a door for him into her life again when she wanted him out, out, out!

Please, God, let him not follow up on it.

Let him shrug it off as a put-down line.

Let him just go on with his life and leave her alone to go on with hers.

That boy...his son? *His* son?

Ari snapped out of the wave of shock rolling through

his mind, swung on his heel, and stared after the woman who had just declared herself the mother of his child. Christina Savalas wasn't waiting around to capitalise on her claim. Having delivered her bombshell she was fast making an exit from any fall-out.

Was it true?

He quickly calculated precisely *when* he had been in Australia. It was six years ago. The boy's age would approximately fit that time-frame. He needed to know the actual birth date to be sure if it was possible. That could be checked. The name was Theo. Theo Savalas. Who looked very like himself as a child!

A chill ran down Ari's spine. If Theo was his, it meant he had left Christina pregnant, abandoned a pregnant woman, left her to bring up his child alone. But how could that happen when he was always careful to sheath himself against such a consequence? Not once had he ever failed to use protection. Had there been a slip-up with her, one that he didn't remember?

He did remember she'd been an innocent. Unexpectedly and delightfully so. He hadn't felt guilty about taking her virginity. Desire had been mutual and he'd given her pleasure—a good start to her sexual life, which he'd reasoned would become quite active as time went by. Any man would see her as desirable and it was only natural that she would be attracted to some of them.

But if he had left her pregnant… That would have messed up her career, messed up her life—reason enough for those extremely expressive dark eyes of hers to shoot black bolts of hatred and contempt at him with her punishing exit line.

Impossible to ignore what she'd said. He had to check it out. If the boy was his son... Why hadn't Christina told him about his existence before this? Why go it alone all these years? Why hit him with it now? There was a hell of a lot of questions to be considered.

'Ari...'

His teeth automatically gritted. He hated that whiny tone in Felicity's voice.

'What are you standing there for? She's gone.'

Gone but not forgotten.

'I was remembering my time in Australia, which was where I'd met Christina,' he said, forcing himself to return to his chair and be reasonably civil to the woman he had invited to be his companion.

'What were you doing in Australia?'

'Checking out the wine industry there. Seeing if any improvements could be made to the Santorini operation.'

'Was this Christina connected to the wine industry?'

The tone had changed to a snipe.

He shrugged. 'Not really. She was part of an advertising drive for the Jacob's Creek label.'

One eyebrow arched in knowing mockery. 'A model.'

'She was then.'

'And you had fun with her.'

He grimaced at her dig, which he found extremely distasteful in the circumstances. 'Ancient history, Felicity. I was simply surprised to see her here in Dubai.'

'Well, she's loaded down with a child now,' she said with snide satisfaction. 'No fun at all.'

'I can't imagine it is much fun, being a single mother,' he said, barely containing a wave of anger at Felicity's opinion.

'Oh, I don't know. Quite a few movie stars have chosen that route and they seem to revel in it.'

Ari wanted this conversation finished. He heaved a sigh, then mockingly drawled, 'What do I know? I'm a man.'

Felicity laughed, leaned over and stroked his thigh. 'And a gorgeous one, darling. Which is why I don't like you straying, even for a minute.'

The urge to stray to Christina Savalas had been instant.

He'd had his surfeit of self-centred women like Felicity Fullbright and the flash of memory—a sweet, charming time—had compelled him out of his seat. But it wasn't the same Christina he'd known. How could it be, given the passage of years? A different person, she'd said. He would need to get to know her again if she was the mother of his child.

He would track her down in the very near future. Obviously she was on a tourist trip with her mother and would be on the move for a few weeks. Best to wait until she was back on home ground. In the meantime, he had to sever any further involvement with Felicity, attend his cousin's wedding, then free himself up to pursue the big question.

Was Theo Savalas his son?

If the answer was a definitive yes, changes to his life had to be made.

And Christina Savalas would have to come to some accommodation with him, whether she liked it or not.

A father had rights to his child, and Ari had no qualms about enforcing them.

Family was family.

CHAPTER THREE

TINA felt continually tense for the rest of their short stay in Dubai, knowing Ari Zavros was in the same city. Although she didn't think he would pursue the paternity issue, and a second accidental encounter with him was unlikely, she only felt safe on the red tour bus in between its stops at the various points of interest; the gold souks, the spice markets, the shopping centres. It was a huge relief to board their flight to Athens on the third day, not having had any further contact with him.

They were met at the airport by Uncle Dimitri, her father's older brother. After a brief stop to check in at their hotel, he took them on to his restaurant which was sited just below the Acropolis and where all their Greek relatives had gathered to welcome them home. It wasn't home to Tina or Theo, both of whom had been born in Australia, but it was interesting to meet her mother's and father's families and it was a very festive get-together.

Her mother revelled in the company and Theo was a hit—*such a beautiful grandchild*—but Tina couldn't help feeling like an outsider. The women tended to talk about her in the third person, as though she wasn't there at all.

'We must find a husband for your daughter, Helen.'

'Why did she cut her hair? Men like long hair.'

'She is obviously a good mother. That is important.'

'And if she is used to helping in a restaurant...'

Not helping, *managing,* Tina silently corrected, observing how Uncle Dimitri was managing his. He was constantly on watch, signalling waiters to wherever service was required. All the patrons were treated to a plate of sliced watermelon at the end of their meals—on the house—a nice touch for long hot evenings. People left happy, which meant return visits and good word-of-mouth. It was something she could copy at home.

Most of the tables were out on the sidewalk, under trees or umbrellas. Herbs were grown in pots, their aromas adding to the pleasant ambience. The food was relatively simple, the salads very good. She particularly liked the olive oil, honey and balsamic vinegar dressing—a combination she would use in future. It was easy to relax and have a taste of Athens.

There'd been a message from Cassandra at the hotel, saying she and her fiancé would join them at the restaurant, and Tina kept looking for their arrival, eager to meet up with her sister again. Cass had brought George home to Sydney with her six months ago, but had been working a heavy international schedule ever since. They had just flown in from London and were spending one night in Athens before moving on to the island of Patmos where George's family lived.

'Here they come!' her mother cried, seeing them first.

Tina looked.

And froze in horror.

There was her beautiful sister, her face aglow with happy excitement, looking every inch the supermodel she had become.

Hugging her to his side was George Carasso, grinning with pride in his bride-to-be.

Next to him strolled Ari Zavros.

Her mother turned to her. 'Tina, isn't that the man we saw...'

She heard the words but couldn't answer. Bad enough to find herself confronted by him again. It was much, much worse with him knowing about Theo!

People were on their feet, greeting, welcoming, hugging and kissing. Ari was introduced as George's cousin who was to be his best man at the wedding. *His best man!* And she was Cass's only bridesmaid! The nightmare she had made for herself was getting more torturous by the second and there was no end to it any time soon. It was going to be impossible to enjoy her sister's wedding. She would have to suffer through being Ari's partner at the ceremony and the reception.

If she hadn't opened her mouth in Dubai and let her secret out, she might have managed to skate over their past involvement. There was little hope of that now. No hope at all, given the look Ari Zavros had just turned her way, a dangerously simmering challenge in the riveting amber eyes.

'And this is your sister?' he prompted Cass, who immediately obliged with the formal introduction.

'Yes. Tina! Oh, it's so good to see you again!' she bubbled, dodging around the table to give her a hug. 'George and I are staying in Ari's apartment tonight and when we told him we were meeting up with you, he insisted on coming with us so you won't be strangers to each other at the wedding.'

Strangers!

He hadn't let the cat out of the bag.

Tina fiercely hoped it suited him not to.

Cass swooped on Theo, lifting him up in her arms and turning to show him off to Ari. 'And this is my nephew, Theo, who is going to be our page boy.'

Ari smiled at him. 'Your Aunty Cassandra told me it's your birthday this week.'

He'd been checking, Tina thought grimly.

Theo held up his hand with fingers and thumb spread. 'Five,' he announced proudly.

'It's my birthday this month, too,' Ari said. 'That makes us both Leos.'

'No. I'm Theo, not Leo.'

Everyone laughed at the correction.

'He didn't mean to get your name wrong, darling,' Cass explained. 'We're all born under star signs and the star sign for your birthday is Leo. Which means a lion. And you have amber eyes, just like a lion.'

Theo pointed to Ari. 'He's got the same colour eyes as me.'

Tina held her breath. Her heart was drumming in her ears. Her mind was screaming *please, please, please don't claim parentage now.* It was the wrong place, the wrong time, the wrong everything!

'There you are, then,' Ari said with an air of indulgence, taking Theo's outstretched hand and giving it a light shake. 'Both of us are lions and I'm very glad to meet you.' He turned to Tina. 'And your mother.'

Relief reduced her to jelly inside. He wasn't pushing his fatherhood yet. Maybe he never would. She should be saying *hello,* but she was so choked up with nervous tension it was impossible to get her voice to work.

'Tina?' He gave her a slightly quizzical smile as he offered his hand to her. 'Short for Christina?'

'Yes.' It was a husky whisper, all she could manage.

Then she was forced by the occasion to let his strong fingers close around hers. The jolting sensation of electric warmth was a searing reminder of the sexual chemistry that had seduced her in the past. It instantly stirred a fierce rebellion in her mind. No way was she going to let it get to her again, making her weak and foolish. If there was to be a fight over custody of Theo, she couldn't let Ari Zavros have any personal power over her. She wriggled her hand out of his as fast as she could.

Seating was quickly re-arranged so that Cass and George could sit beside her mother. Uncle Dimitri produced an extra chair for Ari at the end of the table, right next to her and Theo. It was impossible for Tina to protest this proximity, given they would be partners at the wedding and apparently Ari had already stated his intention to *make her acquaintance.*

The situation demanded polite conversation. Any

failure to follow that course would raise questions about her behaviour. As much as Tina hated having to do it, she adopted the pretence of being strangers, forcing herself to speak to George's *best* man with an air of natural enquiry.

'When did you meet my sister?'

It was a good question. She needed information and needed it fast to help her deal with Ari in the most sensible way. If it was possible to avoid a showdown with him over Theo, grasping that possibility was paramount.

'Only this evening,' he answered with a wry little smile. 'I knew of her, of course, because of her engagement to George, but within the family she was always referred to as simply Cassandra since she is famously known by that name in the supermodel world. I'd never actually heard her surname. I chanced to see it written on her luggage when she set it down in the apartment. Very opportune, given the circumstances.'

The fact that he'd immediately seized the opportunity for a face-to-face meeting with her gave no support to the wishful thought of avoiding an ultimate showdown.

'So you proceeded to draw her out about her family,' Tina said flatly, feeling as though a trap was closing around her.

'Very enlightening,' he drawled, his eyes mocking the secrecy which was no longer a secret to him.

Fear squeezed her heart. Sheer self-defence demanded she ignore his enlightenment. 'You live in Athens?'

'Not really. The apartment is for convenience. Anyone in the family can use it, which is why George felt free to bring Cassandra there for tonight. More private for her than a hotel.'

'Very considerate of him,' she dryly remarked. 'Where do you normally live then?'

All she'd previously known about him was he belonged to a wealthy Greek family with an involvement in the wine industry. During the time they'd spent together, Ari had been more interested in everything Australian than talking about himself.

He shrugged. 'Various business interests require quite a bit of travelling but my family home is on Santorini.'

'We're going to Santorini,' Theo piped up, looked at Ari as though he was fascinated by the man.

Ari smiled at him. 'Yes, I know. Perhaps we could do something special together on your birthday.'

Tina's stomach contracted. He was intent on moving in on her, getting closer to their son.

'Like what?' Theo asked eagerly.

'Let's wait and see what we might like to do, Theo,' Tina cut in firmly, inwardly panicking at spending any more time than she absolutely had to with Ari Zavros. She didn't know if it was curiosity driving him or he was dabbling with the idea of claiming Theo as his flesh and blood. She turned hard, quelling eyes to him. 'You said *family home*. Does that mean you're married with children?'

He shook his head and made an ironic grimace. 'Much to my father's vexation, I am still single. It's his home I was referring to.'

'Not exactly single, Ari,' she tersely reminded him.

He knew she'd seen him with a woman in Dubai. She didn't have to spell that out. If he thought he could start playing fast and loose with her again, cheating on the beautiful blonde, he was on an ego trip she would take great satisfaction in smashing.

'I assure you I am, Christina,' he replied without the blink of an eyelid.

Her teeth gnashed over the lilted use of her full name—a reminder of intimate moments that were long gone. She raked his steady gaze with blistering scepticism. The amber eyes burned straight back at her, denying the slightest shift in what he had just declared.

'Another *charming episode* over?' she sliced at him.

He frowned, probably having forgotten how he had described his relationship with her. Whether he recollected it or not, he shot her a look that was loaded with determined purpose. 'Not so charming. In fact, it convinced me I should free myself up to look for something else.'

His gaze moved to Theo, softening as he said, 'Perhaps I should become a father.'

Tina's spine crawled with apprehension. This was the last thing she wanted. The very last! Somehow she had to fight him, convince him that fatherhood would not suit him at all.

'I don't have a father,' Theo gravely informed him. 'I had a grandfather but he got sick and went to heaven.'

'I'm sorry to hear that,' Ari said sympathetically.

'I think people should be aware there's a very real and lasting responsibility about becoming a parent,'

Tina quickly stated, hoping to ward off any impulsive act that would end up badly.

'I agree with you,' Ari said blandly.

'Fly-by-night people shouldn't even consider it,' she persisted, desperately determined on pricking his conscience.

'What are fly-by-night people, Mama?' Theo asked curiously.

Ari leaned forward to answer him. 'They're people who come and go without staying around long enough to really be an important part of your life. They don't stick by you like your mother does. And your grandmother. And your friends. Do you have some friends, Theo?'

'I have lots of friends,' Theo boasted.

'Then I think you must be a happy boy.'

'Very happy,' Tina cut in, giving Ari a look that clearly telegraphed *without you.*

'Then you must be a very special mother, Christina,' he said in his soft, seductive voice. 'It could not have been easy for you, bringing him up alone.'

She bridled at the compliment. 'I wasn't alone. My parents supported me.'

'Family,' he murmured, nodding approvingly. 'So important. One should never turn one's back on family.'

The glittering challenge in his eyes spurred her into leaning over to privately mutter, 'You turned your back first, Ari.'

'I never have to any blood relative I knew about,' he shot back, leaning towards her and keeping his voice low enough for Theo not to hear his words. 'We can do this the easy way or the hard way, Christina.'

'Do what?'

'Fighting over him is not in our son's best interests.'

'Then don't fight. Let him be.'

'You expect me to ignore his existence?'

'Why not? You've ignored mine.'

'A mistake. Which I will correct.'

'Some mistakes can never be corrected.'

'We shall see.'

The fight was on!

No avoiding it.

The rush of blood to her head as she'd tried to argue him out of it drained away, leaving her dizzy and devastated by his resolute counter to everything she'd said.

He straightened up and smiled at Theo who was tucking into a slice of watermelon. 'Good?' he asked.

Theo nodded, his mouth too full to speak but his eyes twinkling a smile back at Ari. Tina seethed over his charming manner to her son. He'd been so very charming to her once. It meant *nothing!* But it was impossible to explain that to a five-year-old boy.

Ari turned his attention back to her. 'Cassandra told me you now manage a restaurant at Bondi Beach.'

'Yes. It was my father's. He trained me to take over when…when he could no longer do it himself.' Another bad time in her life but she had coped. The restaurant was still thriving.

'That surely means working long hours. It must be difficult, being a mother, too.'

She glared at him, fiercely resenting the suggestion

she might be neglecting her son. 'We live in an apartment above the restaurant. Theo attends a pre-school,
which he loves, during the day. He can be with me or
my mother at all other times. And the beach is his playground, which he also loves. As you remarked, he is a
happy boy.'

And he doesn't need you. For anything.

'Mama and I build great sandcastles,' Theo informed
him.

'There are lots of beaches on the Greek islands,' Ari
said.

'Can anyone go on them?' Theo asked.

'There are public beaches which are for everyone.'

'Do they have chairs in rows like we saw in Dubai?'

'The private beaches do.'

'I don't like that.'

'There's one below where I live on Santorini that
doesn't have chairs. You could build great sand-castles
there.'

'Would you help me?'

Ari laughed, delighted he had won Theo over.

'I don't think we'll have time for that,' Tina said
quickly.

'Nonsense!' Ari grinned triumphantly at her.
'Cassandra told me you're spending five days on
Santorini, and Theo's birthday is two days before the
wedding. It would be my pleasure to give Theo a wonderful time—a trip on the cable-car, a ride on a donkey...'

'A donkey!' Theo cried excitedly.

'...a boat-ride to the volcanic island...'

'A boat-ride!' Theo's eyes were as big as saucers.

'...and a trip to a beach where we can build the biggest sandcastle ever!'

'Can we, Mama? Can we?'

His voice was so high-pitched with excitement, it drew her mother's attention. 'Can you what, Theo?' she asked indulgently.

'Ride a donkey and go on a boat, Yiayia. For my birthday!'

'I said I would take him,' Ari swiftly slid in. 'Give him a birthday on Santorini he will always remember.'

'How kind of you!' Her mother beamed at him—the man gorgeous enough to be a movie star, giving his time to make her grandson's stay on Santorini so pleasurable!

The trap was shut. No way out. With both her mother and Theo onside with Ari, Tina knew she would just have to grit her teeth and go along with him. Being a spoilsport would necessitate explanations she didn't want to give. Not at this point. He might force her to make them in the very near future but she would keep it a private issue between them as long as she could.

Cass didn't deserve to have her wedding overshadowed by a situation that should never have arisen. With that one crazy urge to slap Ari with the truth in Dubai... but the damage was done and somehow Tina had to contain it. At least until after the wedding.

With the whole family's attention drawn to them, she forced herself to smile at Ari. 'Yes, very kind.'

'Cassandra mentioned you'll be staying at the El Greco resort,' he said, arrogantly confident of her agreement to the plan. 'I'll contact you there, make arrangements.'

'Fine! Thank you.'

With that settled, conversation picked up around the table again and Theo plied Ari with questions about Santorini, which were answered with obvious good humour.

Tina didn't have to say anything. She sat in brooding silence, hating Ari Zavros for his facile charm, hating herself for being such a stupid blabbermouth, gearing herself up to tolerate what had to be tolerated and savagely vowing that Ari would not get everything his own way.

Eventually Cass and George excused themselves from the party, saying they needed to catch up on some sleep. To Tina's huge relief, Ari stood up to take his leave, as well. She rose from her chair as he offered his hand which she had to be civil enough to take in front of company.

He actually had the gall to enclose her hand with both of his with a show of enthusiastic pleasure. 'Thank you for trusting me with Theo's birthday, Christina.'

'Oh, I'm sure I can trust you to give the best of yourself, Ari,' she answered sweetly, before softly adding with a touch of acid mockery, 'For a limited time.'

Which told him straight out how very little she trusted him.

He might have won Theo over—for a day—but he'd won nothing from her.

'We shall see,' he repeated with that same arrogant confidence.

General goodnights were exchanged and finally he was gone.

But he'd left his presence behind with her mother raving on about him and Theo equally delighted with the nice man.

No relief from the trap.

Tina had the wretched feeling there never would be.

CHAPTER FOUR

MAXIMUS ZAVROS sat under the vine-covered pergola at one end of the vast patio which overlooked the Aegean Sea. It was where he habitually had breakfast and where he expected his son to join him whenever Ari was home. Today was no exception. However he was taking no pleasure in his surroundings and none in his son, which was obvious from the dark glower of disapproval he directed at Ari the moment he emerged from the house.

'So, you come home without a woman to marry again!' He folded the newspaper he'd been reading and smacked it down on the table in exasperation. 'Your cousin, George, is two years younger than you. He does not have your engaging looks. He does not have your wealth. Yet he can win himself a wife who will grace the rest of his life.' He threw out a gesture of frustration. 'What is the problem with you?'

'Maybe I missed a boat I should have taken,' Ari tossed at his father as he pulled out a chair and sat down, facing him across the table.

'What is that supposed to mean?'

Ari poured himself a glass of orange juice. This was

going to be a long conversation and his throat was already dry. He took a long sip, then answered, 'It means I've met the woman I must marry but I let her go six years ago and somehow I have to win her again. Which is going to prove difficult because she's very hostile to me.'

'Hostile? Why hostile? You were taught to have more finesse than to leave any woman hostile. And why *must* you marry her? To saddle yourself with a sourpuss will not generate a happy life. I credited you with more good sense than that, Ari.'

'I left her pregnant. Unknowingly, I assure you. She gave birth to a son who is now five years old.'

'A son! A grandson!' The tirade was instantly diverted. His father ruminated over this totally unanticipated piece of news for several minutes before speaking again. 'You're sure he is yours?'

'No doubt. The boy not only has a strong resemblance to me but the birth date places the conception during the time I was with Christina.'

'Who is this Christina? Is it possible she could have been with another man?'

Ari shook his head. 'I can't even entertain that as a possibility. We were too intimately involved at the time. And she was a virgin, Papa. I met her when I was in Australia. She was at the start of a promising modelling career...young, beautiful, utterly captivating. When I concluded my business there I said goodbye to her. I had no plans for marriage at that point in my life and I thought her too young to be considering it, either. I thought her life was just starting to open up for her.'

'Australia…' His father frowned. 'How did you meet again? You haven't been back there.'

'George's wife-to-be, Cassandra…when they stayed overnight in the apartment at Athens, I discovered that she was Christina's sister. Christina is to be brides-maid at the wedding and her son, Theo—*my* son—is to be page boy. They were already in Athens en route to Santorini and I went to a family party to meet them.'

'Is it known to the family that you are the father?'

'No. They were obviously in ignorance of my in-volvement. But I cannot ignore it, Papa. Christina wants me to. She is appalled to find herself caught up in a sit-uation with me again.'

'She wants to keep the boy to herself.'

'Yes.'

'So… her mind-set against you has to be changed.'

It was a relief that his father had made a straight leap to this conclusion, although it had been fairly predict-able he would arrive at it, given the pull of a grandson.

'I intend to make a start on that tomorrow. It's Theo's fifth birthday and I managed to manipulate an agree-ment for the two of them to spend it with me.'

'She was not a willing party?'

'I made it unreasonable for her to refuse. The fact that she doesn't want to reveal to her family that I'm Theo's father gives me a lever into her life. At least until after the wedding. I suspect she doesn't want to take any focus off her sister at this time.'

'Caring for her family… I like that. Will she make you a good wife, Ari?'

He made an ironic grimace. 'At least she likes children which cannot be said for Felicity Fullbright. I still find Christina very attractive. What can I say, Papa? I've made my bed and I shall lie in it. When you meet the boy you'll know why.'

'When do they arrive on Santorini?'

'Today.'

'Staying where?'

'The El Greco resort.'

'I shall call the management personally. All expenses for their stay will be paid by me. Fresh fruit and flowers in their rooms. A selection of our best Santorini wines. Everything compliments of the Zavros family. They need to be acquainted with our wealth and power. It tends to bend people's minds in a positive manner.'

Ari kept his own counsel on this point. His father could be right. Generosity might have a benign influence. However, he was well enough acquainted with the Australian character to know they had a habit of cutting down tall poppies. However high people rose on their various totem poles, it did not make them better than anyone else. Apart from which, Christina had already demonstrated a strong independence. He doubted she could be bought.

'The mother might be favourably impressed,' he commented. 'Her name is Helen and she is a widow. It might help if you and Mama pay her some kind attention at the wedding.'

His father nodded. 'Naturally we will do so. As a grandparent she should be sympathetic to those who wish to be. I will make my feelings on the subject known.'

'She is Greek. So was her husband. The two daughters were born and brought up in Australia, but she would be familiar with the old ways…arranged marriages between families. If she understands it could be best for Christina and Theo to have the support and security our family can give them…'

'Leave it to me. I shall win over the mother. You win over the daughter and your son. It is intolerable that we be left out of the boy's life.'

That was the crux of it, Ari thought.

Whatever had to be done he would do to be a proper father to his son.

Ten hours was a long ferry ride from Athens to Santorini. Theo was fascinated by the wake of the boat so Tina spent most of the time on the outer rear deck with him while her mother relaxed inside with a book. They passed many islands, most of them looking quite barren and unattractive, and to Tina's mind, not the least bit alluring like the tropical islands back home. It was disappointing. She had expected more magic. However, these islands were obviously not the main tourist drawcards like Mykonos, Paros, Naxos, and most especially Santorini.

When the ferry finally entered the harbour of their destination, she easily understood the stunning attraction of the landscape created from the volcanic eruption that had devastated ancient civilisations. The water in what had been the crater was a gorgeous blue, the semicircle of high cliffs was dramatic, and perched on top of them the classic white Greek island townships glistened in the late afternoon sunshine.

She wished Ari Zavros did not live on this island. She had looked forward to enjoying it, wanted to enjoy it, and decided she would do so in spite of him. If he had any decency at all, he would let the paternity issue drop, realizing he didn't fit into the life she'd made for herself and Theo, and they were not about to fit into his with his obvious bent for a continual stream of *charming episodes*.

Transport was waiting for them at the ferry terminal. Theo was agog with how the mini-bus would negotiate the amazing zig-zag road which would take them from the bottom of the cliff to the top. As it turned out, the trip was not really hair-raising and the view from the bus-window was beautiful.

The El Greco resort faced the other side of the island, built in terraces down the hillside with rooms built around the swimming pools on each terrace. The buildings were all painted blue and white and the gardens looked very tropical with masses of colourful bougainvillea and hibiscus trees. The reception area was cool and spacious, elegantly furnished and with a view of the sea at the far end. A very attractive place, Tina thought. A place to relax. Except relaxation switched instantly to tension when they started to check in at the reception desk.

'Ah, Mrs Savalas, just a minute please!' the receptionist said quickly, beaming a rather unctuous smile at them. 'I must inform the manager of your arrival.' He ducked away to call through a doorway, 'The Savalas party has arrived.'

A suited man emerged from a back office, beaming a similar smile at them as he approached the desk.

'Is there a problem with our booking?' her mother asked anxiously.

'Not at all, Mrs Savalas. We have put you in rooms on the first terrace which is most convenient to the restaurant and the pool snack-bar. If there is anything that would make you more comfortable, you have only to ask and it will be done.'

'Well, that's very hospitable,' her mother said with an air of relief.

'I have had instructions from Mr Zavros to make you most welcome, Mrs Savalas. I understand you are here for a family wedding.'

'Yes, but...' She threw a puzzled look at Tina whose fists had instinctively clenched at the name that spelled danger all over this situation. 'It's very kind of Ari Zavros to...'

'No, no, it is Maximus Zavros who has given the orders,' the manager corrected her. 'It is his nephew marrying your daughter. Family is family and you are not to pay for anything during your stay at El Greco. All is to be charged to him, so put away your credit card, Mrs Savalas. You will not need it here.'

Her mother shook her head in stunned disbelief. 'I haven't even met this Maximus Zavros.'

It did not concern the manager one bit. 'No doubt you will at the wedding, Mrs Savalas.'

'I'm not sure I should accept this…this arrangement.'

'Oh, but you must!' The manager looked horrified at the thought of refusal. 'Mr Zavros is a very wealthy, powerful man. He owns much of the real estate on Santorini. He would be offended if you did not accept his hospitality and I would be at fault if I did not persuade you to do so. Please, Mrs Savalas… I beg you to enjoy. It is what he wishes.'

'Well…' Her mother looked confused and undecided until a helpful thought struck. She shot Tina a determined look. 'We can talk to Ari about this tomorrow.'

Tina nodded, struggling with the death of any hope that Ari might disappear from her life again. She couldn't believe this was simply a case of a rich powerful Greek extending hospitality. The words—*family is family*—had been like a punch in the stomach. She couldn't dismiss the sickening suspicion that Ari had blabbed to his father. It was the only thing that made sense of this extraordinary move.

'Let me show you to your rooms. A porter will bring your luggage.' The manager bustled out from behind the reception desk. 'I want to assure myself that all is as it should be for you.'

Their adjoining rooms were charming, each one with a walled outside area containing a table and chairs for enjoying the ambience of the resort. Complimentary platters of fresh fruit and a selection of wines were provided. The gorgeous floral arrangements were obvious extras, too. Her mother was delighted with everything. Tina viewed it all with jaundiced eyes and Theo was only interested in how soon he could get into the children's swimming pool.

Their luggage arrived. Tina left her mother in the room Cassandra would share with her the night before the wedding and took Theo into theirs. Within a few minutes she had found their swimsuits in her big suitcase, and feeling driven to get out of the Zavros-permeated room, she and Theo quickly changed their clothes and headed for the water.

She sat on the edge of the shallow pool while Theo dashed in and splashed around, full of happy laughter. Her mind was dark with a terrible sense of foreboding and it was difficult to force an occasional smile at her son. Ari's son. Maximus Zavros's grandson.

Did they intend to make an official claim on him?

People like them probably didn't care how much they disrupted others' lives. If something was desired, for whatever reason, they went after it. And got it. Like the rooms in this resort. Almost anything could be manipulated with wealth.

She couldn't help feeling afraid of the future. She was on this island—their island—for the next five days and it would be impossible to avoid meeting Ari's family at the wedding. Ironically, throwing his fatherhood in his face in Dubai was no longer such a hideous mistake. He would have figured it out at the wedding. There would have been no escape from his knowing. She'd been on a collision course with Ari Zavros from the moment Cassandra had agreed to marry his cousin.

The big question was…how to deal with him?

Should she tell her mother the truth now?

Her head ached from all the possible outcomes of revealing her secret before she absolutely had to. Better to wait, she decided, at least until after she'd spent tomorrow with Ari. Then she would have a better idea of what he intended where Theo was concerned and what she could or couldn't do about it.

Tomorrow… Theo's fifth birthday.

His first with his father.

Tina knew she was going to hate every minute of it.

CHAPTER FIVE

TINA and Theo were about to accompany her mother to breakfast in the nearby restaurant when a call from Ari came through to her room. She quickly pressed her mother to go ahead with Theo while she talked to *the nice man* about plans for the day. As soon as they were out of earshot she flew into attack mode, determined on knowing what she had to handle.

'You've told your father about Theo, haven't you?' she cried accusingly.

'Yes, I have,' he answered calmly. 'He had the right to know, just as I had the right to know. Which you denied me for the past five years, Christina.'

'You made it clear that you were finished with me, Ari.'

'You could have found me. My family is not unknown. A simple search on the Internet…'

'Oh, sure! I can just imagine how much you would have welcomed a cast-off woman running after you. Any contact from me via computer and you would have pressed the delete button.'

'Not if you'd told me you were pregnant.'

'Would you have believed me?' she challenged.

His hesitation gave her instant justification for keeping him in ignorance.

'I thought I had taken care of contraception, Christina,' he said, trying to justify himself. 'I would certainly have checked. However, we now have a different situation—a connection that demands continuation. It's best that you start getting used to that concept because I won't be cut out of my son's life any longer.'

The edge of hard ruthlessness in his tone told her without a doubt that he was intent on making a legal claim. A down to the wire fight over Theo was inevitable. What she needed to do now was buy time. Quelling the threatening rise of panic, she tried bargaining with him.

'You said in Athens we could do this the easy way or the hard way, Ari.'

'Yes. I meant it. Is there something you'd like to suggest?'

'You messed up my life once and I guess nothing is going to stop you from messing it up again. But please…don't make a mess of my sister's day in the sun as a bride. That would be absolutely rotten and selfish, which is typical of your behaviour, but… I'll make it easy for you to get to know your son over the next few days if you hold back on telling everyone else you're his father until after the wedding.'

The silence that followed her offer was nerve-wracking. Tina gritted her teeth and laid out *the hard way.* 'I'll fight you on every front if you don't agree, Ari.'

'When was I ever rotten or selfish to you in our relationship?' he demanded curtly, sounding as though his self-image was badly dented.

'You made me believe what wasn't true… for your own ends,' she stated bitingly. 'And may God damn you to hell if you do that to Theo.'

'Enough! I agree to your deal. I shall meet you at the resort in one hour. We will spend the day happily together for our son's pleasure.'

He cut the connection before Tina could say another word. Her hand was shaking as she returned the telephone receiver to its cradle. At least Cass's wedding wouldn't be spoiled, she told herself. As for the rest… the only thing she could do was deal with one day at a time.

It took Ari the full hour to get his head around Christina's offensive reading of his character. Anger and resentment kept boiling through him. He wasn't used to being so riled by any situation with a woman. It was because of Theo, he reasoned. It was only natural that his emotions were engaged where his son was concerned.

As for Christina, her hostility towards him was totally unreasonable. He remembered romancing her beautifully, showering her with gifts, saying all the sweet words that women liked to hear, wining and dining her, not stinting on anything that could give her pleasure. No one could have been a better first lover for her.

Was it his fault that the contraception he'd used had somehow failed to protect her from falling pregnant?

He had never, *never* intended to mess up her life. He would have dealt honourably with the situation had he known about it. She could have been living in luxury all these years, enjoying being part of a family unit instead of struggling along with single parenthood.

That was her decision, not his. She hadn't allowed him a decision. If there was any condemnation of character to be handed out on all of this, it should be placed at her door. It was *selfish* and *rotten* of her to have denied him the joys of fatherhood.

Yet…there was nothing selfish about not wanting anything to spoil her sister's wedding.

And he could not recall her ever making some selfish demand on him during the time they'd spent together. Not like Felicity Fullbright. Very, very different to Felicity Fullbright. A delight to be with in every sense.

Gradually he calmed down enough to give consideration to her most condemning words… *You made me believe what wasn't true…for your own ends.*

What had he made her believe?

The answer was glaringly simple when he thought about it. She'd been very young, inexperienced, and quite possibly she'd interpreted his whole seduction routine as genuine love for her. Which meant she'd been deeply hurt when he'd left her. So hurt, she probably couldn't bear to tell him about her pregnancy, couldn't bear to be faced with his presence again.

And she thought he might hurt Theo in the same way—apparently loving him, then leaving him.

He had to change her perception of him, make her

understand he would never abandon his child. He had to show her that Theo would be welcomed into his family and genuinely loved. As for winning her over to being his wife…trying to charm her into marrying him wasn't likely to work. Those blazing dark eyes of hers would shoot down every move he made in that direction. So what would work?

She had just offered him a deal.

Why not offer her one?

Make it a deal too attractive to refuse.

Ari worked on that idea as he drove to the El Greco resort.

'He looks just like a Greek God,' her mother remarked admiringly as Ari Zavros strode across the terrace to where they were still sitting in the open-air section of the restaurant, enjoying a last cup of coffee after breakfast.

Tina's stomach instantly cramped. She had thought that once—the golden Greek with his sun-streaked hair and sparkling amber eyes and skin that shone like bronze. And, of course, it was still true. The white shorts and sports shirt he wore this morning made him look even more striking, showing off his athletic physique, the masculine strength in his arms and legs, the broad manly chest. The man was totally charismatic.

This time, however, Tina wasn't about to melt at his feet. 'Bearing gifts, as well,' she said ironically, eyeing the package he was carrying under his arm.

'For me?' Theo cried excitedly.

Ari heard him, beaming a wide grin at his son as he

arrived at their table and presented him with the large package. 'Yes, for you. Happy birthday, Theo.'

'Can I open it?' Theo asked, eagerly eyeing the wrapping paper.

'You should thank Ari first,' Tina prompted.

'Thank you very much,' he obeyed enthusiastically.

Ari laughed. 'Go right ahead. Something for you to build when you have nothing else to do.'

It was a Lego train station, much to Theo's delight.

'He loves Lego,' her mother remarked, finding even more favour with the Greek God.

'I thought he would,' Ari answered. 'My nephews do. Their rooms are full of it.'

'Talking of family,' her mother quickly slid in. 'Your father has apparently insisted on paying for all our accommodation here and...'

'It is his pleasure to do so, Mrs Savalas,' Ari broke in with a smile to wipe out her concern. 'If you were staying on Patmos, George's family would see to it. Here, on Santorini, my father is your host and he has asked me to extend an invitation to all of you for dinner tonight at our family home. Then we will not be strangers at the wedding.'

Her mother instantly melted. 'Oh! How kind!'

Tina glared at Ari. Had he lied about keeping the deal? And what of his parents? Had he warned them not to reveal their relationship to Theo? He was pursuing his own agenda and she wasn't at all sure he would respect hers. Far from melting at his *kindness,* every nerve in her body stiffened with battle tension.

Ari kept smiling. 'I've told my mother it's your birthday, Theo. She's planning a special cake with five candles for you to blow out and make a wish. You've got all day to think about what to wish for.'

All day to worm his way into Theo's heart with his facile charm, Tina thought grimly. She knew only too well he could be *Mr Wonderful* for a while. It was the long haul that worried her—how *constant* Ari would be as a father.

'Are you coming with us today, Mrs Savalas?' he asked, apparently happy to have her mother's company, as well, probably wanting the opportunity to get her even more onside with him.

'No, no. It sounds too busy for me. I shall stroll into the township in my own time, take a look at the church where the wedding is to be held, do a little shopping, visit the museum.' She smiled at Tina, her eyes full of encouraging speculation. 'Much better for you young people to go off together.'

Tina barely stopped herself from rolling her own eyes at what was obviously some romantic delusion. Gorgeous man—unmarried daughter—Greek island in the sun.

'I shall look forward to the family dinner tonight,' her mother added, giving whole-hearted approval to Ari's plans for the whole day.

Tina smothered a groan.

No escape.

She had agreed to letting him into their lives in return for his silence until after the wedding, but if he or his parents let the cat out of the bag tonight, she would

bite their heads off for putting their self-interest ahead
of everything else.

After a brief return to their room to put the Lego gift
on Theo's bed, refresh themselves, and collect hats and
swimming costumes, they re-met Ari and set off for
the five-minute walk into the main township of Fira.
Tina deliberately placed Theo between them. He held
her hand, and unknowingly, his father's. She wondered
how she was going to explain this truth to him—another nail in her heart.

'Are your parents aware of our deal?' she asked Ari
over Theo's head.

'They will be in good time,' he assured her.

She had to believe him…until his assurance proved
false, like the words he had spoken to her in the past.
Would he play fair with her this time? She could only
hope so. This wasn't about him. Or her. It was about
the life of their child.

The view from the path into town was spectacular,
overlooking the fantastic sea-filled crater with its tower-
ing cliffs. Two splendid white cruise ships stood in the
middle of the glittering blue harbour and Theo pointed
to them excitedly.

'Are we going to ride in one of those boats?'

'No, they're far too big to move close to land,' Ari
answered. 'See the smaller boats going out to them?
They're to take the people off and bring them to the
island. We'll be riding in a motor-launch that can take
us wherever we want to go. You can even steer it for a
while if you like.'

Theo was agog. 'Can I? Can I really?'

Ari laughed. 'You can sit on my lap and be the captain. I'll show you what to do.'

'Did you hear that, Mama? I'll be captain of the boat.'

'Your boat, Ari?' Tina asked, anxiously wondering what other goodies he had up his sleeve, ready to roll out for Theo's pleasure.

'A family boat. It will be waiting for us at the town wharf.'

His family. His very wealthy family. How could she stop the seduction of her son by these people? He was a total innocent, as she had been before meeting Ari. He was bound to be deeply impressed by them and the outcome might be a terrible tug-of-war for his love.

Tina suffered major heartburn as they strolled on into town. It was so easy for Ari to win Theo over. It had been easy for him to win her over. He had everything going for him. Even now, knowing how treacherous it was, she still had to fight the pull of his attraction. After him, no other man had interested her, not once in the years since he had left her behind. While he, no doubt, had had his pick of any number of beautiful women who had sparked his interest. Like the blonde in Dubai and probably dozens of others.

It was all terribly wrong. He had been the only man in her life and she'd meant nothing to him. She only meant something to him now because she was the mother of his child and he had to deal with her.

On the road up to the beautiful white church dominating the hillside, a statue of a donkey stood outside a tourist shop displaying many stands of postcards. The donkey was painted pink and it had a slot for letters in its mid-section. Over the slot was painted a red heart with the words POST OF LOVE printed on it.

'I didn't get to sit on the camel, Mama. Can I sit on this donkey?' Theo pleaded.

'You'll be sitting on a real donkey soon. Won't that be better?' Tina cajoled, mentally shying from anything connected with *love*.

Theo shook his head. 'It won't be pink. I'd like a photo of me on this one.'

'Then we must do it for the birthday boy,' Ari said, hoisting Theo up on the donkey and standing beside him to ensure he sat on it safely.

They both grinned at her, so much a picture of father and son it tore at Tina's heart as she viewed it through the camera and took the requested shot.

'Now if you'll stand by Theo, I'll take one of the two of you together,' Ari quickly suggested.

'Yes! Come on, Mama!' Theo backed him up.

She handed Ari her camera and swapped places with him.

'Smile!' he commanded.

She put a smile on her face. As soon as he'd used her camera he whipped a mobile phone out of his shirt pocket and clicked off another shot of them. To show his parents, Tina instantly thought. *This is the woman who is Theo's mother and this is your grandson.* It would probably answer some fleeting curiosity about her, but they would zero straight in on Theo, seeing Ari in him—a Zavros, not a Savalas.

'You have a beautiful smile, Christina,' Ari said

warmly as he returned her camera and lifted Theo off the donkey.

'Stop it!' she muttered, glaring a hostile rejection at him. She couldn't bear him buttering her up when he probably had some killing blow in mind to gain custody of his son.

He returned a puzzled frown. 'Stop what?'

Theo was distracted by a basket of soft toys set out beside the postcard stands, giving her space enough to warn Ari off the totally unwelcome sweet-talking.

'I don't want any more of your compliments.'

His gesture denied any harm in them. 'I was only speaking the truth.'

'They remind me of what a fool I was with you. I won't be fooled again, Ari.'

He grimaced. 'I'm sorry you read more into our previous relationship than was meant, Christina.'

'Oh! What exactly did you mean when you said I was special?' she sliced back at him, her eyes flashing outright scepticism.

He gave her a look that sent a wave of heat through her, right down to her toes. 'You were special. Very special. I just wasn't ready to take on a long-term relationship at the time. But I am now. I want to marry you, Christina.'

Her heart stopped. She stared at him in total shock. No way had she expected this. It was Theo, her stunned mind started to reason. Ari thought it was the best way—the easiest way—to get Theo. Who *she* was, and what *she* wanted was irrelevant.

'Forget it!' she said tersely. 'I'm not about to change my life for your convenience.'

'I could make it convenient for you, too,' he quickly countered.

Her eyes mocked his assertion. 'How do you figure that?'

'A life of ease. No fighting over Theo. We bring him up together. You'll have ample opportunity to do whatever you want within reason.'

'Marriage to you is no guarantee of that. You can dangle as many carrots as you like in front of me, Ari. I'm not biting.'

'What if I give you a guarantee? I'll have a prenuptial agreement drawn up that would assure you and Theo of financial security for the rest of your lives.' His mouth took on an ironic twist. 'Think of it as fair payment for the pain I've given you.'

'I'm perfectly capable of supporting Theo.'

'Not to the extent of giving him every advantage that wealth can provide.'

'Money isn't everything. Besides, I don't want to be your wife. That would simply be asking for more pain.'

He frowned. 'I remember the pleasure we both took in making love. It can be that way again, Christina.'

She flushed at the reminder of how slavishly she had adored him. 'You think a seductive honeymoon makes a marriage, Ari? Taking me as your wife is just a cynical exercise in legality. It gives you full access to our son. Once you have that, I won't matter to you. You'll meet other women who will be happy to provide you with a *special* experience. Can you honestly say you'll pass that up?'

'If I have you willing to share my bed, and the family I hope we'll have together, I shall be a faithful husband like my father,' he said with every appearance of sincerity.

'How can I believe that?' she cried, sure that his sincerity couldn't be genuine.

'Tonight you will meet my parents. Their marriage was arranged but they made it work. It was bonded in family and they are completely devoted to each other. I see no reason why we cannot achieve that same happiness, given enough goodwill between us. Goodwill for the sake of our son, Christina.'

'Except I don't trust you,' she flashed back at him. 'I have no reason to trust you.'

'Then we can have it written into the prenuptial agreement that should you file for divorce because of my proven infidelity, you will get full custody of our children, as well as a financial settlement that will cover every possible need.'

Tina was stunned again. 'You'd go that far?'

'Yes. That is the deal I'm offering you, Christina.' As Theo moved back to claim their attention, Ari shot her one last purposeful look and muttered, 'Think about it!'

CHAPTER SIX

ARI was deeply vexed with himself. Christina *had* pushed him too far. He should have stuck to the financial deal and not let her mocking mistrust goad him into offering full custody if he didn't remain faithful to their marriage. It was impossible to backtrack on it now. If she remained cold and hard towards him, he'd just condemned himself to a bed he certainly wouldn't want to lie in for long.

The will to win was in his blood but usually his mind warned him when the price to be paid was becoming unacceptable. Why hadn't he weighed it up this time? It was as though he was mesmerised by the fierce challenge emanating from her, the dark blaze of energy fighting him with all her might, making him want to win regardless of the cost.

The stakes were high. He wanted his son full-time, living in his home, not on the other side of the world with visits parcelled out by a family law-court. But something very strong in him wanted to win Christina over, too. Maybe it was instinct telling him she could make him the kind of wife he'd be happy to live with—

better than any of the other women he knew. She'd proved herself a good mother—a deeply caring mother. As for the sharing his bed part, surely it wouldn't prove too difficult to establish some workable accord there.

She'd been putty in his hands once, a beautiful rose-bud of a girl whose petals he had gradually unfurled, bringing her to full glorious bloom. She was made of much stronger stuff now. The power of her passion excited him. It was negative passion towards him at the moment, but if he could turn it around, push it into a positive flow...

She did have a beautiful smile. He wanted to make it light up for him. And he wanted to see her magnificent dark eyes sparkling with pleasure—pleasure in him. The marriage bed need not be cold. If he could press the right buttons...he had to or he'd just proposed the worst deal of his life.

He took stock of this different Christina as they wandered through the alleys of shops leading up to the summit of the town. The short hair did suit her, giving more emphasis to her striking cheekbones and her lovely long neck. Her full-lipped mouth was very sexy—bee-stung lips like Angelina Jolie's, though not quite as pronounced. She wasn't quite as tall as her sister, nor as slim. She was, in fact, very sweetly curved, her breasts fuller than when she was younger, her waist not as tiny—probably because of childbirth—but still provocatively feminine in the flow to her neatly rounded hips.

Today she was wearing a pretty lemon and white striped top that was cut into clever angles that spelled designer wear—possibly a gift from Cassandra. She'd teamed it with white Capri pants and she certainly had the legs to wear them with distinction—legs that Ari wanted wound around him in urgent need. She could make him a fine wife, one he would be proud to own, one he wouldn't stray from if she let herself respond to him.

He would make it happen.

One way or another he had to make it happen.

Marriage! Never in her wildest imagination had Tina thought it might be a possibility with Ari Zavros, not since he'd left Australia, putting a decisive end to any such romantic notion. But this wasn't romance. It was a coldly calculated deal to get what he wanted and he probably thought he could fool her on the fidelity front.

How on earth could she believe he wouldn't stray in the future? Even as they strolled along the alleys filled with fascinating shops women stared at him, gobbling him up with their eyes. When she stopped to buy a pretty scarf, the saleswoman kept looking at him, barely glancing at Tina as she paid for it.

The man was a sex magnet. Despite how he'd left her flat, she wasn't immune to the vibrations, either, which made it doubly dangerous to get involved with him on any intimate level. He'd only hurt her again. To marry him would be masochistic madness. But it was probably best to pretend to be thinking about *his* deal until after Cass's wedding to ensure he kept *her* deal.

Then the truth could come out without it being such a distracting bombshell and visitation rights could be discussed. She wouldn't deny him time with his son since he seemed so intent on embracing fatherhood, but he would have to come to Australia for it. Greece was not Theo's home and she wasn't about to let that be changed.

They reached the summit of the town where a cable-car ran down to the old port. Alternatively one could take a donkey-ride along a zig-zag path from top to bottom. Tina would have much preferred to take the cable-car. Ari, however, was bent on making good his promise to Theo, and she made no protest as he selected three donkeys for them to ride—the smallest one for their son, the biggest one for himself and an average-sized one for her.

Theo was beside himself with excitement as Ari lifted him onto the one chosen for him. Tina quickly refused any need for his help, using a stool to mount her donkey. She didn't want to feel Ari's hands on her, nor have him so close that he would have a disturbing physical effect on her. She'd been unsettled enough by his ridiculous offer of marriage.

He grinned at her as he mounted his own donkey, probably arrogantly confident of getting his own way, just as he was getting his own way about Theo's birth-day. She gave him a *beautiful* smile back, letting him think whatever he liked, knowing in her heart she would do what *she* considered best for her child, and being a miserable mother in a miserable marriage was definitely not best.

'I'll ride beside Theo,' he said. 'If you keep your

donkey walking behind his, I'll be able to control both of them.'

'Are they likely to get out of control?' she asked apprehensively.

'They're fed at the bottom and some of them have a tendency to bolt when they near the end of the path.'

'Oh, great!'

He flashed another confident grin. 'Don't worry. I'll take care of you both. That's a promise, Christina.'

His eyes telegraphed it was meant for the future, too.

He could work overtime on his deal, making it as attractive as he could, but she wasn't having any of it, Tina thought grimly. However, she did have to concede he kept their donkeys at a controlled pace when others started to rush past them. And he cheerfully answered Theo's constant questions with all the patience of an indulgent father.

Her son was laughing with delight and giving Ari an impulsive hug as he was lifted off the donkey. For Tina, it was a relief to get her feet back on solid ground. She'd been far too tense to enjoy her ride.

'We'll take the cable-car back up when we return,' Ari said soothingly, aware of her unease.

She nodded, muttering, 'That would be good.'

'Which boat is ours?' Theo asked, eagerly looking forward to the next treat.

Ari pointed. 'This one coming into the wharf now.'

'Looks like you already have a captain,' Tina remarked.

'Oh, Jason will be happy to turn the wheel over to Theo while he's preparing lunch for us. It will be an easy day for him. When the boat is not in family use, he takes out charters, up to eight people at a time. Today he only has three to look after.'

The good-humoured reply left her nothing to say. Besides, she was sure everything on board would run perfectly for Theo's pleasure. Ari would not fail in his mission to have his son thinking the *nice* man was absolutely wonderful. He'd been wonderful to her for three whole months without one slip for any doubt about him to enter her head.

The white motor launch was in pristine condition. A blue and white striped canopy shaded the rear deck which had bench seats softened by blue and white striped cushions. Tina was invited to sit down and relax while Jason got the boat under way again and Ari took Theo to fetch drinks and give him a tour of the galley.

She sat and tried to concentrate on enjoying the marvellous view, let the day flow past without drawing attention to herself. Tonight's family dinner would test her nerves to the limit, but at least her mother would be there, helping to keep normal conversation rolling along. And despite the stress this meeting with Ari's parents would inevitably cause, Tina told herself she did need to see the Zavros home environment, check that it would be a good place for Theo to be if visits to Santorini had to be arranged.

She smiled as she heard Theo say, 'I'm not allowed to have Coca-Cola. Mama says it's not good for me. I can have water or milk or fruit-juice.'

Welcome to the world of parenting, Ari. It isn't all fun and games. Making healthy choices for your child is an important part of it. Would he bother to take that kind of care or would he hire a nanny to do the real business of parenting?

Tina mentally ticked that off as an item to be discussed before agreeing to visits.

'Okay, what would you like?' he asked, not questioning her drinks ruling.

'Orange juice.'

'And what does your Mama like?'

'Water. She drinks lots of water.'

'No wine?'

Not since you put intoxicating bubbles in my brain.

'No. It's water or coffee or tea for Mama,' Theo said decisively.

'Well, after our hot walk, I guess iced water would be the best choice.'

'Yes,' Theo agreed.

He carried out jugs of orange juice and iced water, setting them on the fixed table which served the bench seats. Theo brought a stack of plastic glasses, carefully separating them out as Ari returned to the galley, emerging again with a platter containing a selection of cheeses and crackers, nuts, olives and grapes.

'There we are! Help yourselves,' he invited, though he did pour out the drinks for them—water for him, too.

'I love olives,' Theo declared, quickly biting into one.

'Ah! A true Greek,' Ari said proudly.

Tina instantly bridled. 'Theo is an Australian.'

'But Yia Yia is Greek, Mama,' Theo piped up.

'Definitely some Greek blood there,' Ari declared,

a glittering blast from his golden eyes defying Tina's claim.

'True,' she agreed, deciding the point that needed to be made could be driven home when Theo was not present. Australia was their home country. Theo was an Australian citizen. And the family court in Australia would come down on Tina's side. At least she had that in her favour.

Ari chatted away to their son who positively basked in his father's attention. He explained about the volcano as they sailed towards what was left of it, telling the story of what had happened in the far distant past, how the volcano had erupted and destroyed everything. Theo lapped it up, fascinated by the huge disaster, and eager to walk up to the crater when they disembarked there.

Then it was on to the islet of Palea Kameni for a swim in the hot springs—another new exciting experience for Theo. Tina didn't really want to change into her bikini, being far too physically conscious of Ari looking at her to feel comfortable in it, but she liked the idea of letting Theo go alone with him even less. He was *her son* and she was afraid of giving Ari free rein with him without her supervision.

Unfortunately Ari in a brief black swimming costume reduced her comfort zone to nil. His almost naked perfectly proportioned male body brought memories of their previous intimacy flooding back. She'd loved being with him in bed; loved touching him, feeling him, looking at him, loved the intense pleasure he'd given her in so many ways. It had been the best time of her life. It hurt, even now, that it had only been *a charming episode* for him. It hurt even more that she couldn't control the treacherous desire to have him again.

She could if she married him. She probably could anyhow. He'd lusted after her before without marriage in mind. But having sex with him again wouldn't feel the same. She wouldn't be able to give herself to him whole-heartedly, knowing she wasn't the love of his life. There would be too many shadows in any bed they shared.

It was easier to push the memories aside when they were back on the boat and properly dressed again. Ari in clothes was not quite so mesmerising. He and Theo took over the wheel, playing at being captain together, steering the boat towards the village of Oia on the far point of Santorini while Jason was busy in the galley.

They had a delicious lunch of freshly cooked fish and salad. After all the activity and with his stomach full, Theo curled up on the bench seat, his head on Tina's lap and went to sleep. Jason was instructed to keep the boat cruising around until the boy woke. If there was still time to visit Oia, he could then take them into the small port.

'We don't want him too tired to enjoy his birthday party tonight,' Ari remarked to Tina.

'No. I think we should head home when he wakes. We've done all you promised him, Ari. He should have some quiet time, building the Lego train station before more excitement tonight,' Tina said, needing some quiet time for herself, as well. It was stressful being constantly in the company of the man who was intent on breaking into her life again.

'Okay.' He gave her an admiring look. 'You've done a good job with him, Christina. He's a delightful child.'

She gritted her teeth, determined not to be seduced by his compliments, deliberately moving her gaze to the black cliffs ahead of them. 'I think it's important to instill good principles in a child as early as possible,' she said, a sudden wave of resentment towards him making her add, 'I don't want him to grow up like you.'

His silence tore at her nerves but she refused to look at him.

Eventually he asked, 'What particular fault of mine are you referring to?'

'Thinking women are your toys to be picked up and played with as you please,' she answered, wishing he could be honest about himself and honest to her. 'I want Theo to give consideration to how he touches others' lives. I hope when he connects with people he will always leave them feeling good.'

Another long silence.

Out of the corner of her eye she saw Ari lean forward, resting his forearms on his thighs. 'If you had not fallen pregnant, Christina,' he said softly, 'wouldn't I have left you with good memories of our relationship?'

'You left me shattered, Ari,' she answered bluntly. 'My parents had brought me up to be a good girl believing that sex should only be part of a loving relationship. I truly believed that with you and it wasn't so. Then when I realised I was pregnant, it made everything so much worse. I had to bear their disappointment in me, as well as knowing I'd simply been your sex toy for a while.'

In some ways it was a relief to blurt out the truth to him, though whether it meant anything to him or not was unknowable. Maybe it might make him treat her with more respect. She was not a pawn to be moved around at his will. She was a person who had to be dealt with as a person who had the right to determine her own life and this time she would do it according to her principles.

Ari shook his head. He was in a hard place here. He wasn't used to feeling guilty about his actions or the decisions he'd made. It was not a feeling he liked. Christina had just given a perspective on their previous relationship that he'd never considered and quite clearly it had to be considered if he was to turn this situation around.

She was staring into space—a space that only she occupied, shutting him out. Yet her hand was idly stroking the hair of their sleeping son. He was the connection between them—the only connection Ari could count on right now. He was no longer sure he could reach her sexually, though he would still give it a damned good try. In the meantime he had to start redeeming himself in her eyes or she would never allow herself to be vulnerable to the physical attraction which he knew was not completely dead.

He'd felt her gaze on him at the hot springs, saw it quickly flick away whenever he looked at her. She kept shoring up defences against him by reliving how he'd wronged her in the past. Would she ever let that go or would he be paying for his sins against her far into the future?

'I'm sorry,' he said quietly. 'It was wrong of me to take you. I think it was your innocence that made you so entrancing, so different, so special, and the way you looked at me then… I found it irresistible, Christina. If it means anything to you, there hasn't been a woman since whose company has given me more pleasure.'

As he spoke the words which were designed to be persuasive, there was a slight kick in Ari's mind—a jolting realization that he was actually stating the truth. When he'd moved on, he'd mentally set her aside—too young, not the right time for a serious relationship—but the moment he'd recognised her in Dubai, he'd wanted to experience the sweetness of her all over again, especially when he'd just been suffering the sour taste of Felicity Fullbright.

Christina shook her head. She didn't believe him.

'It's true,' he insisted.

She turned to look at him, dark intense eyes scouring his for insincerity. He held her testing gaze, everything within him tuned to convincing her they could make another start, forge a new understanding between them.

'You didn't come back to me, Ari,' she stated simply. 'You forgot me.'

'No. I put you away from me for reasons that I thought were valid at the time but I didn't forget you, Christina. The moment I recognised you in Dubai, the urge to pick up with you again was instant. And that was before you told me about Theo.'

She frowned, hopefully realising the impulse had been there before she had spoken of their son. 'You were with another woman,' she muttered as though that urge was tarnished, too.

'I was already wishing that I wasn't before I saw you. Please…at least believe this of me. It's true.'

For the first time he saw a hint of uncertainty in her eyes. She lowered her long thick lashes, hiding her thoughts. 'Tell me what your valid reasons were.'

'To my mind, we both still had a lot to achieve on our own without ties holding us back from making choices we would have made by ourselves. You'd barely started your modelling career, Christina, and it was obvious you had the promise of making it big on the international scene. As your sister has done.'

Her mouth twisted into a wry grimace as she looked down at their sleeping son. 'If you didn't forget me, Ari, did you ever wonder why I never broke into the international scene?'

'I did expect you to. I thought you had chosen to stay in Australia. Some people don't like leaving everything that is familiar to them.'

'I wasn't worth coming back to,' she murmured, heaving a sigh that made him feel she had just shed whatever progress he had made with her.

'I was caught up dealing with family business these past six years, Christina,' he swiftly argued. 'It's only now…meeting you again and being faced with my own son that my priorities are undergoing an abrupt change.'

'Give it time, Ari,' she said dryly. 'They might change again.'

'No. I won't be taking my marriage proposal off the table. I want you to consider it very seriously.'

She slid him a measuring look that promised nothing. 'I'll think about it. Don't ask any more of me now.' She nodded down at Theo. 'I'm tired, too. Please ask Jason to head back to Fira.'

'As you wish,' he said, rising from the bench seat to do her bidding.

Trying to push her further would not accomplish any more than he had already accomplished today. She didn't trust him yet but at least she was listening to him. Tonight would give him the chance to show her the family environment he wanted to move her and Theo into. He had to make it as attractive as he could.

CHAPTER SEVEN

WHILE Theo was occupied fitting the pieces of the Lego train station together, Tina tried to imagine what her life might have been like if she hadn't fallen pregnant. Would she have picked herself up from the deeply wounding disillusionment of her love for Ari and channelled all her energy into forging a successful modelling career?

Almost certainly.

She had been very young—only eighteen at the time—and having been rejected by him she would have wanted to *show* him she really was special—so special he would regret not holding onto her.

Cassandra would have helped her to get a foot in on the international scene. Given the chance, she would have tried to make it to the top, delivering whatever was required to keep herself in demand and in the public eye; fashion shows, magazine covers, celebrity turn-outs that would give her even more publicity. Ambition would have been all fired up to make Ari have second thoughts about his decision, make him want to meet her again.

When and if he did she would have played it very cool. No melting on the spot. She would have made him chase her, earn her, and she wouldn't have given in to him until he'd declared himself helplessly in love with her and couldn't live without her. He would have had to propose marriage.

Which he'd done today.

Except the circumstances were very different to what might have been if Theo had never been conceived. That completely changed the plot, making the marriage proposal worth nothing to her.

Though Ari's face had lit up with pleasure at seeing her in Dubai.

But that was only a *fond memory* rekindled.

She wasn't the same naive, stars-in-her-eyes girl and never would be again, so it was impossible for him to recapture the pleasure he'd had in her company in the past. Surely he had to realise that. Empty words, meaning nothing.

She shouldn't let herself be affected by anything he said. Or by his mega sex appeal which was an unsettling distraction, pulling her into wanting to believe he was sincere when he was probably intent on conducting a softening-up process so she would bend to his will. It was important to keep her head straight tonight. He had rights where Theo was concerned. He had none over her.

It was still very hot outside their room when it came time to dress for the birthday party. Her mother, of course, was wearing black—a smart tunic and skirt with an array of gold jewellery to make it look festive.

Tina chose a red and white sundress for herself, teaming it with white sandals and dangly earrings made of little white shells.

She put Theo in navy shorts, navy sandals, and a navy and white top with red stripes across the chest. He insisted on having the big red birthday badge with the smiley face and the number 5 pinned onto it. Ari had bought it for him this morning on their stroll around the shops and Theo wore it proudly.

'See!' he cried, pointing to his badge when Ari came to pick them up.

Ari laughed, lifted him up high, whirled him around, then held him against his shoulder, grinning at him as he said, 'It's a grand thing to be five, Theo.'

There was little doubt in Tina's mind that Theo would love to have Ari as his Papa. Her heart sank at the thought of how much would have to change when the truth had to be admitted. Ari's parents already knew. She could only hope they would handle this meeting with care and discretion.

To her immense relief, Ari seated her mother beside him on the drive to his home on the other end of the island. It was near the Santo winery, he said. Which reminded Tina that he had come to Australia on a tour of the wine industry there. As they passed terraces of grapevines, it was fascinating to see the vines spread across the ground instead of trained to stand in upright rows. To protect the grapes from the strong winds, Ari explained to her mother who happily chatted to him the whole way.

Eventually they arrived at the Zavros home. The

semicircular driveway was dominated by a fountain
with three mermaids as its centrepiece, which instantly fascinated Theo. The home itself appeared to
be three Mediterranean-style villas linked by colon-
nades. Naturally it was white, like most of the buildings on Santorini. Ari led them to the central building
which was larger than the other two. It all shrieked of
great wealth. Intimidating wealth to Tina.

'We're dining on the terrace,' he informed them,
shepherding them along a high spacious hallway that
clearly bisected this villa.

The floor was magnificently tiled in a pattern of
waves and seashells. They emerged onto a huge terrace
overlooking the sea. In front of them was a sparkling
blue swimming pool. To the left was a long vine-
covered pergola and Tina's heart instantly kicked into
a faster beat as she saw what had to be Ari's parents,
seated at a table underneath it.

They rose from their chairs to extend a welcome to
their guests. Tension whipped along Tina's nerves as
both of them looked at Theo first. However their attention on him didn't last too long. They greeted her
mother very graciously and waited for her to introduce
her daughter and grandson.

Maximus Zavros was an older version of Ari in
looks. His wife, Sophie, was still quite a striking woman
with a lovely head of soft wavy hair, warm brown eyes
and a slightly plump, very curvaceous figure. Although
they smiled at her as she was introduced, Tina was
acutely conscious of their scrutiny—sizing her up as

the mother of their grandson. It was a relief when they finally turned their gaze to Theo again.

'And this is the birthday boy,' Sophie Zavros said indulgently.

'Five!' Theo said proudly, pointing to his badge. Then he gave Ari's father a curious look. 'Your name is Maximus?'

'Yes, it is. If it is easier for you, tonight you can call me Max,' he invited, smiling benevolently.

'Oh, no! I *like* Maximus,' Theo said with a broad smile back. 'Mama took me to a movie about a girl with very long hair. What was her name, Mama?'

'Rapunzel,' Tina supplied, barely stopping herself from rolling her eyes at what was bound to come next.

'Rapunzel,' he repeated. 'But the best part of the movie was the horse. His name was Maximus and he was a great horse!'

'I'm glad he was a great horse,' Ari's father said, amused by the connection.

'He was so good at everything!' Theo assured him. 'And he saved them in the end, didn't he, Mama?'

'Yes, he did.'

Ari's father crouched down to Theo's eye level. 'I think I must get hold of this movie. Maybe you and I could watch it together sometime. Would you like to see it again?'

Theo nodded happily.

'Well, I'm not a horse but I can give you a ride over to the table.'

He swept his grandson up in his arms and trotted him to the table, making Theo bubble with laughter. It startled Tina that such a powerful man would be so playful. Her mother and Sophie were laughing, too—any awkwardness at meeting strangers completely broken. She glanced at Ari who was also looking on in amusement.

He quickly moved closer to her, murmuring, 'Relax, Christina. We just want to make this a special night for Theo.'

'Have you told them of your plan to marry me?' she asked quickly, wanting to know if she was being sized up as a possible daughter-in-law.

'Yes, but there will be no pressure for you to agree tonight. This is a different beginning for us, Christina, with our families involved, because it is about family this time.'

His eyes burned serious conviction into hers.

It rattled her deep-seated prejudice against believing anything he said. She sucked in a deep breath and tried to let her inner angst go. This *was* a different scenario between them with their families involved. She decided to judge the night on its merits, see how she felt about it afterwards. To begin with she told herself to be glad that Ari's parents were the kind of people Theo could take to because there was no avoiding the fact they would feature in his future.

Maximus Zavros had seated Theo in the chair on the left of his own at the head of the table. Sophie ushered Tina's mother to the chair next to Theo's and to the right of her own chair at the foot of the table. Ari guided Tina to the chair opposite Theo's, putting her next to his father before sitting beside her.

As soon as they were all seated a man-servant appeared, bringing two platters of hors d'oeuvres. Another followed, bringing jugs of iced water and orange juice.

Ari's father turned to her, pleasantly asking, 'Can I persuade you to try one of our local wines?'

She shook her head. 'No, thank you. I prefer water.'

He looked at her mother. 'Helen?'

'I'm happy to try whatever you suggest, Maximus. I've tasted two of the wines that were sent to my room and they were quite splendid.'

'Ah, I'm glad they pleased your palate.' He signalled to the servant to pour the chosen wine into glasses while he himself filled Tina's glass with water and Theo's with orange juice. He beamed a smile at his grandson. 'Ari tells me you can swim like a fish.'

'I love swimming,' was his enthusiastic reply.

'Did your Mama teach you?'

Theo looked at Tina, unsure of the answer. 'Did you, Mama?'

'No. I took you to tadpole classes when you were only nine months old. You've always loved being in water and you learnt to swim very young.' She turned to Maximus. 'It's important for any child to be able to swim in Australia. There are so many backyard pools and every year there are cases of young children drowning. Also, we live near Bondi Beach, so I particularly wanted Theo to be safe in the water.'

'Very sensible,' Maximus approved, nodding to the pool beyond the pergola. 'There will be no danger for him here, either.'

That was just the start of many subtle and not so

subtle points made to her throughout the evening, by both of Ari's parents. They were clearly intent on welcoming their grandson into their life, assuring her he would be well taken care of and greatly loved. And not once was there any hint of criticism of her for keeping them in ignorance of him until now.

She fielded a few testing questions from Maximus about her own life, but for the most part Ari's parents set out to charm and Tina noticed her mother having a lovely time with Sophie, discussing the forthcoming wedding and marriage in general.

After the hors d'oeuvres, they were served souvlaki and salad which Theo had informed Ari on the boat was his favourite meal. Then came the birthday cake and Ari reminded Theo to make a wish as he blew out the candles—all five of them in one big burst. Everyone clapped and cheered at his success.

The cake was cut and slices of it were served around the table. It was a rich, many layered chocolate cake, moist and delicious, and Theo gobbled his piece up, the first to finish.

'Will I get my wish?' he asked Ari.

'I hope so, Theo. Although if you were wishing for a horse like Maximus, that might be asking for too much.'

'Is wishing for a Papa too much?'

Tina's hands clenched in her lap. Her lungs seized up. The silence around the table felt loaded with emotional dynamite.

'No, that's not asking for too much,' Ari answered decisively.

Her mother leaned over and pulled Theo onto her

lap, giving him a cuddle. 'You miss your Papou, don't you, darling?' She gave Sophie a rueful smile. 'My husband died a year ago. He adored Theo. We didn't have sons, you see, and having a grandson was like a beautiful gift.'

'Yes. A very beautiful gift,' Sophie repeated huskily, her gaze lingering on Theo for a moment before shooting a look of heart-tugging appeal at Tina.

'I think with Ari giving him such a wonderful time today...' her mother rattled on.

'Ari is very good with children,' Sophie broke in. 'His nephews love being with him. He will make a wonderful father.'

Ostensibly she was speaking to her mother but Tina knew the words were for her. Maybe they were true. He might very well be a wonderful father, but being a wonderful husband was something else.

'Maximus and I very much want to see him settled down with his own family,' Sophie carried on.

'Mama, don't push,' Ari gently chided.

She heaved a sigh which drew Tina's mother into a string of sympathetic comments about young people taking their time about getting married these days.

Tina sat in frozen silence until Ari's father leaned towards her and asked, 'Who is managing your family restaurant while you are away, Christina?'

She had to swallow hard to moisten her throat before answering, 'The head chef and the head waiter.'

'You trust them to do it well?'

'Yes. My father set it up before he died that both men

get a percentage of the profits. It's in their best interests to keep it running successfully.'

'Ah! A man of foresight, your father,' he said with satisfaction.

Tina *knew* he was thinking the restaurant could keep running successfully without her. 'It needs an overall manager and my father entrusted me with that job,' she said with defiant pride.

'Which is a measure of his respect for your abilities, Christina. But as a Greek father myself, I know it was not what he wanted for you.'

His amber eyes burned that certain knowledge into her heart. There was no denying it. Her father had not been against his daughters having a career of their choice but he had believed a woman was only truly fulfilled with the love of a good husband and the love of their children.

It hurt, being reminded of her failure to live up to his expectations of her, but the big word in her father's beliefs was love, and Ari did not love her. She faced his father with her own burning determination. 'I have the right to choose what I do with my life. My father respected that, as well.'

'I don't think the choice is so unequivocal when you are a mother, Christina,' he shot back at her. 'The rights of your child have to be considered.'

'Papa…' Ari said in a low warning voice.

'She must understand this, Ari,' was the quick riposte.

'I do,' Tina told him flatly. 'And I am considering them.' She lowered her voice so as not to be overheard at the other end of the table as she fiercely added, 'I hope you do, too, because I *am* Theo's mother and I always will be.'

She would not allow them to take over her son. She would concede visits but knew she would hate every minute Theo was away from her. Not all their wealth and caring would make any difference to the hole that would leave in her life until he returned to her. Tears pricked her eyes. Her head was swimming with all the difficulties that lay ahead.

'Please, forgive me my trespasses,' Ari's father said gruffly. 'You're a fine mother, Christina. And that will always be respected by our family. The boy is a credit to you. How can I put it? I want very much to enjoy more of him.'

A warm hand slid over one of her clenched fists and gently squeezed. 'It's all right, Christina,' Ari murmured, 'You're amongst friends, not enemies.'

She stared down at his hand, biting her lips as she tried to fight back the tears. He'd offered his hand in marriage, which was the easiest way out of the custody issue, but how could she take it when she felt so vulnerable to what he could do to her—twisting up her life all over again?

She swallowed hard to ease the choking sensation in her throat and without looking at either man, said, 'I want to go back to the resort now, Ari. It's been a long day.'

'Of course.' Another gentle squeeze of her hand. 'It's been good of you to let us spend this time together.'

'Yes. A wonderful evening,' his father chimed in. 'Thank you, Christina.'

She nodded, not wanting to be drawn into another stressful conversation. She felt painfully pressured as it was. Her gaze lifted to check Theo who was now nodding off on her mother's lap.

Ari rose from his chair. 'Helen, Mama… Christina is tired and it looks like Theo is ready for bed, as well. It's time to call it a night. I'll carry him out to the car, Helen.'

Ari's parents accompanied them out to the car, walking beside her mother who thanked them profusely for their hospitality. All three expressed pleasure in meeting up again at the wedding. Both Maximus and Sophie dropped goodnight kisses on Theo's forehead before Ari passed him over to Tina in the back seat. She thanked them for the birthday party and the car door was finally closed on it, relieving some of the tension in her chest.

Theo slept all the way back to the resort and the conversation between Ari and her mother in the front seats was conducted in low murmurs. Tina sat in silence, hugging her child, feeling intensely possessive of him and already grieving over how much she would have to part from him.

Having arrived at El Greco, Ari once again lifted Theo into his arms and insisted on carrying him to their accommodation. Tina did not protest, knowing that to her mother this was the natural thing for a man to do. The problem came when she unlocked her door and instead of passing Theo to her, Ari carried him straight into her room.

'Which bed?' he asked.

She dashed past him to turn back the covers on Theo's bed and Ari gently laid him down and tucked him in, dropping a kiss on his forehead before straightening up and smiling down at his sleeping son, making Tina's heart contract at the memory of Theo's wish for a Papa. He had one. And very soon he had to know it.

Ari turned to her and she instantly felt a flood of electricity tingling through her entire body. He was too close to her, dangerously close, exuding the sexual magnetism that she should be immune to but wasn't. Being in a bedroom with Ari Zavros, virtually alone with him, was a bad place to be. She quickly backed off, hurrying to the door, waving for him to leave.

He followed but paused beside her, causing inner havoc again. He raised a hand to touch her cheek and she flinched away from the contact. 'Just go, Ari,' she said harshly. 'You've had your day.'

He frowned at her unfriendliness. 'I only wanted to thank you, Christina.'

She forced her voice to a reasonable tone. 'Okay, but you can do that without touching me.'

'Is my touch so repellent to you?'

Panic tore through her at how vulnerable she might be to it. She stared hard at him, desperate not to show him any weakness. 'Don't push it, Ari. I've had enough, today.'

He nodded. 'I'll call you in the morning.'

'No! Tomorrow is *my* family day,' she said firmly. 'Cassandra will be joining us and so will all our relatives from the mainland. We'll meet again at the wedding.'

For one nerve-wracking moment she thought he would challenge her decision. It surprised her when he smiled and said, 'Then I'll look forward to the wedding. Goodnight, Christina.'

'Goodnight,' she repeated automatically, watching him in a daze of confusion as he walked away from her.

He hadn't done anything *wrong* all day. For the most part, he'd been perfectly charming. And she still *wanted* him, despite the grief he'd given her. There had never been any other man who made her feel what he did. But he probably made every woman feel the same way. It meant nothing. It would be foolish to let it cloud her judgement.

When Theo was told that Ari was his Papa, he would want them to be all together, living happily ever after.

But that was a fairy-tale and this story didn't have the right ingredients. The prince did not love the princess, so how could there be a happy ever after?

Tina fiercely told herself she must not lose sight of that, no matter what!

CHAPTER EIGHT

ARI stood beside George in the church, impatient for the marriage service to be over, his mind working through what had to be accomplished with Christina. Theo was not a problem. His son had grinned broadly at him as he had carried the cushion with the wedding rings up the aisle. He would want his Papa. But Christina had only smiled at George, keeping her gaze averted from him.

She looked absolutely stunning in a dark red satin gown. Desire had kicked in so hard and fast Ari had struggled to control the instinctive physical response to instantly wanting her in his bed again. 'She is magnificent, is she not?' George had murmured, meaning his bride, and she was, but Cassandra stirred nothing in him.

There were many beautiful women in the world. Ari had connected to quite a few of them, but none had twisted his heart as it was being twisted right now. He had to have Christina again. Perhaps she touched something deep in him because she was the mother of his child. Or perhaps it was because he had taken her innocence and she made him feel very strongly about righting the wrong he had done her. The reasons didn't matter. Somehow he had to persuade her to be his wife.

His parents certainly approved of the marriage and not only because of Theo.

'She's lovely, Ari, and I could be good friends with Helen,' his mother had remarked.

His father had been more decisive in his opinion. 'Beautiful, intelligent, and with a fighting spirit I admire. She's a good match for you, Ari. Don't let her get away from you. The two of you should have many interesting children together.'

Easier said than done, Ari thought grimly.

She didn't want him to touch her.

Today, she didn't want to look at him.

Was she frightened of the attraction she still felt with him, frightened of giving in to it? She would *have* to look at him at the wedding reception *and* suffer his touch during the bridal waltz. Not just a touch, either. Full body contact. He would make the waltz one of the most intimate dances she'd ever had, force the sexual chemistry between them to the surface so she couldn't hide from it, couldn't ignore it, couldn't deny it.

She was not going to get away from him.

Tina listened to the marriage service as she stood beside her sister. These same words could be spoken to her soon if she said *yes* to Ari's proposal. Would he take the vows seriously, or were they just mumbo-jumbo to him—the means to an end?

He *had* offered the fidelity clause in a prenuptial agreement. She would get full custody of Theo and any other children they might have together if he faltered on that front. Could she be happy with him if he kept faith with his marriage deal?

It was a risk she probably shouldn't be considering. Cass's wedding was getting to her, stirring up feelings that could land her in a terrible mess. Plus all the marriage talk amongst her Greek relatives yesterday had kept Ari's offer pounding through her mind—no relief at all from the connection with him.

Her mother had raved on about how kind he'd been— taking Tina and Theo out for the day, the birthday party at his parents' home—which had reminded the relatives of how attentive he'd been to Tina at the family party in Athens. Comments on how eligible he was followed, with speculative looks that clearly said Helen's daughter might have a chance with him. Being a single mother was…*so unfortunate.*

Little did they know that Theo was the drawcard, not her. They would all be watching her with Ari today— watching, hoping, encouraging. She would have to look at him soon, take his arm as they followed Cass and George out of the church, be seated next to him at the wedding reception, dance with him. The whole thing was a nightmare with no escape, and it would be worse when the truth was told.

Her mother would want her to marry Ari.

Her relatives would think her mad if she didn't.

Only Cass might take her side, asking what *she* wanted, but Cass wouldn't be there. She and George would be off on their honeymoon. Besides, what Tina *wanted* was impossible—utterly impossible to go back to the time when she had loved Ari with all her heart and believed he loved her. How could she ever believe that now?

She felt a sharp stab of envy as George promised to love Cass for the rest of his life. There was no doubting the fervour in his voice, no doubting Cass, either, as she promised her love in return. A huge welling of emotion brought tears to Tina's eyes as the two of them were declared husband and wife. She wished them all the happiness in the world. This was how it should be between a man and a woman, starting out on a life together.

She was still blinking away the wetness in her eyes when she had to link up with Ari for the walk out of the church. He wound her arm around his and hugged her close, instantly causing an eruption of agitation inside Tina.

'Why do women always weep at weddings?' he murmured, obviously wanting her to focus on him.

She didn't. She swept her gaze around the gathered guests, swallowed hard to unblock her voice and answered, 'Because change is scary and you hope with all your heart that everything will work out right.'

'What is right in your mind, Christina?' he persisted.

Christina...he invariably used her full name because it was what she had called herself for the modelling career that had been cut short after he had left her pregnant. During the months they'd spent together she'd loved how that name had rolled off his tongue in a caressing tone. She wished he wouldn't keep using the same tone now, that he'd call her Tina like everyone else. Then she wouldn't be constantly reminded of the girl she had been and how much she had once loved him.

She wasn't that girl any more.

She'd moved on.

Except Ari could still twist her heart and shoot treacherous excitement through her veins.

It was wrong for him to have that power. *Wrong!* And the pain of her disillusionment with him lent a vehement conviction to her voice as she answered him. 'It's right if they keep loving each other for the rest of their lives, no matter what happens along the way.' She looked at him then, meeting the quizzical amber eyes with as much hard directness as she could muster. 'We don't have that basis for marriage, do we?'

'I don't believe that love is the glue that keeps a marriage together,' he shot back at her. 'It's a madness that's blind to any sensible judgement and it quickly burns out when people's expectations of it aren't met. Absolute commitment is what I'm offering you, Christina. You can trust that more than love.'

His cynical view of love was deeply offensive to her, yet she felt the strength of his will encompassing her, battering at her resistance to what he wanted. 'I'd rather have what Cass and George have than what you're offering,' she muttered, resenting the implication that her sister's happiness with her marriage wouldn't last.

'I understand that change must be scary to you, Christina,' he murmured in her ear. 'I promise you I'll do all I can to make the transition easy for both you and Theo.'

The transition! He expected her to give up her life in Australia—all she'd known, all she'd worked for—to be with him. It wouldn't work the other way around. She knew that wouldn't even be considered. She was supposed to see marriage to him as more desirable than anything else, and she would have seen it that way once, *if he'd loved her.*

That was the sticking point.

Tina couldn't push herself past it.

The hurt that he didn't wouldn't go away.

Outside the church they had to pose for photographs. Tina pasted a smile on her face. Her facial muscles ached from keeping it there. Ari lifted Theo up to perch against his shoulder for some shots and everywhere she looked people seemed to be smiling and nodding benevolently at the grouping of the three of them—not as bridesmaid, best man and page boy, but as wife, husband and son. Ari's parents stood next to her mother and Uncle Dimitri. They would all be allied against her if she decided to reject the marriage proposal.

She ached all over from the tension inside her. At least the drive to the reception spared her any active pressure from Ari. Theo rode in their car, sitting between them on the back seat, chatting happily to the man he would soon know as his father. Tina was grateful not have to say anything but she was acutely aware of Theo's pleasure in Ari and Ari's pleasure in his son. How could she explain to a five-year-old boy why they couldn't all be together with the Papa he had wished for?

They arrived at the Santo winery. Its reception centre was perched on top of a cliff overlooking the sea. To the side of the dining section was a large open area shaded by pergolas and normally used for wine-tasting. Guests gathered here while the bridal party posed for more photographs. Waiters offered drinks and canapés. A festive mood was very quickly in full swing.

Tina thought she might escape from Ari's side for a while after the photographer was satisfied but that proved impossible. He led her straight over to George's family who were all in high spirits, delighted to meet their new daughter-in-law's sister and press invitations to be their guest on Patmos at any time.

Then he insisted on introducing her to his sisters and their husbands—beautiful women, handsome men, bright beautiful people who welcomed Tina into their group, making friendly chat about the wedding. Their children, Ari's nephews, all four of them around Theo's age, quickly drew him off with them to play boy games. Which left Tina very much the centre of attention and as pleasant as the conversation was, she knew they were measuring her up as wife material for Ari.

After a reasonable interval she excused herself, saying she should check if Cass needed her for anything.

It didn't provide much of an escape.

'I'll come with you,' Ari instantly said. 'George might require something from me.'

As soon as they were out of earshot, Tina muttered, 'You told them, didn't you?'

'Not the children. Theo won't hear it from them. Keeping it from your family until after the wedding will be respected, Christina. I simply wanted my sisters to understand where you are with me.'

'I'm not anywhere with you,' she snapped defensively, giving him a reproachful glare.

He held her gaze with a blaze of resolute purpose. 'You're my intended wife and I told them so.'

'Why are you rushing into this?' she cried in exasperation. 'We can make reasonable arrangements about sharing Theo. Other people do it all the time. You don't have to *marry* me!'

'I *want* to marry you.'

'Only because of Theo and that's not right, Ari.'

'You're wrong. I want you, too, Christina.'

She shook her head in anguished denial, instantly shying away from letting herself believe him. Cass and George were chatting to a group of their modelling-world friends and Tina gestured to the gorgeous women amongst them. 'Look at what you could have. I'm not in their class. And I bet they'd lap up your attention.'

'You're in a class of your own and I don't want their attention. I want yours.'

'Today you do, but what about the rest of your future, Ari?'

'I'll make my future with you if you'll give it a chance.'

Again she shook her head. There was no point in arguing with him. He had his mind set on a course of action and nothing she said was going to shift him from it.

'It's worth a chance, isn't it, Christina?' he pressed. 'We were both happy when we were intimately involved. It can be that way again. You can't really want to be separated from Theo during the time he spends with me if you insist he has to bounce between us.'

She would hate it.

But she was also hating the way Cass's girlfriends were gobbling Ari up with their eyes, watching him approach the bride and groom. Not that she could blame them for doing it. He was even more of a sex magnet today, dressed in a formal dinner suit which enhanced his perfect male physique, highlighting how stunningly handsome he was. *A Greek God.* Tina had no doubt they were thinking that. And envying her for having him at her side.

Could she stand a lifetime of that with Ari?

Would he always *stay* at her side?

She felt sick from all the churning inside her. Any distraction from it was intensely welcome. Hopefully Cass would provide it for a while. She and Ari joined the celebrity group and were quickly introduced around. One of George's friends, another photographer, took the opportunity to give Tina his business card.

'Come to me and I'll turn you into a model as famous as your sister. No disrespect to you, Cass, but this girl has quite a unique look that I'd love to capture.'

Cass laughed and turned a beaming smile to Tina. 'I've always said you don't have to be a homebody.'

'But I like being a homebody.' She tried to hand the card back, embarrassed by the spotlight being turned on her. 'Thank you, but no.'

'Keep it,' he insisted. 'I mean it. I would love to work

with that wonderful long neck and those marvellous cheekbones. Your short hair sets them off to perfection.'

'No, please, I don't want it. I have nowhere to put your card anyway.'

'I'll keep it for you. You might have second thoughts,' Ari said, taking the card and sliding it into his breast pocket. He smiled around at the group. 'No disrespect to any of you lovely ladies, but I also think Christina is unique. And very special.'

Which was virtually a public declaration of his interest in her, putting off the interest that any of the lovely ladies might want to show in him.

Tina's *marvellous cheekbones* were instantly illuminated by heat.

Cass leaned over to whisper in her ear. 'Mama is right. Ari is very taken by you. Give him a chance, Tina. He's rather special, too.'

A chance!

Even Cass was on Ari's side.

Tina felt the whole world was conspiring to make her take the step she was frightened of taking.

'I think I need some cool air,' she muttered.

Ari heard her. He took her arm. 'Please excuse us, everyone. We're off to catch the sea breeze for a breather.'

He drew her over to the stone wall along the cliff edge. Tina didn't protest the move. It was useless. She was trapped into being Ari's companion at this wedding and he was not about to release her.

'Why did you take that card?' she demanded crossly.

'Because it was my fault that you didn't continue the modelling career you might have had. It's not too late to try again, Christina. You actually have a more individual beauty now. If you'd like to pursue that path you'd have my full support.'

She frowned at him. 'I'm a mother, Ari. That comes first. And isn't it what you want from me, to be the mother of your children?'

'Yes, but there are models who are also mothers. It can be done, Christina.' He lifted his hand and gently stroked her hot cheek, his eyes burning with what seemed like absolute sincerity. 'I destroyed two of your dreams. At least I can give one of them back to you. Maybe the other...with enough time together. '

She choked up.

It was all too much.

Her mind was in a total jumble. She wanted to believe him, yet he couldn't give her back what he had taken. Whatever they had in the future would be different. And was he just saying these things to win her over? She'd trusted him with her heart and soul once and here she was being vulnerable to his seduction again. How could she believe him? Or trust him? She desperately needed to clear her head.

She stepped back from the tingling touch on her cheek and forced herself to speak. 'I'd like a glass of water, Ari.'

He held her gaze for several moments, his eyes searching for what he wanted to see in hers—a softening towards him, cracks in her resistance. Tina silently pleaded for him to go, give her some space, some relief from the constant pressure to give in and take what he was offering.

Finally he nodded. 'I'll fetch you one.'

She stared out to sea, gulping in fresh air, needing a blast of oxygen to cool her mind of its feverish thoughts.

It didn't really work.

Despite her past experience with Ari Zavros, or maybe because of it, one mind-bending thought kept pounding away at her, undermining her resistance to the course he was pressing her to take.

Give it a chance.
Give it a chance.
Give it a chance.

CHAPTER NINE

THE bridal waltz…

Tina took a deep breath and rose to her feet as Ari held back her chair. He'd been the perfect gentleman all evening. The speech he'd made preceding his toast to the bride and groom had contained all the right touches, charming the guests into smiling and feeling really good about this marriage. An excellent Best Man.

Maybe he was the best man for her, given that she'd not felt attracted to anyone else in the past six years. If she never connected with some other man… did she want to live the rest of her life totally barren of the sexual pleasure she had known with Ari?

Give it a chance…

As he steered her towards the dance floor, the warmth of his hand on the pit of her back spread a flow of heat to her lower body. The band played 'Moon River,' a slow jazz waltz that Cass and George obviously revelled in, executing it with great panache; gliding, twirling, dipping, making it look both romantic and very, very sexy.

Little quivers started running down Tina's legs as

she and Ari waited for their cue to join in. It had been so long since he had held her close. Would she feel the same wild surge of excitement when she connected to his strong masculinity? It was impossible to quell the electric buzz of anticipation when their cue came and he swept her onto the dance floor, yet she stiffened when he drew her against him, instinctively fighting his power to affect her so *physically.*

'Relax, Christina,' he murmured. 'Let your body respond to the rhythm of the music. I know it can.'

Of course, he knew. There was very little he didn't know about her body and how it responded. And she had to find out what it might be like with him now, didn't she? *If she was to give it a chance.*

She forced herself to relax and go with the flow of the dance. He held her very close; her breasts pressed to his chest, her stomach in fluttering contact with his groin area, her thighs brushing his with every move he made. Her heart was pounding much faster than the beat of the music. Her female hormones were stirred into a lustful frenzy. She was in the arms of a Greek God who was hers for the taking and the temptation to take whatever she could of him was roaring through her.

Ari made the most of Christina's surrender to the dance, hoping the sexual chemistry sizzling through him was being transmitted through every sensual contact point. She felt good in his arms. She was the right height for him, tall enough for their bodies to fit in a very satisfying way as he moved her around the dance floor. The sway of her hips, the fullness of her breasts impacting with their lush femininity, the scent of her skin and hair…everything about her was firing up his desire to have her surrender to him.

The waltz ended. She didn't exactly push out of his embrace but eased herself back enough to put a little distance between them. Her cheeks were flushed and she kept her eyes lowered, their thick black lashes hiding any vulnerable feelings. He was sure she had been physically affected by the intimacy of the dance but whether that was enough to sway her his way he didn't know.

The Master of Ceremonies invited all the guests to dance to the next song which had been especially requested by the bride. Ari instantly understood its significance when the band started playing the tune. He and Christina had heard Stevie Wonder's version of it on the car radio on one of their trips together.

'You are the sunshine of my life,' he said, recalling how he had applied the words to her. 'It's your father's favourite song.'

'Yes,' she said huskily. 'Cass misses him, too. He would have been very proud of her today.' Her lashes lifted and she gave him a wry little smile. 'I'm surprised you remembered.'

'Special songs can be very evocative. You *were* the sunshine of my life while we were together, Christina.'

The smile twisted into a grimace. 'There's been a long night since then, Ari. Though I'm sure you found plenty of sunshine elsewhere.'

'Not of the same quality.'

Her gaze slid away from his. 'We have to dance,' she muttered.

She allowed him to hold her close again without any initial resistance. It was *some* progress, he thought, though he savagely wished she wouldn't keep harping on the other women who'd been in his life. The past was the past—impossible to change it. If she'd just set her sights on the future, that was the progress he needed.

He bent his head closer to hers and murmured, 'What you and I can have *now* is what matters, Christina.'

She didn't answer.

Hopefully she was thinking about it.

Tina fiercely wished she could forget everything else but *now,* pretend she was meeting Ari for the first time, feeling all that he made her feel, her whole body brilliantly alive to exciting sensations. She wouldn't care about the other women if this was her first experience with him. She'd be blissfully thinking that he was the man who could make her life complete.

Maybe he would if she set the pain he'd given her aside. He'd said he wanted to give her back the dreams he'd destroyed. Yet it was a terribly risky step, trusting his word. If he didn't keep it, she would hate herself for being a fool, hate him for his deceit, and end up a totally embittered woman.

But she could make him pay for it.

He would lose Theo and any other children they might have if he broke his promise of fidelity. She wouldn't have to worry over the custody issue. All rights would be hers. In which case, it was worth taking the chance, wasn't it?

Her father's favourite song came to an end. She saw Cass go over to her mother who had danced with Uncle Dimitri and give her a hug and a kiss. It caused a painful drag on Tina's heart. She knew her father would have wanted her to marry Ari. It might have made him proud of her if she did.

She looked up at the man who was her son's father, and the seductive amber eyes instantly locked onto hers, simmering with the promise of all the pleasure they'd once had together. Her heart quivered over the decision she had made but it *was* made and she wasn't going to fret over it any longer.

'Let's go where we can talk privately,' she said firmly.

He nodded, quickly obliging her by steering her off the dance floor, then taking her arm and walking her out to the large open patio where they'd been before the reception dinner.

'Would you like to sit down?' he asked, waving to the wooden tables under the pergola.

'Yes.' Her legs were feeling wobbly. Besides, sitting across from him at a table would be more comfortable for laying out the deal she would accept.

They sat. Ari spread his hands in an open gesture, inviting her confidence. 'What do you want to say, Christina?'

Her hands were tightly clenched in her lap. This was it—the moment when her life would begin to take a totally different direction. A wave of trepidation mangled her vocal chords. She looked hard at him, forcing her imagination to see him as a caring and committed father and husband. If she could believe it, maybe the marriage would work out right. She desperately wanted it to.

The first step was to say the words.

Say them.

Just do it and have done with the whole nerve-wracking dilemma.

'I… I…'

'Yes?' Ari encouraged, leaning forward, giving her his concentrated attention.

A surge of panic had made her hesitate. Her mind was screaming *wait! Don't commit yet!* But what would she be waiting for? The situation wasn't going to change. This man was Theo's father and she had loved him with all her heart once. If he was serious about forging a good relationship with her, shouldn't she give it a chance?

'I'll marry you,' she blurted out, sealing the decision.

His face broke into a happy grin. His eyes sparkled with pleasure. Or was it triumph, having won what he wanted? 'That's great, Christina!' he enthused. 'I'm glad you've decided it's the best course because it is.'

He was *so* positive it instantly raised doubts in Tina's mind. Was she a fool for giving in? She had to put a high value on the marriage so he would treat her as he should.

'Give me your hand,' he pressed, reaching across the table to take it.

She shook her head, keeping both hands tightly in her lap. 'I haven't finished what I want to say.'

He frowned at her reluctance to meet his offered hand. He spread his fingers in open appeal. 'Tell me what you need from me.'

'I need you to sign the prenuptial agreement you offered me,' she threw back at him, determined that those terms be kept. It was her safeguard against being used to give Ari a stronger paternal position than he had now.

He drew back, his mouth twisting into an ironic grimace. A sharp wariness wiped the sparkle from his eyes. Tina's stomach cramped with tension. If he retracted the offer, she could not go ahead with the marriage, regardless of any pressure from any source. It was risking too much. He might walk away from her again and take Theo with him.

She waited for his reply.

Waited…and waited…her nerves stretching tighter with every second that passed.

Ari's mind was swiftly sifting through Christina's possible motivations. She didn't trust his word. He understood where she was coming from on that score. What concerned him most was if she had a vengeful nature.

The prenuptial agreement he'd offered gave her everything if he didn't remain a faithful husband. What if she planned to be such a cold, shrewish wife, he would be driven to find some pleasure in other company? If she was secretly determined not to be responsive to him, he'd be condemning himself to a hellish marriage. He needed more than her public compliance to a couple of dances to feel secure about winning her over in bed.

Out here alone together, she wouldn't even give him her hand.

What was in her mind?

What was in her heart?

A totally selfish revenge on him...or hope that they could make a happy future together?

He was risking a lot.

He decided she had to meet him halfway before he tied a knot which could not be undone.

'I am prepared to sign it, Christina,' he said, his eyes burning a very direct challenge at her as he added, 'If you're prepared to spend one night with me before I do.'

She stared at him, startled by the provision he was laying down. 'Why? You'll have all the nights you want with me after we're married.'

'I want to be sure that I will want them. I won't sign away my right to my son to a woman who'll turn her back on me. I need you to show me that won't happen, Christina. Right now your attitude towards me is hardly encouraging. You won't even give me your hand.'

Heat surged up her neck and scorched her cheeks. Her eyes glittered a challenge right back at him. 'I think it's a good idea for us to spend a night together before either of us commit ourselves to anything. Maybe you're not as good a lover as you used to be, Ari.'

Relief swept through him at her ready acceptance of a sex-test. He smiled. 'And maybe you'll warm to me once I prove that I am.'

Again her lashes swept down, veiling her feelings. She heaved a sigh, probably relieving tension. 'We're scheduled to leave Santorini the day after tomorrow,' she muttered.

'That can easily be changed.'

She shook her head. 'I'll spend tomorrow night with you.' Her lashes lifted and there was resolute fire in her eyes. 'That can be the decider for both of us.'

She would bolt if he didn't satisfy her. Ari was confident that he could if she was willing to let it happen.

'Agreed,' he said. 'However, our other deal ends tonight, Christina. Tomorrow you tell your mother and Theo that I am his father. Whatever happens between us, this has to be openly acknowledged.'

She nodded. 'I'll do it in the morning.'

'Make sure your mother understands the circumstances, that I was not told you had my child until we met in Dubai. I would have come back to you had I known, Christina.'

She made a wry grimace. 'Since I've decided I might marry you, naturally I'll put you in as good a light as possible to my mother.'

'It's the truth,' he rammed home as hard as he could, wanting her to believe at least that much of him.

'And my truth is you left me and I didn't want you back,' she shot out, her eyes glittering with angry pride. 'Don't you start harassing me, Ari. I'll do what I have to do to smooth the path to a workable future.'

His father's words about Christina were instantly replayed in his mind...*beautiful, intelligent, and with a fighting spirit I admire.* If she shared his own strong desire for everything to turn out well, there was no need to concern himself about her presentation of the past to her mother.

'I'd like to be there when you tell Theo I'm his father,' he said softly, needing to remove the anger he'd unwittingly triggered. 'I've missed so much—not being there when he was born, his first words, his first step, learning to swim, his first day at kindergarten. I want to see the expression in his eyes when he realises I am the Papa he wished for. Will you give me that, Christina?'

Her eyes went blank, probably focussing inward on the memories she hadn't shared with him. He willed her to be more generous now. Yet when she did speak, her whole expression was one of deep anxiety.

'I hope you really mean to be a good father to him, Ari. Please don't lead him on and then drop him, pursuing other interests.'

He knew she felt he had done that to her.

It had been wrong of him, letting temptation overrule good sense. She had been too young, too impressionable. Theo was much more so and she was frightened for him. Her fear evoked a powerful surge of emotion in him. He wanted to say he'd look after them both for the rest of his life. He hated seeing the fretful doubts in her eyes. But laying them to rest would take time.

'Give me your hand, Christina,' he gently commanded, his eyes pleading for her acquiescence.

Very slowly she lifted it from her lap and held it out to him.

He enclosed it with his. 'I promise you I'll do everything I can to win Theo's love and keep it,' he said fervently. 'He's my son.'

Tears welled into her eyes. She nodded, unable to speak. He stroked her palm with his thumb, wanting to give comfort and reassurance, wishing he could sweep her into his embrace but cautious about rushing her where she might not be ready to go.

'If it's okay with you, I'll come to the El Greco resort tomorrow afternoon. We can spend some time with Theo before having our night together,' he quietly suggested.

She nodded again, sucked in a deep breath and blurted out, 'I'm sorry. It was mean of me…leaving you out of Theo's life.'

'You had your reasons,' he murmured sympathetically. 'It's how we take it from here that will count most to Theo.'

'Yes,' she agreed huskily, taking another deep breath before adding, 'He usually takes a nap after lunch. If you come at four o'clock, we'll tell him then.'

'Thank you.'

She gave him a wobbly smile. 'If that's everything settled, we should go back to the wedding reception. We'll be missed. It is Cass's night and I want to be there for her.'

'And I for George.'

Their first deal was still in place. He had to wait until tomorrow before taking what he wanted with Christina, yet her hand was still in his and as he rose from the table, the temptation to draw her up from her seat and straight into his embrace was irresistible. She didn't try to break free but her free hand fluttered in agitation against his chest and there was a heart-piercing vulnerability in the eyes that met his.

He hated her fear. It made him feel even more wrong about what he'd taken from her in the past. He pressed a soft kiss on her forehead and murmured, 'I'll make it right, Christina. For you and for Theo.'

He gave her what he hoped was a reassuring smile as he released her, only retaining her hand, keeping that physical link for the walk back to the wedding reception, wanting her to feel secure with him.

Tonight belonged to Cassandra and George.

Tomorrow was his.

He could wait.

CHAPTER TEN

TINA waited until after their Greek relatives departed
for the mainland so she could have a private chat to her
mother about her connection to Ari. Everyone had still
been revelling in Cass's wedding—such a wonderful
family celebration. Amongst the happy comments were
a few arch remarks about Ari's interest in her.

'He didn't have eyes for anyone else.'

'Never left your side all evening.'

'Such a charming man!'

'And so handsome!'

Tina had shrugged off the curiosity, discouraging
it by refocussing the conversation on her sister's life.
However, she saw the same curiosity in her mother's
eyes, and when they were finally alone together, relaxing on the lounges by the swimming pool, watching
Theo practice diving into it, she didn't have to think
about how to lead into revealing the truth. Her mother
did it for her.

'Are you seeing Ari again today, Tina?'

'Yes. And there's something I have to tell you,
Mama.' She took a deep breath to calm her jumpy

nerves and started at the beginning. 'Ari Zavros and I were not meeting for the first time in Athens. Six years ago he was in Australia on a three-month tour of the wineries in our country. I met him on a modelling assignment and fell in love with him.'

Her mother instantly leapt to the truth, understanding of Ari's behaviour towards them flashing straight into her eyes. 'He's Theo's father.'

'Yes. I didn't expect to ever see him again. It was a shock when he was presented to us as George's best man. I asked him to wait until after the wedding before revealing that my son was also his because it would have been a major distraction from Cass and that wasn't fair, but today we have to deal with it, Mama.'

'Oh, my dear!' Her mother swung her legs off the lounge to face her directly with a look of anxious concern. 'These past few days must have been very difficult for you.'

Tina had to fight back tears. She hadn't expected such a rush of sympathy from her mother. Shock and perhaps criticism for her silence, worry over the situation, fretting over the choices to be made... she'd geared herself to cope with all this but not the caring for her feelings and the quick understanding of the distress she had been hiding.

'I thought...he was gone from my life, Mama,' she choked out. 'But he's not and he never will be again. He's made that very clear.'

'Yes...very clear,' her mother repeated, nodding as she recollected how Ari had inserted himself and his family into their time on Santorini. 'I don't think that's going to change, Tina. He's definitely intent on making a claim on his son.'

'And he has the wealth and power to back it up. There's no point in trying to resist his claim, Mama. I have to give way.'

'Has he said how he wants to deal with the situation?'

Tina's mouth instantly twisted into an ironic grimace. 'He wants me to marry him.'

'Ah!'

There was no real shock in that *Ah!*—more a realisation of the bigger claim being made—one that would completely change her daughter's life, as well as her grandson's.

After a few moments' thought, her mother asked, 'His family knows all this?'

'He told them after our meeting in Athens. He had no doubt that Theo was his child. His age…his eyes…'

'Yes…now I see.' Her mother nodded a few times. 'They have been extending a welcome to join their family because of Theo.'

'He is the main attraction,' Tina said dryly.

'But they have been very gracious to us, as well, Tina. Which shows they are prepared to accept you as Ari's wife. How do you feel about it?'

She shook her head. 'I don't know. He said he would have come back to me had I told him he'd left me pregnant. I didn't tell him because he didn't love me. I was only a…a charming episode…that he could walk away from.'

'But you loved him.'

'Yes. Totally.'

'And now?'

'I doubt there will ever be anyone else for me, Mama, but it's Theo he wants. I can't fool myself that I'm suddenly the woman he loves above all others.'

'Perhaps you are more special to him now because you are the mother of his child. It's a very Greek way of thinking, Tina. And sometimes love grows from sharing the most precious things to both of you.'

Tina choked up, remembering Ari listing how much he had missed of Theo because she had denied him knowledge of his son.

Her mother heaved a sigh. 'It's not for me to say what you should do, my darling. What do you think is best for you?'

'Oh, probably to marry him,' Tina said in a rush, relieved in a way to finally have it out in the open. 'I think he will be a good father. He's asked me to wait until he comes here this afternoon for us to tell Theo together that he does have a Papa. And after that—well, Ari and I need some time alone to…to see how we feel about each other, Mama. He wants to take me somewhere. Will you look after Theo, have him in your room tonight?'

'Oh, dear!' Her mother shook her head in dismay at realising what the all-night arrangement most probably meant. 'There's so much to take in. I wish your father was here.'

'Don't worry, Mama. I have to make a decision and I think this is the best way to do it.'

'Well, of course I will look after Theo, but…do be careful, Tina,' she said anxiously. 'If you decide not to marry Ari…I remember how you were when you were pregnant with Theo.'

'That won't happen again, Mama,' Tina assured her. It didn't matter this time if Ari used a contraceptive or not. She knew she was in a safe period of her cycle. She reached across and took her mother's hand. 'Thank you taking all this so well. I hate being a problem to you.'

'Not a problem, dear. Just… I do so want you to have a happy life and I wish with all my heart that everything turns out well with Ari.'

The fairy-tale happy ending.

Maybe if she could believe in it enough, it might happen. She'd have a better idea of how the future would run after tonight. Right now she couldn't trust Ari's word that he would remain a faithful husband. Even if they did find sexual pleasure with each other, that was no guarantee he would always be satisfied with her. She might begin to believe they really could forge a good marriage together after he signed the prenuptial agreement.

If he did.

Ari spent an extremely vexatious morning with his lawyer who was dead against signing away paternal rights under any circumstances. A financial settlement was fine in the case of divorce but giving up one's children was utter madness, especially since Ari was marrying to have his son.

'I'm not here for your advice,' Ari had finally said. 'Just draw up the agreement I've spelled out to you. It's an issue of showing good faith and I *will* show it.'

'Show it by all means,' his lawyer shot back at it him, 'but don't sign it.'

He hadn't…yet.

He'd done many deals in his life but none as risky as the one he'd proposed to Christina. The money didn't worry him. He would never begrudge financial support for her and their children. But if the response he needed from her was not forthcoming tonight, marrying her might be too much of a gamble.

His head told him this.

Yet his heart was already set on having Christina Savalas as his wife.

She touched him in ways no other woman had. He had been her first lover, almost certainly her only one, which made her his in a very primal sense. Plus the fact she had carried his child made her uniquely special. Besides, his wealth was not a big attraction to her or she would have gone after a slice of it to support their son rather than taking complete responsibility for him. She was only concerned about the kind of person he was. Looks, money…none of that counted. If he didn't measure up as a man she wanted in her life, he'd be out of it.

He'd never been challenged like this. Who he was on the surface of it had always been enough. Christina was hitting him at deeper levels and he felt totally driven to prove he did measure up—driven to remove all fear from her eyes. Winning her over had somehow become more important than anything else in his life.

The compelling tug of having Theo was a big part of it, but she was part of Theo, too. Ari couldn't separate them in his mind. Didn't want to separate them. The three of them made a family. *His* family. He had to make it so by any means possible because he couldn't tolerate the idea of Christina taking their son back to Australia and shutting him out of their lives as much as she legally could.

He lunched with his parents who were eager for another visit with their grandson. 'Tomorrow,' Ari promised them. 'I'll bring Christina and Theo and Helen back here tomorrow to sort out what is to be done.'

He had to stop them leaving Santorini on schedule. Even if Christina rejected his offer of marriage, she had to see reason about discussing future arrangements for their son. If she accepted his proposal, they would have a wedding to plan. More than a wedding. There would be many decisions to be made on setting up a life together—tying up ends in Australia, where best to make their home.

Ari was tense with determination as he drove to the El Greco resort. He told himself the meeting with Theo was relatively uncomplicated. There was no need to be uptight about his son's response. He had wished for a Papa. Revealing who that Papa was would certainly be a pleasure. What happened afterwards with Christina was the critical time. He fiercely hoped that was going to be a pleasure, too. If it wasn't… He instantly clicked his mind off any negative train of thought. This had to work.

Tina and her mother and Theo were sitting at one of the snack bar tables having afternoon tea when Ari arrived. He came striding down the ramp to the pool patio, a hard purposeful expression on his face, and headed straight towards where their rooms were located.

'We're here!' Tina called out, rising from her chair to catch his attention, her heartbeat instantly accelerating at what his arrival meant for both her and Theo.

His head jerked around and his expression immediately lightened on seeing them. Theo jumped off his chair and ran to meet him. Ari scooped him up in his arms and perched him against his shoulder, smiling broadly at his son's eagerness to welcome him.

'I finished the train station. You must come and see it, Ari,' Theo prattled happily.

'As soon as I say hello to your mother and grandmother,' he promised.

He shot a sharp look of enquiry at Tina as he approached their table. She nodded, assuring him her mother had been told. He smiled at both of them but the smile didn't quite reach his eyes. It made Tina wonder how tense he was over the situation. Marriage was a big step and it might not be the best course for them to take. Was he having second thoughts about his proposal?

He addressed her mother directly, speaking in a quiet tone that carried an impressive intensity of purpose. 'Helen, I want you to know I will look after your daughter with much more care than I did in the past. Please trust me on that.'

'Tina and Theo are very precious to me, Ari,' her mother answered. 'I hope your caring will be as deep as mine.'

He nodded and turned his gaze to Tina. 'Theo wants me to see his train station.'

'I'll take you to our room. He did a great job putting all the Lego together.' She smiled at her son. 'It was very tricky, wasn't it, darling?'

'Very tricky,' he echoed, then grinned triumphantly at Ari. 'But I did it!'

'I knew you were a clever boy,' he warmly approved.

'Will you wait here, Mama?' Tina asked.

'Yes, dear. Go on now.'

Theo was full of questions about Ari's nephews whom he'd spent most of his time with at the wedding reception. Tina didn't have to say anything on their walk to her room. She was acutely conscious of the easy bond Ari had already established with their son and felt fairly sure there would be no trauma attached to revealing the truth. If she made it like a fairy-tale to Theo, he might accept it unquestioningly. On the other hand, there could be a host of questions both of them would have to answer.

Her chest ached with tension as she opened the door to her room and stood aside for Ari to carry Theo inside. He paused a moment, giving her a burning look of command as he said, '*I'll* tell him.'

She felt an instant wave of resentment at his arbitrary taking over from her, yet it did relieve her of the responsibility of explaining the situation to Theo. *Let him get it right for their son,* she thought, closing the door behind them, then parking herself on the chair at the writing desk while Ari duly admired the Lego train station.

'Does your Mama tell you bed-time stories, Theo?' he asked, sitting down on the bed beside the fully constructed station.

'Yes. She points to the words in the book and I can read some of them now,' he answered proudly.

'I think you must be very quick at learning things. If I tell you a story, I wonder if you could guess the ending,' Ari said with a teasing smile.

'Tell me! Tell me!' Theo cried eagerly, sitting cross-legged on the floor in front of Ari, his little body bent forward attentively.

Ari bent forwards, too, his forearms resting on his knees, his gaze locked on the amber eyes shining up at him. 'Once upon a time a prince from a faraway country travelled to a land on the other side of the world.'

Tina was totally stunned that Ari had chosen to use a fairy story to convey the truth, yet how much of the truth would he tell? The tension inside her screwed up several notches.

'There he met a beautiful princess and she was like no one else he'd ever met. He wanted to be with her all the time and she wanted to be with him so they were together while he was in her country. But eventually he had to leave to carry out business for his kingdom back home. It hurt the princess very much when he said goodbye to her and when she found out that she was going to have a baby she decided not to send any message to the prince about it. She didn't want him to come back, then leave her again because it would hurt too much. So she kept the baby a secret from him.'

'Was the baby a boy or a girl?' Theo asked.

'It was a boy. And he was very much loved by her family. This made the princess think he didn't need a Papa because he already had enough people to love him. She didn't know that the boy secretly wished for a Papa.'

'Like me,' Theo popped in. 'But I didn't wish for one until I went to school. It was because my friends there have fathers.'

'It is only natural for you to want one,' Ari assured him.

'Does the boy in the story get his?'

'Let me tell you how it happened. After a few years the sister of the princess was to marry a man who came from the same country as the prince, so her family had to travel halfway around the world to attend the wedding. The princess didn't know that this man was a cousin of the prince and she would meet him again. It was a shock to her when she did, and when the prince saw her son, he knew the boy was his son, too. They had the same eyes.'

'Like you and me,' Theo said, instantly grasping the point.

'Yes. Exactly like that. But the princess asked the prince to keep her secret until after her sister's wedding because she didn't want to take people's attention away from the bride. The prince understood this but he wanted to spend as much time as he could with his son. And he also wanted the princess to know that being a father meant a lot to him. It made him very sad that he had missed out on so much of his son's life and he wanted to be there for him in the future.'

'Can I guess now?' Theo asked.

Ari nodded.

Theo cocked his head to the side, not quite sure he had it right, but wanting to know. 'Are you my Papa, Ari?'

'Yes, Theo. I am,' he answered simply.

Tina held her breath until she saw a happy grin break out on Theo's face. The same grin spread across Ari's. Neither of them looked at her. This was their moment— five years in the waiting—and she couldn't resent being excluded from it. It was her fault they had been kept apart all this time. Ari had been fair in his story-telling and she now had to be fair to the bond she had denied both of them.

'I'm glad you're my Papa,' Theo said fervently, rising to his feet. 'After my birthday party I dreamed that you were.'

Ari lifted him onto his knee, hugging him close. 'We'll always celebrate your birthday together,' he promised huskily.

'But I don't want you to hurt Mama again.'

Tears pricked Tina's eyes, her heart swelling at the love and loyalty in Theo's plea to his father.

'I am trying very hard not to,' Ari said seriously. 'I kept her secret until today, and now your Mama and I are going to work out how best we can be together for the rest of our lives. Will you be happy to be with your grandmother while we do that?'

'Does Yiayia know you're my Papa?'

'Yes. Your Mama told her this morning. And now that you know, too, you can talk about it to your grandmother. Tomorrow, if it's okay with your Mama, I'll take you to visit your other grandparents whom you met at your birthday party.'

Theo's eyes rounded in wonderment. 'Is Maximus my Papou?'

'Yes, and he very much wants to see you again. So does my mother. You will have a much bigger family. The boys you played with at the wedding are your cousins.'

'Will they be there tomorrow?'

'Yes.' Ari rose to his feet, hoisting Theo up in his arms. 'Let's go back to your grandmother because your Mama and I need to have some time to talk about all this.'

The face Theo turned to Tina was full of excitement. 'Is it okay with you, Mama?' he asked eagerly.

'Yes,' she said, not yet ready to commit to a mass family involvement until after her night with Ari, but smiling at her son to remove any worry from his mind.

It was enough for Theo.

He was content to be left with her mother, happy to share the news that his birthday wish had come true and ask a million questions about what might happen next. He waved goodbye to Tina and Ari without a qualm.

All the qualms were in Tina's stomach.

She was about to face a new beginning with Ari Zavros or an end to the idea of marrying him.

CHAPTER ELEVEN

ARI took her hand as they walked up the ramp to the courtyard in front of the reception building. The physical link flooded her mind with thoughts of the intimacy to come. For him it was probably just another night of sex—the performance of an act that had been commonplace in his life, varied only by the different women he'd taken to bed with him.

For her…a little shiver ran down her spine…it had been so long, and she wasn't dazzled by him this time.

Could she really shut off her disillusionment with the love she'd believed he'd shared and take pleasure in what he could give her? He'd said he'd try very hard not to hurt her. There was no need to be frightened of him, but she was frightened of the feelings he might evoke in her. This was not a time to be weak or confused. There was too much at stake to blindly follow instincts that had led her astray in the past.

Though she had to concede that Ari had been very good with Theo. He'd also saved her from the dilemma of how to explain the truth to their son. At least that was done with, and done well, which was only fair to acknowledge.

'I liked your fairy story,' she said, slanting him an appreciative little smile.

He flashed a hopeful smile back. 'We have yet to give it a happy ending.'

'To dream the impossible dream…' tripped straight off her tongue.

'Not impossible, Christina. Open your mind to it.'

They reached his car and he opened the passenger door for her. She paused, looking directly at him before stepping in. 'I don't know *your* mind, Ari. That's the problem.'

Intensity of purpose glittered in his amber eyes as he answered, 'Then I hope you'll know it better by tomorrow morning.'

'I hope I do, too.' She gestured to the car. 'Where are you taking me?'

'To Oia, the northern village of Santorini, the best place for watching the sunset. I've arranged for a suite in a boutique hotel which will give us the perfect view. I thought you would like it.'

'That's…very romantic.'

'With you I want to be romantic,' he replied, his whole expression softening with a look of rueful tenderness that twisted her heart.

She tore her gaze from his and quickly settled herself in the passenger seat, silently and furiously chastising herself for the craven wish to be romanced out of all her mistrust of his fairy-tale happy ending. He was going to make it all too easy to surrender to his charm and there was a huge vulnerable part of her that wanted to believe she was special to him this time and there would be no turning away from her ever again.

But it was his child he really wanted. She was the package deal. And she had no idea how long the package would stay attractive to him. Even if Ari romanced her beautifully tonight, she had to keep her head on straight and insist on the prenuptial agreement he'd offered. It was her insurance against making another big mistake with him.

He chatted to her about the various features of the island they passed on their way to Oia, intent on establishing a companionable mood. Tina did her best to relax and respond in an interested fashion. She remembered how interested he had been in Australia, always asking her questions about it whenever they were driving somewhere together.

'Where would you want us to live if I marry you, Ari?' she asked, needing to know what he had in mind.

He hesitated, then bluntly answered, 'Australia is too far away from my family's business interests, Christina. We could base ourselves anywhere in Europe. Athens if you would like to be near your relatives. Perhaps Helen would like to return there. She would see more of Cassandra and George in the future if she did, and put her closer to us, as well.'

It meant completely uprooting herself. And Theo. Though Ari had made a good point about her mother. So much change…she would end up leading an international life like Cass. Her sister had acclimatised herself to it. Loved it. Perhaps she would learn to love it, too.

'It's also a matter of choosing what might be best for our children's education,' Ari added, shooting her a quick smile.

Our children... It was a very seductive phrase. She adored having Theo. She'd love to have a little girl, as well. If she didn't marry Ari, it was highly unlikely that she would have any more children. But if she had them with Ari, she didn't want to lose them to him.

'Are you okay with that, Christina?' he asked, frowning at her silence.

'I'm opening my mind to it,' she tossed at him.

He laughed, delighted that it wasn't a negative answer.

They had to leave the car on the outskirts of the village and continue on foot through the narrow alleys to the hotel. Both of them had brought light backpacks with essentials for an overnight stay. It only took a minute to load them onto their shoulders and Ari once again took possession of Tina's hand for the walk into the village. It felt more comfortable now, especially as they navigated past the steady stream of tourists that thronged the alleys lined with fascinating shops.

Again she was acutely aware of women looking Ari over but the handhold meant he belonged to her, and she firmly reminded herself that not even Cass's beautiful model friends had turned his head last night. If she could just feel more confident that he could be content with only having her, the female attention he invariably drew might not worry her so much. It hadn't worried her in the past. She had been totally confident that he was hers. Until he wasn't hers any more.

But marriage was different to a *charming episode*.

A wedding ring on Ari's finger would make him legally hers.

Very publicly hers.

That should give her some sense of security with him.

In fact, being the wife of Ari Zavros would empower her quite a bit on many levels.

If she could make herself hard-headed enough to set aside any possible hurt from him in the future and simply go through with the marriage, dealing with each day as it came, her life could become far more colourful than she would ever manage on her own. Besides which if it ended in divorce, the financial settlement would give her the means to do whatever she chose. Wanting Ari to love her…well, that was probably wishing for the moon, but who knew? Even that might come to pass if her mother was right about sharing what was precious to both of them.

All the buildings in Oia were crammed up against each other, using every available bit of space. The entrance to the hotel opened straight onto an alley with pot-plants on either side of the door its only adornment. It was certainly boutique size. The man at the reception desk greeted Ari enthusiastically and escorted them to a suite on what proved to be the top level of three built down the hillside facing the sea. The bathroom, bedroom and balcony were all small but perfectly adequate and the view from the balcony was spectacular.

'Sunset is at eight o'clock,' their escort informed them before departing.

Almost three hours before then, Tina thought, dumping her backpack on a chair and gravitating straight to the balcony, suddenly too nervous to face Ari in the bedroom. A spiral staircase ran down the side of the hotel, linked by landings to each balcony, giving guests easy access to the small swimming pool which took up half the courtyard that extended from the hotel's lowest level. A few people were lounging on deck chairs beside it. She stared down at them, wondering where they had come from and what had brought them here. Probably nothing as complicated as her own situation.

Behind her she heard the pop of a champagne cork. A few moments later Ari was at her side carrying two glasses fizzing with the bubbly wine.

'You used to drink this with me. Will you try it again, Christina? It might relax you,' he said kindly.

She heaved a sigh to ease the tightness in her chest and took the glass he offered. 'Thank you. It's been six years since I was in an intimate situation with a man,' she said with a rueful smile. 'This might take the edge off.'

'I guess having Theo made it difficult for you to form relationships,' he remarked sympathetically.

Not Theo. You. But telling him so would let him know she was stuck on him and it was better that he didn't know. She didn't want him taking anything for granted where she was concerned.

'Don't worry that I'll make you pregnant tonight. I'll be very careful,' he assured her.

She shook her head. 'You won't anyway. This is a safe week for me.'

'Ah!' He grinned, the amber eyes twinkling with pleasure. 'Then we may be totally carefree which will be much better.' He clinked her glass with his. 'To a night of re-discovery, Christina.'

She took a quick sip of the champagne, hoping to settle the flock of butterflies in her stomach. Ari's arm slid around her waist, his hand resting warmly on the curve of her hip, bringing his body closer to hers, stirring memories of how well they had fitted together in the past and triggering the desire to re-discover every sweet nuance of her sexuality.

'I don't want to wait until tonight,' she said decisively, setting her glass down on the top of the balcony wall and turning to face him, a wave of reckless belligerence seizing her and pouring into urgent words. 'Let's just do it, Ari. I don't want to be romanced or seduced or…or treated to any other lover routine you've got. This is a need to know thing, isn't it?'

He set his glass down next to hers and scooped her hard against him, his freed hand lifting to her chin, tilting it up, his eyes blazing a heart-kicking challenge right at her. 'A great many needs to be answered on both sides and I don't want to wait, either.'

His mouth came down on hers so hard she jerked her head back, afraid of what she had just invited. He'd been a tender lover to her, never rough. Panic kicked into her heart. What did she know of him now? If he had no real feeling for her…

'Damn!' he muttered, his chest heaving as he sucked in breath, a glint of anguish in the eyes that bored into hers. 'I *will* control myself. Let me start again, Christina.'

He didn't wait for a reply. His lips brushed lightly over hers, back and forth, back and forth, making them tingle to the point where she welcomed the running of his tongue-tip over them. *Yes,* she thought dizzily, the stiffness melting from her body, panic washed away by a soothing flood of warmth. She lifted her arms and wound them around his neck as she gave herself up to a kiss that was more familiar to her, a loving kind of kiss.

She didn't mind opening her mouth to the gentle probe of his tongue, liking the intimate sensation of tangling her own with it, the slow gathering of excitement. It was easy to close her eyes and forget the years of nothing, remembering only the girl she had been in this man's arms, experiencing sexual pleasure for the first time.

His hand slid down over her bottom, pressing her closer to him, and the hardness of his erection filled her mind with giddy elation. He couldn't fake that. He really did want her. She was still desirable to him so it was okay to desire him, too. And she did, quite fiercely, given the confidence that this wasn't just a cynical seduction to weaken her stance against him.

A wild ripple of exultation shot through her when his kissing took on a more passionate intensity, his tongue driving deep, challenging her to meet its thrust, revel in the explosion of need behind it. Her hands slid into his hair, fingers digging in hard to hold his head to hers,

the desire to take possession of him and keep him forever running rampant through her mind.

He couldn't walk away from this.

Not ever again.

She wouldn't let him.

He wrenched his head from her tight grasp, lifting it
back from her mouth enough to gasp, 'Must move from
here. Come.'

He scooped her off the balcony and into the bedroom,
striding for the bed with her firmly tucked to his side.
Tina's heart was pounding with both fear and excitement. This was the moment to undress. She would see
him again fully naked. But he would see her, too. How
did she measure up against the other women who'd been
in his life... the blonde in Dubai whose breasts had been
more voluptuous?

But he *was* aroused, so maybe the *idea* of her made
physical factors irrelevant. And although she was carrying more flesh than when he had been with her before,
her body was still okay—no looseness from having the
baby. It was silly to fret over it. He wanted sex with her.
He was up and ready for it and it was going to happen.

He stopped close to the bed and swung her to face
him, his hands curling around her shoulders, his eyes
sweeping hers for any hint of last-minute rejection. She
stared back steadily, determined not to baulk at this
point.

'You move me as no other woman ever has,
Christina,' he murmured, and planted a soft warm kiss
on her forehead.

Her heart contracted at those words. Whether they

were true or not, the wish to believe them was too strong to fight. She closed her eyes wanting to privately hug the strong impression of sincerity in his, and he gently kissed her eyelids, sealing the positive flow of feeling he had evoked.

She felt his thumbs hook under the straps of the green sundress she'd worn and slowly slide them down her upper arms. He kissed her bared shoulders as he unzipped the back of her bodice. Tina kept her eyes shut, fiercely focussing on her other senses, loving the soft brush of his lips against her skin and the gentle caress of his fingers along her spine as it, too, was bared. She breathed in the slightly spicy scent of his cologne. It was the same as when they were together before. He hadn't changed it. And the thrill of his touch was the same, too.

Her dress slithered down to the floor. The style of it hadn't required a bra so now her breasts were naked. Her only remaining garment was her green bikini pants, but he didn't set about removing this last piece of clothing. His hands cupped her breasts, stroking them with a kind of reverence that she found emotionally confusing until he asked, 'Did you breast-feed Theo, Christina?'

He was thinking of his son. He was not looking at her as a woman but as the mother of his child.

'Yes,' she answered huskily, telling herself it was okay for him to see her in this light. It made her different to the other women who'd been in his life. More special. Her body had carried his child, had nurtured his child.

'He must have been a very happy baby,' he murmured, and his mouth enclosed one of her nipples, his tongue swirling around it before he sucked on it.

Tina gasped at the arc of piercing pleasure that hit her stomach and shot past it to the apex of her thighs. Her hands flew up and grasped his shoulders, fingers digging into his muscles, needing something strong to hold onto as quivers ran through her entire body. He moved his mouth to her other breast, increasing the sweet turbulence inside her. For her it had been a physical pleasure breast-feeding Theo but it hadn't generated this acute level of sexual excitement. Tina was so wound up in it, she didn't know if it was a relief or a disappointment when he lifted his head away.

Almost immediately he was whipping down her bikini pants and her feet automatically stepped out of them. Any concern about how she looked to him had completely disappeared. He scooped her into such a crushing embrace she could feel his heart thumping against his chest-wall and then he was kissing her again; hard, hungry kisses that sparked an overwhelming hunger for him. She wanted this man. She'd never stopped wanting him.

He lifted her off her feet and laid her on the bed. The sudden loss of contact with him instantly opened her eyes. He was discarding his clothes with such haste Tina was in no doubt of his eagerness to join her, and it was thrilling to watch his nakedness emerge. He was a truly beautiful man with a perfect male body. His olive skin gleamed over well-defined muscles. His smooth hairless chest was sculpted for touching, for gliding hands over it. He had the lean hips and powerful thighs of a top athlete. And there was certainly no doubt about his desire for her, his magnificent manhood flagrantly erect.

Yet when he came to her he ignored any urgency for instant sexual satisfaction. He lay beside her, one arm sliding under her shoulders to draw her into full body contact with him, his free hand stroking long, lovely caresses as his mouth claimed hers again, more in a slow seductive tasting than greedy passion. It gave her the freedom to touch him, to revel in feeling his strong masculinity against her softer femininity, the whole wonderfully sensual intimacy of flesh against flesh.

His hand dipped into the crevice between her thighs, his fingers moving gently, back and forth, intent on building excitement until she felt the exquisite urgency he had always made her feel in the past. Tina lifted her leg over his, giving him easier access to her, refusing to let any inhibitions deny her the pleasure she remembered. He changed the nature of his kissing, his tongue thrusting and withdrawing, mimicking the rhythm of what was to come, accelerating the need to have him there.

But still he didn't hurry. He moved down the bed, trailing kisses to the hollow of her throat, then sucking briefly on her breasts, heightening their sensitivity before sliding his mouth to her stomach, running his tongue around her navel.

'Was it a difficult labour with Theo, Christina?' he asked in a deeply caring tone.

She'd been so focussed on feeling, it took a concentrated effort to find her voice. 'Some...some hard hours,' she answered, savagely wishing he wasn't thinking of their son. Yet that was why he was here, with her, doing what he was doing, and she wouldn't be having this if she hadn't had his child.

'I should have been there,' he murmured, pressing his mouth to her stomach as though yearning for that lost time. 'I would have been there. And I will be for the rest of our children,' he said more fiercely before lifting himself further down to kiss her where his son had emerged from her womb.

I'm not going to think of why, Tina decided with wild determination. *I want this. I want him inside me again.*

The tension building in her body obliterated any further thought. Need was screaming through every nerve. It reached the point where she jack-knifed up to pluck at his shoulders, crying out, 'Enough! Enough!' She couldn't bear another second of waiting for him.

To her intense relief he responded instantly, surging up to fit himself between her legs which were already lifting to curl around his hips in a compulsive urging for the action she frantically craved. Her inner muscles were convulsing as he finally entered her and just one deep plunge drove her to an explosive climax, the exquisite torture peaking then melting into wave after wave of ecstatic pleasure as Ari continued the wonderfully intimate stroking.

It was incredibly satisfying, feeling him filling her again and again. Her body writhed exultantly around him. Her hands dragged up and down his back, urging on the rhythm of mutual possession. The sheer elation of it was so marvellously sweet nothing else existed for Tina, not the why or the where or the how.

When Ari cried out at his own climax, it sounded like a triumphant trumpet of joy to her ears. *She* had brought him to this. He shared the same heights of sensation he had led her to. And she revelled in that sense of intense togetherness as all his mighty strength collapsed on her and she hugged him with all her strength. He rolled onto his side, clutching her tightly against him, holding onto the deep connection, clearly wanting it to last as long as possible.

He didn't speak for quite a long time and Tina didn't want to break the silence. She lay with her head tucked under his chin, listening to his pulse-rate slowing to a normal beat. It was the first time today she actually felt totally relaxed. The sex-test was over. He had certainly satisfied her as a lover and if he was satisfied that she wouldn't turn her back on him, maybe they could move towards a commitment to each other.

It might even have a chance of sticking.

If she kept on having his children.

Was that the key to having him come to love her?

If only she could be sure he would in the end…truly love her for herself…and never want any other woman.

Marrying Ari was a terrible gamble.

But having had him again, she didn't want to let him go.

CHAPTER TWELVE

ARI felt happy. Usually after sex he felt satisfied, content, relaxed. Happiness was something more and it made him wonder if it was a temporary thing or whether having Christina would always give him this exultant sense of joy. Maybe it was simply a case of having risen to the challenge and won the response he wanted from her.

It had been damnably difficult to rein himself in to begin with. Having been forced to exercise control on the physical front for the past few days and suddenly being presented with the green light to go ahead, all the bottled-up desire he'd felt had blown his mind. And almost blown his chance with her.

But she wasn't pulling away from him now. He wished she still had long hair. He remembered how much he'd enjoyed running his fingers through it when she'd lain with him like this in the past. Though it didn't really matter. It was so good just having her content to stay where she was—no barriers between them. No *physical* barriers. He hoped the mental resistance she'd had to him had been stripped away, too.

He knew he'd given her intense sexual pleasure. Was it enough to sway her into marrying him? She had to be considering what Theo wanted in his life, too, and there was no doubt he wanted his father. What more could be done to clinch a future together?

He probably should be talking to her, finding out what was in her mind, yet he was reluctant to break the intimate silence. They had all night, plenty of time for talking. It was great being able to revel in the certainty that she would not be cold to him in the marriage bed.

She stirred, lifting her head. 'I need to go to the bathroom, Ari.'

He released her and she instantly rolled away and onto her feet on the other side of the bed, only giving him a back view of her as she walked swiftly to the bathroom, no glimpse of the expression on her face. However, he couldn't help smiling at the lovely curve of her spine, the perkiness of her sexy bottom and the perfect shape of her long legs.

There was nothing unattractive about Christina Savalas. No one would be surprised at his choice of wife. Not that he cared about what anyone else thought but it would make it easier for Christina to be readily accepted as his partner in life. Women could be quite bitchy if they perceived any other woman as not measuring up to what they expected. Felicity Fulbright had sniped about quite a few while in his company.

Of course he would be on guard to protect Christina from any nastiness but there were always female get-togethers when he wouldn't be present. On the other hand, the fighting spirit his father admired in her was undoubtedly a force to be reckoned with in any kind of critical situation. She would have no qualms about setting people straight as she saw it. She'd done it to him repeatedly in the past few days.

All in all, Ari was quite looking forward to a future with Christina now that the sexual question was answered. However, his satisfaction took a slight knock when she re-emerged from the bathroom, wearing a white cotton kimono which covered her from neck to ankle. It signalled that she wasn't about to jump back into bed with him.

'I found this hanging on a peg behind the bathroom door,' she said, putting a firm knot in the tie-belt and not quite meeting his gaze as she added, 'There's another one for you if you want to wear it after your shower. Easier than re-dressing for sitting on the balcony to watch the sunset.'

And easier for undressing afterwards, Ari thought, accepting her plan of action without argument. It was obvious that she had already showered—no invitation for him to join her—so she was putting an end to their intimacy for a while, which raised questions about how eager she was to continue it. An intriguing combination—hot in bed, cool out of it—another challenge that he had to come to grips with.

She wasn't won yet.

'Have a look at the menu on the desk while I shower,' he said invitingly. 'See what you'd like for dinner. We can order it in.'

It stopped her stroll towards the balcony. She paused at the desk to pick up the menu and began to study it, not even glancing at him as he rose from the bed and moved towards the bathroom. Was she embarrassed by her body's response to his love-making? Was she always going to close up on him afterwards? How much was she truly willing to share with him?

Ari mused over these questions while taking a shower. In every one of his relationships with women there had always been mutual desire and mutual liking, at least at the beginning. It had certainly been so with Christina six years ago. In fact, looking back, that had been the only relationship he'd been reluctant to end. Nothing had soured it. Christina had not deceived him in any way, nor done anything to turn him off. The timing had been wrong, nothing else.

He was still sure his reasons for limiting it to his time in Australia were valid, yet his decision then kept coming between them now and he was no longer sure that good sex was the answer to reaching the kind of relationship he wanted with his wife.

Though it still made the marriage viable.

The mutual desire was right.

He just had to work on getting the mutual liking right again.

Having picked up their clothes from the floor and hung them over a chair, Tina took the menu out to the balcony and sat down at the small table for two. She was hungry, having only had a very light lunch, too full of nervous tension to enjoy food. Now that she felt less uptight about spending the night with Ari, a sunset dinner was very appealing.

She studied the list of dishes with interest, thinking this was the first meal she would spend alone with Ari since meeting him again. It was an opportunity to extend her knowledge of his lifestyle, which was an important preparation for being his wife. There was more to marriage than good sex and she wasn't about to let Ari think that was all he had to give her.

Though it was a very powerful drawcard, completely meddling with Tina's common sense when he strolled out to the balcony. His white kimono barely reached his knees and left a deep V of gleaming olive-skinned chest, causing her to catch her breath. He was so overwhelmingly male and so vitally handsome, all her female hormones were zinging as though caught in an electrical storm. Chemistry still humming from the sex they'd just shared, Tina told herself, but the desire for more of it could not be denied.

'Found what you'd like?' he asked, gesturing towards the menu.

'Yes.' She rattled off a starter, a main dish, and sweets, as well.

He grinned approval at her. 'I've worked up an appetite, too. Give me the menu and I'll call in an order now.' He nodded at the lowering sun. 'It will be pleasant to dine as we watch the sunset.'

Both the sky and the sea were already changing colour. Ari tucked the menu under his arm, picked up the half-empty champagne glasses from the balcony wall and returned to the bedroom to make the call. Tina watched the shimmering waves with their shifting shades of light, trying to calm herself enough to conduct a normal conversation without being continually distracted by lustful thoughts.

Ari brought back two clean wine glasses and an ice-bucket containing a bottle of light white wine which he said would go well with their starters. Tina decided she might as well give up her alcohol ban. Wine was part and parcel of Ari's life and it was more appropriate for his wife to partake of some of it.

He was standing by the balcony wall, opening the bottle of wine when he was hailed from below.

'Ari... Ari... It is you, isn't it?'

Tina's nerves instantly twanged. It was a female voice with a very British accent, like that of the woman who'd been with him in Dubai.

He looked down, his shoulders stiffening as he recognised the person. He raised a hand in acknowledgement but made no vocal reply, quickly turning back to the task of filling their glasses. His mouth had thinned into a line of vexation. His eyes were hooded.

Clearly this was an unwelcome intrusion and Tina felt impelled to ask, 'Who is it?' Facing other women who'd been in his life would have to be done sooner or later and it was probably better that she had a taste of it now, know whether or not she could deal with it.

He grimaced. 'Stephanie Gilchrist. A London socialite.'

'Not a fond memory?' she queried archly, pretending it wasn't important.

His eyes blazed annoyance. 'An acquaintance. No more. I see she's here with her current playmate, Hans

Vogel, a German model who's always strutting his stuff. I had no idea they were booked into this hotel.'

Just two people he didn't want to mix with tonight, Tina thought with considerable relief. She didn't really want to be faced with a woman who had shared his bed, not when the intimacies they had just shared were so fresh in her mind, not when her body was still reacting to them. This new beginning would not feel so good. Later on, when she felt more confident about being Ari's partner—when he made her feel more confident—it might not matter at all.

'Ari!' Stephanie called more demandingly.

'Damned nuisance!' he muttered savagely as he swung around to deal with the problem.

Having regained his attention, Stephanie bluntly asked, 'What are you doing here? I thought you had a home on Santorini. I'm sure Felicity told me...'

'This hotel has a better view of the sunset,' Ari swiftly cut in. 'Why don't you and Hans just lie back on your lounges and enjoy it?'

He waved his hand dismissively but Stephanie apparently had some personal axe to grind with him. 'I'm coming up,' she announced belligerently.

Ari cursed under his breath. He turned sharply to Tina, his brow creased with concern, the amber eyes glittering with intense urgency. 'I'm sorry. I can't stop her. The spiral staircase is open to all guests. I will get rid of her as fast as I can.'

Tina shrugged. 'I can be polite to one of your acquaintances for a few minutes,' she said, eyeing him warily, wondering if he had lied to her about the less than intimate connection to this woman.

Ari swiftly rattled out information. 'She's a close friend of Felicity Fullbright. Felicity was the woman you saw me with in Dubai. Since Stephanie is here, I don't know if she's been told I've ended the relationship with her friend. Anything she says... it's irrelevant to us, Christina. Don't let it worry you.'

It worried him.

Here's where I learn if I'm a fool to even consider marrying him, Tina thought, putting a steel guard around her vulnerability to this man.

Her heart started a painful pounding. 'How long were you with Felicity, Ari?' she asked, needing to know more.

'Six weeks. It was enough to decide she didn't suit me,' he answered tersely.

'You haven't been with me for a week yet,' she pointed out just as tersely.

The clip-clop of sandals was getting closer.

Ari frowned, shaking his head at her assertion. 'It's different with you, Christina.'

Because of Theo. But if they married, he would have to live with her, too, and how long would that suit him? They had had a harmonious relationship for three months but still he'd left her. It hadn't been enough to keep him at her side.

Stephanie's arrival on the staircase landing adjacent to their balcony put a halt to any further private conversation. She was a very curvy blonde with a mass of long, crinkly hair, and wearing a minute blue bikini that left little to the imagination. Her very light, almost aquamarine eyes instantly targeted Tina.

'Well, well, off with the old and on with the new,' she drawled. Her gaze shifted to Ari. 'That must be a quick-change record even for you. I ran into Felicity at Heathrow just a few days ago. She was flying in from Athens and Hans and I were on our way here. She said you'd split but she sure didn't know you had a replacement lined up.'

No waiting for an introduction.

No courtesy at all.

Tina sat tight, watching Ari handle the situation.

'You're assuming too much, Stephanie,' he said blandly, gesturing towards Tina. 'This is Christina Savalas whom I met in Australia quite a few years ago. She happens to be Cassandra's sister who married my cousin, George, yesterday. The wedding gave us the opportunity to catch up again, which has been amazingly good.' He smiled at Tina. 'Wouldn't you say?'

'Amazing,' she echoed, following his lead and smiling back at him.

Stephanie arched her eyebrows. 'Australia? Are you heading back there now that the wedding is over?'

Tina shrugged. 'I shall have to go sometime.'

'Not in any hurry since you've snagged Ari again,' came the mocking comment.

The woman's sheer rudeness goaded Tina into a very cold retort. 'I'm not into snagging men. In fact...'

'I'm the one doing all the running,' Ari cut in. 'And having found out what you wanted to know, why don't you run along back to Hans, Stephanie? You're not exactly endearing yourself to a woman I care about.'

'Really care?' She gave Ari a derisive sneer. 'It's not just a dose of the charm you used to bowl over Felicity? You didn't care about her one bit, did you?'

'Not after she displayed a dislike for children, no,' he answered bitingly.

'Oh!' With her spite somewhat deflated, she turned to Tina for a last jeer. 'Well, I've just done you a favour. You'd better show a liking for children or he'll throw you over as fast as he caught up with you. Good luck!'

With a toss of her hair she flounced off their balcony.

Tina stared out to sea as Stephanie's sandals clattered down the spiral staircase. She wondered if it was good luck or bad that had brought her back into Ari's life. Whatever…luck had little to do with making a marriage work. At least, a liking for children was one thing they definitely shared. Ari wouldn't be throwing her over on that issue. But Stephanie had implied he had a quick turnover of women in his life, which meant he wasn't in the habit of holding onto a relationship. What if she didn't *suit* him after a while?

'You hardly know me, Ari,' she said, suddenly frightened that her suitability might be very limited.

'I know enough to want you as my wife,' he whipped out, an emphatic intensity in his voice. 'And not only because you've given me a son. There's nothing I don't like about you, Christina.'

She sliced him a wary look. 'What do you actively *like?*'

He sat down at the table, pushing one of the glasses

of wine over to her, obviously playing for time to think. 'Take a sip. It doesn't have a sour taste like Stephanie,' he assured her.

She picked up the glass and sipped, eyeing him over its rim.

The expression on his face softened, the amber eyes telegraphing appreciation. 'I like how much you care for your family. I like the way you consider others. I like your good manners. I think you have courage and grit and intelligence—all qualities that I like. They make up the kind of character that I want in a partner.'

He wasn't talking love. He was ticking off boxes. She could tick off the same boxes about him. A match-making agency would probably place them as a likely couple, especially since there was no lack of sexual chemistry between them. But there was one big factor missing.

Tina heaved a sigh as she remembered how Cass and George had acted towards each other yesterday. It hurt that she would never have that wonderful emotional security with Ari. What if she married him and he was bowled over by some other woman further down the track? It could happen. She had to be prepared for it, safeguard herself against it, be practical about what she could expect from him and what she couldn't.

'Tell me about your life, Ari,' she said, needing to feel more informed about what a future with him would entail. 'What are the business interests that take you travelling? I only know of your connection to the wine industry.'

He visibly relaxed, happy to have the Stephanie can of worms closed.

Tina listened carefully to the list of property investments the Zavros family had made in many countries as far apart as Spain and Dubai where Ari had so recently been checking up on an estate development. Mostly they were connected to the tourist industry—resorts and theme parks and specialty shops. They had also tapped into the food industry with olives, cheeses and wine.

'You're in charge of all this?' she enquired.

He shook his head. 'My father runs the ship. I report and advise. The decisions are ultimately his. Most of the family is involved in one capacity or another.'

It was big business—far more complex than managing a restaurant. Tina continued to question him about it over dinner which was as tasty as it had promised to be. The sunset was gorgeous, spreading a rosy hue over all the white buildings on the hillside that faced it. For real lovers this had to be a very romantic place, Tina thought, but she couldn't feel it with Ari. As charming as he was, as good a lover as he was, no way could she bring herself to believe she was the light of his life.

Her own experience prompted her to ask, 'Have you ever been in love, Ari? So in love that person mattered more than anything else? Wildly, passionately, out of your mind...*in love?*'

As she'd been with him.

He frowned, obviously not liking the question. His jaw tightened as he swung his gaze away from hers, staring out to sea. She saw the corner of his mouth turn down into a grimace. He had experienced it, she thought, but not with her. A lead weight settled on her heart. He might very well experience it again with someone else.

CHAPTER THIRTEEN

IN LOVE...

Ari hated that memory. It was the one and only time he'd completely lost his head over a woman. He'd been her fool, slavishly besotted with her while she had only been amusing herself with him.

He wished Christina hadn't asked the question. Yet if he wasn't honest with her she would probably sense it and that would be a black mark against him in her mind. Besides, he was a different person to the boy he was then. He just didn't like dragging up that long-buried piece of the past and laying it out but he had to now. He'd left Christina too long without a reply.

He turned to her, the cynicism he'd learnt from that experience burning in his eyes and drawling through his voice. 'Wildly, passionately in love...yes, that happened to me when I was eighteen. She was very beautiful, exotically glamorous, and incredibly erotic. I would have done anything for her and did do everything she asked.'

'How long did it last?'

'A month.'

Christina raised her eyebrows. 'What made you fall out of love?'

'Being faced with reality.'

'Something you didn't like?'

'I hadn't understood what I was to her. I knew she was years older than me. It didn't matter. Nothing mattered but being with her. I thought she felt the same about me. It was so intense. But she was simply enjoying the intensity, revelling in her power to make me do whatever she wanted.'

'How did you come to realise that?'

'Because I was her Greek toy-boy, a last fling before she married her much more mature American millionaire. *It's been fun,* she said as she kissed me goodbye. *Fun...*'

He snarled the word and immediately cursed himself for letting it get to him after all these years.

'You were badly hurt,' Christina murmured sympathetically.

He shrugged. 'I'm not likely to fall in love again, if that's what you're worried about, Christina. Being someone's fool does not appeal to me.'

'You think your head will always rule your heart?'

'It has since I was eighteen.'

Except with her and Theo. His heart was very much engaged with his son and according to his lawyer, he'd completely lost his head in proposing the prenuptial agreement to induce Christina to marry him, ensuring that Theo would be a constant in his life. But he did feel the fidelity clause was not so much of a risk now. And he did like and admire Christina. He would make

the marriage work. They would have more children…
a family…

'I was eighteen when I fell in love with you.'

The quietly spoken words jolted Ari out of his confident mood and sent an instant chill down his spine. Her
dark eyes were flat, expressionless, steadily watching
whether he understood the parallel of what had been
done to him—not only the hurt, the rejection of any
lasting value in the love offered, but also the shadow it
cast over any deep trust in a relationship. Giving one-
self completely to another was not on. He'd never done
it again.

Was this how Christina felt about him? Had he just
ruined every bit of progress he'd made with her, bringing the past back instead of focussing her mind on the
future they could have? Was this why he couldn't reach
what he wanted to reach in her? He had to fix this. It
was intolerable that she cast him in the same mould as
the woman who'd taken him for a ride.

Before he could find the words to defend himself she
spoke again, cocking her head to one side, her eyes alert
to weighing up his reply. 'Did you think it was *fun* at
the time?'

'Not like that!' he denied vehemently. He leaned towards her, gesturing an appeal for fairness. 'There was
no one else in my life, Christina. I wasn't having a fling
with you, cheating on a woman I intended to marry. The
thought of having a little fun with you never crossed my
mind. That was not part of it, I swear. I was enchanted
by you.'

'For a while.' Her mouth twisted with irony. 'I can

imagine an older woman being enchanted by you when you were eighteen, Ari. You would have been absolutely beautiful. But her head ruled her heart, just as yours did with me. Too young…wasn't that how you explained leaving me behind?'

'You're not too young now.' The urgent need to stop this treacherous trawling through the past pushed Ari to his feet. He took Christina's hands, pulling her out of her chair and into his embrace, speaking with a violence of feeling that exploded off his tongue. 'I wanted you beyond any common sense then. And God knows I've lost any common sense since I've met you again. I want you so much it's been burning me up from the moment I saw you in Dubai. So forget everything else, Christina. Forget everything but this.'

He forgot about being gentle with her. The fierce emotion welling up in him demanded that he obliterate any bad thoughts from her mind and fill it with the same all-consuming desire he felt. He kissed her hard, storming her mouth with intense passion. A wild exultation ran through him as she responded with her own fierce drive to take what he was doing and give it right back.

No hesitation.

No holding back.

Frenzied kisses.

Frenzied touching.

Mutual desire riding high, her body pressed yearningly to his, making him even more on fire for her. Primitive instincts kicked in. He needed, wanted, had to have total possession of this woman. He swept her off her feet, crushed her to his chest as he strode to the bed. Even as he laid her down she was pushing her kimono apart, opening her legs wide for him, not wanting to wait, eagerly inviting instant intimacy.

He tore his own robe off, hating the thought of it getting in the way. Then he was with her, swiftly positioning himself. She was slick and hot, exciting him even further with her readiness. Her legs locked around him, heels digging into his buttocks, urging him on. He pushed in hard and fast and barely stopped himself from climaxing at the very first thrust, just like a teenage boy experiencing the ultimate sex fit.

He sucked in a quick breath, savagely telling himself to maintain control. He tried to set up a slow, voluptuous rhythm with his hips but she wouldn't have it, her body rocking his to go faster, faster. He felt her flesh clenching and unclenching around his and her throat emitted an incredibly sexy groan.

His head was spinning, excitement at an intense level. Her fingers dug into the nape of his neck. Her back arched from the bed. He felt the first spasm of her coming and was unable to hold off his own release any longer. He cried out as it burst from him in violent shudders, and the flood of heat from both of them was so ecstatically satisfying he was totally dazed by the depth of feeling.

He'd collapsed on top of her. She held him in a tightly possessive hug. Was she feeling the same? He had to know. Had to know if all the bad stuff from the past had been wiped out of her mind. He levered himself up on his elbows to see her face. Her eyes were closed, her head thrown back, her lips slightly apart, sucking in air and slowly releasing it.

'Look at me, Christina,' he gruffly commanded.

Her long lashes flicked up. Her eyes were dilated, out of focus. A thrill of triumph ran riot through Ari's mind. She was still feeling him inside her, revelling in the sheer depth of sensation. It gave him a surge of confidence that she wouldn't walk away from this— what they could have together. The glazed look slowly cleared. Her tongue slid out and licked her lips. He was tempted to flick his own tongue over them, but that would start them kissing again and this moment would be swallowed up and he wouldn't know what it meant to her.

'This is now, Christina,' he said with passionate fervour. 'The past is gone. This is now and you're feeling good with me. Tell me that you are.'

'Yes.' The word hissed out on a long sigh. She half-smiled as she added, 'I'm feeling good.'

He nodded. 'So am I. And I truly believe we can always make each other feel good if the will is there to do it.' He lifted a hand to stroke the soft black bangs of hair away from her forehead, his eyes boring into hers to enforce direct mental contact with her. 'We can be great partners in every sense there is, starting now, Christina. We look ahead, not back. Okay?'

There was no instant response but her eyes didn't disengage from his. Their focus sharpened and he had the feeling she was trying to search his soul. He had nothing to hide, yet he was acutely conscious of tension building inside him as he waited for her answer.

He'd hurt her in the past and she'd nursed that hurt for years. It had erupted in his face tonight and he was asking her to let it go, leave it behind them. It was a big ask. He recalled the look of heart-piercing vulnerability he'd seen after they'd made the sex-deal last night. But he'd just proved she had nothing to fear from an intimate connection with him. She'd conceded he'd made her feel good.

He willed her to grasp what could be grasped and take it into the future with them. It was best for their son, best for their lives, too. Surely she could see that.

'Have you had the prenuptial agreement you offered me drawn up, Ari?'

It wasn't what he wanted to hear from her. It meant that it didn't matter what he said or did, she still had a basic mistrust of how he would deal with her in the future. He could pleasure her all night but that verbal kick in the gut told him it would make no difference.

'Yes. It's in my backpack,' he said flatly.

'Have you signed it?'

'Not yet.'

'Will you do so in the morning if…if you're still feeling good with me?'

'Yes,' he said unequivocally, though hating the fact it was still necessary in her mind.

She hadn't faked her response to him. There was nothing fake about Christina Savalas and it was clear that she needed a guarantee that if there was anything fake about him, she would not lose her son by marrying him.

She reached up and gently stroked his cheek. 'I'm

sorry I can't feel more secure with you, Ari. I promise you to do my best to be a partner to you in every sense. If I fail and you end up finding someone else who suits you better, I won't deny you a fair share of Theo. I just need protection against your taking him from me.'

'I'd never do that,' he protested vehemently. 'You're his mother. He loves you.'

She heaved a deep sigh as though that claim meant little in the bigger scheme of things. 'It's impossible to know how things will turn out along the track,' she said in a fatalistic tone. 'As sincere as your commitment might be to me now, as sincere as mine is to you, it's in our minds, Ari, not our hearts, and you might not think so now, but hearts can over-rule minds. I know. It's why I never told you about Theo when I should have. My heart wouldn't let me.'

There was sadness in her eyes—the sadness of betrayed innocence—and Ari knew he'd done that to her. Determination welled up in him to replace it with joy—joy in him and the children they would have together.

'Our marriage will be fine, Christina,' he promised her. 'I don't mind signing the prenuptial agreement. I want you to feel secure, not frightened of anything. And given more time, I hope you'll come to trust me, knowing without a doubt that I mean you well and want you to be happy with me.'

It brought a smile back to her face. 'That would be good, Ari.' Her hand slid up and curled around his head. 'I could do with some more of feeling good.'

He laughed and kissed her.

The night was still young. They proceeded to a more

languorous love-making for a while, pleasuring each other with kisses and caresses. It delighted Ari that Christina had no inhibitions about her sexuality and no hesitation in exploring his. He hoped it would always be like this, no holding back on anything.

The commitment was made now.

Ari felt right about it—more right than he'd ever felt about anything else in his life. And he'd make it right for Christina, too. It would take more than a night to do it. It might take quite a long while. But he was now assured of all the time he would need to wipe out her doubts and win her trust. When that day came—he smiled to himself—all of life would be good.

CHAPTER FOURTEEN

Tina was determined not to regret marrying Ari Zavros but to view her time with him—regardless of what happened in the end—as an experience worth having. In any event, she would not lose Theo or any other children they might have. The signed prenuptial agreement was in her keeping.

Everyone was happy that a wedding would soon take place. The Zavros family seemed particularly pleased to welcome her into their clan and Theo was over the moon at belonging to so many more people. Plans were quickly made. Her mother had no hesitation in deciding that Athens would be the best place for her to live— much closer to her daughters—and Maximus immediately offered to find the best property for her while they dealt with winding up their lives in Australia.

Ari accompanied them back to Sydney. He organised the sale of the restaurant to the head chef and the head waiter. Tina suspected he financed the deal. Everything in their apartment was packed up by professionals— also organised by Ari—and stored in a container which would be shipped to Athens. He was a whirlwind of activity, determined on moving them out with the least amount of stress. Her mother thought he was wonderful.

Tina couldn't fault him, either. He was attentive to their needs, carried out their wishes, and to Tina's surprise, even purchased an extremely expensive three-bedroom apartment overlooking Bondi Beach.

'To Theo it's the best beach in the world,' he explained. 'He might get homesick for it. You, too, Christina. We can always take time out to come back here for a while.'

His caring for their son was so evident, so constant, it continually bolstered her decision to marry him. Theo adored him. Her reservations about his constancy where she was concerned remained in her mind but were slowly being whittled away in her heart. He was so good to her, showing consideration for whatever she wanted in every respect.

Within a month they were back on Santorini. Her mother was to be a guest in the Zavros villa until her furniture arrived for her new apartment in Athens. Maximus, of course, had found the perfect place for her. She quickly became fast friends with Ari's mother who had been organising the wedding in their absence. It was almost the end of the tourist season when most places closed down on the island. They only had a week to finalise arrangements—a week before Tina's life began as Ari's wife.

Cass had been informed of the situation via email and was delighted that everything seemed to be working out well. She insisted on buying Tina's wedding dress and kept sending photographs of glorious gowns until Tina chose one. She let Cass select her own bridesmaid dress. George was to be best man—a reversal of their previous roles.

The same church was to be used for the marriage service and the same reception centre. Both places had also been chosen for the weddings of Ari's sisters. Apparently it was customary for the Zavros family and Tina didn't raise any objection although privately she would have preferred not to be following in her sister's footsteps, being reminded of the real love Cass and George had declared for each other.

She didn't feel like a bride. She looked like one on the day. And despite the lateness of the season, the sun was shining. It made her wonder if Ari had arranged that, too, everything right for the Golden Greek. It was a weird feeling, walking down the aisle to him—more like a dream than reality. Everything had happened so fast. But her feet didn't falter and she gave him her hand at the end of the walk, accepting there was no turning back from this moment.

Her ears were acutely tuned to the tone of Ari's voice as he spoke his marriage vows. It was clear and firm, as though he meant them very seriously. Which Tina found comforting. She had to swallow hard to get her own voice working at all, and the words came out in jerky fashion which she couldn't control. But they were said. It was done. They were declared man and wife.

To Tina, the reception was a blur of happy faces congratulating her and Ari and wishing them well. Everyone from both families was there, along with Ari's close business connections and friends. Tina couldn't remember all their names. She just kept smiling, as a bride should. Ari carried off the evening with great panache and he carried her along with him—his wife.

He took her to Odessa for a honeymoon. It was a beautiful city, called The Pearl of The Black Sea, and for the first time since her future with Ari had been decided, Tina could really relax and enjoy herself. There was nothing that had to be done. Theo was undoubtedly having a great time with his doting grandparents. She was free of all responsibility. And Ari was intent on filling their days—and nights—with pleasure.

The weather was still hot and they lazed away mornings on the beach, had lunch in coffee shops or restaurants beside lovely parks, browsed around the shops that featured crafts of the region—marvellous cashmere shawls, beautifully embroidered blouses, and very different costume jewellery.

They went to a ballet performance at the incredibly opulent opera house—totally different architecture and interior decoration to the amazing hotel in Dubai but just as mind-boggling in its richness.

When she commented on this to Ari he laughed and said, 'Europe is full of such marvels, Christina, and I shall enjoy showing them to you. When we go to Paris, I'll take you to Versailles. You'll be totally stunned by it.'

He was as good as his word. In the first six months of their marriage, she accompanied him on many trips around Europe—Spain, Italy, England, France, Germany. All of them were related to business but Ari made time to play tourist with her. He was the perfect companion, so knowledgeable about everything and apparently happy to spend his free time with her.

There were business dinners they had to attend, and parties they were invited to which invariably made Tina nervous, but Ari never strayed from her side whenever they were socialising. He bought her beautiful clothes so that she always felt confident of her appearance on these occasions and he constantly told her she was beautiful, which eased her anxiety about other women.

They had decided on Athens as their home base. Tina wanted to be close to her mother and it was easier for Theo to be enrolled in the same private English-speaking school as his cousins. He accompanied them on trips which didn't interfere with his schooling but at other times he was happy to stay with family while they were away.

However, when Tina fell pregnant, as happy as she was about having a baby, the morning sickness in the first trimester was so bad she couldn't face travelling anywhere and she couldn't help fretting when Ari had to leave her behind to attend to business. Each time he returned she searched for signs that he was growing tired of her, finding her less attractive, but he always seemed pleased to be home again and eager to take her to bed.

She expected his desire for her to wane as her body lost its shape but it didn't. He displayed a continual fascination with every aspect of her pregnancy, reading up on what should be happening with the child growing inside her, lovingly caressing her lump, even talking to it in a besotted manner and grinning with delight whenever he felt a ripple of movement. He always smiled when he saw her naked, his eyes gloating over her as though she presented an incredibly beautiful image to him, pregnant with his child.

Tina reasoned that obviously having children meant a lot to Ari. He had married her because of Theo and being the mother of his children did make her uniquely special to him. If he never fell in love with anyone else, maybe their marriage would become very solid and lasting. She fiercely hoped so because she couldn't guard against the love that she hadn't wanted to feel with him.

It sat in her heart, heavy with the need to keep it hidden. Pride wouldn't let her express it. Sometimes she let herself imagine that he loved her, but he never said it. Their marriage was based on family. That had to be enough.

She was eight months pregnant and looking forward to the birth of the baby when fate took a hand in ending her happy anticipation. She'd been shopping with her mother, buying a few extra decorations for the newly furnished nursery at home; a gorgeous mobile of butterflies to hang over the cot, a music box with a carousel on top, a kaleidoscope to sit on the windowsill.

They planned to finish off their outing with a visit to a hairdressing salon which was located a few blocks away from the department store where they had purchased these items. Tina felt too tired and cumbersome to walk that far, so they took a taxi for the short trip. It was crossing an intersection when a truck hurtled across the road from the hilly street on their right, clearly out of control, its driver blaring the horn of the truck in warning, his face contorted in anguish at being unable to avoid an accident.

It was the last thing Tina saw—his face. And the last thing she thought was *the baby!* Her arms clutched the mound of the life inside her. It was the last thing she did before the impact robbed her of consciousness.

Ari had never felt so useless in his life. There was nothing he could do to fix this. He had to leave it up to the doctors—their knowledge, their skill. He was so distressed he could barely think. He sat in the hospital waiting room and *waited.*

Theo was taken care of. His parents had flown over from Santorini to collect him from school and take him back home with them. He was to be told that Mama and Papa had been called away on another trip. There was no point in upsetting him with traumatic news. When the truth had to be told—whatever it turned out to be—Ari would do it. He would be there for his son.

His sisters had wanted to rush to the hospital, giving their caring support but he'd told them not to. He didn't want their comforting gestures. He was beyond comfort. Besides, it would be a distraction from willing Christina to get through this. She had to. He couldn't bear the thought of life without her.

Cassandra was flying in from Rome to be with her mother. He didn't have to worry about Helen—just bruises, a broken arm, and concussion. Her relatives were sitting with her and she would be allowed out of hospital tomorrow. She was frantically worried about

Christina. They all were, but he didn't want to listen to any weeping and wailing. He needed to be alone with this until the doctors came back to him.

Head injuries, smashed clavicle, broken ribs, collapsed lung, ripped heart, and damage to the uterus, but the baby's heart was still beating when they'd brought Christina into the emergency ward. A drug-induced coma was apparently the best state for her to be in while undergoing treatment for her injuries and it had been deemed advisable to perform a Caesarian section. It wasn't how Christina had wanted the baby delivered but he'd been told there was no choice in these circumstances.

Their second child…

A brother or sister for Theo…

They'd been so looking forward to its birth, sharing it together. Now it felt like some abstract event…in the hands of the doctors. No mutual joy in it. A baby without a mother unless Christina survived this.

She had to, not only for their children, but for him.

She was his woman, the heart of his life, and his heart would be ripped out if she died. Just thinking about it put one hell of a pain in his chest.

One of the doctors he'd spoken to entered the waiting room, accompanied by a nurse. Ari rose to his feet, his hands instinctively clenching although there was nothing to fight except the fear gripping his stomach.

'Ah, Mr Zavros. The Caesarian went well. You're the father of a healthy baby girl.'

The announcement hit the surface of his mind but didn't engage it. 'And Christina?' he pressed.

'Your wife will be in the operating theatre for some hours yet. The baby has been taken to an intensive care ward and placed in a humidicrib. We thought...'

'Why?' Ari cut in, fear for the life of their child welling up to join his fear for Christina. 'You said she was healthy.'

'Purely a precautionary measure, Mr Zavros. She is very small, a month premature. It is best that she be monitored for a while.'

'Yes...yes...' he muttered distractedly, his mind jagging back to Christina. 'The injuries to my wife...it *is* possible that she can recover from them?'

'One cannot predict with certainty but there is a good chance, yes. The surgeons are confident of success. If there are no complications...' He shrugged. 'Your wife is young and healthy. That is in her favour.'

Please, God, let there be no complications, Ari fiercely prayed.

'If you would like to see your daughter now...?'

His daughter. Their daughter. Seeing her without Christina at his side. It felt wrong. There was a terrible hollowness in his heart. It should have been filled with excitement. And that was wrong, too. Their baby girl should be welcomed into this world, at least by her father.

'Yes... please...' he replied gruffly.

He was escorted to the maternity ward and led to where his daughter lay in a humidicrib attached to monitoring wires. She looked so little, helpless, and again Ari was assaulted by a wretched sense of powerlessness. Right now he couldn't take care of Christina or their child. He had to leave them both in the hands of others.

A smile tugged at his lips as he stared down at the shock of black hair framing the tiny face. Christina's hair. Her lips were perfectly formed, too, just like her mother's.

'Would you like to touch her?' the nurse beside him asked.

'Yes.'

She lifted the lid of the humidicrib. He reached out and gently stroked the super-soft skin of a tiny hand. It startled and delighted him when it curled tightly around one of his fingers. Her eyes opened—dark chocolate eyes—and seemed to lock onto his.

'I'm your Papa,' he told her.

Her little chest lifted and a sigh whispered from her lips as though the bond she needed was in place. She closed her eyes. The grip on his finger slowly eased.

'Be at peace, little one. I'm here for you,' Ari murmured.

But she would need her mother, too.

He needed Christina, though he wasn't sure how much that would mean to her. She had accepted him as her husband. He saw the love she openly showered on their son, but whatever was in her heart for him had always been closely guarded.

So he willed her to live for their children.

That was the stronger pull on her.

Her son and her daughter.

CHAPTER FIFTEEN

SIX weeks... They'd been the longest six weeks of Ari's life. The doctors had explained it was best that Christina remain in a coma until the swelling of her brain had gone down and her injuries had healed. They had also warned him she would initially feel lost and confused when they brought her out of it and would need constant reassurance of where she was, why, and what had happened to her.

Most probably any dreams she may have had during this time would be more real to her than reality and it would require patient understanding from him to deal with her responses to the situation. Ari didn't care how much patient understanding he had to give as long as Christina came back to him. Yet as mentally prepared as he was to deal with anything, it hit him hard when she woke and stared at him without any sign of recognition.

Tears welled into her eyes.

He squeezed her hand gently and quickly said, 'It's okay, Christina. Everything's okay.'

'I lost the baby.'

'No, you didn't,' he vehemently assured her. 'We have a beautiful little baby girl. She's healthy and happy and Theo adores her. We've named her Maria—your favourite name for a girl—and she looks very like you.'

The tears didn't stop. They trickled down her cheeks.

Ari told her about the accident and the need for a Caesarian birth and how their daughter was thriving now. She kept staring at him but he didn't think she was registering anything he said. The look of heart-breaking sadness didn't leave her face. After a while she closed her eyes and slid back into sleep.

He took Theo and Maria with him on his next visit, determined to set Christina's mind at rest.

Again she woke and murmured the mournful words, 'I lost the baby.'

'No, you didn't,' he assured her. 'Look, here she is.'

He laid Maria in her arms and she stared at the baby wonderingly as he explained again about the accident and their daughter's birth. Then Theo, super-excited at having his mother finally awake from her long sleep, chattered non-stop, telling her everything about his new sister. She smiled at him and was actually smiling at the baby as her eyes closed. Ari hoped her sleep would be less fretful now.

Yet from day to day she seemed to forget what had been said and he would have to remind her. He started to worry that she might never fully recover from her head injuries. The doctors explained that it could take a while for the drugs to wash out of her system. Until she completely emerged from her dream-state, it was impossible to gauge if there was some negative side-effect that would have to be treated.

Mostly he just sat by her side and prayed for her to be whole again.

It felt like a miracle when one day she woke up and looked at him with instant recognition. 'Ari,' she said in a pleased tone.

His heart kicked with excitement, then dropped like a stone when her expression changed to the darkly grieving one that had accompanied her other awakenings. But her words were slightly different.

'I'm sorry. I lost the baby.'

'No!'

Encouraged by the certainty that she was actually talking to him this time, he explained the situation again. There was an alertness in her eyes that hadn't been there before. He was sure she was listening, taking in all the information he gave, sifting through it, understanding. A smile started to tug at her mouth.

'A daughter,' she said in a tone of pleasure. 'How lovely!'

Elation soared through him. 'She's beautiful. Just like you, Christina,' he said, smiling back.

A frown of concern puckered her brow. 'And Theo? I've been here…how long?'

'Two months. Theo is fine. Missing his Mama but happily distracted by having a baby sister. I'll bring both of them in for you to see as soon as I can.'

'Maria…' She smiled again, a look of blissful relief on her face. 'Oh, I'm so glad I didn't lose her, Ari.'

'And I'm so glad I didn't lose you,' he said fervently.

Her eyes focussed sharply on him for several moments before her gaze slid away to where her fingers started plucking at the bed-sheet. 'I guess that would have been…inconvenient for you.'

Inconvenient!

Shock rattled Ari's mind. It took him several moments to realise she had no idea how much she meant to him. He'd never told her. He reached out and enclosed the plucking fingers with his, holding them still.

'Look at me, Christina,' he quietly commanded.

She did so, but not with open windows to her soul. Her guard was up, as it had been from the day she had agreed to marry him. He had never worn it down. He should have felt grateful for this return to normality, but the need to break through it was too strong for patience in laying out what was very real to him—had been real for a long time although he hadn't recognised it until faced with losing her from his life.

'Do you remember asking me about falling in love and I told you about the American woman I'd met when I was eighteen?' he asked.

She slowly nodded.

'It was nothing but blind infatuation, Christina,' he said vehemently, his eyes burning into hers to make her believe he spoke the truth. 'I didn't love her. I didn't know her enough to love the person she was. Being with you this past year…I've learnt what it is to really love a woman. I love you.'

Her eyes widened but still they searched his warily.

'If you'd died from this accident, it would have left a hole in my life that no one else could ever fill. It wouldn't have been an inconvenience. Christina. It would have been...' He shook his head, unable to express the terrible emptiness that had loomed while he'd waited for the miracle of her return to him. 'I love you,' he repeated helplessly. 'And please, please, don't ever leave me again.'

'Leave you?' she echoed incredulously. 'I've always been afraid of you leaving me.'

'Never! Never! And after this, let me tell you, I'm going to be nervous about letting you out of my sight.'

She gave him a rueful little smile. 'That's how I felt... nervous when you were away from me. Women always look at you, Ari.'

'They don't make me feel what I do for you, Christina. You're my woman, the best in the world. Believe me.'

Tina wanted to. Somehow it was too much...waking up from the dreadful nightmare of loss and being handed a lovely dream. She lifted her free hand to rub her forehead, get her mind absolutely clear.

'My hair! It's gone!'

'It's growing back,' Ari instantly assured her. 'They had to shave it for the operation.'

Tears spurted into her eyes as she gingerly felt the ultra-short mat of hair covering her scalp. Ari had liked it long so she had let it grow after their wedding. She remembered taking the taxi to the hairdressing salon...

'My mother!'

'She's fine. Minor injuries. She was only in hospital for one day. Everything's fine, Christina. Nothing for you to worry about.'

'Who is looking after the children?'

'The housekeeper, the nanny for Maria, your mother, my mother, my sisters, your aunts…our home is like a railway station for relatives wanting to help.'

The sudden rush of fear receded, replaced by a weird feeling of jealousy that a nanny was replacing her for Maria. 'I need to go home, Ari,' she pleaded.

'As soon as the doctors permit it,' he promised.

'I need to see my children.'

He squeezed her hand. 'You rest quietly now and I'll go and get them, bring them here for you to see. Okay?'

'Yes.'

He rose from the chair beside her bed and gently kissed her forehead. 'Your hair doesn't matter, Christina,' he murmured. 'Only you getting well again matters.'

The deep caring in his voice washed through her, soothing the tumult of emotions that had erupted. Everything was all right. Ari always made perfect arrangements. And he'd said he loved her.

She didn't rest quietly. No sooner had Ari gone than doctors came, asking questions, taking her blood pressure, checking tubes and wires, removing some of them. She had questions for them, too. By the time they left she knew precisely what she had been through and how devoted her husband had been, visiting her every day, doing his best to console her whenever she'd shared her nightmare with him.

The doctors had no doubt that Ari loved her.

Tina started to believe it.

Theo came running into the hospital room, his face

lighting up with joy at seeing her awake and smiling for him. 'Mama! Mama! Can I hug you?'

She laughed and made room on the bed for him to climb up beside her. 'I want to hug you, too.' Her beautiful little son. Hers and Ari's. It was wonderful to cuddle him again.

'And here is my sister,' he declared proudly as Ari carried their baby into the room, grinning delightedly at the two of them together.

Theo quickly shuffled aside to let Ari lay the baby in her arms. Tina felt a huge welling of love as her gaze roved over her daughter, taking in the amazing perfection of her.

'Maria's got more hair than you, Mama,' Theo said, and she could laugh about it, no longer caring about the loss of her long, glossy locks.

'She has your mother's hair, and her eyes and her mouth,' Ari said, as though he was totally besotted by the likeness to her.

Tina couldn't help smiling at him. He smiled back and the words simply spilled out of the fullness of her heart. 'I love you, too, Ari.'

His eyes glowed a warm gold. He leaned over and kissed her on the mouth. 'I will thank God forever that you've come back to us, Christina,' he murmured against her lips, leaving them warm and tingling, making her feel brilliantly alive.

A new life, she thought. Not only for the baby in her arms, but for her and Ari and Theo, too.

A family bonded in love.

It was what her father had wanted for her.

No more disappointment.
She had it all.

It was summer on Santorini again and both families had gathered in force to attend Maria's christening. The same church, the same reception centre, but for Tina, this was a much happier occasion than her wedding. Although Ari's family had welcomed her into it before, she really felt a part of it now, and she also felt much closer to her own family, no longer having the sense of being an outsider who had broken the rules.

It was a truly joyous celebration of life and love. The sun shone. There were no shadows between her and Ari. She saw desire for her simmering in his eyes all day and her own desire for him was zinging through her blood. No sooner was the party over and the children finally asleep in their part of the Zavros villa, than they headed off to their own bedroom, eager to make love. But before they did, there was one thing Tina wanted to do.

She'd put the prenuptial agreement in the top drawer of the bedside table and she went straight to it, took it out and handed it to Ari. 'I want you to tear this up.'

He frowned. 'I don't mind you having it, Christina. I want you to feel secure.'

'No. It's wrong. It's part of a bad time that's gone, Ari. If you were asking me to marry you now, I wouldn't insist on a prenuptial agreement. I trust you. I believe what we have is forever. It is, isn't it?'

He smiled. 'Yes, it is.'

He tore it up.

She smiled and opened her arms to him, opened her

heart to him. 'I love you. I love our family. We're going to have a brilliant life together, aren't we?'

He laughed, lifted her off her feet, twirled her around and dumped her on the bed, falling on top of her, although levering his weight up on his elbows as he grinned down at her. 'Brilliant and beautiful and bountiful, because I have you, my love.'

She reached up and touched his cheek, her eyes shining with all he made her feel.

'And I have you.'

* * * * *

BREAKING THE GREEK'S RULES

ANNE McALLISTER

For Nancy

CHAPTER ONE

ALEXANDROS Antonides studied the crumpled receipt, the one with the hastily scrawled name, address and phone number on the back, and was tempted to stuff it right back in his pocket.

Or better yet, throw it out.

He didn't need a matchmaker, for God's sake!

His fingers crushed the already frequently crumpled piece of paper and he stared out the window of the taxi as it headed north on Eighth Avenue. They weren't out of midtown Manhattan yet. It was nearly five-thirty. He should just tell the driver to forget it.

But he didn't. Instead he made himself lean back against the seat and, just as he had done a dozen or more times before, he smoothed out the paper against his palm.

Daisy Connolly. His cousin Lukas had scribbled down her name and address a month ago when he and Lukas had met up at the family reunion out at Lukas's parents' place in the Hamptons. "She'll find you the perfect wife."

"How do you know?" he'd asked Lukas, letting his voice carry his obvious doubt. He'd looked around pointedly, noting Lukas's complete lack of not only a wife, but even a date for their family reunion.

"Seen her do it," Lukas said frankly. "I went to college with her. She did it then. She does it now. She has some uncanny sense of who belongs together." He shrugged. "Who knows how she does it? Hocus-pocus? Tea leaves? Beats me. Give her a call or go see her."

Alex had grunted, not a sound meant to convey agreement.

"Unless you really don't want to get married." Lukas had cocked his head, considering Alex. Then, "Maybe he's chicken," he had said to his brothers.

One of them had made a clucking sound.

Alex had masked his irritation and rolled his eyes. "Fine," he'd said curtly. "If I get desperate enough, I'll look her up."

"I'd say you're already desperate," Lukas had said, grinning. "How many fiancées have you gone through?"

"Two," Alex said through his teeth. "But Imogene doesn't count."

Imogene had been perfect. She hadn't loved Alex any more than he'd loved her. When her long-time boyfriend had got cold feet faced with a lifetime commitment, Alex had grabbed her on the rebound. Unfortunately two days after she'd said yes to Alex, the love of her life had come to his senses and begged her to marry him.

"What can I do?" she'd wailed at Alex. "I still love him!"

The more fool she, Alex had thought. But he'd been polite and wished her good luck. He still did. If she was that besotted, she'd need it.

"I don't know," Lukas had said slowly, studying him. "Two fiancées in a little over a year…" He'd arched his brows in speculation, then looked over at his brothers. "Sounds pretty desperate to me."

His brothers, Elias and PJ, had nodded sagely.

Alex had merely snorted. He didn't want a perfect wife, anyway. He just wanted a suitable one. He was thirty-five years old. Time to get married.

Of course lots of men would disagree. But not Antonides men. Antonides men married. All of them.

Not young, as a rule. Most all of them sowed their wild oats before settling down. But in the end, every last one of them took the plunge.

As a young man Alex had turned his back on the notion. He'd figured to be the exception to the rule. Besides, then the thrill of the hunt and endless variety had enticed him.

Now it often seemed more trouble than it was worth.

Sex? Well, that wasn't too much trouble. But picking up women who wanted a one-night stand seemed tawdry to him now. And while it was fine to play the field when they were young, Alex understood what every Antonides male understood—that there came a time to turn into a responsible, steady, dependable, mature man.

And that meant having a wife.

Elias might have been born responsible. But even PJ, who had been a beach bum for years, was respectably married now. In fact he had been secretly married for years. And Lukas, the youngest of them and definitely a free spirit, would get married, too.

Even Lukas knew it. It was just a matter of time.

Alex's time was now.

He had made up his mind last year. The hunt had begun to bore him and he found he preferred spending his time designing buildings than enticing women into his bed. It wasn't all that difficult, honestly. The difficult part was when he had to convince them he didn't intend to fall in love with them.

It would be easier and more straightforward, he decided, to find a woman he liked, spell out the rules, marry her and get on with his life.

It wasn't as if he had a lot of rules. Basically all he wanted was an easy-to-get-along-with, undemanding woman who wanted an easy-to-get-along-with, undemanding husband. He wasn't looking for love and he wasn't looking for kids. He wasn't looking to complicate his life.

He and his wife would share bed and board when they were in the same country and would attend each other's duty functions when possible. Presently he lived in an apartment he'd restored in Brooklyn above his offices, but it was a bachelor's pad. He wouldn't expect his wife to live there. They could get another place close to her work. She could choose it. He didn't care. He was perfectly willing to be accommodating.

So, really, how difficult could it be to find a woman willing to agree to his terms?

Harder than he thought, Alex admitted now.

His last three dates had seemed promising—all of them were professional women in their thirties. He'd met them at business social functions. They all had high-powered careers, fast-track lives, and nearly as many demands on their time as he had on his.

They *should* have been perfect.

But the lawyer had treated their dinner date as a cross-examination about his determination not to have children. The dentist bored on about how much she hated her profession and could hardly wait to quit and start a family. And Melissa, the stock analyst with whom he'd had dinner with last night, told him point-blank that her biological clock was ticking and she wanted a baby within a year.

At least Alex had had the presence of mind to say just as firmly, "I don't."

But that date, like so many of the others he'd had since he'd decided that it was possible to marry without anything as messy as love complicating the relationship, had gone downhill from there.

Which brought him back to the receipt he held in his hand. Daisy.

He stared at the name Lukas had scrawled on the crumpled paper. It brought with it flickers of memories, a frisson of awareness. Honey-blonde hair. Sparkling blue eyes. Laughter. Gentle, warm words. Soft sighs. Hot kisses. He shifted in the seat of the cab. Once upon a time, for one brief weekend, Alex had known a woman called Daisy.

So maybe this was fate.

The hot-kisses, soft-sighs Daisy had wanted to marry him. Maybe the matchmaking Daisy would find him a wife.

"Think of it as delegating," Elias had urged him pragmatically when he'd balked at Lukas's suggestion. "You do it all the time at work."

That was true. Alex had a whole staff at his architectural firm who did the things he didn't have time for. They did what he told them, checked availability, researched zoning and land use and materials, sorted and sifted through piles of information, then presented their findings and recommendations, and left him to make the final decision.

It was sensible. It was efficient. And Elias was right: a matchmaker could do the same thing. It would be smarter, in fact, than doing it himself.

He would be leaving less to chance if he deputized a disinterested employee to find appropriate candidates. And he'd be spared the awkwardness of future dinners like the one he'd shared with Melissa last night. With a matchmaker vetting the candidates, he would only have to meet the really suitable ones, then decide which one would make the best wife.

It suddenly sounded promising. He should have dropped in on Daisy Connolly before this. But Alex didn't ordinarily get to the Upper West Side. Today, though, he'd been working on a building project in the West Village and, finishing early, he'd had a bit of time to spare before he headed back to Brooklyn. So he'd plucked the paper out of his wallet and hopped in a cab.

Twenty minutes later he consulted it as he got out again on the corner of Amsterdam Avenue and the cross street on which Daisy Connolly had her office.

He hoped she hadn't gone home already. He hadn't made an appointment. It had seemed more sensible to leave himself the option of changing his mind if, when he saw the place, something about it made him want to walk straight on past.

But the street wore the New York City version of homey respectability. It was quiet, lined with four and five story brownstones, a few blocks north of the Museum of Natural History. The trees on either side of the street were all varying shades of gold and orange this early October afternoon,

making it look like a photo op for an urban lifestyle magazine. Alex took his time walking up the block, the architect
in him enjoying the view.

When he'd first bought a place to live in New York three
years ago, changing his base of operations from Europe to this
side of the Atlantic, he'd opted for an apartment in a high-rise
about a mile south on Central Park West. Twenty-odd stories
up, his aerie had given him a useful bird's-eye perspective of
the city, but it had literally kept him above it all. He hadn't
felt connected.

Two years ago, offered a chance to tear down a pre-war office building in Brooklyn not far from where his cousins Elias
and PJ lived with their families, he'd found a purpose and a
place where he was happy at the same time. He'd found another property on which to build what the owner wanted, and
seeing a chance to make a useful contribution to the gentrifi-
cation of a neighborhood in transition, he had snapped up the
pre-war building for himself. Now he had his offices downstairs and his apartment on the fourth floor. He felt more like
he belonged and less as if he were soaring above it.

He got the same feeling here on Daisy Connolly's street.
There was a laundry on one corner, a restaurant on the other.
Between two of the brownstones he passed an empty lot which
now held a small local playground with some climbing equip-
ment, a swing and slide. One brownstone had a small discreet
plaque by the door of the garden floor apartment offering
herbs and organic seedlings. Another had a small sign for a
chiropractor's office.

Did matchmakers have signs? He felt an unwelcome flicker
of awkwardness. When he found the address midblock, there
was no sign. It looked like a version of all the rest—a tall, narrow, five story building with three stories of bay windows and
another two stories above them of more modest windows—
where once servants had dwelt no doubt. It was the color of
warm honey, lighter than the traditional brownstone, and it

sported lace curtains at the first floor bay windows making it look pleasant and professional at the same time.

Besides the lack of signs, there were no astrology signs or crystal balls in sight. No tiny fairy lights flickering in the windows, either. None of the "hocus-pocus" Lukas had mentioned. Alex breathed a sigh of relief.

He straightened his tie, took a deep breath, strode up the steps and opened the outside door. In the tiny foyer, on the mailbox for apartment 1, he saw her name: *Daisy Connolly*. Resolutely he pressed the buzzer.

For half a minute there was no response at all. Alex shifted from one foot to the other and ground his teeth at the thought of wasting the end of an afternoon coming all the way to the Upper West Side for nothing.

But just as he was about to turn away, he heard the sound of a lock being turned. The door opened into the shadow-filled front hall and he could see the silhouette of a slim woman coming to push open the door to admit him.

She was smiling—until their gazes met. Then the smile faded and the color drained from her face.

She stared at him, stricken. "Alex?"

Honey-blonde hair. Deep blue eyes. A memory of scorching hot kisses. *"Daisy?"*

Alex? Here? No!

No. No. No.

But all the time the word was banging around inside Daisy's head, the truth—all six feet of his whipcord-lean, muscular, gorgeous male self—was staring at her in the face.

Why in heaven's name couldn't she have looked out the window before she'd answered the door?

The answer was simple: Alexandros Antonides was so far in her past she never ever considered that he might turn up on her doorstep.

She'd been expecting Philip Cannavarro.

She'd done a photo shoot with the Cannavarro family—

Phil, Lottie and their three children—last month at the beach. A week and a half ago, they had chosen their photos, and Philip had called at lunch to ask if he could drop by after work and pick up their order.

So when the buzzer had sounded at twenty minutes to six, Daisy had opened the door with a smile on her face and an embossed portfolio of photos in her hand—a portfolio that the sight of Alexandros Antonides had let slip from her nerveless fingers.

"Oh, hell."

Her heart hammering, Daisy stooped quickly and began gathering up the photos. Focusing on that gave her a few moments of time and a little bit of space to get her bearings. Ha. *What was he doing here?*

She hadn't seen Alex in years and she had never expected to ever see him again. Only the fact that he seemed as surprised as she was allowed her to breathe at all.

She stopped doing that, though, when he crouched down beside her and began to help pick up the photos.

"Don't do that. Leave them," she said, trying to snatch them away from him. "I can do it!"

But Alex didn't let go. He simply kept right on. He only said, "No."

And there it was—the same single word, delivered in the same implacable tone that he'd said five years ago—that one that had pulled the rug right out from under her hopes and dreams.

Worse, though, was that his rough-edged, slightly accented, unconsciously sexy baritone still resonated all the way to the core of her exactly as it had from the moment she'd first heard him speak. It was as if he had been her very own personal pied piper of Hamelin. And foolishly, mindlessly, Daisy had fallen under his spell.

Then she'd called it "love at first sight." *Then* she had believed in the foolishness of such fairy tales.

Now she knew better. Now she knew the danger of it, thank

God. There would be no falling under his spell again. She
gathered the last of the photos, no longer in any shape to be
presented to Philip Cannavarro, and got to her feet.

"What are you doing here?" she demanded, stepping away
as he rose to his feet, too.

He shook his head, looking as dazed as she felt. "You're
Daisy?" He glanced at a piece of paper he held in his hand,
then frowned. "Well, of course you are, but…Connolly?"

Daisy lifted her chin. "That's right. Why?"

But before she got an answer, another man appeared outside on the stoop, just beyond the heavy front door and looked
past Alex questioningly.

Daisy's knees went weak with relief. "Phil! Come on in!"
He might as well have been the cavalry come to her rescue.
She beamed at him.

Alex turned and stared over his shoulder, his brows drawing down. "Who's he?" he demanded as if he had more right
there than her client.

Fortunately Phil was already pulling the door open, glancing in quick succession at Daisy's relieved face and Alex's
scowl and finally at the photos in Daisy's hands. "Sorry. Didn't
mean to interrupt—"

"You weren't," Daisy said quickly. "But I heard the bell. I
thought it was you, not—" she gestured helplessly toward Alex
who was standing so she could almost feel the heat of his body
"—and I accidentally dropped your photos. I am so sorry."
She gave Phil a hopeful smile. "I need to have them redone."

"Don't worry about it. They're probably just a little frayed
at the edges," Phil said cheerfully. "No problem." He held out
his hand and doubtless would have taken them from her, but
Daisy shook her head and clutched them against her chest
like a shield.

"No," she said. "I guarantee my work. And I don't give less
than my best. You and Lottie deserve my best." He and Lottie
had been one of the first matches she'd made. Lottie had been
a makeup artist she'd met when she first began working as a

photographer after college. Phil used to do her taxes. She felt almost like their mother even though they were older than she was. And she wasn't giving them less than her best.

"I'll put a rush on it," she promised. "You should have them in two days. I'll have them couriered directly to your house."

Phil looked doubtful. "We won't mind," he said. "Lottie will want…"

"Take these then." Daisy thrust them at him. "But tell her they're just until the new ones come in. Tell her I'm so sorry. Tell her—" She shut her mouth, the only way to stop babbling.

Phil fumbled with the photos, too, then stuffed them in his briefcase, shooting Daisy worried sidelong glances. "Are you sure you're okay?"

"I'm fine," she lied.

But she knew why he was asking. Phil and Lottie were used to the unflappable Daisy, the one who rolled with the punches, adjusted on the fly, never worried if life threw pitchforks in her path.

"Daisy always copes," Lottie said. It was like a mantra.

Daisy wasn't exactly coping now. Alex's mere presence created an electricity in the air, a force field of awareness she could never manage to be indifferent to. Damn it.

"She'll be fine," Alex said smoothly now. "She's just had a bit of a shock." He stepped even closer and looped an arm over her shoulders.

Daisy nearly jumped out of her skin. At the same time, though, her traitorous body clamored to sink into his embrace. Muscle memory was a dangerous thing. Daisy held herself rigid, resisting him, resisting her own inclination.

"She'll be all right. I'll take care of her." Alex's tone was all reassurance as he smiled and somehow put himself between her and Phil, edging the other man toward the door, making it clear that Phil didn't need to hang around.

Phil didn't hang around. He understood male territoriality as well as the next guy. "Right," he said, all smiles and cheerful bravado. "I'll tell Lottie."

And he was out the door and down the steps without glancing back.

"Thank you very much," Daisy said drily, slipping out from beneath his arm, which still managed to leave her with a sense that it was still there. She could feel the warm weight of it even though she'd stepped away. Instinctively she wrapped her own arms across her chest.

What was he doing here? The question pounded again in her brain.

"Daisy." The way he said her name was somewhere between musing and caressing. It sent the hairs on the back of her neck straight up. A slight smile played at the corners of his mouth. "It is fate," he murmured.

"What?" Daisy said sharply.

"I was just thinking about you." His tone was warm. He acted as if they were old friends. Well, maybe to him that was all they were.

"I can't imagine why," Daisy said, which was the absolute truth.

"I'm looking for a wife."

She stared at him, her jaw dropping.

He just smiled, expecting no doubt to hear her say, *Oh, yes, please! Pick me.*

Daisy hugged her arms more tightly across her chest. "Good luck with that." She could have said, *You don't want a wife. You made a huge point of telling me you didn't want a wife!*

Now Alex raised his brows. The smile still lurking. "I wasn't proposing," he said mildly.

Mortified, Daisy said stiffly, "Of course you weren't."

She wasn't going to bring up the past at all. It did her no credit. She'd been young and stupid and far too romantic for her own good when they'd met five years ago at a wedding reception.

Daisy had been one of her college roommate, Heather's, bridesmaids, and Alex had been pressed into service as a last-minute substitute for a sick groomsman. Their eyes had met—something wild and hot and amazing had sparked between them—and to Daisy's fevered romantic twenty-three-year-old brain, it had been one of those meant-to-be moments.

They had only had eyes for each other from the moment they'd met. They talked, they danced, they laughed, they touched. The electricity between them could have lit New York City day and night for a week.

So this was love at first sight. She remembered thinking that, stunned and delighted to finally experience it. She had, of course, always believed. Her parents had always told Daisy and her sister that they'd known from the moment they'd met that they were destined to be together.

Julie, Daisy's sister, had felt that way about Brent, the moment she'd met him in eighth grade. They'd married right out of high school. Twelve years later, they were still deeply in love.

Daisy had never felt that way—wasn't sure she believed it—until the day Alex had walked into her life.

That afternoon had been so extraordinary, so mind-numbingly, body-tinglingly perfect that she'd believed. It was just the way her parents had described it, the way Julie had described it—the sense of knowing, of a belief that all the planets were finally lined up, that the absolutely right man had come into her life.

Of course she hadn't said so. Not then. She'd just met Alex. But she hadn't wanted the day to end—and he hadn't, either. She was the bridesmaid who had been deputized to take Heather's car back to Manhattan after the reception.

"I'm coming, too," Alex had said in that rough sexy baritone, and his eyes had met hers. "If that's all right with you."

Of course it had been all right with her. It was just one more reason to believe he was feeling the same thing, too. Together they had driven back to Manhattan. And all the way there, they had talked.

He was an architect working for a multinational firm, but

eager to strike out on his own. He had his own ideas, a desire to blend old and new, to create both beauty and utility and to design buildings that made people more alive, that spoke to their hearts and souls. His eyes had lit up when he'd talked about his goals, and she had shared his enthusiasm.

He had shared hers about her own professional hopes and dreams. She was working for Finn MacCauley, one of the pre-eminent fashion and lifestyle photographers in the country. It was almost like an apprenticeship, she'd told him. She was learning so much from Finn, but was looking forward, like Alex was, to finding her own niche.

"People definitely," she'd told him. "Families, kids, people at work and play. I'd like to shoot you," she'd told him. She wanted to capture the moment, the man.

And Alex had simply said, "Whenever you want."

When they got to the city, she had left the car in the parking garage by Heather's Upper East Side apartment, then she'd taken Alex downtown on the subway to the Soho flat she was subleasing from a dental student on a semester's internship abroad.

On the subway, Alex had caught her hand in his, rubbing his thumb over her fingers, then dipping his head to touch his lips to hers. It was a light touch, the merest promise, but it set her blood on fire. And when he pulled back, she caught her breath because, looking into his eyes, she had seen a hunger there that was as deep and intense as her own.

It had never happened before. A desire so powerful, so intense just grabbed her—and it wouldn't let go. Daisy wasn't used to this sort of intensity. She didn't fall into bed at the drop of a hat, had only once before fallen into bed with a man at all. It had been fevered groping on his part and discomfort on hers.

With Alex, she'd tried telling herself, it would be more of the same.

But it wasn't.

His kisses were nothing like any she'd tasted before. They were heady, electric, bone-melting. They'd stood on the sidewalk nearly devouring each other. Not something Daisy had ever done!

She couldn't get him back to her apartment fast enough.

Once there, though, she'd felt suddenly awkward, almost shy. "Let me take your picture," she'd said.

And Alex had given her a lazy teasing smile and said, "If that's what you want."

Of course it wasn't what she wanted—or not entirely what she wanted. And it wasn't what he wanted, either. It was foreplay. Serious and smiling, goofing around, letting her direct him this way and that, all the way watching her—burning her up!—from beneath hooded lids.

He wanted her. He didn't have to say it. They circled each other, moved in, moved away. The temperature in the room rose. The temperature in Daisy's blood was close to boiling.

Then Alex had reached out and took the camera from her. He aimed, shot, posed her, caught the ferocity of her desire, as well. He stripped off his jacket, she unbuttoned his shirt. He skimmed down the zip of her dress. But before he could peel it off, she had taken the camera back, set the timer and wrapped her arms around him.

The photo of the two of them together, caught up in each other, had haunted her for years.

But at the time she hadn't been thinking about anything but the moment—the man. Within moments the camera was forgotten and in seconds more the rest of their clothing was gone.

And then there was nothing between them at all.

Alex bore her back onto her bed, settled beside her and bent his dark head, nuzzling her breasts, tasting, teasing, suckling, making her gasp and squirm.

And Daisy, shyness long gone, had been desperate to learn every inch of him. She'd prowled and played, made him suck in his breath and say raggedly, "You're killing me!"

But when she'd pulled back he'd drawn her close again. "Don't stop," he'd said.

They hadn't stopped—neither one of them. They'd driven

each other to the height of ecstasy. And it wasn't at all like that other time.

With Alex there was no discomfort, there was no second-guessing, no wondering if she was doing the right thing. It had been lovemaking at its most pure and elemental, and so perfect she could have cried.

After, lying wrapped in his arms, knowing the rightness of it, she had believed completely in her mother's assertion that there was a "right man"—and about knowing instinctively when you met him.

She'd met Alex and—just like her parents, just like her sister and Brent—she had fallen in love.

They'd talked into the wee hours of the morning, sharing stories of their childhood, of their memories, of the best and worst things that had ever happened to them.

She told him about the first camera she'd ever had—that her grandfather had given her when she was seven. He told her about the first time he'd climbed a mountain and thought he could do anything. She told him about her beloved father who had died earlier that winter and about the loss she felt. He understood. He told her about losing his only brother to leukemia when he was ten and his brother thirteen. They had talked and they had touched. They had stroked and smiled and kissed.

And they had made love again. And again.

It was always going to be like that, Daisy vowed. She had met the man of her dreams, the one who understood her down to the ground, the man she would love and marry and have children with and grow old with—

—until she'd said so.

She remembered that Sunday morning as if it had been yesterday.

They'd finally fallen asleep in each other's arms at dawn. When Daisy had awakened again it was nearly ten. Alex was still asleep, sprawled on his back in her bed, bare-chested, the duvet covering him below the waist. He was so beautiful. She could have just sat there and stared at him forever, tracing the strong lines of his features, the hollows made by his collarbone, the curve of muscle in his arms, the long, tapered fingers that had made her quiver with their touch. She remembered how he'd looked, naked and primal, rising above her when they'd made love.

She would have liked to do it again. She had wanted to slide back beneath the duvet and snuggle up against him, to rub the sole of her foot up and down his calf, then let her fingers walk up and down his thigh, and press kisses to the line of dark hair that bisected his abdomen.

But as much as she wanted to do that, she also wanted to feed him before he had to catch his plane. She knew he had an early evening flight to Paris where he would be spending the next month at the main office of the firm he worked for. She'd hated the thought of him leaving, but she consoled herself by hoping that when he started his own company he would bring it stateside. Or maybe she would follow him to Paris.

Daisy had tried to imagine what living in Paris—living in Paris with Alex—would be like while she made them eggs and bacon and toast for breakfast. The thoughts made her smile. They made her toes curl.

She'd been standing at the stove, toes curling as she turned the bacon when hard muscled arms had come around her and warm breath had touched her ear.

"Morning," Alex murmured, the burr of his voice sending a shiver of longing right through her.

"Morning yourself." She'd smiled as he had kissed her ear, her nape, her jaw, then turned her in his arms and took her mouth with a hunger that said, *The hell with breakfast. Let's go back to bed.*

But she'd fed him a piece of bacon, laughing as he'd nibbled her fingers. And she'd actually got him to eat eggs and toast as well before they'd rolled in the sheets once more.

Finally in the early afternoon he'd groaned as he sat up and swung his legs out of bed. "Got to grab a shower. Come with me?" He'd cocked his head, grinning an invitation that, despite feeling boneless already, Daisy hadn't been able to refuse.

The next half hour had been the most erotic experience of her life. Both of them had been wrung out, beyond bone-less—and squeaky clean—by the time the hot water heater had begun to run cold.

"I need to go," he'd said, kissing her thoroughly once more as he pulled on a pair of cords and buttoned up his shirt.

"Yes," she agreed, kissing him back, but then turning away long enough to stuff her legs into a pair of jeans and pluck a sweater from the drawer. "I'll go out to the airport with you."

Alex had protested that it wasn't necessary, that he was per-fectly capable of going off by himself, he did it all the time.

But Daisy was having none of it. She'd smiled saucily and said, "Yes, but now you have me."

She'd gone with him to the airport, had sat next to him in the back of the hired car and had shared long drugging kisses that she expected to live off until he returned.

"I'll miss you," she'd told him, nibbling his jaw. "I can't believe this has happened. That we found each other. I never really believed, but now I do."

"Believed?" Alex lifted his head from where he'd been kiss-ing her neck long enough to gaze into her eyes. "In what?"

"This." She punctuated the word with a kiss, then looked deeply into his eyes. "You. Me. It's just like my mother said. Love at first sight." She smiled, then sighed. "I just hope we get more years than they did."

There was a sudden stillness in him. And then a slight movement as he pulled back. A small line appeared between his brows. "Years? They?"

"My parents. They fell in love like this. Took one look at each other and fell like a ton of bricks. There was never any-one else for either of them. They were two halves of the same soul. They should have had fifty years. Seventy-five," Daisy said recklessly. "Instead of twenty-six."

Alex didn't move. He barely seemed to breathe. The sparkle in his light green eyes seemed suddenly to fade.

Daisy looked at him, concerned. "What's wrong?"

He'd swallowed. She could remember the way she'd watched his Adam's apple move in his throat, then the way he'd shaken his head slowly and said, "You're talking a lifetime, aren't you?"

And ever honest, Daisy had nodded. "Yes."

There had been a split second before the world tilted. Then Alex had sucked in a harsh breath. "No." Just the one word. Hard, decisive, determined. Then, apparently seeing the look on her face, he'd been at pains to assure her. "Oh, not for you. I'm not saying you won't have a lifetime…with someone. But…not me."

She remembered staring at him, stunned at the change in him. He seemed to have pulled inside himself. Closed off. Turned into the Ice Man as she'd watched. "What?" Even to her own ears her voice had sounded faint, disbelieving.

Alex's jaw set. "I'm not getting married," he'd told her. "Ever."

"But—"

"I don't want to."

"But—"

"No." His tone was implacable. Yet despite the coldness of his tone, there was fire in his eyes. "No hostages to fortune," he'd said. "No wife. No kids. No falling in love. Too much pain. Never again."

"Because…because of your brother?" She had only barely understood that kind of pain. Her parents had been gloriously happily married until her father's death a month before. And she had witnessed what her mother was going through after. There was no doubt it was hard. It was hard on her and on her sister, too. But her parents had had a beautiful marriage. It had been worth the cost.

She'd tried to explain that to Alex in the car. He hadn't wanted to hear it.

"It's fine for you if that's what you want," he'd said firmly. "I don't."

"But last night…this morning…?" Daisy had been grasping desperately at straws.

"You were great," he'd said. Their gazes had met for a moment. Then deliberately Alex looked away.

By the time they'd arrived at the airport, there were no more kisses, only a silence as big and dark as the Atlantic that would soon stretch between them. Alex didn't look at her again. His fingers were fisted against his thighs as he stared resolutely out the window.

Daisy had stared at him, willed him to reconsider, to believe—to give them a chance!

"Maybe I was asking for too much too soon," she ventured at last as their hired car reached the airport departure lanes. "Maybe when you come back…"

Alex was shaking his head even as he turned and looked at her. "No," he said, his voice rough but adamant.

She blinked quickly, hoping he didn't notice the film of unshed tears in her eyes as she stared at him mutely.

"I won't be back, Daisy. A lifetime is what you want," he'd said. "I don't."

It was the last thing he'd said to her—the last time she'd seen him—until she'd opened the door a few minutes ago.

Now she dared to stare at him for just a moment as she tried to calm her galloping heart and mend her frayed nerves, tried to stuff Alexandros Antonides back into the box in the distant reaches of her mind where she'd done her best to keep him for the past five years.

It wasn't any easier to feel indifferent now than it ever had been. He was certainly every bit as gorgeous as he had been then. A shade over six feet tall, broad-shouldered in a pale blue dress shirt and a gray herringbone wool sport coat, his tie loosened at his throat, Alex looked like the consummate successful professional. His dark hair was cut a little shorter now, but it was still capable of being wind-tossed. His eyes were still that clear, light gray-green, arresting in his tanned face with its sharply defined cheekbones and blade-straight nose. And his sensuous mouth was, heaven help her, more appealing than ever with its hint of a smile.

"Why are you here?" she demanded now.

"Lukas sent me," he said.

"Lukas?"

Alex's cousin Lukas had been her official "other half" at the wedding where she'd met Alex. He'd insisted she stay by his side at the reception long enough so that his mother and aunts wouldn't fling hopeful Greek girls at his head. Once he'd established that he wasn't available, he'd given her a conspiratorial wink, a peck on the cheek and had ambled off to drink beer with his brothers and cousins, leaving her to fend for herself.

That was when she'd met Alex.

Now Alex pulled a piece of paper out of his pocket and poked it in front of her face. "He said I should talk to his friend Daisy the matchmaker."

Yes, there it was—her name, address and phone number—in Lukas's spiky handwriting. But she was more arrested by his words than what he was waving in front of her face. "You're looking for a matchmaker? *You?*"

Alex shrugged. "No doubt you're amazed," he said easily. "Thinking I've changed my mind."

She didn't know what to think.

"I haven't," he said firmly. "I'm not looking for hearts and flowers, kindred spirits, the melding of two souls any more than I ever was."

She wondered if he was being so adamant in case she decided to propose. No fear of that, she wanted to tell him. Instead she pressed her lips into a tight line.

"I want a marriage of convenience," Alex went on. "A woman with her own life, doing her own thing. She'll go her way, I'll go mine. But someone who will turn up if a business engagement calls for it. And who's there…at night."

"A sex buddy?" Daisy said drily.

Was that a line of color creeping above his shirt collar? "Friends," he said firmly. "We'll be friends. It's not just about sex."

"Hire a mistress."

"I don't want a mistress. That *is* just about sex."

"Whatever. I can't help you," she said flatly.

"Why not? You're a matchmaker."

"Yes, but I'm a matchmaker who does believe in hearts and flowers, kindred spirits, the melding of two souls." She echoed his words with a saccharine smile. "I believe in real marriages. Love matches. Soul mates. The kind you don't believe in." She met his gaze steadily, refusing to look away from those beautiful pale green eyes that she'd once hoped to drown in forever.

Alex's jaw tightened. "I believe in them," he said harshly. "I just don't want one."

"Right. So I repeat, I can't help you." She said the words again, meant them unequivocally. But even as she spoke in a calm steady tone, her heart was hammering so hard she could hear it.

Their gazes met. Locked. And with everything in her, Daisy resisted the magnetic pull that was still there. But even as she fought it, she felt the rise of desire within her, knew the feelings once more that she'd turned her back on the day he'd walked out of her life. It wasn't love, she told herself. It was something else—something as powerful and perverse and demanding as anything she'd ever felt.

But she was stronger now, and no longer an innocent. She had a life—and a love in it—that was worth resisting Alex Antonides.

"I hope you find what you're looking for," she said, holding his gaze. "It was nice to see you again."

It was, she hoped, a clear dismissal. It was also a blatant lie. She could have gone the rest of her life without seeing Alex again and died a happy woman. She didn't need a reminder of the stupidest thirty hours of her life. But in another way, she was aware of owing him her unending gratitude.

That single day had forever changed her life.

"Was it?" he asked. His words were as speculative as his gaze. He smiled. And resist as she would, she saw in that smile the man who once upon a time had melted her bones, her resolve, every shred of her common sense, then broken her heart.

She turned away. "Goodbye, Alex."

"Daisy." His voice stopped her.

She glanced back. "What?"

The smile grew rueful, crooked, far too appealing. "Have dinner with me."

CHAPTER TWO

"WHAT? *No!*" She looked panic-stricken. Horrified.

Not at all like the Daisy he remembered. And yet she was so much the Daisy he remembered that Alex couldn't just turn and walk away. Not now. Not when he'd finally found her again. "Why not?"

"Because…because I don't want to!" Her cheeks had grown red in the throes of passion. Her whole body had blushed when he'd made love to her. His body—right now—was already contemplating doing the same thing again.

Which was a profoundly stupid idea, considering what he wanted, what she wanted, considering the present—and their past.

"Do you hate me?" he asked. He remembered the way they had parted. She'd looked devastated, about to cry. Thank God she hadn't. But what she'd wanted—the hope of a lifetime of love—was his worst nightmare. It brought back memories that he'd turned his back on years ago. What had begun happening between them that weekend was something he wasn't ready for. Would never be ready for.

So there was no point in making her hope in vain. He regretted having hurt her when he'd left her. But he could never bring himself to regret that weekend. It was one of the best memories of his life.

"Of course I don't hate you," she said briskly now. "I don't care at all about you."

Her words were a slap in the face. But he supposed he had it coming. And it was just as well, wasn't it, that she didn't care? It meant he hadn't hurt her badly after all.

"Well, then," he suggested easily, "let's share a meal." He gave her his best engaging grin. "For old times' sake," he added when he could see the word *no* forming on her lips.

"We don't have old times."

"We have one old time," he reminded her softly.

Her cheeks grew brighter yet. "That was a long, long time ago. Years. Five or six at least."

"Five," he said. "And a half." He remembered clearly. It was right after that weekend that he'd made up his mind to stay in Europe, to buy a place in Paris.

It made sense businesswise, he'd told himself at the time. But it wasn't only business that had made him dig in across the pond. It was smarter to put an ocean between himself and the temptation that was Daisy.

She was still tempting. But a dinner he could handle. "It's just a meal, Daisy. I promise I won't sweep you off to bed." Not that he wouldn't like to.

"You couldn't," she said flatly.

He thought he could, but emotions would get involved. So he wouldn't go there, as tempting as it was. Still, he wasn't willing to walk away, either. "We have a lot to catch up on," he cajoled.

But Daisy shook her head. "I don't think so." Her smile was brittle. He saw none of the sunny sincerity he'd always associated with his memories of her. Interesting.

He studied her now, wondering what her life had been like over the past five years. He'd always imagined she'd found the true love she'd been seeking, had found a man who'd made her happy. And if the thought occasionally had made him grind his teeth, he told himself a guy couldn't have everything. He had what he wanted.

Now he wondered if Daisy had got what she wanted. Suddenly he wanted to know.

"Another time then," he suggested.

"Thank you, but no."

He knew he was going to get "no" if he asked a hundred times. And the knowledge annoyed him. "Once upon a time we had a lot to say to each other," he reminded her.

"Once upon a time is for fairy tales, Alex. Now, if you'll excuse me, I have to go."

"Let's," he said readily. "I'll walk with you."

"I don't mean go somewhere else," she said. "I mean I have to go back inside. I have work to do. In my office."

"Matchmaking?"

She shook her head. "Not tonight."

"Photography?" He remembered the camera, how it had been almost a natural extension of who she was.

She nodded, smiling a little. It was a real smile.

"You've got your own business then?" he pressed.

"Yes." She nodded. The smile stayed.

"Families? Kids? People of all shapes and sizes?" And at her further nod, he said, "Show me."

She almost moved toward the door, almost started to invite him in. But then she stayed where she was, gave her head a little shake. "I don't think so."

"You took photos of us." Sometimes he'd wished he had one. To take out and remember. But that was stupid. It was better to forget.

She shrugged and looked just a little uncomfortable. He wondered if she still had the photos.

"Why matchmaking?" he asked her suddenly.

She shrugged. "Long story." And no invitation to ask her to tell it.

He lifted a corner of his mouth. "I've got time."

"I don't."

"You're scared."

The color in her cheeks bloomed again. "I am not scared! What's there to be scared of?"

"I don't know. You tell me." He cocked his head. "Temptation maybe?"

She shook her head adamantly. "I'm not tempted. I'm busy. I have things to do. I haven't seen you in five years, Alex. I barely knew you then. We don't have a past to catch up on."

"We had a hell of a lot." He didn't know why he was persisting, but he couldn't seem to leave it alone.

"And we wanted to do different things with it. Goodbye, Alex." She turned away and started to go back inside.

But before she could, Alex caught her arm, and spun her slowly back, then did what he'd been wanting to do ever since he'd realized who she was.

He dipped his head and kissed her.

It was instinct, desire, a mad impetuous hunger that he couldn't seem to control. It was a roaring in his ears and a fire in his veins. It was the taste of Daisy—a taste he'd never forgotten. *Never.* And as soon as he tasted her, he wanted more.

And more.

For a second, maybe two, Daisy seemed to melt under the touch of his lips. She went soft and pliable, shaping her mouth to his. And then, in another instant, it was over.

She jerked away from him, stared at him for one horrified moment, cheeks scarlet, mouth still forming an astonished O. Then she pulled out of his grasp and bolted back inside the foyer.

"Daisy!"

The door slammed in his face.

Alex stared after her, still tasting her. Jolted, intrigued, stunned. Aroused.

Five years ago Daisy had been like a siren he'd followed eagerly, mindlessly, hungrily. He'd wanted her on every level imaginable. And having her that weekend over and over hadn't assuaged his hunger. He'd only wanted more.

Leaving, thank God, had removed the temptation.

And now—within minutes of having seen her again—it was back. In spades.

It was the last thing he wanted. The last thing he needed.

Alex turned and walked down the steps, pausing only to drop the paper with her name and address in the trash.

She had been right to say no. He would be smart and walk away.

Ten minutes later Daisy was still shaking.

She sat at her desk, staring at the photo she was editing, and didn't see it at all. Eyes closed or open, she only saw Alex—older, harder, stronger, handsomer—in every way *more*, even more compelling than the younger Alex had been.

She shuddered and scrubbed at her mouth with her fingers, trying to wipe away the taste of his kiss.

But all the scrubbing in the world wouldn't do that, and she knew it. She'd tried to forget it for years. It hadn't done a whit of good.

She hadn't even tried to forget him. That would have been impossible. But as time passed, at least she'd managed to put him on a shelf in the back of her memory's closet. He was still there, but he couldn't hurt her.

But now Alex was here.

She'd just seen him, talked to him. Been kissed by him. Had almost, heaven help her, kissed him back. It had felt so right, so perfect, so exactly the way it had felt the first time.

But she knew better now.

He had come. He had gone. The other shoe had finally dropped. He wouldn't come back.

"And it wouldn't matter if he did," Daisy said aloud.

Because if one thing was completely obvious, it was that however much more he had become, in fundamentals, Alex hadn't changed a bit.

He might want to get married now, but he obviously didn't want anything more than "friends—with benefits." He didn't want love. He didn't want a real marriage. He didn't want a family.

He didn't want her.

For a nanosecond her traitorous heart had dared to believe he'd finally come to his senses, had learned the value of love, of relationships, of lifetime commitment.

Thank goodness, a nanosecond was all the time it had taken her to realize that there was no point in getting her hopes up.

Of course he had proved he still wanted her on one level—the one he had always wanted her on. She wasn't such an innocent that she didn't know desire when she felt it. And she had felt it hard and firm against her when Alex had kissed her and pressed his body against hers.

But physical desire was just that—a basic instinctive response. It had nothing to do with things that really mattered—love, commitment, responsibility, sharing of hearts and souls, dreams and desires.

It was nothing more than an itch to be scratched.

And she wasn't about to be a matchmaker for a pairing like that. If he was interested in nothing more than a woman to share his bed—but not his heart—he wouldn't be interested in the sort of marriages she believed in. So he wouldn't be back.

And thank God for that—because if her heart still beat faster at the very sight of him and her body melted under his touch, at least her mind knew he was the last person she needed in her life.

Not just in her life, but in the life of the person she loved most in all the world—the one who, at this very moment, she could hear pounding his way up the stairs from the kitchen.

"Mom!" His voice was distant at first, then louder. "Mom!" And louder still as the door banged open. "Mom! Aren'tcha finished working yet? It's time to go."

Charlie.

Four and three-quarter years of sunshine and skinned knees and wet kisses and impatience all rolled up in the most wonderful person she knew.

He skidded to a stop in front of her and looked up at her, importuning. "Mom!"

"Charlie!" She smiled at him, echoing his tone, loving him with all her heart.

"Are you ready?" he demanded.

"Almost." She turned back to close the file she hadn't done a thing to since Alex had shown up on the doorstep. "Almost," she repeated, taking a deep breath to steady her nerves, then shutting the file.

She wished she could shut her memories of Alex down as easily. She couldn't. Particularly she couldn't right now—faced with the small boy staring up at her, all quivering impatience.

Impatience wasn't Charlie's middle name, but maybe it should have been. He'd been eager and energetic since the moment of his birth. Before his birth, in fact. He'd come almost two weeks early, right before Christmas. And he'd been taking the world by storm ever since.

He had a chipped tooth from a fall out of a tree back in May. He had a scab on his knee beneath his jeans even now. Daisy had told him last week she was going to buy stock in the Band-Aid company, and after he'd wrinkled his nose and said, "What's stock?" he'd listened to her brief explanation and said, "Good idea."

His stick-straight hair, the color of honey shot through with gold, was very close to the same shade as her own. But his light eyes were nothing like her stormy dark blue.

He didn't look like Alex—except for the shape of his eyes.

And after nearly five years, she was inured to it. She didn't see Alex in him every time she looked at him. She saw Charlie himself—not Alex's son.

Except today. Today the eyes were Alex's. The impatience was Alex's. The "let's get moving" was Alex down to the ground.

"In good time," she said now, determined to slow Charlie down—a little, at least. But she managed a smile as she shut the computer down. And she was sure she was the only one who noticed her hands were shaking.

"You said we'd go at six-thirty. It's almost six-thirty. The game's gonna start." He grabbed one of Daisy's hands and began to tug her back toward the stairs.

"Coming," Daisy said. But she straightened her desk, made a note to reorder the Cannavarro files, put her pencil in the drawer. All very methodical. Orderly. Step by step. Pay attention to detail. From the day that she'd learned she was pregnant, it was how she'd managed to cope.

Charlie bounced from one foot to the other until she finished and finally held out a hand to him again. "Okay. Let's go." She allowed herself to be towed down the stairs.

"We gotta hurry. We're gonna be late. Come on. Dad's pitching."

Dad. One more reason she prayed that Alexandros Antonides didn't darken her door again.

"Hey, Sport." Cal dropped down beside Charlie on the other side of the blanket that Daisy had spread out to sit on while they watched the softball game.

They had been late, as Charlie feared, arriving between innings. But at least Cal, Daisy's ex-husband, had already pitched in his half, so he could come sit with them until it was his turn to bat.

"We made a fire engine," Charlie told him. "Me 'n' Jess. Outta big red cardboard blocks—this big!" He stretched his hands out a couple of feet at least.

Cal looked suitably impressed. "At preschool?"

Charlie bobbed his head. "You an' me could make one."

"Okay. On Saturday," Cal agreed. "But we'll have to use a cardboard box and paint it red. Grandpa will be in town. I'll tell him to bring paint."

Charlie's eyes got big. "Super! Wait'll I tell Jess 'bout ours."

"You don't want to make him jealous," Cal warned. He grinned at Charlie, then over the boy's head at his mother.

Daisy smiled back and told herself that nothing had changed. Nothing. She and Charlie were doing what they often did—dropping by to watch Cal play ball in Central Park, which he and a few diehards continued to do well after the softball leagues ended in the summer. Now, in early October, there was a nip in the air, and the daylight was already going. But they continued to play.

And she and Charlie would continue to come and watch.

It was the joy of a civilized divorce, Daisy often reminded herself. She and Cal didn't hate each other—and they both loved Charlie.

"—you?"

She realized suddenly that Cal was no longer talking to Charlie. He was talking to her. "Sorry," she said, flustered. "I was just…thinking about something."

"Apparently," Cal said drily. Then he looked at her more closely. "What's wrong?"

"Nothing." She looked around. "Where's Charlie?"

Cal nodded in the direction of the trees where Charlie and the son of another one of the players were playing in the dirt. "He's fine. You're not. Something's wrong."

"No. Why should anything be wrong?" That was the trouble with Cal. He'd always been able to read her like a book.

"You're edgy. Distracted. Late," he said pointedly.

"I didn't realize you were timing me. I've got things on my mind, Cal. Work—"

But he cut her off. "And you're biting my head off, which isn't like you, Daze. And you must've come on the bus."

"The bus?" she said stupidly.

"You always walk, so Charlie can ride his bike." Cal looked around pointedly. There was no bike because, he was right, they hadn't had time to bring it. Charlie wanted to ride his bike everywhere. It was the smallest two-wheeler Daisy had ever seen, but Charlie loved it. Daisy was sure he would have slept with it every night if she hadn't put her foot down. Cal had given it to Charlie for his fourth birthday.

Daisy had protested, had said he was too young, that no four-year-old needed a bike.

"Not every four-year-old," Cal had agreed. "Just this one." He'd met her skeptical gaze with confident brown eyes and quiet certainty. "Because he wants it more than anything on earth."

Daisy couldn't argue with that. If Charlie's first word hadn't been *bike* it had been in the first ten. He'd pointed and crowed, "Bike!" well before his first birthday. And he'd been desperate for a bicycle last winter. She hadn't thought it would last. But Cal had insisted, and he'd been right.

Charlie's eyes had shone when he'd spotted the bike that morning. And over the past six months, his love for it had only grown. Since Cal had helped him learn to balance and he could now ride it unaided, Charlie wanted to ride it everywhere.

Usually she let him ride to the park while she walked alongside him. But they had been late today because…because of her visitor.

She was suddenly aware that Cal was watching her, not the game. "He doesn't have to ride his bike every time," she said testily. "And it's nearly dark."

"True." Cal stretched his legs out in front of him and leaned back, resting his weight on his elbows and forearms as his gaze slowly moved away from her to focus on the game, yelling at the batter to focus. Then, still keeping his gaze on the batter, he persisted quietly, "So why don't you just tell me."

He wasn't going to leave it alone. She'd never won an argument with Cal. She'd never been able to convince him of anything. If he was wrong, he couldn't be told. He always had to figure it out himself—like his "I can love anyone I will myself to" edict. He'd been as wrong about that as she had been about her "love at first sight" belief.

Clearly, when it came to love, the two of them didn't know what they were talking about.

Now he stared at her and she plucked at the grass beside the blanket, stared at it. *Nothing's changed. Nothing's changed.* She tried to make it into a mantra so she could convince herself. But she was no better at lying to herself than she was at lying to her ex-husband. Finally she raised her gaze to meet his as he turned away from the game to look at her. "I saw Alex."

There was the crack of bat hitting ball. Whoops and yells abounded.

Cal never turned his head to see what happened. His eyes never left Daisy's. He blinked once. That was all. The rest of his body went still, though. And his words, when they came, were quiet. "Saw him where?"

Daisy ran her tongue over dry lips. "He came to my office."

Cal waited, not pressing, allowing her to tell the story in her own way, in her own time.

And she couldn't quite suppress the ghost of a smile that touched her lips. "Looking for a matchmaker."

"What!" Cal's jaw dropped.

Hysterical laughter bubbled up just as it had threatened to do when Alex told her. This time Daisy gave in to it. "He's looking for a wife."

"You?" Cal demanded.

"No. He was as surprised as I was when he knocked on my door. He didn't know he was coming to see me."

"Then how—?"

"Lukas sent him."

Cal's eyes widened. His teeth came together. "Lukas needs to mind his own business."

"Of course. But Lukas never does. Besides, he didn't have any idea what he was doing. He never knew about Alex and me. No one did." No one ever had except Cal—and only because when she'd discovered she was pregnant, she'd had to talk to someone. "Don't blame Lukas. He thinks he's doing me a favor sending clients my way. And he is, I suppose. Most of the time. Not this time," she said quietly.

"No." Cal stared down at his fingers plucking at the grass for a moment. Then his gaze lifted and went toward Charlie who was still playing with his friend in the dirt. The question was there, but unspoken.

"I didn't say a word."

"But he—"

Daisy shook her head. "No. That hasn't changed. He wouldn't want to know."

"Still?" Cal persisted.

"No. He doesn't want relationships any more than he ever did," Daisy said firmly. "He doesn't want a real wife—he wants a woman to take to social events and go to bed with. It will save him the effort of having to go out and find one, charm one."

"He charmed you," Cal pointed out.

Cal, of course, knew that. He knew the whole sordid story.

She had met Cal Connolly when she'd taken the job with Finn after college. Cal had been the photographer she'd replaced, Finn's assistant before her.

Even after Cal hung out his own shingle, he had regularly come by Finn's to talk shop. Daisy had been included in the conversation. She learned a great deal from both of them.

Finn was brilliant, mercurial—and impatient. Cal was steadier, calmer, more methodical. He didn't yell quite as much. Finn had a wife and growing family. Cal was single, on his own. So it was Cal she began to spend time with. And while Finn had always remained her mentor, Cal had quickly become her best pal.

When she wasn't working for Finn, she had spent hours working with Cal, talking with him, arguing with him. They argued about everything from camera lenses to baseball teams to sushi rolls, from free will to evolution to love at first sight.

That had always been their biggest argument: did you love because—bang!—it hit you between the eyes? Or did you love because you decided who the right person was and made up your mind?

Because of her parents, Daisy had been a staunch believer in the "love at first sight" notion.

"I just haven't met the right person," she had maintained over and over. "When I do, I'll know. In an instant. And it will be perfect."

But Cal had scoffed at that. Ever the logical realist, he'd said, "Nonsense. I don't believe it for a minute. That makes you nothing but a victim of your hormones."

"It's not hormones. It's instinct."

But Cal had disagreed. "You can will whom you love," he'd told her firmly. "It's a rational decision."

So when he'd proposed to her, he'd been determined to demonstrate just that. "Obviously your way doesn't work," he'd pointed out. "So we'll try it my way now."

And Daisy, because she did love Cal—just not the way she thought she loved Alex—had faced the truth of her own folly. And she'd said yes.

It turned out they were both wrong. But they'd given it their best shot. And Daisy still did believe in love—now she had a codicil: it was apparently for other people.

Now Daisy let out a sigh and wrapped a blade of grass around her finger where Cal's wedding ring once had been.

"So, are you going to do it? Matchmake for him?" Cal asked.

"Of course not."

He grunted. "Good." He stared out across the field. "Was it...the same? Did you feel...this time...what you felt before?"

It was all Daisy could do not to touch her tongue to her lips. Instead she pulled her knees up and wrapped her arms around them, in full cocoon mode. "He's still charming," she admitted.

Cal had been watching the next batter swing and miss. But at her words he turned his head and shot her a sharp glance.

Daisy gave him a quick humorless smile. "Speaking objectively. Don't worry. I'm not a fool anymore."

"So I should hope."

The batter swung and missed. Cal hauled himself to his feet to go pitch another inning. "You all right? Anything I can do?"

"No. He won't be back."

Cal cocked his head. "No?" He didn't sound so sure.

"Why would he? I didn't invite him in. I didn't encourage

him at all." *I didn't kiss him back!* "And he doesn't want me. He wants some woman who won't care."

"And Charlie?"

"He doesn't know about Charlie. I'm doing him a favor, really," she said firmly. "He doesn't want kids. He never did."

"Because he doesn't think he has any," Cal pointed out. "What if he finds out he does?"

"He won't."

"But if—" Cal persisted. It was what she hated about him.

"Charlie is mine! And yours."

She had always told Charlie—not that he understood yet really—that he had two fathers—a birth father who had given him life, and Cal, the father he knew. Charlie didn't question it. Someday he would, no doubt. But by then it would be in-grained in his mind. There would never be a time when she had to "tell him" his father was not Cal.

Because in every way that counted, his father was Cal. Cal was the one who had been there for her. He'd been her hus-band when Charlie was born. Charlie bore his surname. He was the only father Charlie knew.

If someday he wanted to know about Alex, she'd tell him. If someday in the distant future, Alex learned he had a child, perhaps they would meet. But not now. Now Charlie was a child. He was vulnerable. He didn't need a father who didn't want him.

"You don't know what he'll do, Daze," Cal said heavily, "if he finds out."

"He won't find out." She would make sure of that.

Cal's smile was grim. "We hope."

CHAPTER THREE

A DAY went by. Two.

Daisy still kept looking over her shoulder—well, out the window, actually—feeling skittish. Apprehensive.

She checked the caller ID every time the phone rang. Her breath caught whenever she saw a shadow on the front steps.

She actually dropped the kettle she was filling this morning, even though it was just the FedEx man bringing an order to Mrs. Kaminski upstairs.

Now she was filling it again for her friend Nell, who had just brought Charlie home from preschool and was staying for a cup of tea and regarding her curiously all the while.

"Something wrong?"

"No. I just…dropped the kettle this morning. I'm trying to be more careful now." Daisy set it on the burner and turned the gas on.

"Cal giving you trouble?" It was always the first thing Nell thought of because her own ex-husband, Scott, was a continual source of irritation.

"Cal never gives me trouble," Daisy said. She glanced out the sliding door to the garden where Charlie and Nell's son Geoff were playing with trucks.

Nell grimaced. "Lucky you. Scott's driving me crazy."

Daisy wasn't glad to hear that Scott was creating difficulties in her friend's life, but talking about it did avert Nell's further interest in Daisy's edginess. She gave Daisy an earful about her ex while they drank their tea and ate biscotti. Daisy made soothing sounds, but Nell was still grumbling when she decided it was time to go. She called Geoff in and they headed out the front door.

Relieved that her life was nowhere near as complicated as her friend's, Daisy was feeling much more sanguine when the phone rang as the door shut behind Nell and her son.

"Daisy Connolly," she said brightly into the phone.

"Daisy." The voice was warm, slightly gruff and instantly recognizable. The intimate tone of it made the hairs on the back of Daisy's neck stand straight up. Why hadn't she checked the ID this time?

"Yes. This is Daisy," she said crisply. "Who is this?"

"You know who it is." There was a smile in his voice as he called her bluff.

"Alex," she said flatly because playing the fool any longer wasn't going to help matters a bit.

"See. I knew you'd figure it out." He was grinning now. She could hear that, too.

"What do you want?"

"Are you married?"

"What?"

"I remembered you weren't Daisy Connolly back then. Wasn't your last name Harris? Morris?"

"Harris."

There was a brief silence. "So you did marry." It wasn't a question.

"Yes," she said firmly.

"And now?"

"What do you mean, and now?" Why did he have to ask? What business was it of his?

"Are you still…married?"

What kind of question was that? Damn it. She wanted to lie. But she'd never been a good liar, and though her acquaintance with Alex hadn't been long, it had been intense. She was sure he would be able to tell if she did.

"I'm divorced." She bit the words out.

"Ah."

Which meant what? Never mind. She didn't want to know. "Alex," she said with all the patience she could muster. "I'm working."

"This is work."

"No. I told you, I'm not matchmaking for you."

"I got that. You don't want what I want." He parroted her sentiments back to her. "This is photography. Or are you going to turn me down for that, too?"

She opened her mouth, wanting desperately to do exactly that. But she wouldn't give him the satisfaction of knowing he'd rattled her. "What sort of photography?" she said. "I do family stuff."

"And weddings. And bar mitzvahs. And some professional head shots. Some editorial. Recreation. Ice skating," he added. "Frisbee in the park. Baseball games." He ticked off half a dozen scenarios that were all shoots she had actually done.

"How do you know that?"

"You have a website," he reminded her. "The internet is a wonderful thing."

Daisy, grinding her teeth, wasn't so sure. Her fingers tapped an irritated staccato on the countertop. Outside Charlie was making vrooming noises as he pushed his cars around the patio. Any minute he'd slide open the door and want a snack. To prevent it, she latched the sliding door and got some crackers out of the cupboard and cheese from the refrigerator, preempting his demand. "What did you have in mind?" she asked.

"I need photos. An architectural journal is doing a piece on me and some of the work I've done. They've got photos of my projects from all over the world. Now they want some of me on one of the sites." He paused. "They said they could send a photographer—"

"Then let them."

"But I'd rather have you."

She wanted to say, Why? But she didn't want to hear his answer. Besides, asking would open a whole new can of worms.

"Not my line," she said briskly as she slapped cheese between the crackers and made little sandwiches for Charlie.

"You do editorial. I've seen magazine articles."

"Yes. But I don't traipse all over the world. I work in the city."

"The building is in Brooklyn." He gave her a second to digest that, then added, "I seem to remember you cross the river."

They had crossed the river together coming back from the wedding on Long Island. Daisy felt the walls closing in.

"Yes, I cross the river. *If* I have time. I'm busy."

"Any time in the next two weeks," he said smoothly. "And don't tell me that every minute of your life is booked."

Daisy heard the challenge in his voice. It was just another way of saying, *I don't believe you're really over me at all. You still want me. And now that you're divorced you might not believe in that ridiculous "love at first sight" notion anymore. You might be glad for a roll in bed.*

And, if it weren't for Charlie, heaven help her, she might.

"Are you still there? Daisy?" he prompted when she didn't reply.

She drew a breath. "I might have something next week. Let me check." It was the only way she could think of to prove to him—and to herself—that she wasn't a weak-willed fool.

She put the cracker sandwiches on a paper plate, flipped up the latch and slid open the door. Charlie looked up and, at the sight of the plate, grinned and jumped to his feet.

Daisy put a finger to her lips to shush him before he could speak, grateful that she'd taught him almost since he could talk not to blurt things out where people on the phone could hear him. That way, she'd explained, he wouldn't have to have a babysitter as often if she could take calls as if she were in her office when, in fact, she was at home.

Charlie had learned quickly. Now he stuffed a cracker

sandwich into his mouth, then carried the plate back to his trucks. For a moment, Daisy just watched him and felt her heart squeeze with love. Then quietly she slid the door shut and went to look at her appointment book.

"Where in Brooklyn? What sort of photos?" she asked as she flipped through the pages of her day planner.

"Park Slope." Alex gave her the address. "It's a pre-war building."

"I thought you were an architect. Don't you design new buildings?"

"Not this one. I built this one from the inside out. The outside is pretty much intact, except for the windows. I fixed the windows. The place was in really awful shape and the guy who owned it wanted it removed. He wanted me to put up a new building there. But when I got into it, I couldn't see tearing it down. Structurally it was sound. And it had some really strong period architectural features. It fit the block, the surroundings. So I made him a deal. I bought it from him and he bought land a couple of miles away. Then I built him what he wanted there, and I kept this one for myself."

The eagerness and the satisfaction in his voice reminded her of when he'd talked about his hopes for his career. He'd already done some big projects for the company he'd worked for then. But those had been projects he'd been assigned, ones that had been the vision of someone else. Now it sounded like he had taken the reins and was making his own choices, his own decisions.

"Are you your own boss now?" she asked, unable not to.

"For the last five years." He hesitated, then went on so smoothly she might have imagined the brief pause. "There was never going to be the perfect time to leave, so I just… jumped in."

"You like it?"

"Couldn't be happier," he said. "What about you? You've obviously left the guy you were working for."

"Finn? Yes. And I like what I'm doing, too."

"You can tell me all about it—if you can see a way to work me into your schedule?"

He made it sound very straightforward. A job. No more. No less. Maybe this really was all business.

Daisy could almost—but not quite—forget the way he'd kissed her. Deliberately she shoved the thought away. "What sort of thing does the writer have in mind?" she asked. "What do they want to feature?"

"Me," Alex said ruefully. "Up-and-coming architect, blah, blah, blah. I designed a hospital wing—first one I've done— and it's up for some award."

"That's great." And not surprising, really. She imagined that Alex would be good at whatever he did. "Where? Nearby?"

"Upstate a ways. Same side of the river, though," he added drily. "They used staff photos for that. They want ones of me and of the place in Brooklyn because it's a new departure for me. So you'd be shooting it now—plenty of awful 'then' photos already available. And then they want some of me 'in my environment.'" His tone twisted the words wryly. "With a pencil protector in my pocket." She could hear his grin. "Playing with blueprints. I don't know. You will."

If she did it. And maybe she should. Maybe it was exactly what she needed to do—learn about the man, demythologize him, turn him into some digital files and eight-by-ten-inch glossies.

"I can spare a bit of time next Thursday afternoon. Say, around three?"

"Great. I'll pick you up."

"I'll meet you. Just give me the address again." It was business. Just business.

He gave her the address. She wrote it down.

Then he said, "See you Thursday. Bye."

And he was gone. Just like that.

She had second thoughts. And third. And thirty-third. By the time Saturday rolled around, it was all she could think about.

"So call him and tell him you can't," Cal said when he came by to pick up Charlie Saturday morning. Charlie had already given her a smacking kiss goodbye and bolted out the door eager to tell his grandfather about the fire engine they were going to make.

But Cal hadn't followed him. He was eying her curiously as Daisy told him about Alex's call and his offer of the photography job. She also admitted to her qualms.

"It's just...distracting!" She stuck her hands in her hair and tugged.

"Why do it then? Call him up and tell him no."

"He'll want to know why."

"You're not obliged to tell him."

"If I don't, he'll get suspicious."

"About what? Is he going to think you're hiding his son from him?"

"No, of course not. He'll think—" Daisy hesitated "—that I'm still in love with him. That I don't trust myself around him."

"Possible," Cal agreed. "Or maybe you don't trust him."

Maybe she didn't trust either of them. The attraction was still there on a physical level. She hadn't told Cal about Alex's kiss. Or her reaction to it. There were some things better left unsaid. Now she just shrugged. "It'll be all right," she murmured.

Cal gave her a long hard look. She tried to remain indifferent under his gaze, but Cal was a photographer, too. He saw things that other people couldn't see.

"Is it just hormones?" he said at last. "Or something more?"

Daisy flushed, giving him yet another telltale sign. "I'm curious about what he's done with the building. About the sort of work he's doing."

"Uh-huh." Cal wasn't having any of it.

"Really. I wouldn't jeopardize Charlie's future. You know that." She looked at him steadily.

"Keep it in mind," Cal warned.

"No fear. I'm not an airy-fairy fool anymore."

Cal looked as if he doubted that. But at last he shrugged. "If you say so."

"In fact," Daisy added, "I think this may be a good thing. I can learn more about his real life, so I'll be able to tell Charlie about it someday."

"Oh, there's a plus," Cal muttered.

"It'll be fine." She put a hand on his sleeve. "Really, Cal. Don't worry."

Cal let out a slow breath. "I'm trying not to." He started toward the door and then turned back. "Charlie hasn't seen him? He hasn't seen Charlie?"

"No!" She smiled her best reassuring smile.

"Someday…"

"Someday they'll meet. Someday when Charlie is older. Grown-up. Settled. And if he has questions in the meantime, I'll answer them. But I'm not setting him up to be hurt! You know that. We've discussed it." When a man felt about having kids the way Alex did, deliberately introducing him into Charlie's life wasn't a risk she wanted to take.

Besides, he had a perfectly fine father in Cal. And one father was enough—for the moment at least.

"C'mon, Dad!" Charlie poked his head out of the window of the car.

"Go on, Dad," Daisy urged him. "And don't you worry. I'm doing enough for both of us. And it's silly, really. I will be fine. I'll shoot his photos, admire his handsome face and come home. End of story. Trust me. I can take care of myself."

The building Alex had restored wasn't far from Prospect Park. Daisy found it easily. It sat on the corner of a residential street filled with brownstones and trees and a business cross street that was wider, had fewer trees to block the view, and gave her plenty of scope.

She'd arrived early to scope out the neighborhood, wanted to get herself in work-mode before she ever laid eyes on him.

The day was cool and crisp, the trees in their full autumn glory as she walked down the block, studying the building side on.

At a few minutes before three the sun was low enough that the shadows picked out some of the ornate carved relief on the facing of the top floor, sharpening the detail, showing the building to best advantage. Daisy took out her camera before she was halfway down the block, framed and shot. She took a dozen or more, then crossed the main thoroughfare to study the angles.

The building was tall and narrow, a four story redbrick like others in the neighborhood, but, unlike the rest of them, it seemed somehow to draw in the light.

She studied it more closely, trying to understand what she was seeing. The ground floor housed an electronics store which seemed an odd tenant for an old building. But somehow it fit the space easily and looked as if it belonged. Studying it, she began to realize why. The windows were taller than those in other buildings on the block and she remembered Alex saying he had changed the windows. But they still fit the period; they belonged. But he'd made the proportions just that little bit more generous.

Now they fit twenty-first century people. It made all the difference.

The second floor echoed the look with a series of gothic-arched windows and cream-colored facings that contrasted with the dark red brick. Stenciled just above waist height across the central largest window in black sans serif was Antonides Architectural Design. Simple, spare, elegant.

She could see possibilities forming as she moved quickly along the sidewalk. She would shoot Alex standing in that window, looking out, master of his kingdom. And another at his drafting table. She could envision him in her mind's eye bending over a drawing, black hair drifting across his forehead as he studied his work intently.

There would doubtless be plenty of other possibilities inside; an open staircase perhaps or a period elevator or maybe a skylight and, she grinned delightedly—enough light to make it happen.

Suddenly enthused and feeling like a real competent professional photographer for the first time since Alex had asked her to do it, Daisy turned—and came up hard against a solid male chest.

CHAPTER FOUR

"I SAW you wandering back and forth across the street. I thought you might be lost." Alex had caught hold of her when she'd turned and crashed into him. He was still holding on now. Their bodies were touching.

Daisy's heart was going a mile a minute. Hastily she pulled away from his hard chest. "I wasn't lost," she said, hating her sudden breathlessness. "I was studying the building. Looking at all the angles."

She squinted up at him, trying not to be bowled over by the casual magnetism of the man. What was it about Alexandros Antonides that drew her like a moth to a flame?

Well, he was still gorgeous, there was that. Tall, whip-cord lean, broad-shouldered. Masculinity defined. Alex didn't have to flaunt the testosterone. It wasn't a veneer he put on. It was clearly bedrock in him.

"Well, if you're done assessing all the angles, let me show you around." He gave her one of those smiles, too, the one that had, from the beginning, undermined her common sense.

But she was older now, Daisy reminded herself. Made of sterner stuff. And she knew what he was made of, too.

"Fine," she said briskly. "Lead on."

He did just that, but not before he plucked her camera bag and one of the tripods out of her hands, leaving her with only her purse and the smaller tripod. "You could have left that in the building while you were looking around," he said over his shoulder as he crossed the street.

"I suppose."

"How'd you get here?"

"Subway."

He turned as he stepped up onto the sidewalk in front of his building. "With all this stuff? For God's sake, Daisy! They have cabs in Manhattan!"

"It's more efficient to take the subway."

"I'd have paid the cab fare."

"I don't need your cab fare. It's a business expense. When I want to take a taxi, I take one. I prefer the subway when I'm coming to Brooklyn. No bridge tie-ups. Now can we get going?"

She didn't want him fussing over her. He had no right. She didn't need him—of all people—thinking he knew best what was good for her.

Alex grunted, but still he shook his head as if despairing of her as he pushed open the door to the building. The electronics store she'd already spotted had its entrance off this interior vestibule on one side of the building. On the other was a stationer's shop—all fine paper and cards and pens.

"The old and the new," Daisy remarked, looking from the stationer's to the electronics store, nodding. She'd work that in, too.

Meanwhile he was leading her into the electronics store, pointing out the new windows and the old oak paneling, the new built-in oak cabinets and the old tin ceilings now restored. It was an artful blend of the best of both, and it showed off the latest electronic devices spectacularly well. After a quick tour there, he took her into the stationer's shop, and the same was true there, as well.

The exquisite paper products looked appealing against the same oak cabinetry. The displays of calligraphic pens and multicolored inks and artists' tools were equally appealing. Against the tall narrow windows Alex had created window seats which the proprietor had set up as inviting nooks for one or two people to sit and try out the various products. They were all full—and many of the customers were as young and hip as those in the electronics store across the vestibule.

"I'll show you photos of how it was before when we go upstairs," he said. "In the meantime, shoot whatever you want. Den and Caroline—the owners of the stores—have given their permission."

"Great. Thanks. You don't have to hang around," she said when he made no move to go. "I'll shoot down here. Then I can come to your office."

"I've cleared my calendar." He set her bag down, then propped his shoulders against the wall and watched every move she made.

Daisy was used to going about her work single-mindedly forgetting everything and everyone else but the focus of her shots. She was, this time, aware every second of Alex's eyes on her. She tried to tell herself he was just being polite. But he didn't simply watch while she took photos in the stationer's shop and in the electronics store. He followed her outside so she could shoot a couple from down the block.

Daisy shot him a hard look. He smiled back blandly.

"Fine," she muttered, "if you're going to tag along..." Then she raised her voice loud enough for him to hear and motioned him to stand in front of one of the heavy oak and etched glass doors. "Stand there and look 'lord of the manor-ish.'"

He was Greek. What did he know about lords of the manor?

But apparently some things were universal, and he understood perfectly, leaning casually against one of the walls by the front door, a proprietorial air about him that said exactly what she wanted it to—that this was his domain. He owned the place.

"Got it," she said, clicking off half a dozen so she could have her pick.

"Come on upstairs, then." He led the way back inside.

The elevator was utilitarian, so she wasn't sure what to

expect when the doors opened—a hallway and doors to offices, she would have guessed. But that wasn't what she got.

The elevator opened into one big room facing north. There were expanses of gleaming oak flooring broken up by areas covered with dove-gray carpet. In one of the carpeted areas, a woman sat at a desk making some notes while she talked on the phone. Not far away, on another carpet there was soft furniture—sofas and armchairs that invited you to sit and peruse books from floor-to-ceiling bookcases.

Where the floor was wood, she saw several large tables with projects on display, detailed architectural models in place. Around the sides of the room, in their own spaces but accessible to everyone, there were drafting tables, a couple of which had people working at them. They had glanced up when the elevator doors opened, but seeing Alex, they'd nodded and gone back to work.

Daisy's gaze swiveled to take in the whole room. "Wow," she said, impressed. "Very nice."

"I like it. Let me show you around." He introduced her to Alison, his middle-aged office manager. Then he took her to meet the two at the drafting tables. A young dark-haired woman, Naomi, was deeply involved in whatever she'd been assigned and barely glanced up to smile. But the other, an intern named Steve, had some questions about his project, so Daisy was able to take some shots of Alex and Steve, leaning over one of the drafting tables, studying blue prints.

Then, while Alex answered Steve's questions, she wandered around, taking other shots of the room, of Alex on the job.

It was just the way she'd imagined him—in his element, his easy competence apparent. He drew her gaze as he bent over the table, his dark hair falling across his forehead as he pointed out something to Steve. She snapped off a couple of shots. But even when she lowered the camera, she couldn't seem to look away.

"Sorry," he said, coming back to her. "I didn't mean to spend so long with him."

"No problem. I got some good shots. Which is your table?" She nodded toward the vacant drafting tables.

"Upstairs. I'll show you."

He led her to a spiral staircase that ascended in one corner of the room. "We could use the elevator, but this is faster."

It was also a treat. It had caught her eye earlier, a bit of wrought-iron frivolity in stark utilitarian surroundings. And yet it belonged.

"Was it original to the building?" It was a little added lagniappe, and she had already taken a number of shots of it.

"No. But I wanted something to catch the eye," Alex said. "Something that was from the original period. I went to every salvage place in the boroughs, looking. I knew it when I saw it."

"It's perfect." She motioned him to precede her up the steps. "Turn around," she said when he was halfway up. She took several shots of him on the steps, and was seriously tempted to take one of his backside when, afterward, she followed him up. But she didn't need any more reminders of how tempting Alex Antonides was.

His office was out of the mainstream, but connected to it. "I don't let them up here," he said frankly. "I need my space."

"A perk of being the boss," Daisy acknowledged. But she had to admit she liked his private aerie, too. The room in which he had created his office wasn't large. Like the bigger room downstairs, it had tall, narrow, gothic arched windows and polished oak flooring. Floor-to-ceiling bookshelves held vast arrays of architectural titles, books about design, and a lot of history, art and photography books. Daisy studied the titles.

It was disconcerting to find many of the same titles she had on her own shelves. So, whatever it was, it wasn't just physical.

She wished it were. He would be so much easier to resist. Forcing herself to focus on the task at hand, she gave a little wave of her camera, asking permission to take photos. "May I?"

He nodded. "Of course."

"I've heard that there's a movement to minimize windows for energy conservation," she said as she pointed the camera in his direction. "You obviously don't believe that."

"There's a place for that. But light is good, too. And while you can conserve energy by building dark, I like light. So I try to make sure the windows are doing their job, too." He stopped. "Sorry. Boring."

Daisy lowered the camera. "It's not, actually. And I'm a photographer. I like light, too."

"Come on," he said suddenly. "I'll show you the best light of all."

Without looking to see if she followed, he started up to the next level on the same spiral staircase. Daisy followed, expecting more office space. But when he reached the landing and unlocked the door, she knew better.

This was where Alex lived.

If he hadn't said, "Welcome to my place," she would have known it anyway. The light walls, the earth tones, the casual modern but not stark furniture, the plush dark rust and blue and gold oriental rug centered on the polished oak floor created a visual backdrop for the man she had known. Even if he weren't standing there watching her take it all in, she would have known this was where he belonged.

There were, in the furnishings, in the books and papers on the coffee table, in the framed architectural drawings on the walls, signs of Alex everywhere. She was shaken by how instantly she felt at home, as if she, too, belonged here.

No. No, she didn't.

She took a breath, steeled herself and tossed his words back at him, "So show me the best light of all."

He smiled. "Right this way."

Wouldn't you just bloody know that it would be the skylight in his bedroom!

Daisy stopped dead at the door, realizing a split second before she crossed the threshold exactly where they were going. "I didn't mean—"

Alex turned, flashing her a grin. "You asked for it."

Daisy read the challenge in it—the very challenge she'd told Cal she could handle. And she could, damn it. So, deliberately, she stepped in and looked around. The skylight was above the bed. The bed looked to be the size of, perhaps, the Sahara Desert—but vastly more comfortable with its buff-colored duvet and a quartet of dark brown pillows.

"Very nice," she said, doing her best to keep her gaze fixed on the skylight until she turned back to the living room again. "Let me shoot some photos out here."

He smiled, but didn't challenge her further, just let her wander around and look her fill.

Daisy resisted looking her fill. She'd have been here for hours, curious about the man, wanting to know him better, at the same time she knew she shouldn't want to know him at all.

Alex's apartment was not some sterile showplace. There were dishes in the sink, a newspaper on the counter. Two pairs of athletic shoes, a gym bag and a racing bike sat by what she supposed was the main front door—the one that didn't lead down to his office. And one wall of the kitchen was painted as a mural of something that looked like the Greek islands—lots of blue sea and sky, white-washed buildings and blue domed churches. It drew her attention.

"Did Martha paint that?"

Martha was Lukas's twin sister. Daisy had met her several times over the years. She knew Martha now lived part of the year in Montana—of all places—and part of the year on Long Island and wherever her husband, Theo Savas, was sailing boats.

It seemed an amazing exotic existence to Daisy who had been born in Colorado, came to the big city for university, and never left—except to go back home occasionally.

"She did," Alex agreed. "Kind of bowls you over, doesn't it?"

"I like it," Daisy said.

"I didn't," Alex said, surprising her.

"What? Why not?"

He shook his head. "Memories."

That startled her until she remembered him telling her about his childhood, about his brother who had died young.

"You could paint over it," she suggested.

He shrugged. "I got used to it. I just wasn't expecting it. I was heading out of town and I told her to paint whatever she wanted. She thought it would make me happy. Can we get on with this?" he said abruptly, gesturing to her camera.

"Oh! Yes, of course!" Daisy grimaced, feeling a flush of confusion engulf her. That would teach her.

She pointed to the armchair near the window. "Go sit there and look at one of your books."

Alex picked up a book and sat down with it, opened it at random, studied it as if he cared what was in it while Daisy moved and shot, moved and shot.

He turned a page. "I hired a matchmaker."

Daisy's finger slipped on the shutter release. Then, taking a slow careful breath so as not to jar the camera, she clicked off several more shots and lowered it again.

"Did you?" she said, heart pounding. "Good for you. I'm sure you'll find exactly what you're looking for. Turn a little more this way."

He turned. "I found her on the internet."

A breath hissed through Daisy's teeth. "The internet? For heaven's sake, Alex! How do you know she's legitimate? She might be a charlatan—someone hanging out her shingle, looking to make money off poor unsuspecting fools."

He looked up from the book and raised a brow. "Poor unsuspecting fools…like me?"

Daisy's cheeks burned. "I didn't mean that! I never said—" She retreated behind her camera again. "I just meant that not everyone is reliable, honest. Did you get letters of recommendation? What do you know about her background?"

"She has a degree in human relations. She was born and raised in Virginia. She came to the 'big city' when she was just out of college. Reminded me a little of you."

"I'm not from Virginia," Daisy bit out. "And I don't have a degree in human relations."

"So maybe she's more qualified than you are," Alex mused, giving her a sly smile.

"Maybe she is. I've got enough here. Let's go back down to your office." Someplace less intimate. Someplace where she could focus on her work. She didn't want to hear anything more about his matchmaker.

Alex picked up her camera bag, then started down the stairs again. He glanced back. "I went out with one of her suggestions last night."

Daisy pasted on a bright smile. "How nice. Maybe you'll have a wife by Christmas."

He nodded. "Maybe I will. She's a stockbroker. Nice enough. Intense, though," he mused.

Daisy pointed him toward his drafting table. "Put out a drawing and focus," she directed. She did not intend to get sucked into analyzing his date.

"Too intense for me," he went on, even as he obediently pulled out a drawing, spread it on the table and stared down at it. "She'd talked nonstop about everything from chandeliers to parakeets to stock options to astronomy."

"Well, it's early days yet," Daisy said briskly. "Maybe the next one will be better."

If he'd been her client she'd have talked to him about that, tried to learn what he hadn't liked, what was "too intense." But she wasn't finding a wife for Alex Antonides. He was someone else's problem.

He kept his gaze on the drawing. "Maybe. I'm going out with another one tonight."

"Another one?" That fast? Where was the "matchmaking" in that? It sounded more like trial and error.

He glanced around. "Amalie—that's the matchmaker—has got a whole list."

A list. Daisy wasn't impressed. "Is she French? Or fake?" she added before she could help herself.

Alex raised a brow. "Her mother's French. Is that a problem?"

Daisy raised her camera again, refusing to admit she was taking refuge behind it. "Of course not. I just wondered. I suppose she's introducing you to French women then." It made sense. He spent a good part of every year in Paris.

"Career women," Alex corrected. "And I'm not looking for a French one. I live here now."

That was news. Daisy stayed behind the camera. She kept moving.

Alex picked up the drawing and rolled it up. Whether she was finished or not, it was clear that he was. "She has a list as long as my arm," he reported. "She said I need options."

Daisy grunted noncommittedly. She didn't think much of "options." But then, when she helped people find the right mate, she was trying to find their soul mate, not a sex partner who was willing to share a mortgage.

"So," Alex said, "I just have to find the right one."

Good luck with that, Daisy thought. But she kept her skepticism to herself. If she expressed it, he'd tell her she should do it herself.

"All done," she said, and began disassembling her camera and stowing it in her bag. "I'll get to work editing these early next week. I'm going to be out all day tomorrow, and I'm not working this weekend. If you'll give me your business card, I'll email you when I've finished. Then you can let me know whether to send you a disk or email you files or send them directly to the magazine."

Alex fished a card out of his wallet, started to hand it to her, then took it back and scribbled something on the back before pressing it into her palm again. "You can reach me at this number anytime."

Not likely. But Daisy just pocketed it and smiled as she zipped her bag shut, stood up and hoisted it onto her shoulder. Then, deliberately, she stuck out her hand to Alex for a businesslike shake. "Thank you."

He blinked, then stared—at her, at her hand. Something unreadable flickered across his face. Then in slow motion, he reached out and took her fingers in his. Flesh on flesh.

Daisy tried not to think about it. But his palm was warm and firm and there were light calluses on it, as if he didn't only sit in his office and draw. She remembered those calluses, those fingers—the way they had grazed her skin, had traced the line of her jaw, the curve of her hip, the hollow of her collarbone. Other lines. Other hollows.

She swallowed hard.

Still he held her hand. Then abruptly he dropped it. "Thank you, too," he said, his voice crisp. As businesslike as she hoped hers was.

"Goodbye." One more polite smile and she'd be gone.

Alex nodded, his gaze fixed on hers. The phone on his desk rang. He grimaced, then picked it up. "What is it, Alison?" There was barely concealed impatience in his tone. Then he grimaced again. "Right. Okay. Give me a sec." He turned back to Daisy. "I have to take this."

"Of course. I was just on my way."

She was down the steps and out the door without looking back. There. She'd done it—beard the lion in his den.

And survived.

Just like she'd told Cal she would.

Staring at the skylight in his ceiling in the dark didn't have much to recommend it. There were stars. There were a few small clouds scudding along, silvery in the moonlight.

There was Daisy.

Alex flipped over and dragged the pillow over his head. It didn't help. She was on the insides of his eyelids, it seemed.

The whole day had been a bloody disaster. Well, no, that

wasn't true. Before 3:00 p.m., things had been pretty normal. He'd been a little distracted, there had been a lot to do, but he'd got some work done.

And then Daisy had shown up. Exactly as he'd planned.

She was supposed to come, take her photos, and leave again. He was supposed to smile and look professional and competent and disinterested, and see her on her way. Asking her to take the photos was supposed to settle things between them, put them on a business footing.

It was supposed to pigeonhole her—and convince Alex that he wasn't really attracted, that he hadn't been thinking about her fifty times a day since he'd seen her again, that she didn't draw his gaze more than any other woman, that he was perfectly happy to watch her walk out of his office and out of his life.

The operative word was *supposed*. The truth was, well, something else altogether.

And the day hadn't been all that normal before three o'clock, either. He might have got some work done earlier in the day, but shortly before Daisy was due to arrive, he'd found himself walking over to look out the window every few minutes. It was a nice day, sunny, brisk. He was enjoying perfect fall weather. No more, no less.

So why had his heart kicked over at the sight of her down there on the sidewalk, pointing her camera up at his building? Why had he stopped Steve abruptly halfway through a question to go down and intercept her before she came in? Why had his fingers itched to reach out and touch her? And why had he had to fight to suppress the urge to kiss her when she'd turned and bumped straight into his chest?

She drove him crazy. She got under his skin. The minute he saw her, he couldn't seem to focus on anything or anyone else.

The feeling persisted the whole time she was there—this desire to touch her, to smooth a hand over her hair, to pull her against him, to touch his lips to hers. His heart had begun hammering the moment he'd seen her, and it was still banging away when he'd had to take that phone call and she'd left.

He'd wanted to stop her, to say, "Hang on. Wait," because it was too soon, there had been so little time, he had not had enough of her yet.

But at the same time, he knew it was stupid—*he* was stupid. Daisy Harris—Connolly!—was *not* what he wanted—or needed—in his life.

And it didn't matter that she was divorced now. She still apparently wanted things he didn't want. Wanted things he wasn't prepared to give. So the one bit of common sense he had, had kept his mouth shut.

He hadn't said, "Wait." Hadn't stopped her or called her to come back.

It was better she had left. And better still that he had had a date that night with one of Amalie's "options."

Whoever she was, she would erase Daisy from his mind.

Except she hadn't.

Her name was Laura or Maura or Dora. Hell, he couldn't remember. She had been pleasant enough in an airheaded sort of way. But he'd spent the evening making mental comparisons between her and Daisy.

Suffice to say, Dora/Maura/Laura had come up short on all counts.

She didn't have Daisy's charm. She didn't have Daisy's ability to listen. She didn't have Daisy's smile or Daisy's sparkling eyes or Daisy's eager enthusiasm.

She wasn't Daisy. He was bored.

He'd been polite enough. He'd listened and nodded and smiled until his jaw ached. He'd dutifully told her a bit about himself, but his comments were flat and uninteresting even to his own ears. It wasn't hard to tell she was bored, too.

"You win a few, you lose a few," she'd said, smiling and shaking his hand when they'd left the restaurant to go their separate ways.

It was nine-thirty. Shortly after ten he was home.

And that was when he began to realize his mistake. He'd not only lost, he'd lost big-time.

He hadn't vanquished Daisy from his mind by having her come take photos this afternoon. On the contrary he now had a whole host of new images of Daisy—on his turf.

Now when he stood at the window, he could look down at where he'd first spotted her, camera to her eye, taking pictures of his building, her hair loose in the wind. And when he grew tired of pacing his apartment and went back down to his office to do some work, the minute he sat down at his drafting table, he could almost feel her presence just over his right shoulder where she had been that afternoon.

He crumpled up half a dozen attempted drawings before he gave up, stomped back upstairs, stripped off his clothes and took a shower.

She hadn't been in his shower, at least.

Not this one, anyway. But he'd shared a shower with her five years ago, and the memories flashed across his mind with such insistence that he'd cranked the hot water down till only the cold beat down on his body. But his arousal persisted.

He wanted to go for a bike ride, burn off the energy, the edge. But not in Brooklyn. Not at midnight. There was stupid—and then there was stupid.

He was stupid, not suicidal.

He should have known better than to think he could see her again and forget her. He'd never been able to forget her. And he wouldn't be able to, damn it, until Amalie finally found him the right woman.

In the meantime he'd flung himself onto his bed, stared up at the skylight—and discovered the depth of his folly.

Daisy had been in his bedroom. He'd deliberately brought her in here—to show her the "best light"—wanting to get a rise out of her.

Well, she wasn't the one who was rising. Pun intended, he thought savagely. The joke was on him.

* * *

The trouble with doing an hour-long shoot with Alex was that the hour was just the beginning.

Oh, it was over for him. But Daisy had to work with the images, study them, analyze them, choose the best ones, correct them. Spend hours and hours and hours contemplating them.

It drove her insane.

She didn't want to see him in his element hour after hour. She didn't want to feast her eyes on that handsome face. She didn't want to focus on the lithe muscular body as he stretched across the drafting table to point something out to Steve. She didn't want to study the strong profile, the sharp angles, the hard jaw, and hawklike nose as he stared out the window.

He was everything she'd thought he would become.

And she couldn't bear to look at it.

She put the photos away and went to read books to Charlie. The next night she watched a movie instead. The following night she had a new shoot, some high school senior pictures to work on. She'd get to Alex's when the memory of being in his office, in his apartment—in his bedroom—wasn't quite so immediate.

She would do them.

Not now. Not yet.

She needed time. An eon or two.

She needed space. Would a galaxy be enough?

The trouble with the "options" Amalie was providing him with, Alex decided after his fifth disastrous date, was that not one of them—so far—had been worth the trouble.

He'd gone out with half a dozen since he'd contracted with her, and since the intense Gina whom he'd mentioned to Daisy and the airhead whose name he couldn't recall, there had been phlegmatic Deirdre and twitchy Shannon and a politician called Chloe.

But if they'd been bad, tonight's "flavor of the evening" was absolutely no improvement, though Amalie had sworn they would be perfect for each other.

"She's an architecture student. You'll have so much in common!" Amalie had vowed.

He met her at a restaurant near the Lincoln Center. She was at the bar when he got there, a red scarf looped around her neck. That's how he would recognize her, she'd told him on the phone.

He did a double take when he saw her. She looked so much like Daisy. Maybe a little blonder than Daisy, maybe a little taller. And her eyes were a sort of faded gray-green. She beamed at him when he arrived.

"I knew it was you!" She was like bubbly champagne. "You're even more handsome than your picture."

She might have meant it. He didn't know. Didn't care. Her eyes didn't sparkle like Daisy's.

They took their drinks to a table and he said, "Amalie says you're studying architecture."

Not quite. What Tracie knew about architecture she appeared to have memorized from Wikipedia. She started talking about the Acropolis before they ordered and had barely reached the Colosseum by the time their entrees arrived.

It was always interesting to learn which buildings inspired another architect, but Tracie wasn't an architect—or even a student of architecture, Alex was willing to bet. After two hours of her nonstop talking, he'd had enough. If she hadn't looked so much like Daisy, he doubted he'd have lasted that long.

But the truth was, the longer he spent with her, the less like Daisy she seemed. Tracie was nervous, edgy. She had a shrill laugh. Her voice grated on him.

Daisy's laugh made him feel like smiling. Her eyes always sparkled—either with joy or annoyance. It didn't matter which. They drew his gaze. When she was with him, he couldn't stop looking at her. Her voice was always like warm honey.

Not, of course, that he'd heard it since she'd walked out of his place a week and a half ago. She'd taken his picture and said she'd be in touch and he'd never heard from her again.

He set down his fork sharply.

"You're bored," Tracie accused, staring hard at him over his empty plate. He hadn't had to talk, so he'd eaten everything in front of him.

Now Alex shook his head. "No," he lied. "I'm distracted. I just realized I have to be somewhere. I have an appointment."

"Tonight?" Her eyes widened.

"I have to pick up some photos," he said. "I need to get them to an editor in the morning." It wasn't entirely true. But the editor did need them. She'd called him yesterday inquiring about where they were. He'd thought Daisy had sent them in so she wouldn't have to contact him again.

Tracie pursed her lips, then pouted. "But we've only reached the Duomo." Which meant they had about six hundred more years of architecture to cover.

"I'm sorry," Alex said firmly. "I really need to go."

He did finish his coffee, but then called for the bill, saw her into a taxi and watched it drive off. Not until it disappeared around the corner did he breathe a sigh of relief. He was free.

For what?

It was just past nine. Not really late—unless you'd just spent the past two hours being systematically bored to death. Then you wanted some excitement, something to get the adrenaline going.

But the adrenaline was already going—and so were his feet.

They knew exactly where they were headed, and before Alex even realized it, he was on the corner of the street where Daisy's office was.

Daisy—who was, let's face it, the reason he'd been willing to go on five dates in the past ten days—so he would bloody well stop thinking about her.

But he hadn't stopped.

Every night he lay in bed and stared at the damned skylight

and remembered her sparkling eyes, her smooth golden skin, her warm smile. And because he was in bed, he remembered other things, too.

He remembered touching her skin—all over. He remembered kissing her smiling mouth. He remembered stripping off her clothes and running his hands over her body, teasing, tasting—

Hell! He couldn't show up on her doorstep halfway to wanting to bed her. Not that she'd even be there. It was her office, for God's sake. Why would she be burning the midnight oil editing photos? Presumably she had a life.

She probably even went out on dates now that she was divorced. Maybe she had a boyfriend. His jaw tightened and he shoved his hands in the pockets of his jacket as he started walking down the street.

He didn't expect she would be there. So he was taken aback to discover lights on in the bay window of the apartment that was her office.

She didn't have a life, after all? He stopped across the street and stared.

Now what? Turn around and walk back to Columbus? Catch a cab home? And stare at the damn skylight again?

Abruptly Alex crossed the street, took the steps to the front door two at a time, opened the door to the vestibule and punched the doorbell.

He waited. And waited. He shifted from one foot to the other, and wondered if she left the lights on all the time. Maybe she wasn't even there.

He was ready to turn around and leave when all at once he heard the sound of the lock twisting and the door handle rattling. The door opened.

Daisy stared out at him, nonplused. *"Alex?"*

"I came for the photos."

"What?"

"The editor called me. She wants the photos. You said you'd have them ready."

"I said I'd call you when they were ready." She was gripping the door, glaring at him, and by God, yes, her eyes were sparking fire.

He almost smiled as he snaked past her into her office before she could object, then turned and let his gaze run over her again.

She was wearing a pair of jeans and a sweatshirt—about as inelegant as imaginable—and she looked as sexy as hell. Her blonde hair was hanging loose around her face. It was disheveled, as if she—or someone else?—had been running fingers through it.

"Am I interrupting something?" he snapped.

"What?" She frowned. Then she shrugged. "My work. If you want the photos, let me get back to them. They're not done yet. I'm sorry. I've been busy. I'll have them for you tomorrow. I—"

"Let me see them."

"No. Not while I'm still working."

"Why? Afraid of someone else's opinion?"

"Do I offer you opinions about the buildings you design?" she countered with saccharine sweetness. "Of course not. So go away."

But Alex didn't want to go away. He wanted to drop down in the chair and watch her work. He wanted to run his fingers through her hair and pull her close. He wanted to slide his hands down the curve of her spine, cup her buttocks—

He groaned.

"What's wrong?" She was looking at him intently, worriedly.

He ground his teeth, then turned away, knowing he should get the hell out of here, but somehow he couldn't go. It was as if she'd bewitched him, cast some spell that wouldn't let him find the woman he knew had to be out there, the woman who would actually be right for him.

"Alex?" she pressed in the face of his silence.

Finally he snapped. "I've had five dates, and they've all been disasters!"

Daisy's eyes widened. She stared at him, then let out a sound that might have been a laugh. Or a snort.

"What a shame," Daisy said in a tone that told him it had been both a laugh and a snort.

"It is, damn it! And it's a waste of time." Alex cracked his knuckles and spun away to pace irritably around her office. But every step brought him closer to her. And he wanted her. Badly.

She stepped past him and moved toward her desk, and he wheeled to follow her when he found himself face-to-face with the photos on her walls.

None of them, of course, was Daisy.

But they all spoke of Daisy. Of what she wanted and he didn't.

Families. Children. Pets.

He looked at her. Her cheeks were flushed. She ran her tongue over her lips. She watched him warily, worriedly.

"Never mind," he said abruptly. "I have to go."

Ignoring his desire, forcing himself to turn away from the most beautiful woman he'd ever made love to, he stalked out the door. He was halfway down the steps when he turned his head, his heart still hammering. "Send me those photos, damn it."

CHAPTER FIVE

THE next day Alex got an email with a link to a site where he could download the photos Daisy had taken.

Here you are, the email said. Sorry it took so long. Hope they meet with your editor's satisfaction. Thank you for the opportunity to work with you.

Kind regards, Daisy Connolly.

Kind regards? Daisy *Connolly?*

As if he would need her last name to distinguish her from all the other Daisys in his life.

Blast her, anyway! Alex smacked a hand on the desk next to his computer screen. So all it had needed was for him to turn up on her doorstep and make an idiot of himself and Daisy was suddenly inspired to finish editing the photos, send them along and get him out of her life.

Swell.

He'd lain awake half the night—staring at the damned skylight and cursing his own misplaced desire—and wishing Amalie would come up with a viable "option."

In the morning he called her and demanded a better selection. "The last one was a charlatan," he said. "If she was an architecture student, I play center field for the New York Yankees."

"I'm talking to another young woman today," she promised. "You're very discerning. It takes time."

It didn't take time, damn it. That was the trouble. If Daisy wanted what he wanted there wouldn't be any problem at all.

But she didn't. That was perfectly clear. She probably hadn't been stalling. She'd probably actually been busy, too busy to get right to his photos. But once he'd turned up on her doorstep, making demands, she'd outdone herself getting the photos finished so she didn't need to have anything more to do with him.

They were amazing photos, though.

He stood in his office, staring at them now. He'd spread them out on his drafting table, studying them, seeing himself through her eyes.

They were every bit as sharp and insightful as the ones he'd seen on her wall last night. She'd taken most of the shots in black and white which, on first glance, surprised him.

But the more he studied them, the more he saw what she was doing: she had used the monochrome scheme to pare him down to his essence, exactly the way an architectural drawing or a blueprint did.

She caught him clearly—a man who had little patience with subtlety, who knew what he wanted.

He wanted her.

She had to know that. Didn't she know that?

He sighed and scraped the photos into a pile and put them back into the envelope. Of course she knew it.

She didn't want him—not on his terms.

So he'd seen the last of her.

End of story.

Daisy was still taking deep breaths and letting them out slowly a week later. But it was her own fault. She knew she should have got the photos edited and sent off right away. She hadn't.

And so Alex had turned up on her doorstep. An intense, edgy, irritated Alex. An Alex who had looked at her with fire in his normally cool green gaze. An Alex who had shot into her office so quickly, she hadn't even thought about how to stop him. And once he was there, it had felt like being trapped in a cage with a full-grown, very hungry panther.

A panther who had complained about the meals he was being offered at the same time he was looking at her like he intended to make her the next one.

She'd skittered away, crossed the room, needing to put space between them, because the mere sight of him had set her heart to pounding. All her senses went on alert with Alex. Her body wanted him no matter what her brain—and her mother's-heart—told her was wise.

She had been determined to resist—not just Alex, but her own desire.

Then abruptly he had turned and walked out!

And Daisy had been left staring after him as he strode off into the cold dark windy night. Then she'd shut the door and leaned against it, her heart still slamming against the wall of her chest, her pulse racing.

The adrenaline had kept her working half the night.

It took a week to wear off, more for her to be able to say with confidence to Cal that life was back to normal, and still more until she believed it herself.

So it was a blow on the first Saturday evening in November to hear a knock on the door, expect to get the Thai takeaway she'd ordered, and find Alex standing on her doorstep again.

She stared at him, dumbstruck.

"Good evening to you, too," he said cheerfully. His tone was mild, friendly, completely at odds with the Alex who had shown up last time.

"Good evening," she replied cautiously, trying not to look at his smooth-shaven face, his quirking smile, that groove in his cheek she always itched to touch. Deliberately she curled her fingers into the palm of her hand.

He hesitated a split second, then said, "I just wanted to say that I may have found the one."

Daisy blinked. "The one? The one what?"

His smile widened. "Woman." There was a pause. Then, "Wife," he clarified.

Daisy's stomach did an odd sort of somersault. She swallowed, then mustered her best polite smile. "Really. How nice."

She shut her eyes for an instant, and opened them to discover that he'd done it again—slipped past her and was suddenly standing in her office. How did he do that?

"She's a vice president in marketing for an international cosmetics firm," he reported, his handsome face looking very pleased. "She runs campaigns in half a dozen places all over the world. Always on the move. She has two phones. A red one for emergencies." He grinned, as if this were a good thing.

"Does she?" Daisy said drily. "Sounds perfect for you."

"You think so, too?" He was still grinning, so she didn't know if he heard her sarcasm as it had been intended or not. "That's what I thought. I read Amalie the riot act after the first bunch, said if that was as good as she could do, I was finished. And then she came up with Caroline."

Caroline. Even her name was right. Sophisticated, but approachable. She did sound perfect.

"And," Alex went on with considerable enthusiasm, "there are other things, too—she's beautiful, bright, funny, articulate, well-read."

Daisy shut the door but stayed by it, keeping an eye out for the Thai deliveryman and thanking God that Charlie was at Cal's this weekend. "So have you asked her to marry you yet?" she asked Alex flippantly.

"Considering it."

Her jaw dropped. "On the basis of a couple of dates?"

"Three," Alex corrected. He was moving around her office in panther mode, but looking better fed. He picked up an alabaster cat on the bookcase, and examined it while he talked. "Well, two and a half." His mouth twisted wryly. "The red phone rang tonight. She had to leave in the middle of dinner. She's on her way to San Francisco right now."

"You're joking." He had to be joking. *Didn't he?*

But when he didn't immediately agree that he was, Daisy shook her head, torn between despair and the prickling of awareness and wholly useless desire she always felt faced with Alexandros Antonides. Still. Damn it. "You're insane."

He put the cat down again and looked at her quizzically. "Insane? Why?"

"You can't make a decision like that in a few weeks' time!"

"Why not? She's what I want."

"But are *you* what *she* wants?" Daisy didn't know why she was asking that. Didn't know why she was arguing with him.

"That's her problem."

"Yours, too." She couldn't seem to help herself. "If you get married without knowing each other well, without thinking things through—"

"I could end up like you did?"

Daisy rocked with the punch of his words. *"What?"*

"That isn't why your marriage didn't work?"

"No, of course it isn't!" Daisy felt the heat of his accusation. But she denied it, and it wasn't a lie, either. "And we're not discussing my marriage." She wrapped her arms across her chest, as if they would defend her. Fat chance.

"Why didn't it, then?" he persisted.

"This is not about me!"

He raised his brows. "Maybe I'm trying to learn from your mistake."

"You and I are not likely to make the same mistakes."

Alex shrugged. "How will I know if you don't tell me?"

"I'm not going to tell you, Alex! My marriage is none of your business." She shoved away from the door and jerked it open. "I think you should go."

But Alex didn't go anywhere. On the contrary, he turned and flopped down into one of the armchairs, settling in, folding his arms behind his head. "Not yet. I want to hear why I shouldn't pop the question."

Daisy wanted to strangle him. But the quickest way to get him out of her life was to answer his questions. So she did.

"Because," she said slowly and with the articulation of an el-ocution teacher, "you don't want to get a divorce. Do you?" she challenged him. "Maybe you don't care whether you do or not because you won't care about her."

"I don't want a divorce," he said evenly. The green eyes glinted.

Daisy shrugged. "Fine. Then take your time. Make sure you're on the same page. That you want the same things. That… Oh, hell, why am I telling you this? You don't un-derstand!"

He cocked his head. "Weren't you on the same page, Daisy?" He sounded almost sympathetic now.

She pressed her lips together and didn't answer.

He gave her a little half smile. "Are you going to marry again?"

"I doubt it." She turned away, then turned back and shrugged. "Maybe someday. It depends."

"On?"

"On whether or not I'm in love with him."

Alex's jaw clenched.

Daisy smiled. It was a painful smile, hard-earned. "Yes, love. Still. I want the whole package, Alex. Now more than ever."

Alex didn't move. A muscle ticking in his temple was the only betrayal of anything beyond casual interest in what she had to say. Then, with studied nonchalance, he rose slowly. "I wish you the joy of it then."

"And I you," Daisy said automatically.

He gave her a sardonic look.

"No, truly." She almost put a hand on his arm as he passed. But then she laced her fingers together instead. Still, she looked up at him earnestly. "I mean it, Alex. You deserve a wonderful life. I hope…Caroline is the right woman for you. I hope she gives you what you want."

He had stopped and was standing now, quite close. She kept her gaze on the rise and fall of his chest, knew that she could reach out and touch him. Knew she should back away.

But she didn't. She stayed quite still and met his gaze. "Regardless of what you think, marriage is more than you expect. You should...take your time, get to know this...woman you're considering marrying. Make sure it's right for both of you."

Alex stood staring at her as if he couldn't believe the words coming out of her mouth.

Daisy couldn't believe them, either. It wasn't any of her business. But she couldn't seem to stop herself. And maybe she did owe him the benefit of her experience with Cal. Certainly it had taught her something.

"No matter what you think you want out of marriage," she finished, "it can surprise you. You shouldn't take it lightly."

Alex's eyes narrowed further, and she expected he would tell her to mind her own business. But his jaw just tightened again, then he nodded. "I'll keep it in mind."

Their gazes locked—all the electricity flowing through New York City at that moment had nothing on what arced between them.

Then, carefully, consciously, Daisy swallowed. "Have a good life, Alex."

For a long moment he didn't reply, and she couldn't read his gaze. Then he said flatly, "I will. Shall I invite you to the wedding?"

No! It was her gut-level response. But she squelched it. "When you're sure she's the right one," she said slowly, "I would be delighted to come."

Alex's lips pressed together in a thin line. He nodded, then walked past her wordlessly out the door.

She closed it after him, leaned back against it, knees wobbling. Only after the sound of his footsteps had long faded away, did Daisy breathe again.

Moving on.

That's what her father always used to say when Daisy or her sister got all wrought up about something they could do nothing about. He'd listen to them anguishing for, oh, maybe thirty minutes, and then he'd say, "Can you do anything about it?"

They'd say, "No."

And he'd flash them his sunny grin and say, "So…moving on…"

He didn't mean, *get over it.* He meant, *stop dwelling on it. Get past it.*

You might still ache with disappointment. You might remember it forever. But you'd done all you could do. Now it was time to pull up your socks and move on.

Daisy moved on.

She still thought about Alex. How could she not? She had loved him once. He was the father of her child, even if he didn't know it. She owed him for that—for Charlie. And she wished things could have been different.

But they weren't.

Life moved on, and determinedly Daisy moved on with it. She did her work. She introduced a great couple, Debbie whom she'd met at a yoga class and Mark, who played baseball with Cal, and was delighted when they seemed to hit it off. She wasn't losing her touch with other people at least. Cal bought Charlie a point-and-shoot camera, and she went with the two of them for walks in the park and on the streets and took loads of pictures. It was fun to discover Charlie's interest, and restful to be with him and Cal.

Every time her thoughts drifted to Alex and she wondered if he'd proposed yet, she deliberately focused them elsewhere. So she wasn't even thinking about him the Sunday evening before Thanksgiving when Cal came into the kitchen and asked, "Whatever happened with Alex?"

Her ex had stopped by that afternoon to take Charlie for a bike ride in the park. When they'd come back, Daisy had invited him to stay for leftovers. After, he'd helped Charlie build a fire station with his Legos. Now Charlie had gone upstairs to get ready for his bath while Daisy put dishes in the dishwasher.

She felt a moment's jolt at the sound of his name. But then

she just shrugged. "No idea. Haven't seen him for a while. I believe he's got a woman in his life. He seems to think she's 'the one.'" Daisy couldn't help adding that.

Cal looked at her closely. "I'm sorry."

"I'm not," Daisy said, dropping forks in the silverware slots. "He was never the man I thought he was. He still isn't."

"Life sucks," Cal said with a faint grin.

"It has some good bits," Daisy countered, nodding toward the stairs where they could both hear Charlie banging around in the upstairs hall.

Cal's grin widened. "You're right. It does." He shoved away from the doorjamb and flexed his shoulders. "I'll be going then. Thanks for letting me take him to the park."

"Anytime." She walked to the front door with him and kissed him on the cheek and he gave her a hug. Then he shrugged on his jacket. "I'll pick Charlie up Thursday morning. I told my folks we'd be up there by noon."

Daisy nodded and forced a smile even as she felt her throat tighten. "He'll have so much fun."

Cal was taking Charlie to his parents' upstate for Thanksgiving. They wouldn't be back until Sunday morning. The thought of rattling around by herself for four days was horrible. But it was good for Charlie and for Cal and his family. It was a part of the life they'd made.

"My folks are really looking forward to it," Cal said. He looked at her closely. "You can come if you want." He must have seen some of the hollowness she felt.

Daisy shook her head. "Thanks, but I can't. You know that."

If she did Cal's parents might think there was hope of them getting back together. They had been upset when she and Cal divorced. Now they seemed to be coming to terms with the way things were. It wouldn't do to get their hopes up again.

"You're probably right. No, you are right. It's just—I'm sorry. Especially this year."

Daisy shrugged. "Don't worry. I'll be fine. I'm going to

Finn and Izzy's. It will be chaos. I'll never miss you. What do you have planned?"

"Going fishing if the weather stays warm enough. Chopping wood otherwise. Getting ready for winter." He grimaced.

"You'll have fun."

"Charlie will make it fun. He and Dad are something else when you get them together." Cal shook his head, grinning. "Like two kids."

"I'd guess there were three." Daisy cocked her head and smiled at him.

Cal rubbed a hand against the back of his neck. "Well, yeah."

Their eyes met, both of them rueful.

"Moving on," Daisy said with all the briskness she could muster.

And Cal nodded resolutely. "Moving on."

He went out, and Daisy locked the door after him. Then she went back into the living room, rubbing her hands up and down her arms. Was Alex having Thanksgiving with the woman in his life? Or was he working on one continent while she was on another?

What did she care? Daisy asked herself irritably.

She didn't, damn it. But sometimes moving on felt curiously like walking through molasses with her shoelaces tied together. Hard and lonely.

She felt suddenly very, very cold.

CHAPTER SIX

FINN and Izzy's at Thanksgiving *was* chaos. Finn's nieces, Tansy and Pansy, were both there, along with Rip and Crash, Finn and Izzy's sons, and a dozen or so other friends, several slightly giddy from having spent the night before over by the Museum of Natural History where all the gigantic balloon floats for the annual parade were being inflated.

Daisy had gone to the MacCauleys' early and she'd stayed late. Friday she'd spent the entire day catching up on photo editing. More often than she'd liked, she'd been tempted to open the folder where Alex's photos were.

Every time, she'd steeled herself against it and had resisted.

Saturday was harder. Her backlog of work was gone. The house was reasonably clean. The laundry was done, folded, put away. The rugs vacuumed, the furniture dusted. She supposed she could clean the oven, but that seemed like taking things too far.

Instead she took the dog Murphy for a long walk in the park, then decided to do some Christmas shopping. Closer to Christmas, stores would be jammed. Of course, they were on Saturday, too. But it wasn't as lonely as being home by herself, wondering if Charlie and Cal were having a good time.

Wondering what Alex was doing.

It was a relief when Cal and Charlie got back late Sunday afternoon. Charlie was full of stories about hiking in the woods and stacking firewood.

"No, I didn't let him chop it," Cal said before she could ask.

"An' we caught fish," Charlie told her, hopping from one foot to the other. "We got pictures. Look."

Daisy admired the pictures Cal had taken of Charlie and the fish. One of them, though, startled her as his expression in it was so much like Alex's. She never thought he looked like Alex. She really didn't know who he looked like, except that he had her color hair. But in that photo of him grinning up at his grandfather she could see that he had Alex's profile. It made her catch her breath.

"What's wrong?" Cal asked.

"Nothing," she said, papering over her surprise. "I was just amazed at the size of the fish."

"It was huuuuuge," Charlie told her proudly. He spread his arms to their fullest extent.

"Well, maybe not quite that big," Cal said.

But to Charlie it was the biggest fish in the world, and he'd had the best time in the world. And he proceeded to tell Daisy all about it after Cal went home and all through dinner and during his bath.

And Daisy nodded and smiled as she listened to her son's nonstop commentary. He'd had a wonderful time. She was glad he had gone. Glad Cal and his parents had had the joy of him.

Mostly, though, she was glad he was home again.

And when she went to bed that night, she thought, *I can do this. I'm going to be fine.*

She and Cal could cope with trading Charlie back and forth. Charlie wasn't a basket case. He was a normal happy little boy. Life was good.

She didn't think about Alex—or his perfect woman.

At least she tried not to.

"How much longer till Christmas?" Charlie asked. He'd been asking for the past four days, ever since he'd got back from Cal's parents'.

"Oh, a long time," Daisy said, tucking him into bed. She'd been saying the same thing every day since, too, because a person who was Almost Five had no concept of time, and she'd quickly discovered that if she said "soon," Charlie expected it to be "right after lunch."

"And my birthday?"

"Not quite as long."

Charlie made a face. "They should hurry up."

"All in good time." Even though she had caught up on things over Thanksgiving already, four days later, she felt her to-do lists getting longer by the minute. Lots of people suddenly remembered they wanted family photos for Christmas, and Daisy, understanding the desire, tried not to disappoint any of them.

She had other jobs, too. Most were from repeat customers who wanted her to do some editorial work, and a promo for a boutique in Soho. But one phone call the day after Thanksgiving had surprised her.

"This is Lauren Nicols," the woman had said when Daisy answered. "You did the photos for my piece on Alexandros Antonides."

"Oh! Yes, of course. I hope they were suitable," Daisy said, her heart quickening.

"More than," Lauren Nicols said warmly. "I was delighted. Alex told me you'd be good, but they were better than I'd hoped. The black and white surprised me, but it was perfect. You caught the man."

"I hope so," Daisy said honestly. "I tried."

"Oh, you did," the other woman assured her. "I wondered if you'd be willing to do some more for me."

"Of Alex?" Daisy asked, startled.

"No, Alex's article is in production. But I do other personality pieces for trade periodicals, usually three or four a month. Would you be interested in working with me on a couple of them at least?"

"I—" Daisy stopped herself before she could refuse, because really, why should she? She had enjoyed doing the photo shoot of Alex, and what better way to make sure her brain kept him in the "business" folder of her mind than to start filling it with other assignments, as well? "Yes," she had said. "I'd like that."

And so she had two shoots for Lauren to do before the holidays, as well.

"Go to sleep," she told Charlie now. "It will get here sooner."

"How much sooner?"

Daisy bent and kissed him good night. "You'll just have to wait and see."

Charlie made a face. But eventually he screwed his eyes shut, and Daisy, knowing that was going to be his best attempt, smiled and turned out the light. "Night, Chaz," she said softly. Then she pulled the door and went down the hall to her office where she'd be working until midnight at least.

First on the docket were the wedding photos she'd taken last night. Wednesday night weddings weren't common, but this had been a small intimate affair to which Daisy had been thrilled to be invited—and eager to take the photos.

They were her wedding present to the couple because both the bride and the groom were "hers."

Seeing Rafaela Cruz, a tech at Murphy's veterinarian's office, and Gino Martinelli, a cop who lived in Finn MacCauley's building, standing at the altar together made Daisy's heart sing for she had helped them find each other.

When she'd learned that besides being a photographer, Daisy was a matchmaker, Rafaela had said, "Huh. Not sure I believe in that."

"Some people don't," Daisy had replied. She wasn't in the market to twist anyone's arm. But Rafaela had wanted to know more because, as she said, "I don't believe there's any good men left." So Daisy had spent time talking to her, trying to discover who, beneath her bluster, Rafaela really was.

Even when she finally said she wanted to try it, Rafaela had had her doubts.

And she and Gino had definitely not been "love at first sight."

Gino, who was Rip MacCauley's soccer coach, had been badly burned in an earlier relationship. But somehow he was the one Daisy had thought of when Rafaela had challenged her to "prove there's one good man."

"Come watch him coach," Daisy had suggested.

Rafaela had dismissed the idea. "I don't want a coach. I want a husband."

"You want a patient man," Daisy said. "A man who works hard and values kids and will be there for you and your family no matter what."

"Yes, but—" Rafaela had protested.

"Maybe Gino could be that man. Unless you're afraid to try?" Daisy had challenged her right back. Then she'd turned around and challenged a reluctant Gino, too.

"She's too pretty," Gino had said. "She'll want some hotshot stud."

Daisy had just looked him up and down. "And you're not a stud?"

Gino had laughed at that. "All right. Bring her on."

They'd been cautious to the point that Daisy sometimes wanted to bang their heads together. But gradually Rafaela and Gino had faced their doubts, had given each other a shot. Had discovered in each other what Daisy had seen from early days. Over the summer they had fallen in love.

And now they were married.

Daisy's gift to them was going to be a book of photos she'd taken throughout their courtship and at their wedding. She just needed to get it finished. The pages from the courtship were done. Now she picked up the wedding invitation and set it on the flatbed scanner. It was high rag content paper, heavy and elegant.

Daisy remembered when she'd plucked it out of the mailbox right before Thanksgiving. She had stared at it, feeling an odd sinking sensation in the pit of her stomach because she hadn't thought it was Rafaela and Gino's invitation at all.

She'd thought it was Alex's.

She'd been shocked at the relief she'd felt upon opening it to discover Rafaela's and Gino's names inside.

Of course, she'd told herself logically, even if Alex had run right out and asked his perfect woman to marry him the minute he'd left her that night, they wouldn't have been sending out invitations right away.

But logic had never had much to do with anything where her relationship with Alex was concerned.

Now, taking an expansive breath, Daisy smoothed the invitation flat and lowered the lid, then pushed the scanning button.

The phone rang as it was appearing on her screen. She picked it up absently. "Daisy Connolly."

"Daisy." The voice was gruff and instantly recognizable. "I have a favor to ask."

"Alex," she said as soon as she could breathe again. "What do you want?"

"A date."

Once more Daisy's breath caught in her throat. Then she realized what he was really asking for. "I am not matchmaking for you."

"I don't want you to fix me up with a date. I want you."

I want you. She knew he didn't mean it the way it sounded. She didn't *want* him to mean it the way it sounded. But she didn't know what he did mean, either. *"What are you talking about?"*

"I need a date for Saturday night."

"Need a date?" That had to be a first.

"There's a big charity fundraising dinner and dance at the Plaza. Remember I told you I designed a new wing for a hospital? Well, I'm on the guest list—and they're giving me some plaque or something—so I have to show up. With a date."

Daisy waited a beat. "What happened to Caroline?"

"Caroline had to fly out to Hong Kong this afternoon. Unexpected breakdown of some project she'd been overseeing. She won't be back for a week. I can't show up alone. I've already committed for two. They expect me to bring someone. Head table and all that."

"Head table?"

He grunted. "So I need a replacement." And apparently in his mind it was perfectly logical that she would drop everything and accompany him to some society event in another woman's place.

Daisy focused on the wedding invitation on her screen. "Get your matchmaker to find you one."

"Can't."

"Of course you can."

"No," Alex said tersely. "I can't. Thanks to you."

That startled her. "Me? Why me?"

"Because, damn it, you're the one who told me to take it slow. 'Don't ask her to marry you yet. Get to know her,' you said. Make sure she's 'the one.'"

He'd listened?

"So I have been. It isn't easy because half the time I'm out of town or she is. But we've gone out more."

"As well you should," Daisy said firmly, still surprised that he'd done it.

"So I can't ask Amalie to find me a date, can I?" Alex said. "If I went out with someone else now—someone new—what would that say to Caroline? Not to mention that I'd be creating false expectations in whoever Amalie found."

Daisy was somewhere between dazed and amazed. "You thought of that all by yourself?" Since when had Alex put thought into the repercussions of relationships?

"Can I help it if you put ideas in my head?"

"Good for me." She grinned in spite of herself.

"So you see the problem. It has to be you."

Daisy pressed back against the desk chair she sat in and asked, "Why won't I upset Caroline?"

"She knows I need a date. I told her I was going to ask you. She'll be glad I've found an old friend to go with."

"Old friend?" Daisy echoed.

"You know what I mean. So," he went on briskly, "Saturday night. Black tie. The equivalent for you. I'll pick you up a little before eight. Where do you live?"

"What? No! Wait. I didn't agree."

"So you don't stand behind your own advice?"

Daisy opened her mouth to object, and couldn't find words to convince herself, let alone ones that would convince as stubborn a man as Alex.

"I can't," she said feebly.

"Why not?"

Because I don't have a babysitter. She didn't say that, even though it was certainly true. "I— My wardrobe doesn't run to that sort of thing."

"Get something suitable," he directed. "I'll pay for it."

"You will not. I can't—"

"Did you or did you not tell me to take my time, get to know Caroline?"

"Yes, but—" She stopped, waiting for him to cut her off, but he didn't. He waited in silence for her next reason she couldn't go. And she didn't have one—other than self-protection.

Maybe she was protesting too much. Maybe going with him would be the best self-protection there could be.

Maybe spending an evening with Alexandros Antonides, going on a date with him, would actually force her to "move on" once and for all.

Last time she'd felt like Cinderella going to the ball—and she'd believed she'd found Prince Charming. If she went now, she would go with no illusions at all.

She could even dance with him—but know it ended there—know that her happy ending was waiting at home in her life with her son.

She would be in no danger of succumbing to airy-fairy fantasies. She would enjoy the evening and come home at midnight—unlike Cinderella—with both shoes on and her heart intact.

Daisy took a breath. "Yes, all right. I'll do it."

"Great." He sounded pleased. "What's your address?"

"I'll meet you there."

Alex argued. Daisy was adamant. He said she was being silly. She said she didn't care.

"I'm not your real date. I don't need to act like one. I will see myself to the Plaza and I'll see myself home afterward."

"Daisy, that's ridic—"

"Take it or leave it."

There was a long silence, then an exasperated sigh. "Fine. Quarter to eight. Front steps of the Plaza. This Saturday. Don't be late."

She was out of her mind.

Absolutely insane.

She couldn't go out with Alex! She didn't have a babysitter. And even if she could find one, she didn't have a dress. Nor did she have a fairy godmother and some talented singing mice who could whip one up in an afternoon.

She was in a complete dither the next afternoon when Izzy and the boys stopped by for a visit after Rip's orthodontist appointment.

Izzy took one look at Daisy pacing around the kitchen and demanded, "What's the matter with you?" Her boys went running out back to play with Charlie, but Izzy stood right where she was and studied Daisy with concern.

"Nothing's wrong with me."

"Really?" Izzy's tone dripped disbelief. "You're pacing the floor. You're tearing your hair."

True, but Daisy stopped long enough to put the kettle on. "I have to go out tomorrow night. To the Plaza."

Izzy's eyes widened. "A date? At last!" She beamed and rubbed her hands together.

"Not a date! Nothing like that," Daisy said quickly. "It's business. Well, sort of business." She couldn't quite explain.

"Who with?" Izzy demanded.

"A cousin of Lukas's. An old…friend." Which was the truth, wasn't it? Alex had even called her "an old friend." "I knew him years ago. He's interested in getting married. Wanted me to matchmake for him. I said no. Now he's got a serious girlfriend, but she's out of town. So he asked me to go in her place."

It sounded quite believable to Daisy.

Izzy immediately caught the snag. "Why wouldn't you matchmake for him? I thought you loved matching people with their soul mates."

"Yes, but—" She wasn't going into what Alex thought about soul mates. "I didn't feel I knew him well enough." Daisy turned away and started rearranging the forks in her silverware drawer. A Tarzan-like yodel from the backyard turned her around in time to see Izzy's oldest son, Rip, hurtle out of the tree at the end of the garden. He and his younger brother, Crash, were Charlie's heroes.

"Mountain goats," Izzy muttered. "I can make them stop if you want."

Daisy shook her head, grateful the conversation had veered away from Alex. "It's all right. Charlie loves trying to keep up with them. And it's good for him to have them. He needs older brothers."

"Not these two." Izzy winced as Crash followed his brother's leap with one of his own. "What's he like? This cousin of Lukas's," Izzy elaborated at Daisy's blank stare. "Your 'old friend'? One of the dark handsome Antonides men, is he?"

Daisy did her best at a negligent shrug. "I guess."

"Not a wild man like Lukas, I hope."

"No. He's not like Lukas," she said. "He's very…driven."

"Is that why you're chewing your nails?"

"I'm chewing my nails because I can't find a babysitter. I already called your girls."

"Tansy and Pansy are hopeless now they're in college," Izzy agreed cheerfully. "They have lives." She sighed. "But no worries. I'll keep him."

Daisy blinked. "You will? Are you sure?"

"Absolutely. If you don't mind me having him at our place." Izzy picked up the kettle and began pouring boiling water because Daisy wasn't doing it. "He can even spend the night. In case you don't want to turn into a pumpkin right after the Plaza." She grinned.

Daisy flushed and shook her head. "Not a chance. I am a pumpkin. Home before midnight. This is not a date. But Charlie would love to go to your place, if you're sure."

Izzy waved a hand airily. "I'll never notice he's there." She zeroed back in. "What are you wearing?"

"That's my other problem," Daisy admitted. Nothing in her wardrobe lent itself to upscale fundraisers at the Plaza. And despite his brusque "Get something. I'll pay for it," she had no intention of allowing herself to feel beholden to Alex.

Izzy was thoughtfully silent for a long moment. Then, "I might have something," she said, looking Daisy up and down assessingly. "Ichiro Sorrento," she said.

"What?"

"That new designer whose collection Finn shot last year. Japanese-Italian. You remember him?"

Daisy did. But she shook her head. "No way I can afford anything with his label."

"You don't have to. You can wear mine. Remember that gorgeous dress and jacket I wore to Finn's opening last spring?"

Daisy's eyes widened. "*That* dress?" The dress had been a deep-sapphire-blue silk, spare and elegant, with an exquisitely embroidered jacket in the same deep blues, emerald-green and hints of violet. "You don't want me wearing your gorgeous dress. I'd spill something on it."

"I already have. It doesn't show," Izzy said cheerfully.

"I'm taller than you are."

"Everyone is taller than I am," Izzy countered. "So what? You'll just show more leg. I doubt anyone will mind. Especially—" she grinned "—not a male Antonides."

"Not. A. Date," Daisy reiterated firmly. "I'm not trying to show off my legs."

"Of course not. But you're not a nun, either. You need to knock Mr. Driven Antonides's socks off. Make him forget all about his serious girlfriend and run off to Vegas with you!"

It was as if a little devil called Izzy was sitting on her shoulder tempting her. "Dream on," Daisy scoffed.

"A little dreaming never hurt anyone," Izzy retorted.

Daisy let her have the last word.

But in her heart she begged to differ.

Where the hell was she?

Dozens of hired cars and limos and taxis slid up to the Plaza's entrance Saturday evening while Alex stood on the steps, shifting from one foot to the other, watching and waiting. There were snowflakes in the air. Alex could see his breath, and his shoulders were getting damp as the snow melted, but he couldn't bring himself to go inside and wait and pace.

There were scores of black-tie-clad men and elegantly dressed women getting out of taxis and limos—and not one of them was Daisy.

He'd told her quarter to eight. It was almost ten after. He'd got here early, to be sure he was here when she arrived, and she was nowhere to be seen.

He should never have given in to her demand that she come on her own, that he neither pick her up nor take her home after. He'd agreed only because she would have refused to come otherwise. The sweet and malleable Daisy he had known five years ago might still be somewhere inside this Daisy Connolly, but he hadn't caught a glimpse of her in a long, long time.

Was this her revenge? Was standing him up payback for

his having said he wasn't interested in marriage all those years ago?

He shouldn't have asked her to come. It was a damn fool idea. When Caroline had said she couldn't make it, but suggested he invite his friend Daisy, he'd been surprised.

"My friend Daisy?" he'd echoed, puzzled.

Caroline had shrugged. "I assume she's your friend. You talk about her all the time."

Did he? Surely not. But he could hardly deny their friendship if it came across that way to Caroline because how could he justify talking about her if she wasn't a friend? What would Caroline think if he said she wasn't a friend at all, she was…a thorn in his side, an itch he never quite managed to get rid of. Like poison ivy, perhaps.

So he'd shrugged and told Caroline he'd ask. And, hell, why not? He could prove to Daisy that he'd listened, that he hadn't gone straight home and asked Caroline to marry him. He'd done what Daisy suggested and got to know her.

He hadn't fallen in love with her. That wasn't going to happen. He knew it. Caroline knew it.

They had seen each other as often as their schedules allowed. They always had a good time. Relationship-wise they were on the same page—and perfectly happy to be there. And if they still hadn't managed to make it to bed together, well, the time had never been right.

She'd had an early meeting or he was flying off to Paris. She was in Rio or he was in Vancouver. It had nothing to do with memories of Daisy in his bed. She hadn't been in this bed.

Only in his bedroom. And the fact that he couldn't forget that was still driving him nuts.

"Alex!" A hearty booming voice from the doorway startled him back to the present—back to the lack of Daisy anywhere in sight. He turned to see Tom Holcomb, the hospital's vice president in charge of building development.

Tom was grinning broadly, holding out a hand to shake.

"Good to see you. Big night for you." He pumped Alex's hand, then looked around. "Where's your date?"

Alex opened his mouth, hoping that a suitable polite reply would come out when, all of a sudden, from behind a hand caught his.

"Sorry," Daisy said, catching her breath.

Alex turned his head, saw her smiling up at him, and felt his heart do some sort of triple axel in his chest. There was a glow to her cheeks, as if she'd been running, but she was smiling.

And so was he. His heart which, after the triple axel, had seemed to stop all together as he looked at her, began beating again. "About time," he said gruffly, swallowing his relief. She was gorgeous. She wore a long black wool dress coat and he could barely get a glimpse of the dress beneath it, but what he could see seemed to sparkle—just as Daisy did. Her eyes were alight, electric almost, taking in everything. She'd pinned her hair up in some sort of intricate knot which reminded him of the way she'd worn it at the wedding when he'd met her. He remembered taking it down, running his fingers through it. Felt a quickening in his body at the temptation to do it again now. It was, after all, already slightly askew, as if she had been running.

"My cab got stuck in traffic. Think I stood you up?" She laughed.

"No." He wiped damp palms down the sides of his trousers. He wasn't admitting anything.

"Your date, I presume?"

Alex was suddenly conscious of Tom Holcomb still standing beside him, looking with interest at Daisy.

Alex nodded and drew her forward. "This is Daisy Connolly. Daisy, Tom Holcomb. He is the VP in charge of building development, the man I worked with on the hospital design."

"The man who rubber-stamped his terrific ideas," Tom

corrected, shaking the hand Daisy offered. "I'm delighted to meet you. Are you an architect, too?"

"No. A photographer," Daisy said, shaking the hand he held out. "I recently did a photo shoot of Alex at a building he restored in Brooklyn."

"A man of many talents," Tom agreed. He drew Daisy with him into the hotel, asking questions about her own work which she answered, still smiling. And Daisy, with a glance back at Alex, went with him.

Alex stood watching, bemused, and somehow a little dazed.

Dazed by Daisy. Dazzling Daisy, he thought, smiling wryly at his own foolishness. But it was true. And he didn't mind following, it gave him a chance to admire her from another angle.

From any angle tonight she was elegant, sophisticated, tailored, stylish. She would never be the stunning classical beauty that Caroline was. Daisy's nose still had a spattering of freckles, her cheekbones were not quite as sharply pronounced. Her mouth was less sculpted than impish. And you could never say that Daisy had every hair in place.

But everything about her was alive—from her unruly hair to her lively sparkling eyes to her kissable lips.

Alex tried not to think about her kissable lips. It wasn't as if he was going to be tasting them again this evening. Furthermore, he reminded himself, he shouldn't even want to. He was this close to buying Caroline an engagement ring.

But Caroline's kisses had never intoxicated him. They'd never made him hot and hard and hungry in a matter of an instant. He'd lost every bit of his common sense that weekend with Daisy—and she hadn't had any at all.

There had never been anything cool, calm and collected about her. She was a lead-with-her-heart, damn-the-torpedoes, full-speed-ahead sort of woman.

Basically the anti-Caroline. And Caroline was what he wanted.

Wasn't she?

"Are you coming?"

Alex jerked his brain back into gear to see that Tom had disappeared into the hotel, but that Daisy was still standing at the top of the stairs by the revolving door, waiting.

"Got distracted. Sorry." He bounded up the steps, feeling awkward, caught out. And feeling that way, he challenged her. "Been running?" he asked her gruffly.

"I told you," she said with some asperity. "The cab was caught in traffic. I left it in the middle of Columbus Circle."

"You *walked* from Columbus Circle?" Wide-eyed he stared at her high pointy-toed heels.

"No," she said flatly. "I ran."

Definitely the anti-Caroline. Alex shook his head, dazed and amazed, and unable to keep from grinning. "Of course you did."

Daisy glared, her eyes flashing. "You said not to be late!"

"So I did." His grin widened briefly, then he met her gaze. "Thank you."

Their eyes locked. And Alex felt the electricity arc between them exactly the way it always did. It didn't seem to matter that she was all wrong for him. He jerked his gaze away from hers, but it only went as far as her lips. Nervously she licked them.

Alex's body went on full alert.

Daisy tore her gaze away. "It sounded like the sort of occasion where it wouldn't do to waltz in late," she said, a little ragged edge to her voice. "Not if you're at the head table."

She was right, of course. He was being a fool—again.

Impatient with his own weakness, Alex gestured her brusquely into the revolving door. "Well, let's not waste your sacrifice, then. We'll go in."

Daisy was in complete control.

She might as well have had a squadron of singing mice and a fairy godmother the way everything had fallen into place. Izzy was keeping Charlie, the glitzy shimmery dress fit perfectly, the sophisticated black dress coat her mother had given her for her birthday was beautifully appropriate. Other than the stupid traffic jam and having to run quarter of a mile and that she could feel her hair slipping from its knot, she didn't have a care in the world.

Granted her first glimpse of Alex in formal attire, complete with black tie, pristine white shirt, checking his watch impatiently as he waited for her, had made her mouth dry and her heart gallop. But, Daisy assured herself, that was because she'd just been running, not because of the man himself.

Still, once in the hotel, on the arm of the handsomest man in the room, it was hard not to believe she was channeling Cinderella.

Daisy had been to the Plaza before. But she'd never been to An Event.

This was An Event—in a cavernous room that despite its immensity, managed somehow to seem warm and appealing and elegant with matte gold walls, burgundy drapes, glimmering sconces and crystal chandeliers. The dozens of tables wore pristine white damask linens, sported napkins folded by origami experts, and had settings of gleaming china and rows of delicate stemware.

Not a bowl of mac and cheese in sight.

When she worked for Finn, Daisy had gone to plenty of glitz-and-glamour events. In the fashion industry they'd been brasher and flashier, not to mention, thousands of decibels louder than this one. A girl from small town Colorado had been very much out of her league. But after the first half dozen or so, she had become blasé and soon she began waltzing through them without batting an eyelash.

Of course those rarely required her to look suave and elegant and remember which fork to use. Tonight there looked to be a surfeit of forks. But it wasn't the number of forks that was making her blood race. It was Alex.

"Can I get you something to drink? Wine? A cocktail?"

"I'll have a glass of wine," Daisy decided. "Red."

They'd drunk a smooth dark burgundy when they'd first

met. If she was going to rewrite the ending of their encounter, she would begin tonight the way they'd begun before. But this time she wouldn't let herself embroider the circumstances with airy-fairy fantasies of happily ever afters.

"Burgundy," Alex said, surprising her. Did he remember? But she couldn't—wouldn't—ask.

"I'll be right back." He headed toward the bar.

When he returned, drinks in hand, Daisy was standing near the wall right where Alex had left her. She drew his eye clear across the room. The dress he'd glimpsed before she'd shed her coat definitely lived up to its promise. Its blue-green iridescence sparkled like northern lights as it molded her every curve. The short embroidered jacket covered more than he wished, hinting at bare shoulders beneath, smooth shoulders he remembered kissing all too well.

But it was more than the dress that drew his gaze, more than the dress that made the woman. There was a warmth and a vibrant energy in Daisy—as if she were the only person there in three dimensions. Everyone else seemed flat by comparison.

She had been alone when he'd left her, but now she was chatting with hospital CEO Douglas Standish and his wife. Daisy's expression was animated, interested. He remembered her that way from the moment he'd first seen her. She engaged with people, drew them out. She had drawn him.

Never particularly social, Alex had attended the wedding with the intent of leaving as soon as it was reasonable to do so. He'd drifted around the periphery of the room, keeping his eye on the exit—until he'd seen Daisy.

Then he'd only had eyes for her. It was still that way.

Now he wound his way through the crowds of people, heading toward her as determinedly as he had that long-ago day.

"Here you go." He handed the drink to Daisy, then turned to Standish's wife. "May I get you a drink?"

"No, thank you, dear. Douglas will do that. I just wanted to meet your lovely lady—and tell her how lovely you are—"

her eyes twinkled merrily when Alex opened his mouth to protest "—and what an amazing gift you've given us with the design for the hospital wing."

"Thank you for saying so."

She patted him on the sleeve. "Have a wonderful evening. You deserve it. So nice to meet you, dear," she said to Daisy, before taking her husband's arm and guiding them into the crowd.

"So," Daisy said, looking him in the eye when the other woman had left, "you're the guest of honor. And you couldn't be bothered to tell me?"

Alex shrugged. "It's no big deal."

Daisy's eyes glittered. "It's a huge deal," she contradicted him. "Huge. Apparently your hospital wing has broken new ground in patient services. It's celebrated worldwide." She had gone beyond glitter to glare now. "They're giving you an award."

"I told you that when you did the photos for the article."

"An award, you said. You didn't tell me anything about it. It might have been for perfect attendance at meetings for all I knew! This is wonderful!" And now her wonderful eyes sparkled with warmth and delight, and in spite of himself, Alex felt a rush of pleasure. "Did you tell Caroline?"

"No," he said, surprised.

"Why not?"

He shrugged. "It's nothing to do with her."

"Of course it is!"

Baffled, he shook his head. "Why?" She hadn't done anything. He hadn't even known her when he'd done it himself.

"Because *you* did it! Because you're her man."

But he *wasn't* Caroline's man. He wasn't anyone's man. But he wasn't going to have that argument with Daisy now. Fortunately people were beginning to head to their seats. So he just said, "Come on. We need to go sit down." He took her arm, more aware of touching her than he was whenever he touched Caroline. He led her to the table where they would be sitting, then pulled out her chair.

Daisy flounced down into it, but she still wasn't done. She looked up at him, her expression annoyed. "She'd be thrilled," she told him. "And proud. I am—proud," she said, "and it's nothing at all to do with me."

Alex felt a warm flush of pleasure at her admitting that. What he didn't do was tell her that it wasn't entirely true.

He would never have taken the commission at all if something she'd said to him hadn't stuck with him for the past five years. Initially he'd said no. He had no interest in hospital design. He didn't like hospitals. Hated them, in fact.

After his brother had got leukemia, Alex had spent far too much time in hospitals watching his brother suffer and become more and more remote. It had devastated him. Even now Alex associated hospitals with the most painful period of his life.

After Vass's death, Alex had never set foot in one again. Even when he broke his arm playing lacrosse in college, he'd insisted on having it set at a doctor's office. "No hospital," he'd said firmly. It was the last place he wanted to be.

He didn't talk about hospitals, either. Didn't talk about Vass. Never had to anyone. Except that weekend when Daisy had got under his skin.

He supposed it was because she was just getting her equilibrium back after losing her father. Barely fifty, he'd been born with a heart defect that had grown worse over time. He'd been in and out of the hospital often, she'd said. And the sad wistful look on her face had prompted Alex to confide that he, too, hated hospitals.

"They take away your life," he'd said harshly, remembering how remote and sterile they had seemed, how they'd isolated his brother, how Vass had wanted to come home so badly, to be out, to be anywhere but there. "They don't save it."

He'd expected her to agree.

Instead she'd shaken her head. "It wasn't the hospital's fault. Without the care my dad got there, we'd have lost him sooner.

But it was hard for him to feel connected. He felt so isolated, like he wasn't really a part of things anymore."

Vass had said the same thing.

"There was only one window," she'd gone on. "But he couldn't see outside from his bed. So we used to pretend. We'd close our eyes and pretend he was home or we were going fishing in the San Juan or even doing chores, chopping wood for the fireplace. He loved that fireplace..." Daisy had swallowed then, and her eyes had glistened with unshed tears. She'd blinked them back rapidly. "It wasn't the hospital's fault," she repeated. "But it could have been better. It could have been more."

Her words had made Alex think.

What if Vass had had a chance to spend time in a hospital that had allowed him to feel connected. What if he'd been able to do, at least virtually, the things he wanted to do—like go back to the beach near their island home, or drive a race car, or sail over the Alps in a hot-air balloon?

Once Alex opened the floodgates, the ideas wouldn't stop coming. And what hadn't been possible twenty-five to thirty years ago was within reach now.

Alex's hospital wing was full of windows—floor-to-ceiling in many rooms. Even treatment rooms, wherever possible, brought the outside in. If a patient wanted to see the world beyond the walls, he could. The semirural setting just across the river north of the city provided views of the countryside as well as the city skyline. And it wasn't just about the visuals. Alex worked in sound systems and even olfactory ones, connecting senses to the world beyond the hospital's confines.

He had provided virtual worlds, as well. Patients in the wing he'd designed could close their eyes as Daisy's father had, but they could also use modern electronics to create the sights, sounds and smells of the seashore, the woods, the inside of a race car or the ballroom of a fairy-tale palace.

He told her about it now, aware of the way she looked at him, as if he could hang the moon. The salads that had been in front of them when they'd sat down remained virtually untouched.

"It sounds like an amazing place." Daisy smiled, a smile that went all the way to her eyes, that touched—as it always did—a place hidden somewhere deep inside him that no one ever reached but her.

He cleared his throat. "If you have to be in a hospital," he agreed gruffly, "if you can't have what the rest of the world takes for granted, I guess it will do."

Their eyes met. And Alex knew that whether or not he mentioned his brother or her father, Daisy remembered. Daisy knew.

What surprised him, though, was her withdrawal. One minute she'd been gazing at him with warmth and admiration. The next some shadow seemed to settle over her, her expression shuttered.

"I'm sure that all the children will appreciate it." Her tone was polite, but she seemed suddenly more remote. She turned to her salad and began to eat.

Alex was more nettled by her withdrawal than he would have liked. But really, what difference did it make? He hadn't done it for her. He'd done it for people like her father, his brother. He dug into his own salad.

Neither of them spoke until the salads were taken away and the entree was set before them. Then Daisy turned toward him again. "What sort of building are you working on now?"

So they were going to be polite and proper and distant. Fine by him. Alex was glad to talk about the present so he told her about the office building he was designing on the edge of Paris.

Daisy had never been to Paris. And as he talked, he saw her eyes begin to sparkle again. Her remoteness vanished. Her questions came more quickly, and her enthusiasm was contagious. He wanted to make her smile, wanted to have her cock her head and listen eagerly. Alex found himself telling her not just about his work in Paris, but about the city itself, about places he liked, things he'd seen, galleries he visited, buildings he admired.

"You used to live there, didn't you?" It was the first time she'd alluded to the past.

"Yes. And then I was here for a while. But I went back four or five years ago," he said. He knew precisely when he'd gone—and why. After the disastrous end to his weekend with Daisy, New York had more memories than he wanted. Paris seemed like a far safer place to be.

It was only in the past six months or so—when he'd made up his mind to marry, in fact—that he'd returned to live more or less permanently in New York. Even now, though, he kept his small flat in the fifth arrondissement.

Their talk moved from Paris to the Riviera, to other places he'd been. Daisy asked about all of them. The women Amalie had set him up with had asked questions, too, but not like Daisy. Not as if they cared about the answers.

Daisy did. And her interest and enthusiasm drew him out. He would have liked to show her Paris, to walk the wide boulevards and narrow lanes with her, to sit at a tiny table in an outdoor café and drink strong dark coffee with her, to wander through the museums and the galleries hand in hand with her, to walk along the Seine with her and kiss her there, to run through a rainstorm with her.

To take her back to his little garret flat and make love with her. He could imagine Daisy there, letting him strip off her little embroidered jacket, then letting him find the zip at the back of her dress and lower it slowly. He'd kiss his way down—inch by luscious inch and—

"And what?" Daisy was looking at him, curious and impatient.

Hot. God, he was hot. And hard. And suddenly aware that he was in the middle of a crowded room with the object of his fantasy studying him worriedly. Her eyes were still bright and eager, but she was looking at him with puzzlement.

"What happened? You stopped talking," Daisy said. "Did you just get distracted?"

Alex's heart was still hammering, his body still feeling the effects of what he'd been thinking about—her. He shifted in his chair and cleared his throat. "I did, yes." He gave a quick shake of his head. "Sorry about that."

He didn't let it happen again, even though he was still intensely aware of her. It was almost a relief when dinner ended. Except then the speeches began, and Alex knew he would have to say something when the award was presented.

Public speaking wasn't his forte. He preferred to speak with his work, with his design, with his buildings, not his words.

But when the time came, Daisy clapped madly and beamed at him encouragingly when Douglas Standish beckoned him to the podium to accept his award.

Alex made it brief. He gripped the podium and stared into the bright lights as he thanked the hospital board who had given him the opportunity to design the wing and the committee who had given him the award. It was what he had prepared, and it was all he had intended to say.

But before he could walk away, his gaze slid across the hundreds of people in the room and, looking down, he didn't see the lights. He saw Daisy.

His mouth went dry at the sight of her upturned face, at her avid expression, her tantalizing smile. And he didn't walk away. He looked at her, spoke to her.

His voice was less stilted and more ragged as he said, "I hope this wing makes a difference to the patients. I hope it gives them the safe haven they need to get well and—" he paused, his eyes still locked with hers "—the connections to the world outside to keep them strong."

Like your father never had. Like my brother never had. And you're the only one who knows why I did it.

He could see that in her eyes, the realization dawning, her lips parting in a silent O.

Alex jerked his gaze away and abruptly shut his mouth.

Then, clutching the award in a sweaty hand, he said hoarsely, "Thank you all," and strode back to his chair and sat down.

His heart was crashing in his chest. He didn't look at Daisy. He didn't have to. He could sense her eyes on him. The awareness, the emotion vibrated between them. So damn much emotion it felt like being swept off by a tidal wave. He kept his gaze resolutely on the platform where Douglas was coming back to speak.

With a few brief words he thanked Alex again, then thanked all the hospital's staff and benefactors for their support. Then the doors opened to the adjoining ballroom and the small live orchestra just beyond those doors began to play.

People stood up, couples headed toward the dance floor. Alex breathed again.

Abruptly he stood and held out a hand. "Let's dance."

CHAPTER SEVEN

PUTTING her hand in his was like touching a live wire.

A current of electricity seemed to flow between them, one even stronger than the flickering awareness she'd felt all night.

Daisy was aware of the pressure of Alex's strong fingers wrapping around hers as he led her through the doors and onto the dance floor. But it was nothing compared to her awareness when he took her in his arms.

She almost stumbled against him as she tried to do the opposite and keep a respectable distance between them. It was a battle because every instinct in her went to him like a moth to the proverbial flame.

Every touch was memorable. His fingers encased hers warmly. She was exquisitely aware of his hand pressing lightly at the small of her back. She was close enough that she could catch a faint hint of soap and aftershave. And a quick glance showed her how smooth-shaven his jaw was. She remembered it rougher, had loved to stroke her hand over it, stubbled one way, smooth the other.

Abruptly she turned her head, trying to follow his lead at the same time and nearly tripped over his foot. He caught her, pulled her closer. And Daisy knew the sensation of her body melting into his, as if she belonged there, wrapped in his arms.

She had danced with lots of other men. She had felt other men's hands on her body. None—not even Cal's—evoked such strong reactions.

Even now, knowing he was not for her, knowing for a fact that she and Alex had no future, Daisy could not deny that Alex's touch, Alex's smile, Alex's gaze brought to life something inside her that no other man's ever had.

Dancing with Alex was, just as it had been five years ago, the Cinderella experience that Daisy had remembered.

She understood now how she had been swept away by it. There was a feeling of rightness, of perfect understanding, that she'd never had with anyone else. And it scared her to feel it again and know how wrong it had been.

She forced herself to remain clearheaded and sane. She looked away from his hard jaw to study the room, determined to commit it to memory. She focused on the music, tried to think of the title, the composer, to isolate the instruments. And all the while she was aware of the man who held her in his arms.

His breath teased the tendrils of her hair. His trouser-clad legs brushed the silk of her dress. And every touch, every brush set off a hum of something electric. And the study of the room and the music and everything else faded away.

It was all right, she told herself. Nothing was going to happen on a dance floor. He couldn't sweep her off her feet. She couldn't slide a hand between the buttons of his shirt.

So where was the harm in appreciating the feel of hard muscles under her fingertips? Why not give in, just for the moment, to the instinctive rhythm they seemed to engage in when they moved to the music? As long as she didn't allow herself to remember the instinctive rhythm they'd brought to their lovemaking...

There was a point beyond which lay foolishness. Daisy had been there once. Never again.

Careful, she warned herself. Be careful.

But her head turned and so did his. Her lips brushed his jaw. His touched her ear. A shiver ran from the hairs on her neck to the tips of her toes. Her body trembled. Her knees wobbled. And deep in the center of her, something ached with the desire she refused to admit.

She took a breath. "So," she said, "tell me about Caroline."

She was gratified when Alex seemed briefly to stumble. But then he caught himself and without even looking directly at him, she saw his jaw ease as if he were smiling.

"Caroline is amazing," he said. "She's quick. Witty. Beautiful."

His voice was warm, animated. Of course it was. Caroline was his woman. *Remember that,* Daisy told herself sharply and kept asking him Caroline-related questions.

Maybe it was masochistic. Maybe it was just the only way to keep her common sense. Whatever it was, it helped. Daisy made herself listen as he told her all about the ad campaign Caroline was developing that had taken her to Hong Kong. Alex told her about how Caroline had been headhunted by five different companies in the past two years.

"She's amazingly successful. Definitely making her mark. She's even thinking she might go out on her own in the next couple of years." He clearly approved of her ambition and her talent. Daisy forced herself to think about that and not about the way his legs brushed against hers.

"So what are you waiting for if she's so wonderful?" She ventured a glance at his face, wanting to see his expression.

A tiny crease appeared between his brows. The muscles in his shoulder tensed beneath her hand, and hard green eyes looked down into hers. "I thought you weren't in favor of quick decisions these days," he said sharply.

"Yes, well, I'm not you."

Alex grunted. He didn't say anything else. Didn't answer. Didn't talk about Caroline anymore, either.

Daisy tried to stifle her irritation. She told herself it didn't matter, but for some reason it did. It would be easier if he were engaged. Easier to stop thinking about how damned appealing he still was.

Well, fine, if he wouldn't help her out by talking about

Caroline, she'd talk about the pulmonologist whose photos she'd taken for Lauren Nicols.

"I have to thank you for sending Lauren my way," she said. She didn't really want to be beholden to him. But it was her own work that had caused Lauren to call, nothing he'd done. So she talked about that. And Alex seemed grateful enough to take up that topic of conversation. Then the dance was over, and Douglas Standish asked to partner her for the next one.

She danced with half a dozen men, and only reaffirmed that no one's touch affected her the way Alex's did. She seemed to be aware of him—where he was, who he was dancing with—even when he was nowhere near. Actually though, he always seemed to be somewhere fairly near. Wherever her partners danced her, Alex was never far away.

She tried not to look at him, tried not to envy the women he held in his arms, tried not to gauge if he had held them as closely as he'd held her. But she couldn't help noticing that while he danced and chatted with them, his gaze often sought her.

It didn't mean anything. It couldn't.

But she couldn't quite stifle the gratification she felt every time she felt his eyes on her. She didn't dare catch his eye, though. It would be playing with fire. And Daisy had no intention of playing with fire, though there seemed to be one kindling somewhere just south of her midsection, and every time she looked his way, the fire grew.

The evening passed quickly. It was nine-thirty. Ten. Then nearly eleven. They danced. They visited with people Alex had worked with. They danced again. And this time the flames burned even hotter than before.

His eyes seemed to bore into hers whenever she looked at him. Their legs brushed. Their bodies touched. Against her breasts, she could feel the beat of his heart. With everyone else they spoke easily, casually. But when they danced, they had little to say to each other, and the conflagration continued to build.

It wasn't yet midnight, not even eleven-thirty. But Daisy knew she needed to be sensible. While she wouldn't turn into a pumpkin at midnight, and Izzy was keeping Charlie until the morning, a woman could stand just so much temptation.

But one more dance wouldn't hurt, she thought as the music began again and, wordlessly, Alex drew her once more into his arms. They hadn't danced with each other two dances in a row. But it seemed natural now. Right.

Inevitable.

Just as, inevitably, in a few minutes she would say thank-you for a nice evening and take her leave.

But now—just for a few moments more, Daisy allowed herself the luxury of lingering close to him, to luxuriate in the warmth and the nearness of his body, to relish the shiver she felt at his warm breath against her hair.

It's all right, she assured herself. It's just now. Just this moment. Not forever. She had no expectations this time. She was only making memories that would last her through the years.

Her body trembled. Vibrated. Particularly her hip.

Her hip? For a moment she didn't know what was happening. The vibration stopped, thank God. But almost instantly, it started again.

Daisy stumbled, realizing that this vibration had nothing to do with the nearness of Alex and everything to do with the tiny mobile phone she'd tucked into the on-seam pocket of the dress.

"You won't need it," Izzy had said.

But Daisy had insisted. Most glitzy high-fashion dresses clung so tightly that anything more than underwear—and sometimes even that—was too much. But Izzy's gorgeous kicky swirly dress flared at the hips, and Daisy had put her phone into one of its tiny pockets.

"Just in case," she'd said, patting it.

"Suit yourself. I won't be calling you," Izzy had vowed.

But someone was calling her now.

Alex caught her when she stumbled. "What's wrong?"

"It's my phone."

His brows drew together. "Your *phone*? Who the hell do you need to talk to tonight?"

Daisy didn't answer that. "Sorry." She shrugged, half apologetic, half worried as she slipped out of his arms and moved to the edge of the dance floor. "I have to get this."

Alex followed her. "One of your clients out on a hot date and need advice?" he growled.

Daisy glanced at the caller ID. It was Izzy. She answered at once. "Is it Charlie? What happened? What's wrong?"

"He's fine," Izzy said quickly. She sounded as out of breath as Daisy felt. "Well, not entirely fine. But nothing life-threatening. Really. Don't panic."

"What *happened*?" Daisy pressed the phone hard against her ear, trying to hear above the music.

"He was following Rip," Izzy reported ruefully. "Doing what the big boys do. They were climbing on the bunk beds. Rip has this notion that he can move all around their bedroom without touching the floor—"

"Oh, God."

"Well, he can," Izzy admitted. "Of course he's bigger than Charlie. He has longer arms and legs. More wingspan."

Daisy didn't need to have it spelled out. "Oh, God," she said again, knees wobbling.

"Charlie's a pretty impressive climber," Izzy said with the calm that came from having got sons through the first decade of their adventurous lives. "And jumper— but he didn't quite make it to the top of the chair from Rip's bunk. He's broken his arm. I'm so sorry, Daisy. I feel terrible. I—"

"Where is he? St. Luke's?"

"Yes. Finn's taking him. We're on a first-name basis with the emergency room staff."

"I'll meet him there." Daisy was already headed for the nearest exit so she could grab her coat and then a cab.

"I'm so sorry," Izzy repeated. "And Rip is devastated."

"Tell him not to worry. I'm sure it will be fine." She just needed to get there. Now.

"I feel so responsible. Or, as Finn says, irresponsible."

"Don't. It's not your fault."

"It is. I forget how much younger Charlie is. Call me as soon as you've seen him. Promise?"

"I promise." Daisy stuffed the phone back into her pocket and headed for the cloak room.

"What is it? What happened?"

Dear God, she'd forgotten about Alex!

Daisy shot him a quick glance and apologetic smile over her shoulder. "I— It's…an emergency. A friend…" She gave a vague wave of her hand as she skirted around groups of people in the foyer. "I'm sorry. I have to go."

"I figured that out," Alex said gruffly. "Not a client."

"No."

"Your ex?" he bit out.

Daisy blinked at him. "What?"

"Guess not. A new boyfriend?" His gaze narrowed. When she didn't answer, it narrowed further. "Did you tell him you were coming out with me?"

There were no answers to anything he was likely to ask now. "I need to go, Alex," she repeated, then forced herself to stop and face him squarely, even managing to paste a smile on her face. "Thank you for this evening. I enjoyed it."

"I did, too," he said, a grim set to his mouth. Then he stepped around her to present the claim check for her coat to the lady behind the desk.

"Thank you. You don't have to wait. I'll just catch a cab."

He didn't reply. But he didn't leave, either. And moments later, when the lady brought her coat and she reached for it, Alex was there first, shaking it out and holding it so she could slip it on.

"Thank you." As the coat settled on her shoulders, Daisy flicked a grateful smile in his general direction. "I'm sorry to run off. I did have a lovely evening." She paused, hoping he'd say, *Of course, I understand. Thank you for coming.* Then, niceties observed, she could dart away.

He said, "I'll come with you."

"No! I mean, no, thank you. It's not necessary. Really, Alex. I mean it," she said when she saw his jaw tighten. "Thank you for everything, but I'll say good-night here." There was a moment's silence. Then, not knowing what else to do, she thrust out a hand for him to shake.

He looked at it as if she'd offered him a poisonous snake.

Hastily Daisy withdrew it. "Good night, Alex." And without giving him time to reply she turned and darted out of the hotel to catch a cab.

He should just let her walk away and get on with his life.

It was clearly what she wanted. Whatever the hell she was doing, dropping everything and running off at the drop of a hat, it wasn't any of his business.

Alex knew that.

She didn't want him there. He knew that, too.

But he couldn't let her go and face whatever the hell she was about to face when the mere thought of it turned her white-faced and stricken.

So what if it was a boyfriend? Once he saw that she was all right, he'd leave her to it. To him—the boyfriend. Though he couldn't help grinding his teeth at the thought.

The cab he'd grabbed outside the Plaza took a right on Fifty-seventh and headed west. It was Saturday night in midtown, and the traffic was bumper-to-bumper traffic. The theaters had just disgorged people by the hundreds onto the streets. Progress was excruciatingly slow.

He should have just followed her straight out the door. But she'd got a head start on him, and then Standish had called his name. There was no way to pretend he hadn't heard, and impossible to be impolite and brush the older man off—not without being able to offer a convincing excuse.

And what was he going to say? "My date had to rush to

the hospital because she thinks her ex-husband...or maybe her boyfriend...or some guy she knows called Charlie needs her?"

Damn it. Didn't she have any pride?

He glared out at the traffic, willing it to move. At least Standish had told him where St. Luke's was. It wasn't that close to Daisy's office, though perhaps it was near where she actually lived.

He didn't even *know* where she lived. Something else she hadn't shared with him. And something else to fume about until the driver dropped him off outside the emergency services department and sped away.

Facing it, Alex's feet suddenly felt rooted to the pavement.

He didn't do hospitals. Of course he'd been in and out of the hospital he'd designed the wing for. But he'd never been in it other than for work. He'd never been in a hospital for anything resembling a medical reason—for anyone—since the day Vass died. Everything in him wanted to walk away.

Only the memory of Daisy's stricken face made him take a breath, then another deep one, and stride straight in.

It was a zoo. There were people everywhere, sitting, standing, crying, bleeding, filling out forms.

Not one of them was Daisy.

Alex stood by the door, cracking his knuckles. He didn't even know who to ask for. Charlie Somebody.

Hell, he didn't even know the guy's last name. He got in line anyway. Maybe he'd spot her before he had to come up with a name.

He was two cases from the desk when he heard the sound of her voice. His head jerked around, his heart lurched at the sight of her drawn pale face.

She stood in the doorway of one of the examining rooms, her expression intent as she listened to a white-coated doctor. Whatever he said, she nodded, still looking fragile. The doctor patted her arm, then went into the room. Daisy started to go after him.

Alex went after her. "Daisy!"

She jerked as if she'd been shot. Then she spun around, white as a sheet.

He started to go to her, but instead she hurried toward him. "What are you doing here?" Her voice was thready, strained.

He just looked at her. "You're here."

She swallowed. Something shuttered in her gaze. "You don't need to be here."

"You look like hell."

"Thank you so much."

He moved closer. She moved back until he'd cornered her between a chair and the wall. Then he put a hand on her arm so she couldn't pull away. "I came to see if I could help, Daisy."

She shook her head almost fiercely. "I don't need your help. I told you that. It'll be all right."

"Charlie will," he clarified, needing to see her reaction to his name. He tried to keep his voice even, nonjudgmental, but he didn't like it when she flinched.

Her jaw tightened. Her fingers knotted.

"Is it bad?" he asked. He didn't want the guy to die, for heaven's sake. He just didn't want Daisy dropping everything to race across the city for him.

"He has a broken arm."

"A broken arm?" Alex almost laughed with relief at the same time he felt a surge of annoyance. "All this hysteria for a broken arm?"

"I'm not hysterical!" Daisy said indignantly. There was color in her cheeks again.

He couldn't help grinning. "No? Taking a phone call in the middle of a dance? Rushing out of the hotel? For a broken arm?"

"I apologized," Daisy said tightly. She hugged her arms across her chest. "You didn't have to come. I certainly didn't invite you!"

"I thought he might be dying. You looked devastated. I didn't want you to have to face it alone."

Something flickered across her features. She hesitated for

a moment, as if she was giving him the benefit of the doubt. Then she nodded. "That was kind of you. Thank you. But it really wasn't necessary." She straightened, pulled her arm out of his grasp, and gave him what he supposed was a dismissive smile. "It will be fine. *He* will be. I just… Maybe I overreacted. Don't worry. No one's going to die. Now, please excuse me." She tried to slip around him.

But Alex was in no mood to be dismissed and he blocked her way. "Who is he, Daisy?"

She didn't answer. He didn't think she was going to. But then a nurse poked her head out of the examination room. "Mrs. Connolly, Charlie's asking for you. Doctor is going to put the cast on now."

Once more Daisy started to move away, but Alex caught her arm. "He's *asking* for you?" he said mockingly. "To what? Hold his hand?"

Her teeth came together. Her eyes flashed. "Maybe. He's a little boy," she snapped, her eyes flashing anger. "He's my son."

Her *son*? Daisy had a *son*?

But before he could do more than reel at her words, Daisy had jerked her arm away, cut around him and stalked back into the examination room. The door shut behind her with a resounding bang.

A dozen people stopped talking and looked around in surprise.

Alex felt as if he'd been punched. *Where the hell did she get a son?*

Well, of course, he supposed she'd got the boy the time-honored way—she and her ex. But why hadn't she mentioned him?

Not that it was his business. But still…

Alex glared at all the people who were still murmuring and staring at him as if it were his fault she'd stormed away and slammed the door. He wouldn't have minded slamming one or two himself. Instead he stalked over to an empty chair by the windows and flung himself down.

He didn't know how long he waited. Long enough to have plenty of second thoughts. Daisy wasn't going to be happy to come out and find that he had waited. She'd made that perfectly clear.

And did he really want to meet Daisy's child?

It was annoying enough to think that she had professed to love him, then turned around and married someone else. To be honest, Alex had felt a certain satisfaction knowing her rebound marriage hadn't lasted.

That it had resulted in a child was somehow disconcerting.

A child. Charlie.

Alex tried to imagine a little boy who looked like Daisy. Would he have her mischievous grin, a dimple in one cheek, freckles across his nose and a mop of honey-colored hair?

Or would the boy look like her ex-husband? Was the ex holding Charlie's other hand in the exam room with them now? Alex straightened in the chair, scowling at the thought.

Maybe he was going to be sitting here when all three of them came out of the room together. And wouldn't that be awkward as hell?

The noise of a crying baby, a croupy cough, a parent and teenager arguing washed right over him. Alex paid no attention. So it would be awkward. So what? He'd walked out on her and their child, hadn't he?

Alex almost hoped the S.O.B. was here. He'd like to see what was so wonderful that Daisy had ever married him. Scowling, he shifted irritably in the chair, then looked up to see Daisy coming out of the examining room.

On her hip was a little boy with a mop of brownish-blonde hair and one arm in a bright blue cast. He'd expected a two- or three-year-old. But this boy looked bigger. Alex leaned forward, studying him intently. But he couldn't see much. There were people in the way.

Daisy was listening to the nurse. They were standing just

outside the exam room door. The boy was listening, too. Then he turned his head to look out at the waiting room.

Alex's breath caught. His heart seemed to stutter even as he stared.

Charlie's jaw was squarer than Daisy's, his lower lip fuller, his nose a little sharper, his cheekbones higher. His eyes weren't blue, they were green.

He didn't really resemble Daisy at all. Even his hair was actually a deeper gold than Daisy's. But Alex knew exactly who he was. He had known another boy with those eyes, that jaw, whose hair had been exactly that color.

His brother. Vassilios.

CHAPTER EIGHT

FOR a moment Alex couldn't move. Couldn't think. Could only stare.

And understand the implication. It hit him like a fist to the gut.

He moved on automatic pilot, putting himself between Daisy and the door. And all the while, he couldn't take his eyes off the child.

The boy was Vass all over again. Alex's heart squeezed in his chest. His throat tightened. He couldn't swallow. He barely had a toehold on his composure when Daisy finished talking to the nurse and turned—and saw him.

She stopped, rooted right where she was.

Their eyes locked and he watched her color fade. Her lips parted and trembled. Her arms tightened around the boy in her arms and she glanced around as if looking for another way out.

Dad luck, Daze, Alex thought grimly. Nowhere to go but through me.

She understood that, for a second later she straightened her shoulders, lifted her chin and walked straight toward him.

"I told you that you didn't need to wait."

Alex felt a muscle in his temple tick. He swallowed, seeking words. There were none. Only a well of pain.

How could you? His eyes asked her. The boy—his son!—was close enough to reach out and touch.

He balled his fingers into fists, every fiber of his being

wanted to reach out to the little boy, to take him in his arms and never let him go. But the boy didn't know, wouldn't understand. Even Daisy seemed to think he was behaving oddly.

"Are you all right?" she asked when he didn't reply.

She had no idea. Didn't realize what he knew. Of course, she wouldn't. She had no idea Charlie could've been Vass's clone. Alex managed a curt nod. "Fine." Poleaxed, in truth.

"Good." She smiled briefly. "It was kind of you to bother," she said. "But not necessary."

It was necessary. Alex knew that down to his toes. He just looked at her. For a moment neither of them spoke, neither moved.

"Mommy."

Daisy shifted at the sound of the small plaintive voice. She hugged the little boy close. "This is Charlie," she said. "Charlie, this is Mr. Antonides."

Your father.

God, how he wanted to say the words. He didn't. He just studied the boy up close. His cheeks were fuller than Vass's had been. But at that age, maybe his brother had had round cheeks, too. Alex would have been too young to recall. But Charlie had the same freckles across his nose that Vass had had, the same long lashes.

"I got a brok'n arm," the boy told him in a froggy little voice.

Alex nodded and met his chocolate gaze. "Yeah, I see that you do."

Daisy shifted under the boy's weight. "I need to get him home. Thank you. I'm sorry that the evening ended this way."

I'm not. Alex didn't say that, either. He dragged his gaze away from the boy long enough to meet hers. It all made sense now—her distance, her coolness, her determination to shut him out.

But he wasn't out any longer—and he had no intention of ever being out of this child's life again.

"Come on," he said. "Let's get you into a cab." He stepped

back to let Daisy go through the door. It was late, well after midnight, and the snow was still falling. Charlie couldn't put his arm in his jacket, and Daisy was trying to pull it more closely around his shoulders.

"Let me." Alex took the boy's puffy red down jacket and settled it around small bony shoulders. His hands trembled as he brushed them over him, then tucked the jacket close between Charlie's body and his mother's. "There you go." Even to his own ears, his voice sounded hoarse.

"Thank you." Daisy flicked him a quick smile.

There were no taxis right outside. So he strode off to the corner to flag one down. He half expected Daisy to have vanished by the time he got back with it. But sanity must have prevailed. Either that or she was too shattered by the events of the evening to pull a disappearing act.

Alex opened the door to the taxi. "After you. I'll take him." He held out his arms.

"I can manage." She tried to get in with the boy in her arms, but she nearly lost her balance, and Alex scooped him away.

And the moment the boy's solid body settled in his arms, Alex felt something in him change. Something strong and protective took root, dug in. Instinctively he moved his face closer to the boy's soft hair, drawing in the scent of antiseptic, bubble-gum shampoo, laundry soap and earthy little boy.

His breath caught, his grip tightened.

"I can take him now." Daisy's hollow-eyed gaze locked with Alex's as she held out her arms to the little boy.

Slowly, carefully—reluctantly—Alex settled him on the seat next to her. Then, not giving her a chance to tell him he didn't need to come along, he slid into the backseat as well and shut the door.

There was silence except for the taxi's public service babbling. The car didn't move.

"You'll have to tell him where we're going," Alex said at last. "I don't know."

Daisy hesitated for a split second, then in a low voice gave the cab driver the address. It was the same address as her office.

As the cab lurched forward, he narrowed his gaze at her. Daisy kept hers focused straight ahead. Charlie huddled between them. Alex could feel the little boy's bony shoulder pressed against his arm. He angled his gaze down to see the top of the boy's head, the burnished gold of his hair, the sharp little nose and what looked like a stubborn chin. Looking at him, Alex felt his throat tighten with so many emotions he couldn't name them all.

Charlie.

His son.

Alex turned the notion over in his mind. Tested it. Tasted it. Wrapped his entire being around it. Then he lifted his gaze and looked over the top of Charlie's head at the woman who hadn't even bothered to tell him and felt his whole body stiffen with anger.

As if he were aware of something wrong, Charlie stiffened, too. He edged closer under his mother's arm.

Was he scared? Certainly he sensed something was amiss. Kids could do that, Alex remembered. He certainly had.

He'd read his parents' body language for years. He had sensed their worry about Vass, even when they'd tried to say everything would be fine. He'd felt their pain, their hurt at his brother's illness. He'd felt, without needing words, their emotional withdrawal.

He didn't blame them. His brother had been his idol. His hero. He knew as well as they had that Vass was the best person in the world. And he instinctively felt what they felt: that if they had to lose one of their sons, it should not have been Vass.

Moody, temperamental, fidgety, less-than-perfect Alex was the one who should have died.

Of course no one said so. No one had to. Kids could read body language. They could hear the feelings in the silences— as Charlie could no doubt hear his now.

Consciously Alex relaxed his body and stopped glaring at

Daisy. Instead he shifted slightly away so that he could look down at Charlie more easily.

"I'm not Mr. Antonides. I'm Alex," he said.

The boy flicked a quick glance up at him and dipped his head in acknowledgment.

"Want to shake left hands?" Alex asked.

Charlie's gaze lifted again to meet his. Alex could feel Daisy's eyes on him, as well. Wary, suspicious. Charlie hesitated a moment, then nodded and stuck out his left hand. Small fingers gripped his.

And Alex knew that this first mutual touch was momentous, and that the feel of that small warm hand in his was a memory he would carry with him to his grave.

"I broke my arm once, too," he told the boy, "when I was ten."

"Did you jump off a bunk bed?"

So that was what Charlie had done. Alex smiled and shook his head. "I was climbing some cliffs. One crumbled and I fell."

If he had been on the cliffs near their Santorini home, he didn't think it would have happened. He knew those cliffs like he knew the inside of his bedroom. He and Vass had climbed them their whole lives.

But they hadn't been in Santorini. They had been at a place they were renting in Athens while Vass was in the hospital for treatments. Alex had hated it there, hated the hospital, hated the house, hated having to play by himself all the time because Vass was too ill to do anything.

And he'd only made things worse when he fell.

"You don't think!" his mother had raged. "You never think!"

"You should be glad it hurts," his father had said sternly. "Maybe you will not be so inconsiderate again."

"I wish I'd been with you," Vass had whispered when Alex finally got to see him. His brother's eyes had had dark circles under them. But they had still glittered with urgency and desire.

And Alex had said fervently, "Me, too."

Now, trying to push aside the painful memory, he smiled at the little boy who was looking up at him with Vass's eyes. "Did you break yours jumping from a bunk?"

"I was tryin' to get to the dresser like Rip does."

"Who's Rip?" Whoever he was, Alex liked his name.

"One of Finn and Izzy MacCauley's boys," Daisy said. "Rip is Charlie's hero. He tries to do whatever Rip does, in this case, apparently, to get around the house without touching the floor," she said despairingly.

Alex grinned. "I used to do that, too."

Charlie's eyes widened. "You did?"

"It's something all boys do?" Daisy looked dismayed.

"It's a challenge," Alex told her. "Boys like challenges. How old is Rip?"

"Almost twelve," Daisy said. They were speeding down Central Park West. There was little traffic now and they were hitting the lights. It would be a matter of minutes until they were at Daisy's office.

"That explains it," Alex told the little boy. "You've just got to get bigger."

"Mom says I can't do it again."

Daisy looked mulish. "I don't want him killing himself."

"He won't," Alex said. He smiled at Charlie. "You look like a pretty tough guy."

The boy's head bobbed. "I am. My dad says so."

"Your dad?" Alex lifted his gaze to look from Charlie to Daisy. "His dad?" he said to her.

"His dad." Daisy's look was even more mulish and her tone even firmer than before. "My ex-husband. Cal."

Alex's jaw tightened at the lie. He stared at her.

And just as if she were telling God's own truth, Daisy stared defiantly back. Their gazes were still locked when the cab turned the corner on Daisy's street and pulled up midblock in front of her place. He understood it was more than her office now. She damned well lived here, too.

"Here's where we get out," Daisy said briskly. She reached into the pocket of her coat and pulled out money for the cab.

"I'm paying," Alex said flatly.

Daisy opened her mouth as if to protest, but then shrugged. "Thank you."

He paid the driver, then opened the door and got out, reaching back in and lifting Charlie carefully up into his arms, settling him against his hip. Charlie looped an arm over his shoulder.

Daisy scrambled out and looked disconcerted to see the boy in Alex's arms and not standing on the sidewalk where she had apparently expected to see him.

Alex nodded toward the building. "After you."

He wasn't surprised when Daisy fished a key out of her pocket and, instead of going up the stoop, led the way through a wrought-iron gate and down the steps to the door below. Her movements were jerky as she fumbled the key, but finally unlocked the outer door and pushed it open, then did the same with the lock on the front door, and turned to hold out her arms for her son.

Still carrying Charlie, Alex pushed straight past her into a tiny foyer filled with jackets and boots and roller skates and the smallest bicycle he'd ever seen.

"Yours?" he asked Charlie.

The boy's head nodded against Alex's shoulder.

"Can you ride it?"

Another nod, this one firmer than the last.

"Good for you. I had a bike when I was your age." Alex smiled. Bikes had been his thing—never Vass's. And already Charlie rode one. So there was that bit of himself in his son. "We'll have to go riding."

"He has a broken arm," Daisy said sharply.

"Not now." Alex turned and faced her. "There will be time."

He watched that register in her brain before he said to Charlie, "Plenty of time."

"Alex," Daisy protested faintly.

He turned his stare back on her until her gaze slid away.

"You got a bike?" Charlie asked, interested.

"Yep. I race bikes."

Charlie looked fascinated. Daisy looked dismayed. She shook her head, as if resisting everything. Then quickly and deliberately she stripped off her coat and hung it on one of the hooks in the foyer and crossed the room, holding out her arms.

"Give him to me. He needs to get ready for bed. Now."

Alex wanted to argue. Wanted to defy her, hang on to his son. But for all that he was furious with Daisy, none of it was Charlie's fault. But his jaw was tight, his whole body felt rigid as he loosed his grip and eased the boy into his mother's arms. He took special care not to jar Charlie's arm. And once he'd let go, he smoothed a hand over Charlie's hair, letting it linger.

"You're a brave guy," he said, keeping his gaze on Charlie. The boy nodded solemnly.

"We'll ride bikes together sometime soon," Alex promised, his smile crooked. "Okay?"

Another nod and a tentative smile.

He could hear Daisy's indrawn breath. "Good night, Alex." She paused, then added evenly, "Thank you for…everything."

For everything? His eyes asked her.

For giving you a son?

"Who's he?" Charlie asked as Daisy carried him up the stairs.

"A man I used to know. A…friend." But she was distracted as she spoke, remembering Alex's narrowed gaze as he'd watched her carrying Charlie across the emergency room.

He didn't know, she assured herself. He couldn't.

It was Charlie's mere existence that had surprised him—that *she* had a son. And his terseness simply meant that he was annoyed she hadn't told him.

In Charlie's room, she flicked on the light and deposited

him gently on the bed. She rarely carried him anywhere these days, and having done so now, she was almost out of breath, surprised at how big he'd gotten since she used to carry him all the time.

"My arm hurts."

"I know. I'm sorry." She bent to kiss his soft hair, then smoothed her hand over it, pulling back as she remembered that Alex had just done the same thing. "I guess maybe you won't leap from bunk beds anymore?"

Charlie pursed his lips, considering. "Not till I'm bigger," he decided. "Crash can do it."

"Maybe you should wait till you're nine or ten then." She got his pajamas off the hook behind the door.

"Maybe." Charlie took the pajamas, then tried to wriggle out of the jacket he still had over his shoulders and one arm.

"I'll help you tonight," Daisy said. "But you're going to have to figure out how to do it yourself, too." She eased off the jacket, then lifted the hem of his shirt and began to slide it up and over his good arm and his head.

"Maybe Alex could teach me."

"What?" She jerked back, then stared at the pair of bright eyes that popped into view as the shirt came off. "Why would he?"

"'Cause he broke his arm," Charlie said simply. "He'd know how."

"Oh. Well…" Daisy made a noncommittal sound. "I'm pretty sure you can figure it out without Alex's help." She finished getting his clothes off and his pajamas on. "Go wash your face and brush your teeth."

Charlie flopped back on the bed. "But I'm tired. Do I hafta?"

"Yes. Even boys who fall off bunk beds have to maintain a minimum of civil decorum."

"I didn't fall," Charlie protested. But he allowed her to pull him up. "I jumped. An' what's 'civil deck-somethin'?" Charlie loved big words.

"Civil decorum," Daisy repeated. It was what she had tried to maintain for the past hour and a half. She said, "Behaving like a well-brought-up *clean* child."

"Ugh." But Charlie slid off the bed and padded toward the bathroom while Daisy gathered up his clothes. "Oh!" she heard him say brightly. "Hi."

"Hi." The unexpected sound of Alex's voice right outside the door sent Daisy hurrying out. She skidded to a halt a second before she collided with his chest.

"You didn't leave."

"No." He had propped a shoulder against the wall outside Charlie's bedroom door and stood there meeting her gaze, then his eyes dropped to Charlie, and Daisy felt more than a flicker of unease.

He didn't say anything. But even quiet and unmoving, his presence seemed to overpower everything else. He was too big. Too close. The space was too intimate. And the situation didn't bear thinking about. She didn't want him here.

But she didn't know how to get rid of him without causing Charlie to wonder what was going on. He already had to wonder. No man but Cal had ever been upstairs.

But Alex was, right here in the hallway, his dark hair disheveled, as if he had run his fingers through it. He looked incongruous here in his formal evening wear, but even as she thought it, she realized the formal evening wear wasn't so formal anymore. He'd removed his tie—it dangled from his pocket—and he'd undone the top two buttons of his shirt.

It had the effect of making him look more masculine and primal than ever—with the added misfortune of reminding her of how he'd looked five years ago when she'd brought him into her tiny apartment after the wedding. He was all the things he'd been then and all the things she'd been at pains to resist earlier this evening—too broad-shouldered, too imposing and too damned predatorily male.

"I came to say good night to Charlie." His tone was measured, his words easy, understandable and, to Charlie, un-threatening.

But Daisy knew a threat when she heard one. She took a quick breath. "Say good night, Charlie."

Charlie tipped his head back to look up at Alex, but instead of saying good night, he said, "Can you teach me to get my shirt on an' off over my cast?"

Alex nodded. "I can."

"No, he can't. It's after one in the morning. You need to go to bed," Daisy said firmly.

"I'll show you," Alex promised smoothly. "Tomorrow."

"But—" Charlie began.

"Your mother's right," Alex said firmly. "You need to sleep."

"I can't sleep. My arm hurts," Charlie argued.

"But you're tough," Alex reminded him. The two of them looked at each other. Two men understanding each other—even though one of them was only four.

"Teeth, Charlie," Daisy said firmly. "And wash your face. Now." She took hold of his shoulders and steered him past Alex, doing her best not to brush against him in the narrow hallway. If she'd hoped he'd take the hint and go, she was out of luck.

He didn't budge, just waited until Charlie had brushed his teeth—awkwardly because he had to do it left-handed—and scrubbed at his face with a washcloth. He didn't use soap, but Daisy didn't make him do it again. She just wanted him in bed.

"Right," she said briskly. "Off to bed."

Obediently Charlie headed back down the hall, but stopped directly in front of Alex. He looked up again. "G'night."

And Daisy remembered when she'd seen the photo of Charlie looking up at Cal's father and had realized how similar her son's profile was to Alex's. They were indeed remarkably alike.

Was that how Alex had known? Or was it some scary primal innate recognition between father and son? She didn't know. She only knew that the still-deep emotion that she could sense simmering in Alex was more elemental than just a response to discovering she had a child she hadn't told him about.

The question was no longer: *Did he know?*

The question was: *What was he going to do now?*

He reached out a hand and brushed the top of Charlie's head once more. "Good night," he said gravely. "It was nice meeting you, Charlie." His fingers lingered for a moment, then he withdrew them and tucked them into the pocket of his trousers and brought his gaze up to meet Daisy's. "At last."

She suppressed a shiver, then swallowed. With her eyes she beseeched him to be silent, and was relieved when he didn't say anything else. Giving him a fleeting grateful smile, she slipped past him to follow Charlie into his bedroom where she shut the door with a solid click.

Whatever Alex might have to say to her—and she had no doubt he had plenty to say—he could say it tomorrow. Or next month. Not now.

Her priority was Charlie. It was the middle of the night and he'd been hurt, and it didn't matter that her brain was whirling a million miles a minute. If she pushed him, he would balk and take even longer.

So she did everything in his bedtime routine. She tucked him in, then read him a bedtime story. She listened as he told her about his day, including a long involved account of everything he'd done at Rip and Crash's house, what he didn't like about the emergency room, and ultimately, as she'd feared, questions about Alex.

"Do you think he'll ride bikes with me?"

"I don't know," she said. "He's a busy man."

"He said he would."

"Yes. And maybe he will."

"Remind him."

Daisy made a noncommittal sound. "Prayers," she reminded him, and when he'd finished, she added a desperate silent one of her own. Then she kissed her son good-night.

Charlie clutched her hand when she got up to leave. "Stay."

"Charlie."

"My arm hurts. Sing to me," he pleaded.

That wasn't part of the regular nightly routine, but sometimes when he was sick and irritable, she could calm him with some silly songs. "You're tired."

His big eyes drooped even as he nodded. "I'll sleep. Sing."

So Daisy turned out the light, determinedly shut out the turmoil roiling around in her mind, and sat back down on the bed beside him.

Maybe it would soothe them both, she thought as she began to sing. There was a boat song, and a campfire song, and a bus, train and truck song. She had made them up about Charlie's life when he was a toddler. He knew them by heart. Now he settled against her, his eyes shut, the blue cast dark against the pale blanket that covered him. His breathing slowed.

Her voice slowed, too, and finally stopped. Waited. Watched him. And finally when she was sure he was asleep, she dipped her head and kissed him.

"I love you," she whispered, brushing a hand over his hair. Then she put out the bedside light and slipped quietly out of his room, shutting the door after her.

The clock in her bedroom said five minutes of two. Daisy felt as if she'd been up for two days. Or weeks.

Wearily, she stripped off Izzy's dress. It still sparkled in the soft bedside light. It had made her sparkle in the beginning. She didn't sparkle now. She felt as if she'd been run over by a truck. She flexed her bare shoulders and shivered as she stared into the mirror over her dresser. A pale, hollow-eyed, haunted version of herself stared back.

She felt ill. Exhausted. And scared.

Alex knew. And soon he would confront her about Charlie. He would say whatever he had to say about the son he hadn't known he had. The son he never wanted. She felt a tremor run through her.

Whatever he said, he could say it to her. He wasn't going to say it to Charlie. Charlie wasn't ever going to hear that he wasn't wanted. Ever!

Maybe, with luck, Alex would pretend he didn't know. Maybe he would simply walk away. She could hope.

Quickly pulling on her nightgown, she wrapped up in her fuzzy chenille robe and tiptoed down the hall to brush her teeth and wash her face. Then she went downstairs to let Murphy out. She would have done it when she first got home, but Charlie had taken precedence.

Murphy wagged his tail, delighted to see her. She rubbed his ears and kissed the top of his head. Then she slid open the door to the back garden, Murphy went out, and she slid it closed against the snowy December night. Then, while he was out there, she went to put the dead bolt on the front door. Alex couldn't have done it when he left.

If he had left.

He hadn't. He was sprawled, eyes closed, on the sofa.

CHAPTER NINE

For a moment Daisy didn't even breathe, just pressed a hand protectively against her breasts and felt her heart pound wildly beneath it.

She dared hope he was asleep—because hoping he was a figment of her imagination was not a possibility. But even as she did so, Alex's eyes fluttered open and he rolled to a sitting position.

"What are you doing here?" she asked.

Alex rolled his shoulders, working the stiffness out. He had taken off his coat and the stark white of his shirt made his shoulders seem broader than ever. He looked at her levelly. "Waiting for you."

"It's late!"

His eyes bored into her. "Five years late."

"I don't know what you mean," she said. Her fingers knotted together.

"You know." His gaze was steady, his eyes chips of green ice.

"Alex," she protested.

"We're done playing games, Daisy."

"I'm not—"

"We're going to talk." There was a thread of steel in his voice now, and as he spoke, he stood up. Slightly more than six feet of whipcord muscle and testosterone somehow filled the room.

Daisy stepped back. "I have to let the dog in."

He shrugged. "Go ahead. I'm not going anywhere."

Exactly what she was afraid of. She hurried through the kitchen and fumbled with shaking fingers to open the sliding-glass door for Murphy. It wasn't just her fingers shaking, her whole body was trembling, and it had nothing to do with the cold December night. The cold in Alex's stare was a different story.

Murphy trotted in, wagging his tail cheerfully. Daisy shut the door and slid the bolt home, then cast a longing look at the stairs that led up to her room. But retreat wasn't an option. So, wiping damp palms down the sides of her robe, she went back to the living room.

Alex was standing by the mantel, holding the photo of her and Charlie and Cal taken last Christmas. At her footsteps, he took one last look and he set it back on the mantel, then looked over at her. "Is this your ex?"

She nodded. "That's Cal."

"Very cozy."

"It was Christmas. Christmas is cozy."

"You look happy."

"We were happy." She hugged her arms across her chest.

"You were still married to him then?"

"No."

One dark brow arched in surprise. "But you had a picture taken together?"

"Yes." She wasn't giving him any explanations. She didn't owe him any.

"He's not Charlie's father."

"Yes, he is." She had been married to Cal when Charlie was born. He was the father on Charlie's birth certificate. He was the father that Charlie called Dad. He was a father to Charlie in every way that mattered.

"Not by blood, he's not."

Daisy swallowed, then lifted her chin. "And you know this how?"

He reached into his back pocket and pulled out a thin black leather billfold. Opening the wallet, he took out a photo, crossed the room and handed it to her. It was a small color snapshot of two young boys, grinning at the camera.

Daisy saw only one. He could have been Charlie.

He was older than Charlie, maybe nine or ten. But his eyes were Charlie's—the same shape, the same light color. He had the same sharp nose, spattered with freckles, the same wide grin. He even had the same straight honey-blonde hair that she'd always assured herself had come from her side of the family.

She clutched the photo so tightly, her fingers trembled. Her throat tightened and she shut her eyes. She couldn't breathe.

Alex didn't seem to be breathing, either. He was stone silent and unmoving. Waiting for her to speak?

But what could she say?

Slowly she opened her eyes again and began to study the picture more carefully. The two boys were standing on a beach, bare-chested and wearing shorts, the sea lapping bright blue behind them. They had their arms slung around each other's shoulders and they were laughing into the camera. The older boy was the one who looked like Charlie. The other was younger, maybe six or seven, with a front tooth missing. He had dark shaggy hair and light eyes. Daisy knew those eyes.

Slowly, cautiously, she looked up at them now. "It's you..." she said so softly she doubted he could hear her. Her thumb stroked over the dark-haired boy's face. "And your brother."

A muscle ticked in his jaw. He nodded. "Vassilios."

Of course it was. His beloved brother, his hero, the beautiful loving boy whose death had destroyed his family looked almost exactly like Charlie.

Dear God, what a shock seeing his son must have been.

Outside a siren wailed as a fire truck went up Central Park West. Inside, the room was so silent she could hear the old oak mantel clock tick. She could hear Murphy two rooms away in the kitchen lapping up water. It was the calm before the storm.

"Why the hell didn't you tell me?" His voice accused her, anguished, ragged, furious. He plucked the photo back out of her hand, his fingers fumbling as he slid it back in his wallet and shoved it into his pocket.

She heard the pain, the anguish, the accusation. On one level she understood them. But she remembered pain and anguish of her own.

"Why the hell should I?" she countered, stung by his fury. "You didn't want a child. You said so! I babbled about marriage and family and you were quite clear. No marriage. No family! Why should I have told you?"

"That was before I knew I had one! How could I say I didn't want my son when I didn't even know he existed?"

"You didn't want him to exist!"

His nostrils flared and his jaw clamped shut. He balled his fingers into fists, as if he were trying to control what he did with them. Like strangle her. "You kept my son from me!"

"I took you at your word!"

"Damn it!" Alex let out a harsh breath. He glared at her, then raked his fingers through his hair and paced the room. At the far end, he whirled around. "You knew how I felt about my brother!"

Yes, she had known. She knew that Vassilios had been the favorite son, the star, the heir. She knew that everyone had loved him. Even Alex. Especially Alex. Vassilios had been bright, funny, caring, social. Everything, Alex had told Daisy five years ago, that he himself was not.

But Vass had been so wonderful that Alex hadn't envied him. He'd only wanted to be like him. He had loved his brother deeply. Vassilios's death had irrevocably changed his life.

She had known that losing his brother was the main reason Alex never wanted children. It was the reason Alex had originally never wanted to marry. He didn't want to love, he'd told her. Love hurt.

Dear God, she could agree with that. She'd hurt more in the aftermath of his leaving and her discovering she was having his child than she could ever have imagined. She'd loved him—and lost him—and for nearly five years now had Charlie to remind her of that loss.

But she couldn't regret it. She couldn't even regret marrying Cal. At least they'd had some sort of love. They'd tried.

Alex had refused to even try. Not then. Not now. He still wanted a marriage on his terms, a marriage without love. And children had still been a deal breaker. He'd made that clear.

So now she met his accusation squarely and told him the honest truth. "Yes, I knew," she agreed. "But mostly I knew you didn't want children. I did what I had to do. I did the best that I could for my son."

"Really? And you and dear Cal have such a spectacular marriage." His tone mocked her, infuriated her.

Daisy had to fight her own inclination to look away. Even so she felt her face heat. "Cal is a great father."

"And I wouldn't have been?" His challenge was loud and clear. Mostly loud.

"Not if you didn't love him! And be quiet. You'll wake him up."

Alex's teeth came together with a snap. She could hear his harsh breathing, but he didn't claim he would love Charlie. How could he? He'd already hardened his heart.

"Why would I think you'd be a good father to a child you didn't want?" she said. "Cal was. Cal was there when he was born—"

"Because you damned well didn't tell me!"

"Cal loves him," she finished quietly.

"And I've never had a chance to!"

"You didn't want one. You'd already made your choice. And when I found out I was pregnant, I had to make choices, too. I chose to do what I thought was best for Charlie. He needed love. He needed parents. A family. You didn't want that. You said, 'No entanglements, no hostages of fortune.'"

He had actually used those terms, and when she repeated

them now, she saw him wince. "You said love hurt too much. You wanted nothing to do with it."

They glared at each other. Daisy wrapped her arms across her chest and stared unblinkingly at him. She knew what he had said, and Alex would be lying if he denied it now.

He didn't deny it. He didn't say anything at all. His jaw worked. His eyes reflected his inner turmoil. Seconds passed. Daisy could hear Murphy's toenails clicking down the hallway as he came out from the kitchen to look at them inquiringly.

Alex didn't notice. He was cracking his knuckles, then kneading the muscles at the back of his neck. He paced the room like an agitated animal trapped in a cage. Finally he flung himself down on the sofa and rubbed his hair until it stuck up all over his head. He dragged his palms down his face and stared at her bleakly over the top of them. "Hell."

In a word, yes.

It was a hell she was already familiar with. The confusion, the anguish, the damned-if-you-do, damned-if-you-don't choices she had faced when she'd discovered she was pregnant. She remembered the hollowness she'd felt at Alex's flat-out rejection of any sort of relationship. In the face of her hopes and dreams and—let's face it—fantasies, he had been crystal clear.

She hadn't even wanted to imagine what he would have said if she'd turned up on his doorstep and announced she was expecting his child. The very thought had made her blood run cold. Even now she shivered inside the thick robe she was wearing. Tucking her hands inside the opposite sleeves, she chaffed her arms briskly, trying to warm them.

Alex just sat there. He didn't speak. He didn't move, except for the rise and fall of his chest. His expression was grim as he stared across the room. He wasn't looking at her now.

She wondered what he was seeing in his mind's eye. His dying brother? His unknown son? The parents who had rejected him and each other? His life, as carefully designed as any building he'd ever planned, going down the drain?

She couldn't imagine. Didn't want to.

Murphy stood between them, looking from one to the other as if wondering what they were doing in his living room in the middle of the night. Finally, accepting it as dogs always did, he curled up on his bed in front of the fireplace and put his head between his paws.

Alex looked up and met her gaze. "I want my son."

"Want your...?" Daisy stared at him, breathless, as if he had punched her in the gut. "What does that mean? You can't take him!" she blurted, anguished. "You don't have any right!"

"I didn't say I was going to take him." Icy green eyes collided with hers. "But I'm not walking away, either."

Daisy swallowed, tried to think, to fathom what Alex's "not walking away" meant. For Charlie. For her. She didn't have a clue.

She only knew what she must not let happen. "You're not hurting him," she said fiercely. "I won't let you."

Alex rubbed a hand over his hair. His brows drew down. "Why the hell would I want to hurt him?"

Daisy had started to pace, but she stopped and turned to face him. "I didn't say you would intend to. But it could happen. He's only four, Alex. He won't understand. Besides, he has a father."

Alex's jaw tightened. "Cal." He spat her ex-husband's name. "Did you marry him because of Charlie?"

Daisy ran her tongue over her lips as she tried to decide how to answer it, how to be honest and fair to both Alex and to Cal.

"Did you?" Alex persisted when she didn't reply.

She sat down in the armchair across from the sofa where he was leaning toward her, his elbows on his knees, his fingers laced. "Yes," she admitted. "But it wasn't as simple as that. I didn't go find the nearest eligible man and ask him to marry me."

"No?" He mocked her.

Daisy tried not to bristle. "No," she said firmly. "Cal asked me."

"And you jumped at it."

In fact she'd been shocked. It had never occurred to her. They'd been friends. Nothing more. "I thought about it. He insisted we could make it work."

"Sounds passionate," Alex drawled.

"Cal and I had been friends for a long time. He said love wasn't just a matter of passion. It was a matter of choice. I thought he was right. He wasn't. But—" she met his mockery defiantly "—I love Cal."

"You thought you loved me."

"I did," Daisy agreed. "But that was before I found out you didn't give a damn."

Alex stiffened as if she'd slapped him, then surged to his feet and loomed over her. "So you fell out of love with me and in love with What's His Face in, what? Six weeks? Less?"

"It wasn't like that."

"No? So, what was it like?"

She knew he didn't really want to hear the answer. He was angry and he just wanted to put her on the defensive, pick a fight.

But Daisy wasn't buying into that. "Sit down," she said, and pointed at the sofa when he didn't move. "Sit down and I'll tell you what it was like," she repeated sharply.

His gaze narrowed on her, but when she kept pointing, he dropped onto the sofa, still staring at her unblinkingly.

When he had settled again, Daisy tucked her feet under her and tried to find words that would make him understand.

"I was hurt when you didn't feel what I did that weekend," she began.

Alex started to interrupt, but she held up a hand to stop him. "I know you think I shouldn't have been. You think I presumed too much, And—" she took a steadying breath "—you were right. I presumed far too much. But I was young and foolish, and nothing like that had ever happened to me before."

Alex's mouth was a thin line, but he was listening at least.

Daisy twisted the tie of her bathrobe between her fingers,

staring at it before lifting her gaze again. She shrugged and told him helplessly, "I fell in love with you. It was a mistake, I admit that." She laced her fingers in her lap and dropped her gaze to stare at them. If she looked at him, she'd realize that she was actually saying these things—and she didn't want to be saying any of them.

She wanted her life back—the way it had been before she had gone to the dinner with him tonight, the way it had been before everything she'd worked so hard to build and hold together for the past five years had all come apart at the scams.

"When you walked out, I was humiliated," she said. "I felt like an idiot. Sick."

Alex's jaw bunched. She knew he wanted to argue. He shifted uncomfortably. Daisy didn't care. She was uncomfortable, too. They could suffer through this together.

"Weeks went by," she continued. "Two, three, four—and instead of being able to put it behind me, I just felt sicker. And sicker. I started throwing up every morning. And that," she said, lifting her eyes to look at him squarely now, "was when I realized that it wasn't the memory of my idiocy that was making me sick. It was being pregnant."

He flinched, then let out a slow breath.

"I didn't even think about trying to find you," she said levelly. "You'd made it quite clear you weren't interested in any sort of involvement at all."

"You could've —"

"No," she said flatly "I couldn't." She hesitated, then just told him the truth. "I was afraid you might want me to get an abortion."

He stared at her, shocked. "How could you think—?"

"Why wouldn't I?" she demanded. "You didn't want to care! I was afraid you'd say, 'Get rid of it before *anyone* cares.' Well, *I* cared. Even then I cared!" She could feel tears stinging the back of her eyes.

"Jesus," he muttered.

"Exactly," Daisy said, understanding the desperation that

made him say it. "I did a lot of praying. You can believe that. I was scared. I didn't know how I was going to cope. I could keep working for Finn while I was pregnant, but after the baby came, I thought I might have to go back to Colorado and stay with my mother till I could work something out. And then—" she breathed deeply "—Cal proposed."

"Your savior. He was just standing around, waiting in the wings, for exactly that moment?" Alex demanded bitterly. "Ready to take some other man's woman?" Alex ground out. "His *pregnant* woman?"

"I was *not* your woman! And he was my friend. He *is* my friend."

"And yet you couldn't stay married to him," Alex said derisively.

Her jaw tightened. "It didn't work out." She folded her hands in her lap.

"Why not?"

"That's not your business."

Alex scowled blackly. "He married you, then dumped you? It doesn't make sense. None of it makes sense."

"He didn't dump me! And it made sense," Daisy insisted. "We hoped it would work. We wanted it to work. Cal's a good man," she said, looking over at the photo on the mantel. She stared at it for a long moment, then turned her gaze and met Alex's, smiling a little sadly. "He's been a good father."

"But not Charlie's only father!" Alex insisted.

"He knows he has a biological father. Well, as much as any four-year-old understands that. He knows he has two fathers. I figured I could explain you more to him as he got older."

"I'll explain myself to him now."

"No," Daisy said. "Not until I know how you feel."

"You know damn well how I feel. I want my son!"

Their gazes locked, dueled. And in the silence of battle, the stairs creaked.

"Mommy?"

Daisy's head jerked up to see Charlie peering over the bannister halfway down them. Alex stared up at him, too. Dear God, had he heard?

Daisy hurried up the stairs and scooped him up into her arms. "What is it, sweetie?"

"My arm hurts," he whimpered, and tucked his head between her jaw and her shoulder. He clung to her, but his gaze was fixed on Alex who was slowly coming to his feet.

Daisy shifted so that her body blocked his view. "I know." She kissed his hair and cuddled him close. "I wish it didn't. I'll take you back upstairs and sing to you. Okay?"

Charlie nodded. "Can Alex come, too?"

"Alex was just leaving." But she turned and carried Charlie down the stairs. "We'll just say good-night and see him out the front door." She smiled into Alex's suddenly narrowed gaze. "That will be nice, won't it?" she said to her son.

Solemnly Charlie nodded. He looked at Alex.

Alex looked back with an intensity that made Daisy quiver. Then Charlie lifted his head off her shoulder. "Night, Alex."

Daisy held her breath as, slowly, Alex shrugged into his suit jacket and crossed the room, stopping mere inches from them. He didn't look at her. He had eyes only for Charlie. To Daisy he looked dark, forbidding and positively scary.

But then he lifted a hand to touch Charlie's cheek and his expression softened, a smile touched the corner of his mouth. "Good night, son."

CHAPTER TEN

I⟊ was like waiting for the other shoe to drop.

Daisy half expected to find Alex standing on the stoop when she got up. But a peek out the curtains as soon as she got up proved that no one was there.

He didn't call, either, though she jumped every time the phone rang.

Charlie, pushing his scrambled eggs around his plate, wanted to know what the matter was with her. "You're all jumpy," he remarked when a sound on the sidewalk made her flinch.

"Nothing's the matter." Daisy turned away, busying herself putting the dishes in the dishwasher. "Izzy said she and the boys were coming by."

Izzy's had been the first phone call she'd got this morning.

"How is he?" her friend had demanded even before Daisy had dragged herself out of bed.

"Still asleep," Daisy reported. In fact he was asleep on the other side of her bed. She'd got him back to sleep after Alex had finally left, but he'd awakened and come into her room again at five-thirty. Barely able to pry her eyes open, Daisy had taken the easy way out and let him clamber into bed with her. Fortunately he'd gone straight back to sleep, and when Izzy had rung at eight, he was still dead to the world.

"Sorry. We've been up for hours thinking about him."

"He's going to be fine," Daisy assured her. At least his

arm was. How his life was going to change now that Alex was going to be part of it, she didn't know. But at least Alex had been kind last night. He'd actually behaved—toward Charlie—very well. Maybe, given that, he would be fine. And kids were resilient.

It was her own resilience Daisy was worried about.

How was she going to deal with Alexandros Antonides in her life?

She didn't want to think about it. So when Izzy asked if they could come and see Charlie in the afternoon, Daisy said yes without hesitation. The distraction would do them both good.

By midafternoon with no Rip and no Crash, Charlie was getting restless. Daisy had watched a Disney DVD with him, then read him a couple of dozen picture books. She tried unsuccessfully to talk him into a nap.

"I'm too big for naps," he told her. "An' I'm not tired."

No, just cranky. She had a photo shoot to finish editing before tomorrow afternoon. So she brought her laptop down to the living room and worked on it there while Charlie played with his cars and his Legos on the floor.

"Maybe that Alex will come back," he said hopefully, looking up from his cars.

"Mmm." Daisy didn't encourage that line of thinking. A man who had been as adamant as Alex had been about not wanting children might have had a brief change of heart when faced with a little boy who looked very much like his beloved deceased brother.

But having a son was a huge responsibility. And it wasn't one that you could just pick up and put down as the whim struck you. Alex wasn't a fool. He had to realize that. It was possible that Alex had gone home in the early hours of the morning, thought about the implications of having a son, and come to the conclusion that he'd made the right decision five years ago. Whatever he decided, Daisy was determined that she wouldn't let him upset Charlie's life to suit himself.

She didn't have time to think about it more because finally the doorbell rang.

"They're here!" Charlie scrambled up from the floor and raced to open the door.

Daisy unlocked the door, and Charlie tugged it open.

Rip MacCauley took one look at Charlie's cast and said, "Oh, wow. Your cast is blue? That's cool."

The first smile of the day flickered across Charlie's face. "You think?"

"Oh, yeah," Rip said, coming in and taking off his jacket. "I only ever had a white one."

"Mine was purple when I broke my ankle," Crash announced. "Here. This is for you." He thrust a package wrapped in newspaper comics into Charlie's hand.

"A little something to keep him busy," Izzy told Daisy as the boys headed instinctively for the cars and the Legos on the floor and she followed Daisy into the kitchen. "Rip and Crash have been really worried. They seem to think they're indestructible, but when Charlie got hurt, they were, like, 'Oh, no! What if he dies?' They felt very responsible. As well they should, Finn says."

"Finn being such a pattern card of model behavior." Daisy grinned.

Izzy laughed. "That's what I said." She perched on a bar stool while Daisy made them coffee. "I was amazed when Finn got home so quickly last night. Why didn't you let him stay for a bit and help you with Charlie?"

"No point. We were fine." And she was very glad he hadn't been there to witness the meeting of Alex and his son.

"I'm sorry we interrupted your evening. How was the Plaza? Tell all." Izzy leaned forward eagerly.

It took Daisy a moment to even begin to remember the details, so much had happened in the meantime. "It was…fine," she said vaguely. "The Plaza is elegant, of course. The dinner was wonderful," she added dutifully, because "fine" wasn't going to satisfy Izzy.

"And the dress?"

"It was fantastic."

"Knocked his socks off?" Izzy's eyes were bright.

"It wasn't supposed to knock his socks off," Daisy reminded her. "He's got a girlfriend."

Izzy looked disappointed. But then she shrugged philosophically. "So you had a good time."

Daisy did her best to sound bright and enthusiastic about the evening. She didn't tell Izzy that Alex had turned up at the hospital. She didn't mention anything that happened after that. Until she had some idea of what Alex intended, she wasn't borrowing trouble—or discussing him with anyone.

She was glad Izzy and the boys came because it took the edge off Charlie's boredom and irritability. The matchbox cars that Rip and Crash brought him were a big hit. But Daisy was, honestly, glad when they left again because it was hard to give the impression of cheerful equanimity when she felt edgy and stressed and as if her world was splintering into a million pieces. She left Charlie playing with his cars on the floor in the living room and retreated to the kitchen to wash up the cups and plates from the MacCauleys' visit.

And then the doorbell rang.

"It's Alex!" Charlie yelled, jumping up and running to the door.

Wiping nervous hands on the sides of her jeans, Daisy followed him to answer it. She dragged the door open a few inches and, as always, felt her heart do a somersault in her chest at the mere sight of him.

Gone, of course, was the formal wear of last evening. This afternoon Alex was in jeans and a hunter-green down jacket, his dark hair windblown and dusted with snowflakes, his jaw stubbled. His eyes were bloodshot, but they met hers squarely.

"Daisy." His voice was soft but firm, and gravelly as if he hadn't slept.

"Alex," she replied, holding herself rigid, trying to relax, but unable to. Still she swallowed and tried to sound cordial and polite.

"Hi, Alex." Charlie poked his head around to beam up at the man on the doorstep. "Come 'n' see my new cars."

"Cars?" Alex grinned and stepped across the threshold.

Daisy backed up hastily. "Charlie's much better," she said as he brushed past. "You didn't have to come."

He gave her a look so intense it could have leveled buildings. "I wanted to come." Then he turned his attention to Charlie. "You're better, are you?" he said, his tone far lighter. "Good. I thought maybe we could go to the park."

"The park?" Daisy echoed doubtfully.

But Charlie cheered. Obviously no one had told him he was an invalid.

"But let's see your new cars first." Alex was already shedding his jacket, dropping down onto the floor next to Charlie, making himself at home.

Charlie was clearly delighted to have the attention. He showed Alex the new set of Matchbox cars that Rip and Crash had given him. "Sports cars," he told Alex eagerly. "They go really fast. See?" He raced them around on the floor, making car noises.

Alex stretched out his long legs and leaned back on an elbow, watching, not just indulgently, but with real interest. He picked up the cars by turn, examining them, commenting knowledgeably because, of course, he knew all about cars. It must come standard issue with the Y chromosome.

Daisy stood there, watching, unable to pull herself away. Seeing the two of them together—father and son—was something she'd barely ever dreamed of. Hearing Charlie's eager chatter and Alex's low baritone in reply set something deep inside her quivering, aching.

Wanting. Far too much.

Abruptly she wheeled away. "I'll be upstairs," she said. "I have work to do."

He had come to see Charlie, not her. And while it was

hardly an honest introduction to the demands of fatherhood, if he came looking for reinforcements in fifteen minutes, she'd know it wasn't going to last.

Charlie came in half an hour later. "Alex an' me want to go to the park. He says to ask if you want to go along."

Annoyed that he would presume to decide what he and Charlie were going to do without consulting her, Daisy hurried downstairs.

The Legos and Matchbox cars had been neatly put away and Alex was zipping up his jacket. "Good," he said. "You're coming, too."

"You don't presume. You should have asked!"

"Charlie did ask."

Charlie bobbed his head. "I said we wanted to go, and did you want to come."

Daisy opened her mouth, then closed it again. "Fine," she said shortly. "I'll come."

It was torture, seeing him with Charlie, being with him herself, acting as though they were some lovely happy family, all the while knowing it was a sham.

"Take it easy," Alex said in an undertone as she jerkily shoved her arms into her jacket. "I'm not going to steal my son."

My son, she wanted to correct him. *And no, you're damned well not!*

But Alex had turned and was helping Charlie with his jacket. Daisy wanted to push him away and do it herself. But one look told her that Charlie was more patient with Alex helping than he would have been with her. And Alex did take the time to show him how to do it himself—except for the zipping up part.

"Guess we'll have to help with that," he said easily, then zipped the jacket up to Charlie's chin. Then rising again, he reached down to ruffle the little boy's hair.

It was a casual movement, but it already spoke of a connection that made Daisy's insides clench, especially when Charlie flashed him a happy grin.

Turning abruptly, she called Murphy and snapped on his leash. Then the four of them went out the door and headed to the park—just like a family.

She shouldn't have come. She should have stayed back in her office and got more work done. But the temptation of watching Alex with Charlie was too great. It was terrifying, too. But Charlie was having such a good time.

There was still lots of snow on the ground. Once they got to the park, they built a snowman. And they had a snowball fight. Then Charlie made snow angels.

"A snow devil more like," Daisy said, laughing as she watched him, then taking photos with the small pocket-size camera she always carried. She got quite a few of Charlie and Alex rolling balls to make the snowman, then more of Alex lifting Charlie onto his shoulders so he could put an old hat on the snowman's head.

They were laughing as they did it, Alex lurching around in the snow while Charlie gripped Alex's hair with his free hand and laughed madly. Then Alex tipped his head back to grin up at his son, and the look they shared made Daisy feel as if she'd caught a snowball square in the heart.

Later she nearly did as she helped Charlie pelt Alex with snowballs. She got several shots of Charlie and Alex throwing them at each other. Then Alex took the camera out of her hand.

"What are you doing?" She tried to grab it back.

But Alex held it out of her reach, his green eyes mischievous. "Go play with your son."

Self-consciously at first, Daisy did. But then she got caught up in Charlie's enthusiasm. And while she pushed Charlie on a swing and helped him build a little snow dog to go with the snowman, Alex took pictures. Finally, when Daisy said it was time to leave, he set the camera's timer and hauled them all into a picture together, scooping Charlie up into one arm while he flung the other around Daisy.

And once more when his arm pulled her close, Daisy felt the hum of electricity between them. She felt desire all over again, and knew it for the hopeless feeling it was. It was a relief when the timer went off, the shutter clicked, and he let her go, slung Charlie onto his shoulders and they all walked home.

On the doorstep, when Alex set him down, Daisy smiled politely. "Thank you. He enjoyed that."

"Did you?" Alex asked.

She heard the pointedness of his tone and chose to ignore it. "Of course." She fumbled to get the key in the lock. He was wearing sunglasses and before she'd turned away she couldn't read his expression, but she could still feel the intensity of his gaze.

"Good." He took the key out of her hand and opened the door himself. Then he pushed it open, let them go in, then followed and shut it behind him.

"I need to get dinner started. Don't let us keep you. I'm sure you have things to do." Daisy said briskly and, slipping off her jacket, started toward the kitchen.

"We can get takeout. What do you like?"

"I'm making stew. Charlie likes it."

"So do I." Alex smiled guilelessly.

"Alex can stay, can't he?" Charlie asked.

What was a mother to do? Of course she had to be polite. She was teaching Charlie to be polite.

The evening was interminable. Dinner. Then Charlie's bath. Then bedtime stories. And awareness of Alex at every single moment. Watching him with Charlie, catching him looking at her when he thought she wasn't noticing. Charlie's stories took forever, even though Alex read several of them. Prayers were longer, too, because Alex, of course, was added to them.

"No singing tonight," Daisy decreed before Charlie could even suggest it. "You need to go to sleep. Remember, your class is going to the zoo tomorrow." The preschool trip to the Bronx Zoo—and a program about animals in winter—had been much anticipated.

Now Charlie looked up from his pillow and asked, "Can Alex come?"

"No," Daisy said without giving Alex a chance to reply.

"But—"

"I have to work," Alex said, sounding regretful. "But we had fun today. We'll do this again."

Charlie popped up. "When?"

"That depends on how well and how fast you go to sleep now," Daisy said, no stranger to manipulative children. She gave him a speaking look.

Charlie sighed, sank back against the pillow and shut his eyes. "I'm sleepin'."

"So I see," Daisy said drily, bending to kiss him. "Good night, Mr. Sleepyhead."

"Night," Charlie murmured, not opening his eyes.

She stepped back, and found that Alex had taken her place at Charlie's bedside. He brushed a hand over Charlie's head, then dropped to one knee and pressed a light kiss on Charlie's forehead.

The boy's eyes popped open and small hard arms and one very hard blue cast wrapped themselves around Alex's neck.

Alex stiffened. And Daisy held her breath.

Then slowly his posture eased, and his arms went around Charlie, too. He scooped the boy up for a fierce hug, burying his face in the crook of Charlie's neck. Then slowly he drew back and lowered the boy to the pillows again. "G'night, sport." His voice was rough. He straightened and stood looking down at the little boy for a long moment.

Then his gaze turned to Daisy. Their eyes met. She shut off the light and headed down to the kitchen.

If he wanted to talk, he could do it while she washed the dinner dishes. But frankly, she didn't know what else there was to say. She began to run water in the sink, all the while aware of exactly where he was, hip propped against the counter beside the refrigerator, watching her.

"Sorry I didn't get here earlier," he said over the running water.

"You didn't need to come at all." Daisy set the plates in the soapy water.

"Of course I needed to come. But I had to get hold of Caroline. I needed to tell her first."

Daisy did turn then. "That you had a son? How did she take that after your 'no children ever' edict?"

Alex's mouth twisted wryly. "She was…surprised."

"I'll bet." Daisy turned away again, picking up a mug and scrubbing it so furiously that the tiny sprays of yellow primroses on it threatened to disappear.

"But she understands."

Daisy's teeth came together as she swallowed half a dozen remarks that were far snarkier than the previous one. "I don't want her *understanding*. If she's like you, she doesn't want kids around!"

"She won't have them. We've broken it off."

Daisy stared at him. "What?"

Alex lifted his shoulders. "Circumstances changed. I called Amalie, too. Told her I was cancelling the rest of our agreement. My matchmaker," Alex said when Daisy stared at him blankly.

She was still processing Caroline's departure. "Why?"

"Because I don't need one now. Obviously. She gets her money anyway, so she doesn't care. She wished me all the best." He paused, then exhaled slowly and said, "So, the decks are clear."

There was a moment's stark silence as the implication of his words set in. Daisy felt a sudden chill but it started inside her, not out.

"Clear," she echoed. "Clear for what?"

But as soon as she asked, she knew she couldn't let him answer. She already knew—and she didn't want to hear it. "For you to be noble? For you to do something stupid like ask me to marry you?"

Alex stared at her, taken aback. "Damned right I want to marry you. Why the hell not? It makes perfect sense."

Exactly what she wanted to hear. Daisy wasn't cold any longer, she was burning up. She wouldn't have been surprised if steam was coming out of her ears.

"You're just like Cal! What is it with men, anyway? Why do you always think you can make the world act the way you want it to?"

"Daisy—"

"It's all control with you, isn't it?"

"Daisy, stop it! Stop being stupid. And this has nothing to do with your ex or anyone else." He shoved away from where he was leaning against the countertop and came toward her. "Be sensible, Daisy. I want to—"

"No. Don't do it, Alex," she said fiercely. "Don't say it. I don't want to hear it." She flung the sponge away and put her hands over her ears. "I won't!"

Of all the bloody-minded females!

Alex couldn't believe it! But Daisy was glaring at him, her cheeks flushed, her eyes flashing. She'd flung the sponge into the sink and put her hands over her ears, defying him to…what?

Propose?

Of course he was damned well going to propose. It was the right thing to do. If he had fathered a child—and he quite obviously had—it was his duty to marry his child's mother, be her husband, a father to their child and…and then what?

Live happily ever after?

He wouldn't let himself think about that.

Because in his experience, people didn't get to. Well, maybe some did. But how did you know? How could you ever be sure?

You couldn't. But the decision was no longer his. He'd made it five years ago when he'd made love to Daisy. He'd spent all night coming to terms with what that meant, and he was ready to do it. Determined to do it.

And now...

Now he didn't have to.

Just like that, Daisy had popped his balloon of self-righteous nobility before he'd even had a chance to let it fly.

He should be relieved, Alex told himself. Somewhere deep down, he supposed he *was* relieved. But at the same time, he was madder than hell. He didn't like being dismissed, being told his presence wasn't needed, wasn't valued.

And if she expected he would just turn around and walk away, she was bloody well out of her mind. At least she'd taken her hands off her ears now and had turned back to the pots and pans with which she was making an almighty racket.

Alex scowled at her back. "I seem to recall," he pointed out, "that you wanted marriage."

The pots continued to clatter. She shot him a quick furious glance over her shoulder. "Five years ago, yes. When I was besotted, yes. When I thought you loved me, too. Not now! I don't want you now!"

It surprised him that her words actually hurt. They made him stiffen as if he could defend himself against them, against her. His jaw felt as tight as a steel trap. "Fine," he said tersely. "You don't have to 'have' me."

Daisy turned, a look of consternation flicked across her features, followed by a faint sheepish smile of relief. "Well, um, good. Thank you," she said gruffly.

"But that doesn't mean you're getting rid of me."

She blinked. "But—"

"For God's sake, Daisy. You have my son! You might not have seen fit to tell me, but I know it now. And I'm not going to walk out of his life. I want to be part of it. I want him to be part of mine."

"For how long? Are you going to be buddies like you were today? For as long as it suits you? Are you going to be here when he needs you or are you going to walk when the going gets tough? Do you imagine you can be here and not *care,* Alex? You said—you told me plainly—brutally—that you didn't want to care—about anyone!" Her eyes flashed with accusation.

"You never let me care," he pointed out, trying to sound calmer than he felt. "You didn't even tell me he existed!"

"To protect him! To protect him from the knowledge that for you love is a one-way street!"

Stung, for a moment Alex didn't reply. Deliberately he swallowed his discomfort at the truth of her words. But at the same time, he lashed back. "Is that what it is?" he challenged her. "Or maybe—" he flung at her because, damn it, he wasn't the only one in the wrong "—it's all about protecting yourself!"

"I don't need to protect myself from you anymore. I know the score now. But Charlie doesn't. He'll give his love, wholly and completely, to you! To a man who can't let himself care— to a man who thinks love is worth nothing! And how do you think that's going to make him feel? I know what that's like, remember? And I wasn't four! I know what's right for my son!"

"And you're the arbiter of all things 'right' in Charlie's life?"

"I know him better than anyone. I love him more than anyone. I want the best for him."

"The best thing would be if he had a family," Alex told her flatly. "And you know it."

Daisy didn't reply. She just stared at him stonily. Then she reached for a towel, dried her hands on it, and marched past him, heading straight into the living room where she twisted the locks and yanked open the door. "I think it's time you left now."

Alex followed her into the living room, but he stopped there, staring at her, trying to fathom what was going on in her head. She wasn't being sensible, wasn't being rational.

"You know I'm right, Daisy."

She just looked at him, then at the door. When he still didn't move, she yanked his jacket off the hook where he'd hung it and thrust it at him. "Goodbye, Alex."

Wordlessly he reached out and took it, shrugged it on and zipped it up. "Fine. I'll go. But this isn't over. I'll be back. And while I'm gone, don't just think about Charlie. Think about what you want, too."

And he pulled her into his arms and took her mouth with his.

He'd been wanting to do this all day, all yesterday, every minute, it seemed, since he'd kissed her last. The hunger was so fierce he ached with it.

Now he felt her whole body stiffen. She raised her arms between them, her forearms pressing against his chest as if to hold him off. It didn't matter. While he would have liked to feel her body melt against him, to have her arms wrap around him, to know her eagerness matched his, he didn't need it to prove his point.

He had his lips to convince her, to taste her, to tease her. He had his tongue to touch her lips, to part them, to slip between and find her sweetness. God, she made him crazy, made his whole being quiver with need, made the blood sing in his veins.

He wasn't going to let her pretend that it meant nothing. Kissing Daisy *never* meant nothing. Kissing Daisy was amazing, wild, always potent, always drugging. Kissing Daisy always made his heart slam against the wall of his chest, made his loins tighten and his body hum with desire.

And damn it, he knew—absolutely knew—it was the same for her.

She fought it. He could feel her resisting. But she was fighting herself, not him. Her lips trembled, pressed together, denied him. But she denied herself, as well.

So he touched them anyway. He drew a line with his tongue, coaxed, teased. And they gave, opened just a fraction. He took advantage, darted within. He heard her whimper, and her fingers opened to clutch his jacket, hanging on. Her lips softened, parted farther. And he felt a jolt as her tongue tangled with his.

Yes, like that. It was always like that between them. Always had been. Alex wanted to cheer, to exult, to press his advantage and take them where they both wanted to go. He wanted to slide his fingers beneath her sweater and stroke her curves, her breasts, her very bones. He wanted to tease beneath the waistband of her jeans, slide his fingers south, touch her— there. Damn she was killing him. His breath came hard and fast. He wanted to taste, to tease, to sample and suckle. He wanted to devour. He wrapped her in his arms, thrust his fingers in her hair, kissed her hard one more time.

Then he pulled back, dragging in lungfuls of air as he looked down into her stunned feverish gaze. "While you're thinking," he said roughly, "think about that."

Her palm connected with his cheek so fast he didn't even see it coming.

"What the hell was that for?" he demanded. His fingers curled. He jammed his hands in his pockets.

"What was the kiss for?" she countered furiously.

His gaze narrowed. "*That's* why you slapped me? For reminding you that we had something good?"

"I don't need any reminders, thank you very much. And it turns out we didn't have anything at all."

"You don't believe that."

"I do. And I don't need you trying to bribe me with sex."

He gaped at her. "Bribe you?"

Her eyes flashed. "Bribe me, get around me, coerce me, make me do what you want because I'm somehow susceptible to you! Call it what you like. It's not going to work."

"For God's sake, Daisy." He raked fingers through his hair. "I was trying to show you it isn't all about Charlie."

"No, it isn't. It's all about you—what you want, when you want it, and not when you don't. You don't love Charlie. You don't love anyone. You don't want to. You push people away. At least Cal wanted to," she spat at him furiously.

"Cal?" he retorted. "This is all about Cal? All about your 'failed' marriage? Has it really made you that bitter?"

"I'm not bitter at all. Not at Cal. Not at our marriage." She lifted her chin as if defying him to argue. "We went into it with our eyes open."

He watched her, saw a host of conflicting expressions cross her face. Then she lifted a shoulder as if shrugging off a burden and said, "Cal is gay."

Alex stared at her.

"He's my friend. And he didn't have a lover. So when he saw what I was going through, he tried to make it easier for me." She ran her tongue over her lips. "He was convinced that he could will himself to love whoever he wanted to love." She shrugged. "He believes in the same things I do—commitment, long-term relationships, responsibility. Love."

Alex's gaze narrowed.

"He never lied to me. And I didn't lie to him. He knew I loved you. He knew you didn't love me. He offered his name, his support, everything he could. And I did the same for him. But—" she lifted her shoulders "—it wasn't enough. We tried to make it work. It didn't. In the end we knew that. We'll always be friends. But there's more to real love, real marriage than that. And we both wanted…more."

"I'm offering you more," Alex pointed out indignantly.

Daisy just looked at him. She took a slow breath, then swallowed and shook her head. "No, Alex. You're not. You're offering far, far less."

She pushed him out the door and closed it after him.

CHAPTER ELEVEN

DAISY leaned against the door, tears blurring her eyes. She dashed them away with a shaking hand. Of course he thought she was mad. The way he'd looked at her, patent disbelief in his eyes.

He was offering her marriage, wasn't he? Hadn't that been her heart's desire five years ago?

Yes, then. Not now.

Because this was exactly the sort of "marriage" he would have been offering Caroline. A wedding, a legal, convenient version of friends with benefits. Now as she stood with her back to the front door, still hearing Alex's footfalls moving quickly away, Daisy wiped a hand over her face, touched the tears, wanted to deny them. Knew she couldn't.

They were as real as the truth she'd just told Alex: marriages of convenience didn't work. Not for her. She and Cal had done their best. But friendship and responsibility only went so far.

They were only a part of the deep abiding fullness of heart, soul, mind and body that real love was.

She knew it wasn't easy. She knew, just as Alex knew, that real love hurt.

She didn't care. If she could have the love, she could endure the pain. She'd been raised in the real love of her parents' marriage. She remembered their joys and their sorrows. She remembered all too well her mother's pain at her father's death.

But she remembered, too, the sight of her mother smiling through her tears as she'd said, "I don't regret it for an instant. Loving Jack was worth all of this."

This was sometimes heartache, sometimes pain, sometimes joy, sometimes the simple act of heart-deep sharing.

Daisy wanted that.

She had the pain part down pat, she thought, tears streaming down her face.

But she knew she'd done the right thing—even if Alex had been right, that she'd been protecting herself. If marrying Cal had been a mistake, marrying Alex would be a disaster—because she could not stop loving him, and he didn't know what real love was.

He couldn't draw a straight line.

He broke the lead in all his mechanical pencils. He snapped the nib off his best drawing pen. His hands shook so badly as he sat at his desk and tried to find the calm he always felt designing, that he crumpled up page after page of the paper in his sketchbook.

Finally Alex threw the whole damn thing out and went to stand and stare out the window, dragging in deep breaths. But for once even the sight of the spectacular Manhattan skyline didn't soothe his furious soul.

He pressed his forehead against the cold glass of the window, then lifted a hand and rubbed it against his stubbled cheek.

The physical sting of Daisy's palm was long gone. But the emotional sting was imprinted on his soul. So were the words she'd flung at him: *It's all about you. You don't love Charlie. You don't love anyone. You don't want to.*

His throat tightened. His eyes blurred. He sucked in another breath and shook his head, wanting to deny it.

But he couldn't. Not entirely. At least a part of what she said was true: He *hadn't* wanted to.

For years—ever since Vass's death and his parents' divorce—Alex had done his best to make sure that anything as messy and painful as love would not be a part of his world. He'd deliberately built himself a life without it. He had his business, his design projects, his friends, and recently he'd figured that he could do marriage as long as it was on his terms, where his wife didn't want anything deeper or more demanding than he did.

He'd wanted a world he could control.

Which was why he had turned his back on Daisy five years ago.

She had threatened his control. She had bowled him over that weekend, had loved and given and enchanted in equal measures. He'd never met anyone so unguarded, so genuine, so warm and real.

Letting Daisy into his life would have been opening himself up to a tidal wave of emotions he couldn't control, a future he couldn't predict, the possibility for pain he didn't ever want to experience again.

God knew what would happened if he let down his guard.

So he hadn't. He'd turned away from her warmth, rejected her love, shut her out of his life. And having done so, he'd thought he was safe.

He was wrong.

But she was wrong, too.

Daisy had thought he *couldn't* love, and Alex had believed he *wouldn't*.

But God help him, he did. He loved Charlie. He'd only had to see the boy, watch the joy of life in his eyes, listen to him, hold his hand, touch his hair—and he loved. But more than that, before he recognized that he loved Charlie, he knew he loved her.

Daisy.

In spite of himself and his determined intentions, the day Daisy had come into his life, she had created a tiny rent in his armor. She had pierced his defenses, had touched his heart and planted a seed deep in his soul. For two days she had given him a glimpse of what life could be like if he had dared to let it grow.

He hadn't. He'd turned his back. But while he thought he'd walked away heart-whole, it wasn't true.

The minute he'd seen her again this autumn, everything he had felt when he'd been with her the first time—the need, the emotion, the connection—the sense that the world was a brighter, warmer, fuller, more welcoming place—had broken through.

He hadn't given in, of course. Though he had felt the attraction all over again, he'd still tried to do it his way—to control it. To control her.

He couldn't.

She wouldn't let him.

He knew what she wanted. Demanded. A real future, a no-holds-barred willingness to love and, admitting that love, to face the possibility of pain, of loss of control, of helplessness—all the things he'd said no to.

He didn't know if he could do it now.

But he loved. He had no choice. It was simply there—in him. For better or worse. But he knew he couldn't face the future until he was able to face the past.

Rubbing a hand over his face, Alex turned away from the window, from the cool remote perfection of the distant skyline, to the emotional minefield that he carried inside him. He padded into his bedroom.

The room was spare, unadorned. It held a wide bed, a tall oak chest of drawers, a closet. Nothing more. He went to the chest of drawers, then crouched down and pulled open the bottom drawer.

It was empty except for one thing—a single sturdy, flat, dark green cardboard box, perhaps a foot-square, two inches deep.

For a long minute, he just looked at it. Didn't immediately reach for it. Didn't really want to touch it even yet.

He hadn't touched it except when he'd moved it, since he'd

left for university at the age of eighteen. He hadn't opened it since he'd put the lid on it when his parents separated, when they sold the house, when his mother moved to Athens and his father to Corfu.

"Don't look back," his father had said as he'd sold off everything and buried himself in his scholarly books.

But Alex had put the things that mattered in that box, the things he couldn't let go of, even if he couldn't bring himself to look at them.

He'd carried the box with him ever since. He'd taken it to university in London, to his first job in Brussels, to the dozen or so places he'd lived in his adult life. He had brought it with him here.

Wherever he was, he always put it carefully in its own drawer where he wouldn't accidentally stumble across it when he was looking for something else. He didn't want to be blindsided when he wasn't prepared.

Someday, he always promised himself, he would open it. When the time was right he would once again let himself remember. But as time had passed, he'd learned to cope, he'd shut off the past, had refused to give it the power to hurt him. It was easier to forget. The time had never been right.

Until now.

Now he hurt anyway. Now Daisy's words had cut right through his protective shield, had looked inside him and found him wanting.

His hands shook as he drew the box out of the drawer and carried it over to sit on the bed with it. He was surprised how light it was. In his imagination it was the heaviest thing he owned.

He ran his fingers over the top, then carefully eased the lid off and set it aside. There were only a handful of things within—and just as he had feared, the sight of them brought a thousand memories flooding back.

There was the postcard of the Matterhorn that Vass had sent him when he was six and Vass was nine. Vass had been with their father in Switzerland. "It's s'cool," he had written. "You and me will climb it someday."

They hadn't, of course. But when Vass came home, they'd begun climbing the cliffs by their island home with eager purpose. Just as they'd earnestly practiced tying ship's knots in the two feet of line that lay in the box, as well.

"Learn to tie the knots and I'll teach you to sail," their father had said.

Now Alex drew the piece of line out of the box and his fingers moved automatically to make a Spanish bowline, a clove hitch, a figure eight while in his mind's eye he saw the summer days they'd spent on the water, the three of them. He remembered the heat and the sun and the wind—and the stories and the laughter that came with them.

He picked a small reddish-brown pottery shard out next, rubbing his thumb over its worn contours and remembering Vass finding it and saying he was going to grow up and be an archaeologist like Indiana Jones. And there were two very well-used Star Wars figures—Luke and Han, of course— they'd played with for years. There was a painstaking drawing of the Battlestar Galactica that Vass had drawn while he was in the hospital, and a far more precise elegant one that Alex had drawn at the same time because, after all, he was the one who was going to be the architect, not Vass.

And then there was a single silver Porsche Matchbox car.

Alex had faced all the other bits of memorabilia with a tight jaw, a strained smile, blinking eyes.

But the silver Porsche felt like a dagger to his heart.

They had fought over the silver Porsche, he and Vass. It had been his brother's, but Vass had been indifferent until Alex wanted it. And they had fought—actually came to blows— and Vass had punched him in the stomach and he had given Vass a bloody nose.

He stared at the small car now, picked it up and ran his hands over the lines of its frame. Then he closed his fingers around it until he felt the cold metal bite into his hand. He wanted to feel it. Needed the pain.

It hadn't been Vass's first bloody nose. He'd had several that summer. But this one they hadn't been able to stop. Not until they'd taken him to the doctor. And then there had been murmurs of concern. His mother's worry. His father's pacing. More doctor visits. A flight to Athens to see a specialist. A hospital. Tests.

A diagnosis. Leukemia.

Because of a bloody nose. A bloody nose that was Alex's fault.

It wasn't, of course. He knew that now. But at the time, he was not yet nine years old. He hadn't known—and no one had bothered to reassure him. They'd all been far too worried about Vass. He had been worried, too.

But he'd swallowed his worry and his guilt because there hadn't been time for it, there hadn't been room for it. His parents hadn't even seen it.

When Vass had come home from the hospital the first time, Alex had been scared to go into his room, afraid he might do more damage.

But Vass had said scornfully, "You can't give somebody leukemia. You're not that powerful, brat." Then he'd grinned, Vass's old wonderful "I can do anything" grin, and Alex had had his brother back.

Then he'd believed Vass would recover. Then he'd hoped for the best. Two and a half years later, there was no best.

The last time he'd been in Vass's hospital room, Vass had said, "Keep the Porsche. It's yours."

"I don't want it," Alex had protested, tears streaming down his face.

Now slowly, painfully, he unbent his fingers, and stared at the little car. He rubbed his fingers over it, remembering Vass doing the same thing. He squeezed his eyes shut and saw Vass's frail body and thin pale face, and he let the pain wash over him.

But other memories came, too. Along with the pain, he remembered the good times, the joy, the sharing and laughter. And he knew you couldn't have one without the other.

For years he'd put the Porsche and the memories in a box and tucked them away, unable to face them.

You don't love anyone. You don't want to. Daisy's words echoed in his mind. He heard them again, along with her parting shot: *You're offering far, far less.*

Alex knew what he had to do.

He just hoped to God he could do it.

"'S Christmas!" Charlie jiggled Daisy's shoulder, waking her, peering wide-eyed into her sleep-gritted ones. "An' Santa came!"

The pure joy of youth and belief beamed at her. She rolled over and shoved herself to a sitting position, then reached out to pull him into a fierce hug. "Of course he did. Were you worried?"

Charlie gave her a quick, hard, fierce hug in return, then wriggled out of her grasp, his head shaking to and fro. "Nah. I knew he'd come." He held out a hand to her and Daisy let him pull her to her feet.

"I did, too," she confided, snagging her bathrobe as he dragged her toward the living room, toward the Christmas tree which was already lit with small bright multicolored lights, because obviously Charlie had been there first, poking around.

But he hadn't opened any gifts. He had waited for her. Now he looked at her expectantly.

And deliberately, mustering all the joy she could manage, Daisy put her game face on. "Let me put the coffee on. Then we'll see what Santa brought."

There was no time to brood on Christmas morning. There were gifts to unwrap and ooh-and-aah over. Santa made a just-turned-five-year-old boy very happy. There was a set of Legos and some action figures, three new books, a soccer ball, and a floor mat with the outline of streets and buildings—a city to drive his cars around in. Daisy's mother had sent him a build-it-yourself racetrack for his little cars and a stash of art supplies for rainy days.

Charlie was thrilled. He wanted to play with all of it now. Daisy wanted to let him. But Cal was coming to get Charlie at noon. His parents were already here from Cooperstown and were looking forward to spending the day with Cal and their grandson. All of Cal's siblings and their families were coming, too.

"They'd be happy to see you, too," Cal had assured Daisy last week when they'd discussed plans. "You don't have to be alone."

But Daisy had shaken her head. "I'll be all right. I've booked a photo shoot." She had done it deliberately, agreeing to a plea from one of her old college classmates that she do a four-generation family shoot on Christmas afternoon.

"They're all only here for the day," Josie had apologized when she'd asked. "I know it's probably impossible being Christmas and all...but just in case..."

"Sounds great," Daisy had said firmly. It would keep her from sitting at home alone and miserable. "It'll be fun." She'd pasted a bright determined smile on her face. "If it's nice and there's snow on the ground, we can shoot it in the park."

It was nice. There was even, amazingly enough, a few inches of new snow on the ground. And more was drifting down by the time Cal appeared at the door.

He was smiling and looked happier than she could remember. She knew he'd met someone. It was early days yet, he'd told her last week. But there was a light in his eyes she hadn't ever seen before.

He took one look at her pale face and the dark circles under her own eyes and said, "You look awful."

Daisy laughed wryly. "Thank you very much."

But Cal frowned. "I shouldn't be taking him away from you today. Come with us."

Adamantly Daisy shook her head. "I'm meeting Josie's

family at their place at one to do some indoor shots, then we're going to shoot at the Bow Bridge in the park if it's still snowing."

"Come after you finish."

"I'll be fine," she insisted. "Go on. Have a good time." She gave Charlie a hug and a kiss. "Behave."

"I always behave," he said stoutly. "I'm bringin' my new guys to show Grandpa."

"He'll like that." Daisy gave him one more squeeze, then stood up. Her smile was strained. Of course Charlie didn't notice. She hoped Cal didn't, either. "See you tomorrow," she said with all the cheer she could manage. Then she shut the door behind them, leaned back against it, and pressed her hands to her eyes.

It was letting Charlie go, she told herself. This was, after all, the first Christmas that she hadn't had him with her all the time. Always before, after their divorce, Cal had come here and they'd celebrated together. But they both knew that couldn't last. He had a life now—and she had to get one.

Now she scrubbed at her eyes and took a deep, hopefully steadying breath, then she went upstairs to get ready to go, picking out the lenses and filters she wanted to take, determined to keep her mind busy so she wouldn't think about where Charlie was and what he was doing and...

...about Alex.

She *had* to stop thinking about Alex.

It had been two weeks since they'd had their confrontation. Two weeks since she'd spurned his offer of marriage before he could even make it, since she'd told him exactly what she thought of it—and of him—and had shoved him out of the door and out of her life.

He hadn't been back.

Was she surprised? Of course not. It was for the best, really, and she knew it.

What surprised her was how much she cared.

She didn't want to care! She didn't want to miss him,

didn't want to remember him sitting on the floor playing with Charlie, didn't want to think about him telling their son a story, didn't want to close her eyes and be plagued by images of him with Charlie in his arms or on his shoulders, the two of them grinning at each other.

She didn't want to remember how proud she'd felt the night he'd got the award for his hospital design, how intently she'd listened when he'd told her about his inspiration for it, how much she heard and understood what he didn't ever say.

She didn't want to think about him—and she couldn't seem to stop.

Now she finished packing her gear bag, slipped on her puffy, bright blue down jacket and headed toward the park.

It was Christmas. A time of hope. A time to put the past behind her and move on. She squared her shoulders, and picked up her bag. Maybe after she'd finished Josie's family's photo shoot, she would go ice skating, meet the man of her dreams, fall in love.

Fairy tales. Would she never learn?

Daisy sighed and headed for Josie's place.

Four generations of the Costello family were ready and waiting. Josie swept Daisy into their Fifth Avenue sixth floor apartment overlooking the park, equal measures eager and apologetic. They were so glad to have her take photos of their family holiday, they were so sorry they were taking her away from her own family today of all days.

"It's all right," Daisy assured them. "I'm glad to do it."

It was every bit the distraction she had hoped. The seven children—cousins who didn't see each other often—along with their parents, grandparents and two great-grandparents, were a noisy energetic mob. And Daisy, intrigued by the possibilities, threw herself into the work.

She did a series of family groups, then gathered them around the table, shot Josie's grandfather slicing the turkey, her grandmother helping the youngest grandson fill his plate.

She caught two cousins playing chess in front of the fire, three little girl cousins playing dress-up with the small trunk of fancy clothes one had got for Christmas.

It was the perfect family Christmas, the kind she'd seen in movies and on TV. The kind she'd always wanted for herself. And especially for Charlie.

She shot their preening and their giggling. She shot four generations of Costello men watching football on television, simultaneously cheering or groaning. She had all the children make a human pyramid that mimicked the Christmas tree.

Then, as soon as she shot that, she said, "Let's go to the park," before things got rowdy, which the human pyramid showed signs of becoming.

The snow was still falling, picture-perfect, when they got to the Bow Bridge. She posed them there and did a couple of formal shots for posterity while passersby, walking off their Christmas dinners, stopped and watched then, smiling, moved on.

Daisy didn't pay them any mind. She glanced their way, then turned back to shoot a series of photos of great-grandpa and grandpa and two little grandsons building a snowman. The girls were making snow angels, their colorful scarves flung out against the snow as they moved their arms and legs. They danced and played and she captured it all—the grace, the laughter—mothers and daughters, grandmothers, great-grandmother and granddaughters. The boys were wrestling in the snow now, pelting each other with snowballs, laughing madly.

Family.

How she envied them their family. She tried to shove the thought away even as it tightened her throat, made her swallow hard. She blinked hard and stopped shooting for a moment, needing to turn away.

Several people who had been watching, smiled at her and scuffed their feet and moved away. She got a grip, started to turn back, then caught a glimpse of someone else out of the corner of her eye.

Her gaze stopped, jerked back, dismissed it. She turned to shoot the snowball-throwing boys again. But her heart was beating faster as she edged around to get a different angle, to look west without turning her head.

He was still there, standing in the shadows beneath the trees.

Lean, tall. Dark wind-blown hair. Wearing jeans and a hunter-green down jacket.

"Lookit me!" one of the Costello boys shouted. He had scrambled up into the crook of a tree and peered down at her.

Daisy turned, focused, shot. Then she swivelled again, taking more shots of the snowball fight, but not even looking at what she was shooting.

She was trying to squint past the camera, to get a better look. He was too far away to be sure. But the last time she'd seen Alex he'd worn a jacket like that.

Surely it wasn't. It couldn't be. It was her stupid fairy-tale-obsessed mind playing tricks on her.

She turned and aimed her shots at the snowman builders now. Grandpa had the littlest boy on his shoulders to loop a scarf around the snowman's neck. Daisy shot it all. That was what she was here for.

When she turned around again, she expected the man to be gone. He was leaning against the tree, hands in his pockets, staring steadily at her.

Daisy raised her camera and pointed it. She zoomed in, and caught her breath.

Slowly Alex nodded at her.

But he didn't move, didn't come closer. Just leaned against the tree, as if he was waiting for a bus or something!

"Are your fingers freezing? Daisy? Daisy?"

She turned, realizing that Josie had been talking to her. "N-no. I'm fine. I— Fine." She glanced back.

He was still there.

"I think we'll call it quits if you've got enough," Josie said. "The little ones and great-grandma are getting cold. I am, too," she admitted, blowing on her hands. "But it's been such fun. Will you come with us? We're going to make cocoa for the kids and hot toddies for the grown-ups."

The panicky desperate part of Daisy wanted to jump at the invitation. Whatever Alex was doing there, he was there on purpose. He had something to say. And Daisy was sure she didn't want to hear it.

But if she didn't hear it now, he'd find another time. And at least she wouldn't have to worry about Charlie overhearing.

"Thanks," she said to Josie. "But I'll just go on home. I loved doing it, though. I'll have the proofs for you by the end of the week."

"Fantastic." Josie gave her a hug. "You were brilliant. And we had a blast. We'll remember it always."

Daisy smiled wanly. She had a feeling she would, too.

With cheery goodbyes and fierce hugs from several small children and a couple of great-grandparents, Daisy began to pack up her gear while the Costellos headed back across the park.

She focused securing the lenses in her camera bag. She didn't look around, ignored the sound of footsteps through the snow. But her heart was going like a jackhammer in her chest. She straightened just as a shadow fell across her.

"Daisy." His voice was soft and gruff, surprisingly hesitant.

Steeling herself, she turned. The sight that met her eyes was a surprise, too. This wasn't the smooth confident man she expected to see. This Alex's jaw was stubbled with at least a day's worth of beard. This Alex's eyes were bloodshot and shadowed. As she stared, his jaw bunched and tightened. He ran the tip of his tongue between his lips, then pressed them together again.

"Alex." She nodded carefully, determinedly giving nothing away, particularly encouragement. The last thing she needed was to fight this battle again.

For a long moment he didn't speak, either, and Daisy wondered if she ought to just step around him, head home. Maybe he'd just been walking in the park, had happened on her by accident. God knew perverse things like that could happen.

"You were right," he said abruptly. "What you said."

Daisy blinked. What she'd said? What had she said? Uncertainly she shook her head.

"That I didn't want to love. That I pushed people away." He answered the question before she even had to ask. He said the words quickly, as if he needed to get past them. Then he said again more slowly, "I didn't want to. Then." Pale green eyes met hers.

Then? Which meant…what? Daisy felt herself tense, but didn't move. She searched his gaze, tried to hear the words he never said.

Then he took a breath and said them. "I loved my brother," he said, the words coming out on a harsh breath. "And I thought I killed him."

"What?" She stared at him, aghast.

He shook his head. "We had a fight…over a car. A toy. I was *eight*," he said harshly. "And I gave him a bloody nose. He bled and bled. They said he had leukemia. I thought…" He shook his head, anguished. "I wasn't even nine," he said. "I didn't know."

"Oh, Alex." She just looked at him. She'd known about his brother. She hadn't known this.

"He said I didn't. But he just kept getting sicker. And…then he died." Now she could hear him dragging the words out. "My parents were shell-shocked. Destroyed. They couldn't help each other. They couldn't even look at me."

"It wasn't your fault!"

"I know that now. But we don't talk much in my family, not about…" He swallowed, then looked past her over her shoulder, staring into the distance, his eyes bright with unshed tears. Whatever he was seeing, Daisy was sure it wasn't in Central Park.

He brought his gaze back to hers, his eyes filled with pain. "When I was ten years old I thought I'd killed my brother and ended our family." His throat worked. "I loved all of them."

And she had told him he didn't love anyone.

"I'm sorry." Her words came out as brokenly as his. She wanted to reach out, to touch his sleeve, to put her arms around him. She had no right. "I'm so sorry."

He nodded almost imperceptibly. He took a breath and then another. "I put it away, shut it out of my mind, didn't deal with it. I never talked to anyone about it—except you. Five years ago."

Her eyes widened. "You never—?"

"No. I shut it all out." There it was, the sharp hard edge. She could hear it. It was the way he always shut people out.

He bent his head. "But I couldn't shut you out." His voice was ragged. A faint smile touched his beautiful mouth.

"You certainly did," Daisy reminded him. She remembered his words all too well.

Alex had the grace to grimace. "I tried," he allowed. "Because you got under my skin. Made me feel things that scared the hell out of me."

"What?" Daisy blinked, confused.

"I was…falling in love with you—even back then, that first night." He pulled a hand out of his pocket and rubbed it against the back of his neck. "I was falling in love with you," he repeated, wonderingly, as if he was amazed he could admit it not only to her but to himself. "And it scared me to death. When you started talking about it like it was a good thing— loving—all I could think was, 'I've got to get out of here. I'll destroy her, too.'" His tone was harsh, anguished. And when she looked close she could see his eyes glistening. He blinked rapidly, then gave a quick shake of his head. "So I did." He swallowed. "Hell of a lot safer that way."

Daisy digested that. Drew in a breath, then another, and cocked her head, then asked him gently, "Was it?"

A corner of his mouth quirked up. "It was until I ran into

you again back in September. Then, short answer—no. You're under my skin. I can't get rid of you. Wherever I go, wherever I am, there you are." He made it sound awful, but Daisy suddenly couldn't stop smiling.

Despairing, Alex shook his head. "I couldn't get you out of my mind, though God knows, I tried. I told myself I needed a woman who didn't make me feel all the things you made me feel. But you must have noticed, I couldn't stay away."

"Every time I thought I'd seen the last of you, you came back," Daisy realized. "It made me nervous."

"Because of Charlie?"

"Partly. But really, I suppose, because I'd…never quite got over you." She didn't want to admit it, but if they were being honest, she owed him that. The heat of his gaze was warming her, making her tingle all the way to her toes. At the same time she was still trying to get a grip on the notion that five years ago he'd been falling in love with her, too.

"I wanted you as soon as I saw you again," he told her.

"On your terms."

"Hell, yes. Safer that way. And Caroline was safe. I never felt for her the tiniest bit of what I feel for you. I never wanted her. Never missed her. I knew I could live without her. I can't live without you."

"Alex." She touched his cheek with her palm and he turned his face to press his lips into it, his kiss making her shiver.

"I couldn't ask her to marry me," he admitted. "I was going to, but I never could."

"You must have realized she needed someone else."

He reached up a hand to press her palm against his cheek. He looked down into her eyes, his full of an emotion she'd never dared hope to see there. "Yeah, maybe that was it." He gave a self-deprecating laugh. "No, damn it. I was still in love with you."

Daisy stared at him in astonishment.

"And then I discovered Charlie."

"And you wanted Charlie."

"Yes. I love Charlie," Alex said with an intensity that made her believe it. "Not just because he reminds me of Vass, though God knows he does. I love him because he's yours. And mine. Because he's bright and inquisitive and fun and just knowing he's alive gives me joy." He shook his head slowly. "And I would give my life for him—and for you. I will go to the ends of the earth for you. I will slay dragons for you. I will get hurt for you. I swear it, Daisy." There was wonder in his voice.

Daisy opened her mouth, then closed it again. She didn't know what to say. Her eyes brimmed. So did her heart. Dear God, she'd loved this man for years, but never more than she loved him now, now that he had discovered the love he was capable of, the love he was willing to dare to share.

He reached out and touched her cheek, stroking away a tear she didn't even know was there. Then he wrapped his arms around her and drew her close, let her feel the pounding of his heart, the warmth of his love, the shelter of his embrace.

She leaned against him, letting herself sink into him, loving his strength, his steadiness. She rested her head in the crook between his shoulder and his chin.

"I would have been here sooner," Alex went on. He spoke softly, his lips against her hair. "But I didn't think you probably wanted to talk to me again after what you said the last time."

Daisy raised her eyes to look up at him, feeling guilty. "I didn't know—"

But Alex shook his head. "No, you were right. It was my problem. You gave me a reason to confront it, to deal with it. And I needed to before I could come back. So I did. I had to go to Paris for work anyway. It was a commitment. I spent ten days there. Then I went to see my parents."

Daisy took a quick look into his eyes.

He bent his head, held her closer. "We've…barely talked in years. It was, I suppose, easier for all of us that way. Not to be reminded."

Daisy slid her arms around his back, holding him close, feeling the tension in him.

He cleared his throat, scuffed his boot in the snow, then pulled back a little so he could look down into her eyes. "They're both in Greece these days. Not together. My mother's divorced a third time. My dad is still buried in his books. But I…talked to both of them. About Vass. About…what happened, about what I thought. They were shocked. They had no idea." His eyes were brimming again. He shook his head. "I'm glad I went. And I…expect I'll see them again." He hesitated. "I told them about you…and Charlie. They'd like to meet you both someday…if you're agreeable."

"Of course," Daisy said faintly, her heart spilling over with love for him, thrilled that he'd taken the step to reconnect with his parents, delighted that they might all now find a beginning to their healing.

Alex pressed a kiss into her hair. "Thank you."

Then he drew back and dug into the pocket of his jacket. "Will you give this to Charlie?" He took out a small silver Matchbox car and handed it to her. "I have real Christmas presents for him, but he's got them already. I left them with Cal."

"Cal?" She stared at him in wonder. "You've never even met Cal."

"I have now. I went to your place from the airport. You weren't there. I didn't know where you were. I thought you might be with him."

"How do you know where he lives?"

"I told you once before—" Alex's mouth quirked "—the internet is a wonderful thing."

Apparently it was. "But I wasn't there."

"No," Alex said. "But he knew where you were."

"And he told you?" That didn't sound like Cal. He was generally very protective.

"After he'd threatened me within an inch of my life. Said I'd be sorry if I hurt you. And I believed him. I liked him.

And...I don't ever want to hurt you, Daze." His voice was rough and warm and intense.

And he wasn't hurting her, he was killing her, Daisy thought desperately. She looked down at the tiny car in her hand. Without having to be told, she knew what it was.

"The car you fought over," she said.

He nodded. "It was Vass's. He gave it to me before...before he died." Alex choked on the words. "I've carried it with me ever since."

"Your hair shirt?" Daisy asked gently.

"I didn't think so then, but yes, it was. I lived with the guilt a long time. I might have lived with it forever—without you."

"Oh, Alex." She nestled close again.

"Charlie should have it. He doesn't need to know its past. Only that it's for him—a gift from the uncle he'll never know. Vass—" Alex swallowed "—would have loved him."

Daisy blinked furiously, her fingers tightening around the tiny car. "Yes." She tucked it into the pocket of her jacket. "Oh, yes."

"I have something for you, too." He fished in his other pocket and pulled out a small box, the sort that jewelry came in. A ring box?

Daisy's heart hammered furiously. More manipulation? Or were they past that?

Alex held it out to her. "This is for you. I saw it at a little shop in Paris and I thought of you. Of us. It's the way I'd like us to be." He looked into her eyes and pressed it into her palm, then closed her fingers over it. Snowflakes dusted his dark lashes, settled on his midnight hair. He smiled gently. "I love you, Daisy. I hope someday you believe it."

Then he drew away from her, turned and set off through the snow.

Numbly, Daisy stared after him. *What?*

He was just going to leave her here? He was going to tell her he loved her, give her his heart, then walk away?

No insistence? No demand? No renewed proposal?

She looked down at the tiny box in her hand, then fumbled to open it. Inside was a silver necklace—real silver, unlike the Porsche—of two interlocking, entwined open hearts.

I thought of you, he'd said. *Of us.*

Two open hearts entwined.

Daisy bit down on her lip. Her fingers trembled. She clutched the box with the necklace in one hand and her camera bag in the other and broke into a run. "Alex! Alex, wait!"

He stopped, turned. Looked at her, half stricken, half hoping. She recognized that look now. She skidded to a halt bare inches in front of him, blinking furiously into the sun, into the dawning hope in those beautiful pale green eyes. "Ask me."

He frowned. "Ask what?"

"You know what!"

He raised a brow. A corner of his mouth quivered, almost smiled.

"Ask," Daisy demanded.

Then he took a breath. "Will you let me love you?" he asked. "Forever?"

"Yes." She threw her arms around him.

"Will you love me?" he asked as she kissed him. His voice was suspiciously hoarse.

"Yes!" She breathed the word against his lips.

"Will you marry me, Daze?" He barely got the words out because now he was kissing her back.

"Yes, Alex. Oh, yes, yes. Yes."

Daisy didn't miss Charlie that night as much as she'd thought she would. She took Alex home and didn't even open the other Christmas present he'd brought her from Paris.

She put on her necklace—or, rather, he put it on for her. Then she took him upstairs to her bedroom. There, slowly, he took off her sweater, her jeans, her shirt, her socks. Then he lowered her to the bed, and, smiling, began to take off everything else she wore.

Everything but the necklace. Daisy wouldn't let him take off that. But the rest—oh, yes. She shivered with pleasure at the way his fingers traced the lines and curves of her body, the way his lips followed and his tongue, as well.

When he unfastened her bra and slipped it off her shoulders, then bent his head to kiss her breasts, she lifted her hands and threaded them in the silky softness of his hair.

Alex kissed his way across her breasts, laved her nipples, made her tremble with longing. Then, smiling at her reaction, he dropped kisses down the line between her breasts, on down to her navel and beyond. And Daisy quivered with need for him.

"Alex!" She squirmed when he peeled her panties down, tossed them aside, then ran his fingers back up her calves, then her thighs, then touched her—there. "Wait. My turn. You're overdressed."

He lifted his head and smiled. "Am I?"

"Oh, yes." And then Daisy set about unwrapping the Christmas present she wanted more than anything—him.

"I love you," she whispered as she tugged his sweater over his head. "I've never forgotten doing this." She tossed his sweater on the bedside chair, then quickly disposed of the buttons of his shirt.

"You're faster at that than I remember." Alex kept his hands at his sides as he watched her, but there was a flame of desire in his eyes.

"Practice," Daisy said, beginning to work on the zip of his jeans.

"Practice?" Alex frowned.

"Charlie couldn't always dress himself."

He grinned, then sucked in a quick breath when she made quick work of the zipper and her fingers found him. He swallowed hard, then shrugged off his jeans and came to her on the bed, settled next to her, stroked his hands over her with an almost hesitant wonder.

And Daisy felt the same. "I love you," she whispered, glorying in being able to say it, to acknowledge it, and to know that he wanted to hear the words.

"I know. But not as much as I love you," he said, a tremor in his voice and another in the hands that stroked her sensitive skin.

"I'll show you," she insisted, and rolled onto her back, drawing him on top of her, wrapping herself around him.

"And I'll show you," Alex countered, teasing, tasting, touching. He was so exquisitely gentle, yet possessively so. His fingers found her, knew her, parted her. And then he slid in. "Daze!" His body tensed, froze. And then—at last—he began to move.

"Alex!" Her nails dug into his buttocks. Her head thrashed on the pillow. Her body tightened around him. He made her shiver, he made her quiver, he made her shatter. And he shattered right along with her, his face contorting, his body going rigid, then collapsing to bury his face against her neck.

She stroked his sweat-slick back, then turned her head and kissed his ear and along the whisker-roughened line of his jaw.

When at last he lifted his head it was to look down into her eyes with wonder. "Why did it take me so long to realize?" he murmured, sounding awestruck.

Daisy shook her head. She didn't need to ask why anymore. She had the answer she needed. "I'm just glad you did."

He rolled onto his back then and pulled her on top so that she rested her head on his chest and felt the gallop of his heart beneath her cheek. Softly, rhythmically, Alex stroked her hair.

Daisy didn't know how long they lay like that. She might have slept a little. She thought he did. But when they roused and began to touch, to love again, he raised his head from the pillow and peered down his nose at her. "Is this the sort of match you try to make?" he asked, giving her his heart with his eyes.

Daisy returned his gift full measure. But then she shook her head no.

"It's better," she told him, rising up to meet his lips, to love him, to share the wonder once more.

* * * * *

THE GREEK'S
ACQUISITION

CHANTELLE SHAW

CHAPTER ONE

ATHENS at two-thirty on a summer's afternoon baked beneath a cloudless sky. A heat haze shimmered above the steps leading to the entrance of Kalakos Shipping, and the glare from the sun seemed to set the office block's bronze-tinted glass windows aflame.

The automatic doors parted smoothly as Louise approached them. Inside, the décor was minimalist chic, and the air-conditioned atmosphere was as hushed as a cathedral. Her stiletto heels reverberated excruciatingly loudly on the black marble floor as she walked up to the desk.

The receptionist was as elegant as the surroundings, impeccably dressed, her face discreetly made up. Her smile was politely enquiring.

'My name is Louise Frobisher. I'm here to see Dimitri Kalakos.' Louise spoke in fluent Greek. One of the only good things to come from her nomadic childhood was that she had developed a flair for learning languages.

The receptionist glanced at the appointments diary on the desk and her expertly shaped brows drew together in a faint frown.

'I'm sorry, but Mr Kalakos does not appear to have an appointment with you, Miss Frobisher.

Louise had planned for such a response. 'My visit is on

a personal, not a business matter. I assure you Mr Kalakos will be delighted to see me.'

The statement strained the truth thinner than an over-stretched elastic band, she acknowledged. But she had gambled on the fact that Dimitri had a reputation as a playboy, and that with luck the reception staff would believe she was one of his—according to the gossip columns—numerous mistresses. That was the reason she was wearing a skirt several inches shorter than she had ever worn before, and killer heels that made her legs look as if they went on for ever.

She had left her hair loose for once, instead of bundling it into a knot on top of her head, and she was wearing more make-up than usual; the smoky grey shadow on her eyelids emphasised the deep blue of her eyes and her scarlet lipgloss matched exactly the colour of her skirt and jacket. The diamond *fleur-de-lis* pendant suspended on a fine gold chain around her neck had been her grandmother's. It was the only piece of jewellery she owned, and she had chosen to wear it in the hope that if her *grand-mère*, Céline, was looking down on her she would send her good luck.

She had read somewhere that confidence tricksters were successful because they acted with absolute self-assurance. And so when the receptionist murmured that she would just check with Mr Kalakos's PA, Louise laughed and tossed her blond curls over her shoulders as she strolled towards the lift. Many years ago she had visited Kalakos Shipping, when her mother had been Kostas Kalakos's mistress, and she felt certain that Dimitri now occupied the luxurious office suite on the top floor of the building that had once been his father's.

'There's no question that Dimitri will want to see me. And I promise you he won't want us to be disturbed for quite a while,' she drawled.

The receptionist stared at her uncertainly, but to Louise's relief she made no further attempts to detain her. However, the moment the lift doors closed her bravado disappeared and she felt as awkward and unsure of herself as she had been at nineteen. She could recall as clearly as if it had happened yesterday the bitter confrontation that had taken place between her and Dimitri seven years ago, and the memory of his anger and her humiliation induced a churning sensation in the pit of her stomach.

The lift seemed horribly claustrophobic, but she took a deep breath and forced herself to stay calm. Dimitri represented her best hope of helping her mother, and it was vital she remained composed and in control of the emotions that had been see-sawing between apprehension and anticipation at the prospect of coming face to face with him again after all this time.

She should have expected that getting past his PA would prove to be far more difficult than the receptionist in the downstairs lobby. To give Aletha Pagnotis—her name was on the door of her office—due credit, she did phone through to her boss and relay Louise's request for five minutes of his time.

The request was met with a blank refusal.

'If you could tell me the reason for your visit, Miss Frobisher, then perhaps Mr Kalakos will reconsider his decision,' the PA murmured, after half an hour had passed and she was no doubt as tired of having a stranger sitting in her office as Louise was tired of waiting.

Her reason for wanting to see Dimitri was too personal and too important to discuss with anyone but him, but it suddenly occurred to Louise that on Eirenne she had been known as Loulou—the nickname her mother always called her by. And because she had a different surname from Tina maybe Dimitri did not realise her identity.

His PA looked mystified as she double-checked the new message Louise asked her to give to her boss, but she duly disappeared into his office.

The aroma of freshly brewed coffee assailed Dimitri's senses and told him without him having to check the platinum Rolex on his wrist that it was 3:00 p.m. His PA served him coffee at exactly the same time every afternoon. Aletha had been with him for five years, and she ensured that his office ran with the smooth efficiency of a well-oiled machine.

'Efkharistó.' He did not lift his eyes from the columns of figures on his computer screen, but he was aware of her setting the tray down on his desk. Subconsciously he listened for the faint click of the door to indicate that she had left the room.

The click did not come.

'Dimitri—if I could have a word?'

Frowning at the unexpected interruption, he flicked his gaze from the financial report he was working on and glanced at his PA. 'I asked not to be disturbed,' he reminded her, impatience edging into his voice.

'Yes, I'm sorry…but the young woman who arrived earlier and asked to see you is still here.'

He shrugged. 'As I explained earlier, I don't know Louise Frobisher. I've never heard of her before, and unless she can give a reason for her visit I suggest you call Security and have her escorted from the premises.'

Aletha Pagnotis read the warning signs that the head of Kalakos Shipping was becoming irritated. Nothing was more likely to trigger Dimitri's temper than disruption to his routine. But running a billion-pound business empire must put huge demands on him, she conceded.

At thirty-three, Dimitri was one of the country's most

powerful businessmen. Even before he had taken up the reigns of Kalakos Shipping, after the death of his father, Dimitri had set up an internet company which specialised in selling designer goods to the rapidly expanding Asian market, and within only a few years he had become a self-made millionaire. His drive and determination were phenomenal, and his brilliance and ruthlessness in the boardroom legendary.

Aletha sometimes had the feeling that he was trying to prove something to his father, even though Kostas had been dead for three years. The rift between father and son had been public knowledge, and she had always thought it a pity that they had never resolved their differences.

Whatever was behind his motivation, Dimitri set himself a demanding work schedule, and paid his staff generous salaries to see to it that his life ran like clockwork. Ordinarily she would not have bothered him about a visitor who had turned up without an appointment and refused to explain why she wanted to see him. But beneath the Englishwoman Louise Frobisher's quiet determination Aletha had sensed an air of desperation, which had prompted her to ignore Dimitri's orders that he was not to be disturbed under any circumstances.

'Miss Frobisher has asked me to tell you that you knew her several years ago by her nickname—Loulou. And that she wishes to discuss Eirenne.'

Aletha was sure she had repeated the message correctly, but now the words sounded rather ridiculous, and she braced herself for an explosion of Dimitri's anger.

His eyes narrowed and he stared at her in silence for several seconds, before to her astonishment he said tersely, 'Inform her that I can spare her precisely three minutes of my time and show her in.'

* * *

It was so quiet in the PA's office that the ticking of the clock seemed to be in competition with the thud of Louise's heart. The window offered a spectacular view over the city, but the Athens skyline did not hold her attention for long. Her nerves were frayed, and the sound of a door opening made her spin round as Aletha Pagnotis reappeared.

'Mr Kalakos will see you very briefly,' the PA said calmly. She was clearly intrigued by the situation but far too professional to reveal her curiosity. 'Please come this way.'

Butterflies leapt in Louise's stomach. *If you act confident he won't be able to intimidate you*, she told herself. But the butterflies still danced, and her legs felt wobbly as she balanced on her four-inch heels and entered the lion's den.

'So, when did Loulou Hobbs become Louise Frobisher?'

Dimitri was seated behind a huge mahogany desk. He did not get to his feet when Louise walked in and his expression remained impassive, so that she had no idea what he was thinking, but he exuded an air of power and authority that she found daunting. Her brain also registered that he was utterly gorgeous, with his dark, Mediterranean colouring and sculpted features, and as she met his cool stare her heart jolted against her ribcage.

After his PA had slipped discreetly from the room Dimitri leaned back in his chair and surveyed Louise in a frank appraisal that brought a warm flush to her cheeks. She fought the urge to tug on the hem of her skirt to try and make it appear longer. It wasn't even *that* short—only an inch or so above her knees, she reminded herself. But her elegant, sophisticated outfit, yes, a little bit provocative—chosen deliberately in the hope of boosting her self-confidence—was very different from the smart but practical navy suit she wore every day to the museum.

Unlike her mother, who had been an avid attention-seeker, Louise was quite happy to blend into the background. She wasn't used to being looked at the way Dimitri was looking at her—as if she was an attractive woman and he was imagining her without any clothes on! Her face burned hotter. Of *course* he was not picturing her naked. That wasn't a glint of sexual awareness in his olive-green eyes. It was just the sunlight slanting through the blinds and reflecting in his retinas.

He had found her attractive once before, whispered a voice in her head. And if she was absolutely honest hadn't she chosen her outfit because she'd hoped to impress him—to show him what he had lost? Once he had told her she was beautiful. But that hadn't been real, her common sense pointed out. It had been part of the cruel game he'd been playing with her, and the memories of what had happened between them on Eirenne were best left undisturbed.

'Are you married? Is Frobisher your husband's name?'

The curt questions took her by surprise. Dimitri's face was still inscrutable but she suddenly sensed an inexplicable tension about him.

She shook her head. 'No—I'm not married. I have always been Louise Frobisher. My mother called me by that silly nickname when I was younger, but I prefer to use my real name. And I was never Hobbs. I was given my father's surname, even though Tina wasn't married to him. They split up when I was a few months old and he refused to support her or me.'

Dimitri's face hardened at the mention of her mother. 'It doesn't surprise me to hear that your father was one of a long list of Tina's lovers. You're lucky she even remembered his name.'

'You're hardly one to talk,' Louise shot back, instantly defensive.

In truth Tina had *not* been the best parent in the world.

Louise had spent much of her childhood dumped in various boarding schools, while her mother had flitted around Europe with whichever man she'd hooked up with at the time. But now Tina was ill, and it no longer mattered that as a child Louise had often felt she was a nuisance who disrupted her mother's busy social life. Even in today's world of advanced medical science the word cancer evoked a feeling of dread, and the prospect of losing her mother had made Louise realise how much she cared about her.

'From what I've seen in media reports you relish being a billionaire playboy with an endless supply of beautiful mistresses. I accept that my mother isn't perfect, but are you any better, Dimitri?'

'I don't break up marriages,' he said harshly. 'I've never stolen someone's partner or wrecked a perfectly happy relationship. It is an irrefutable fact that your mother broke my mother's heart.'

His bitter words hit Louise like bullets, and even though *she* had nothing to feel guilty about she wished for the millionth time that her mother had not had an affair with Kostas Kalakos.

'It takes two people to make a relationship,' she said quietly. 'Your father chose to leave your mother for Tina…'

'Only because she chased him relentlessly and seduced him with every trick in her no doubt extensive sexual repertoire.' Dimitri's voice dripped with contempt. 'Tina Hobbs knew exactly who my father was when she "bumped into him" at a party in Monaco. It was not the chance meeting she convinced you it was. She knew Kostas would be there, and she managed to wangle an invitation to that party with the absolute intention of catching herself a rich lover.'

Dimitri's nostrils flared as he sought to control the anger that still burned inside him whenever he thought of his father's mistress. The first time he'd set eyes on Tina Hobbs he had seen her for what she was—an avaricious harlot who attached herself like a leech to any rich man stupid enough to fall for a pair of big breasts and the promise of sexual nirvana.

That was what had got to him the most. The realisation that his father hadn't been as clever or wonderful as he had believed had hurt. He'd lost respect for Kostas, who had been his idol, and even now he still felt a hard knot inside when he remembered how his illusions had been shattered.

Anger filled him with a restless energy, and he scraped back his chair and jerked to his feet. He frowned when Louise immediately edged backwards towards the door. It wasn't *her* fault that her mother was a greedy, manipulating bitch, he reminded himself. Louise had been a child when Tina had met Kostas—a gawky kid with braces on her teeth and an annoying habit of staring down at the ground as if she hoped she would sink through it and become invisible.

To tell the truth he hadn't taken much notice of her on the occasions when he had visited his father on the Kalakos family's private Aegean island and she had been staying there with her mother during the school holidays.

It had been a shock when he had gone to the island that final time—after the row with his father—and the girl he had known as Loulou had been there alone. Only she hadn't been a girl. She had been nineteen—on the brink of womanhood and innocently unaware of her allure. He'd had no idea when exactly the awkward teenager who had been too shy to say a word to him had transformed into an articulate, intelligent and beautiful adult. For the first time in his life his usual self-assurance had deserted him and he had found himself struggling to know what to say to her.

He had resolved the problem by kissing her...

Dimitri hauled his mind back to the present. Trips down memory lane were never a good idea. But as he stared at the unexpected visitor who had interrupted his tightly organised work schedule, he acknowledged that in the past seven years Loulou—or Louise—had realised the potential she had shown at nineteen and developed into a stunner.

He ran his eyes over her, taking in her long honey-blond hair which was parted on one side so that it curved around her heart-shaped face and fell halfway down her back in a tumble of glossy curls. Her eyes were a deep sapphire-blue, and her red-glossed lips were a serious temptation.

Desire corkscrewed in his gut as he lowered his gaze and noted the way her fitted scarlet jacket moulded the firm thrust of her breasts and emphasised her narrow waist. Her skirt was short and her legs, sheathed in pale hose, were long and slender. Black stiletto heels added at least three inches to her height.

He trailed his eyes slowly back up her body and lingered on her mouth. Soft, moist lips slightly parted... He felt himself harden as an image flashed into his mind of slanting his lips over hers and kissing her as he had done many years ago.

Louise's breath seemed to be trapped in her lungs. Something was happening between her and Dimitri—some curious connection had made the atmosphere in the room almost crackle with electricity. She could not look away from him. It seemed as if an invisible force had locked her eyes with his, and as she stared at him she felt her blood pound in her ears, echoing the frantic rhythm of her heartbeat.

When she had walked into his office her first thought had been that he hadn't changed. He still held his head at that arrogant angle, as if he believed he was superior to everyone else. And although he must be in his thirties now there was no hint of grey in his dark-as-ebony hair.

But of course there were differences about him. In the

seven years since she had last seen him his sleek, hand-some, could-have-been-a-model-in-an-aftershave-advert looks had grown more rugged. His face was leaner, harder, with razor-sharp cheekbones and a square jaw that warned of an implacable determination to always have his own way. The boyish air that she remembered had disappeared, and now he was a blatantly virile man at the prime of physical perfection.

Now that he was standing she was conscious of his exceptional height. He must be four or five inches over six feet tall, she estimated, and powerfully built, with the finely honed musculature of an athlete. Superbly tailored grey trousers hugged his lean hips, and at some point during the day he had discarded his tie—it was draped over the back of his chair—and undone the top buttons of his shirt to reveal a vee of darkly tanned skin and a smattering of the dark hair that she knew covered his chest.

Memories assailed her—images of a younger Dimitri, standing at the edge of the pool at the villa on Eirenne, wearing a pair of wet swim-shorts that moulded his hard thighs and left little to the imagination. Not that she had needed to imagine him naked. She had seen every inch of his glorious golden-skinned body. She had touched him, stroked him, felt the weight of him pressing her into the mattress as he lowered himself onto her…

'Why are you here?'

His abrupt question was a welcome interruption to her wayward thoughts. She released her pent-up breath on a faint sigh.

'I need to talk to you.'

'That's funny,' he said sardonically. 'I remember saying those exact words to you once, but you refused to listen to me. Why should I listen to you now?'

Louise was startled by his reference to the past. She'd

assumed that he would have forgotten the brief time they had spent together. They had been magical, golden days for her, but she had meant nothing to him—as she had later found out.

She moistened her dry lips with the tip of her tongue. 'I think you'll be interested in what I have to say. I'm putting Eirenne up for sale—and I thought you might want to buy it.'

Dimitri gave a harsh laugh. 'You mean buy back the island that belonged to my family for forty years before your mother persuaded my father on his deathbed to amend his will and leave Eirenne to her? Morally, it is not yours to sell.' He frowned. 'Nor do you have the right to sell it. Kostas named Tina as his beneficiary, and the island belongs to her.'

'Actually, I *am* the legal owner. My mother transferred the deeds into my name and I can do what I like with Eirenne—although Tina is in agreement with my decision to sell it.'

The first part of that statement at least was true, Louise thought. Her mother had been advised by her accountant to transfer ownership of the island for tax purposes. But Louise had never regarded Eirenne as hers, and her decision to sell it was a last resort to raise the huge sum of money needed to pay for Tina to have lifesaving pioneering medical treatment in the U.S. She had not discussed it with her mother, who was too ill to cope with anything more than getting through each day. Tina's chances of survival were slim, but Louise was determined she would *have* a chance.

She held Dimitri's gaze and tried not to feel intimidated by the aggression emanating from him. 'The island has been valued at three million pounds. I'm prepared to sell it to you for one million.'

His eyes narrowed. 'Why?'

She understood his surprise. The real-estate agent had clearly thought she was mad when she'd told him she was prepared to offer the small but charming Greek island set amid the turquoise waters of the Aegean Sea for considerably less than its market value.

She shrugged. 'Because I need a quick sale.'

She did not attempt to explain that she had never felt comfortable with the fact that Kostas Kalakos had left the island to her mother rather than to his family. For one thing she doubted Dimitri would believe her, and for another she did not want to bring personal feelings into what was essentially a business proposition. She needed to sell Eirenne and she was sure Dimitri would be keen to buy it. End of story.

'I know you tried to buy the island from my mother shortly after Kostas died, and she refused to sell it. Now I'm giving you the chance to own it again.'

Dimitri snorted. 'Let me guess. Tina wants you to sell Eirenne because she has spent all the money my father left her and has decided to cash in her remaining asset.'

His comment was painfully close to the truth, Louise acknowledged heavily. Since Kostas's death her mother *had* lived an extravagant lifestyle, and failed to heed warnings from the bank that her inheritance fund was running out.

'I don't intend to discuss the reason for the sale. But if you turn down my offer I will advertise Eirenne, and I've been told that it should attract a lot of interest.'

'Interest, possibly. But in case you hadn't noticed the world is in the middle of an economic recession and I doubt you'll sell quickly. Businesses in the leisure industry won't be attracted to Eirenne because it isn't big enough to be developed as a tourist destination—thankfully.'

Dimitri's words echoed what the real-estate agent had told Louise. 'Buying a private island is not a top priority for most people right now. Even billionaires are being cautious in this uncertain economic climate, and it could be months before a buyer comes forward.'

Panic coiled in her stomach. Her mother did not have months.

Dimitri studied Louise speculatively, curious when he saw the colour drain from her face. She gave the impression of self-confidence, but he sensed a vulnerability about her that reminded him of the younger woman he had known seven years ago.

She had been in her first year at university, just stepping out into the world and brimming with enthusiasm for life. Her passion for everything, especially the arts, had captivated him. Although he'd only been in his twenties, he had already been jaded by a diet of sophisticated socialites who fell into his bed with a willingness that he'd begun to find tedious. But the Loulou he had met on Eirenne that spring had been different from any other woman he'd ever known—just as she had been different from the shy teenager he'd largely ignored on the few previous occasions when he had seen her at his father's villa.

He had been intrigued by her new maturity, and they had talked for hours. Not pointless small-talk, but interesting conversations. As the days had passed he'd found that he valued her friendship and her honesty as much as he was entranced by her beauty, which was not just skin-deep but truly came from within her.

He had thought he had found something special—*someone* special. But he had been wrong.

Dimitri was conscious of a faint feeling of regret, which he immediately dismissed as he slammed the door on his memories.

'There's more to this than you're telling me,' he guessed intuitively. 'Why are you prepared to sell the island for significantly less than it's worth?'

When she did not reply he shrugged dismissively. 'Thanks for the offer, but I am no longer interested in Eirenne.' He shot her an intent look. 'It holds too many memories that I'd prefer to forget.'

Louise wondered if he deliberately meant to hurt her. He could have been referring to his father's affair with her mother, of course. Kostas had left Dimitri's mother to live with Tina on Eirenne. But somehow she knew he had been talking about more personal memories—of the few wonderful days they had spent together and that one incredible night.

He drew back his shirt-cuff and glanced at his watch. 'Your three minutes are up. A member of my security staff will escort you from the building.'

'*No...* Wait!' Shocked by his abrupt dismissal, Louise jerked forward and reached out to prevent him from picking up the phone on his desk. Her fingers touched his and the brief contact sent a quiver of electricity shooting up her arm. She could not restrain an audible gasp and snatched her hand back.

She felt his eyes on her, but she was so shaken by her reaction to him that she could not bring herself to meet his gaze. She was stunned by his refusal to buy the island. She had been sure he would agree.

Her mind whirled. If Dimitri did not want to buy Eirenne she could advertise it at the same below-value price she had offered it to him. But there was still no guarantee that it would be sold quickly, and time for Tina was running out.

She pictured her mother's painfully thin face the last time she had visited her. The slash of bright lipstick Tina still applied every day with the help of a nurse had looked garish against her grey skin.

'I'm scared, Loulou,' Tina had whispered, when Louise

had leaned over the bed to kiss her the day before she had flown to Greece.

'It's going to be all right—I promise.'

She would do everything in her power to keep the promise she had given her mother, Louise vowed. Somehow she had to raise enough money for Tina to have that treatment in the U.S., and her best chance of doing that was to persuade Dimitri to buy back the island that she believed in her heart should be his.

That was why she had offered Eirenne to him for less than it was worth. Her conscience was torn between wanting to help her mother and a desire to be fair to Dimitri. The figure she had quoted him would cover Tina's medical costs at the specialist cancer clinic in Massachusetts, and would leave enough for her to live on once she was well again.

She *had* to believe it was going to happen, Louise thought emotionally. She refused to contemplate that Tina would not survive. But Dimitri's declaration that he was not interested in the island was a serious blow to her hopes.

CHAPTER TWO

'I THOUGHT you would jump at the chance to own Eirenne.' Louise prayed that Dimitri could not hear the desperation in her voice. 'I remember you told me it meant a lot to you because you'd spent happy times there as a child.'

His jaw tightened. 'They were happy times—for me, my sister and my parents. We spent every holiday on Eirenne. Until your mother destroyed my family. Now you have the gall to want me to buy back what should have been mine? My father had no right to leave our island to his whore.

'I presume you would give the money to Tina, so that she can continue to fund her extravagant lifestyle?' His lip curled in disgust. 'What kind of sucker do you take me for? Why don't you suggest she finds herself another rich lover? Or do what every other decent person does and find a job so that she can support herself? That would be a novelty,' he sneered. 'Tina actually working for a living. Although I suppose she would argue that lying flat on her back *is* a form of work.'

'*Shut up!*' The vile picture he was painting of her mother ripped Louise apart—not least because she could not deny there was some truth in his words. Tina had never worked. She had lived off her lovers and shamelessly allowed them to keep her—until a richer man came along.

But she was her mother, faults and all, and she was

dying. Louise refused to criticise Tina or allow Dimitri to insult her.

'I've told you—I am the legal owner of Eirenne and I'm selling it because I need to raise some capital.'

He frowned. 'You're saying the money would be for *you*? Why do you need a million pounds?'

'Why does anyone need money? A girl has to live, you know.'

Unconsciously she touched the diamond *fleur-de-lis* pendant and thought of her grandmother. Céline had not approved of the way her daughter lived her life, but she would have wanted her granddaughter to do everything possible to help Tina. Louise had even had the pendant valued by a jeweller, thinking that she could sell it to raise funds for Tina's treatment. But the sum she would have made was a fraction of the cost of medical expenses in America, and on the jeweller's advice she had decided to keep her only memento of her grandmother.

She flushed beneath Dimitri's hard stare. The contempt in his eyes hurt like a knife in her chest, but it was vital that she convinced him she was selling the island for her own benefit. If he guessed that Tina needed money there wasn't a hope in hell he would agree to buy Eirenne. She was not being dishonest, she assured herself. She was giving Dimitri the opportunity to buy the island that had once belonged to his family at a bargain price. It was no business of his how she chose to spend the proceeds of the sale.

'From what I remember of Eirenne it is a pleasant enough place, but I'd rather have hard cash than a lump of grey rock in the middle of the sea,' she told him.

Dimitri felt a sensation like a lead weight sinking in his stomach. It was stupid to feel disappointed because Louise had turned out like her mother, he told himself. Tina Hobbs was the ultimate gold-digger, and it should be no surprise that her daughter shared the same lack of moral integrity.

Seven years ago he would have sworn that Louise was different from Tina, but clearly she was not. She wanted easy money. From her appearance—designer outfit and perfect hair and make-up—she was obviously high-maintenance and had expensive tastes. Her necklace was not some cheap trinket. Diamonds which sparkled with such brilliance were worth a fortune.

How was she able to afford couture clothes and valuable jewellery? Dimitri frowned as the thought slid into his head that perhaps a man had paid for her outfit in return for her sleeping with him. Her mother had made a career out of leeching off rich lovers, and he was sickened to think that Louise might be doing the same.

Seven years ago she had been so innocent, he remembered. Not sexually—although it *had* crossed his mind when he had taken her to bed that she was not very experienced. At first she had been a little shy with him, a little hesitant, but she had responded to him with such ardent passion that he had dismissed the idea that he was her first lover. Sex with her had been mind-blowing, and even now the memory of her wrapping her slender limbs around him, the soft cries of delight she had made when he had kissed every inch of her body and parted her thighs to press his mouth to her sweet feminine heart, caused his gut to clench.

Her unworldly air had probably been an act, Dimitri thought grimly as he dragged his eyes from her face and turned to stare out of the window. Even if she had been as sweet and lovely as he'd believed all those years ago, she was patently her mother's daughter now.

So why was he so fiercely attracted to her? The question mocked him, because however much he hated to admit it he felt an overwhelming urge to stride around his desk and pull her into his arms. He felt a tightening in his groin as he imagined kissing her, pictured himself thrusting his tongue between her red-glossed lips and sliding his hand beneath her short skirt.

Gamoto! He cursed beneath his breath. The girl Loulou he remembered from years ago had gone for ever. Perhaps she had never existed at all except for in his mind. He had made her out to be special, but he had been kidding himself.

The woman standing in his office was beautiful and desirable—and he was a red-blooded male. He wasn't going to beat himself up because she fired him up. But he was not some crass youth with a surfeit of hormones. Louise was off-limits for all sorts of reasons—not least because she was history and he had no wish to revisit the past.

Confident that he had regained control of his libido, he swung round and regarded her dispassionately. His first instinct when she had offered to sell him Eirenne had been to tell her to go to hell. But now his business brain acknowledged that he would be crazy to turn down the proposition. The island was easily worth double the amount Louise was asking. He did not know why she was prepared to sell it for less, and frankly he didn't care.

Three years ago his lawyers had contested Kostas's will and argued that Eirenne should remain the property of the Kalakos family, but to no avail. There had been no legal loopholes and Dimitri had had to accept that he would never own the island he believed was rightfully his. Now he had the chance to buy it at an exceptionally good price. He would be a fool to allow his pride to stand in the way of a good deal.

'I need some time to consider whether or not I want to buy Eirenne,' he said abruptly.

Louise hardly dared to breathe, afraid she had misheard him or misunderstood, and that the fragile thread of hope he seemed to be offering would be snatched away. A few moments ago he had told her he was not interested, but now, miraculously, he appeared to be having second thoughts.

'How much time?' She did not want to push him, but Tina needed to start the treatment in America as soon as possible.

'Three days. I'll contact you at your hotel. Where are you staying?'

'I'm not—I arrived in Greece yesterday evening and I'm leaving tonight. I can't be away from home for too long.'

Why not? Dimitri wondered. Did she live with a lover who demanded her presence in his bed every night? Was he the same man who had bought her the diamond pendant that sparkled so brilliantly against her creamy skin? Heat surged inside him—an inexplicable feeling of rage that boiled in his blood. It was none of his business how Louise lived her life, he reminded himself. He didn't give a damn if she had an army of lovers.

'Give me details of where I can contact you,' he instructed her tersely, handing her the notepad and pen from his desk.

She quickly wrote something down and handed the pad back to him. He glanced at her address and felt another flare of anger. Property in the centre of Paris was expensive. He knew because a couple of years ago he had purchased an apartment block on the *Rue de Rivoli* to add to his real-estate portfolio.

She could have a well-paid job, his mind pointed out. He shouldn't leap to the assumption that she allowed a man to keep her just because her mother had always done so. But she had told him she was selling Eirenne because she needed the money. So, had a rich lover grown tired of her? She would have to have a damn good job to afford the rent on a prime city-centre address so close to the Champs-Élysées.

Incensed by the thoughts ricocheting around his brain—about a woman he had not the slightest interest in—Dimitri strode across the room and pulled open the door for her to leave.

'I'll be in touch.'

Louise's eyes flew to his face, but she could read nothing in his hard expression. Patently their meeting was at an end. The next three days were going to seem an eternity, but she could do nothing now except wait for Dimitri's decision.

'Thank you.' Her voice sounded rusty and her legs felt as unsteady as a newborn foal's as she walked out of his office. As she passed him, she caught the drift of his cologne, mingled with another subtly masculine scent that was achingly familiar even after all this time. She hesitated, swamped by a crazy urge to slide her arms around his waist, to rest her head against his chest and feel the beat of his heart next to her own as she had done a long time ago.

Of their own volition, it seemed, her eyes were drawn to his face, and just as when she had first entered his office some unseen force seemed to weld her gaze to his. Unconsciously she moistened her lips with the tip of her tongue.

Dimitri's eyes narrowed. *Theos*, she was a temptress—and he was a mere mortal with a healthy sex drive. Despite his determination to ignore the smouldering chemistry between him and Louise he was conscious of an ache low in his gut, and his mouth twisted in self-disgust when he felt himself harden.

For the space of a heartbeat he almost gave in to the temptation to pull her back into the room, close the door and push her against it, so that he could grind the swollen shaft throbbing painfully beneath his trousers against her pelvis. It was a long time since he had felt such an urgent, almost primitive desire for a woman. He prided himself on the fact that he was always in control, always coolly collected. But he did not feel cool now. Molten heat was surging through his veins, and as he stared into her sapphire-blue eyes every sensible thought in his head was overruled by a sexual hunger that was so strong it took all his considerable will-power not to succumb to it.

'Antio.' He bade her goodbye in a clipped tone, his teeth gritted.

The sound of Dimitri's voice shattered the spell. Louise tore her eyes from his. She discovered that she had been holding her breath and released it on a shaky sigh. She forced her feet to continue moving, and the instant she stepped into the corridor she heard the decisive snick of the door being closed behind her.

For a few seconds she leaned against the corridor wall and dragged oxygen into her lungs, conscious of her heart hammering beneath her ribs. She was shocked by the effect Dimitri had had on her. He was just a man, she reminded herself. Sure, he was good-looking, but she had met other handsome men and hadn't felt as if she had been hit in the solar plexus.

She had never met another man as devastatingly sexy as Dimitri, a voice in her head taunted. No other man had ever turned her legs to jelly and evoked shockingly erotic images in her mind that caused her cheeks to burn as she hurried into the lift. Seven years ago she had been utterly overwhelmed by Dimitri, and she was dismayed to realise that nothing had changed.

Dimitri walked back across to his desk and drummed his fingers on the polished wooden surface. He could not forget the expression of relief that had flared in Louise's eyes when he had told her he would consider buying the island. Maybe she had debts and that was why she needed money in a hurry, he brooded. That would explain why she couldn't wait for a buyer who would pay the full value of Eirenne.

He dropped into his chair and stared at his computer screen, but his concentration was shot to pieces and his mood was filthy. Sexual frustration was *not* conducive to work productivity, he discovered. With a savage curse he gave up on the financial report, snatched up his phone and put a call through to a private investigator whose services he used occasionally.

'I want you to check out a woman called Louise Frobisher—I have an address in Paris for her. The usual information. Where she works—' *if* she works, he thought to himself '—her friends…' his jaw hardened '…boyfriends. Report back to me in twenty-four hours.'

It was past midnight when Louise arrived back at her apartment in the Châtelet-Les-Halles area of Paris. Ideally located close enough to the Musée du Louvre that she could walk to work, it had been her home for the past four years, and she let out a heartfelt sigh as she walked through the front door. Her flat was on the sixth floor, in the eaves of the building. The sloping ceilings made the compact interior seem even smaller, but the view over the city from the tiny balcony was wonderful.

The view was the last thing on her mind, however, as she dumped her suitcase in the hall and kicked off her shoes. The past forty-eight hours—in which she had flown to Athens and back again, and had that tense meeting with Dimitri—had been tiring, not to mention fraught with emotions.

As she entered the living room Madeleine, her Siamese

cat, stretched elegantly before springing down from a cushion on the wide windowsill.

'Don't give me that look,' Louise murmured as she lifted the cat into her arms and Madeleine fixed her with a reproachful stare from slanting eyes the colour of lapis-lazuli. 'You weren't abandoned. Benoit promised he would feed you twice a day, and I bet he made a fuss of you.'

Her neighbour, who lived in the flat below, had been a great help recently, offering to feed Madeleine while Louise spent time with Tina at the hospital. She would visit her mother after work tomorrow. For now, she knew she should eat something, but her appetite was as depleted as the interior of her fridge. A quick shower followed by bed beckoned, and half an hour later she slid between crisp white sheets and did not bother to make even a token protest when Madeleine sprang up onto the counterpane and curled up in the crook of her knees.

Sleep should have come quickly, but it eluded her as thoughts chased round inside her head. Seeing Dimitri again had been so much more painful than she had been prepared for. It had been seven years, she reminded herself angrily. She should be over him by now—*was* over him. And what was there to be over, anyway? The brief time they had spent together had hardly constituted a relationship.

But as she lay in bed, watching silver moonbeams slant through the gap in the curtains, she could not hold back her memories.

She had gone to Eirenne for the Easter holidays. Her friends at university had tried to persuade her to stay in Sheffield, but she'd had exams coming up and had guessed she wouldn't get any studying done if her flatmates planned to hold parties every night. Besides, she had planned to spend her nineteenth birthday with her mother.

But when she had arrived at the island she'd found Tina

and Kostas about to leave for a holiday in Dubai. It wasn't the first time Tina had forgotten her birthday, and Louise hadn't bothered to remind her. All her life she had taken second place to her mother's lovers. At least she would be able to get her assignment finished, she'd consoled herself. But she had been lonely on Eirenne with only the villa's staff for company, and she had missed her new university friends.

One afternoon, bored with her studies, she had decided to ride around the island on her pushbike. Eirenne was a small island, but on previous visits she had never strayed far from the grounds of the opulent villa that Kostas had built for his mistress.

The road that ran around the island was little more than a bumpy track and Louise had been carefully avoiding the potholes when a motorbike had suddenly shot round the bend and swerved to avoid hitting her. In panic she had lost her balance and fallen, scraping her arm on the rough ground as she landed.

'*Theos*, why weren't you looking where you were going?'

She had recognised the angry voice, even though she had only met Kostas's son Dimitri a handful of times when he had happened to visit his father at the same time as she had been staying on Eirenne. She had never really spoken to him before, although she had overheard the arguments he'd had with Kostas about his relationship with Tina.

'You nearly crashed into me,' she'd defended herself, her temper rising when he grabbed her arm none too gently and hauled her to her feet. 'Road hog! Some birthday this is turning out to be,' she had added grumpily. 'I wish I'd stayed in England.'

For a moment his unusual olive-green eyes darkened. But then he threw back his head and laughed.

'So you *do* speak? You've always seemed to be struck dumb whenever I've met you.'

'I suppose you think I'm over-awed by you,' she said, flushing. Not for the world would she allow him to know that since she was sixteen she'd had a massive crush on him.

He stared down at her, his eyes glinting with amusement in his handsome face. 'And *are* you over-awed, Loulou?'

'Of course not. I'm annoyed. My bike's got a puncture, thanks to you. And I'm going to have a lovely bruise on my shoulder.'

'You're bleeding,' he said, noticing where she had scraped her arm. 'Come back to the house and I'll clean that graze and fix your tyre.'

'But the Villa Aphrodite is that way,' she said in a puzzled voice when he turned in the opposite direction. 'Where are you staying, anyway? I haven't seen you around. I thought Kostas had banned you from the villa after your last row with him.'

'It suits me never to set foot inside that tasteless monstrosity my father has built for his tart.' The anger returned to Dimitri's voice. 'I'm staying at the old house my grandfather built many years ago. He named the house Iremia, which means tranquillity. But the island is no longer a tranquil place since your mother came here.'

Leaving his motorbike by the side of the track, he pushed Louise's bicycle. She followed him in silence, daunted by the rigid set of his shoulders. But his temper had cooled by the time they arrived at the house, and he was a polite host, inviting her in and instructing his butler to serve them drinks on the terrace.

The house was nestled in a dip in the land, surrounded by pine trees and olive groves so that it was hidden from view. It was not surprising that Louise had never seen it before. Unlike the ultra-modern and to Louise's mind unattractive Villa Aphrodite, Iremia was a beautiful old house built in a classical style, with coral-pink walls and cream-coloured wooden shutters at the windows. The gardens were well-established, and through the trees the cobalt-blue sea sparkled in the distance.

'Hold still while I put some antiseptic on your arm,' Dimitri instructed after he had led her out to the terrace and indicated that she should sit on one of the sun-loungers.

His touch was light, yet a tiny tremor ran through Louise at the feel of his hands on her skin. His dark head was bent close to hers, and she was fiercely aware of the tang of his aftershave mingled with another subtly masculine scent that caused her heart to race.

He glanced up and met her gaze. 'I hardly recognised you,' he said, his smile doing strange things to her insides. 'The last time I saw you, you were the proverbial ugly duckling.'

'Thanks,' she muttered sarcastically, flushing as she remembered the thick braces she'd worn on her teeth for years. Thankfully she'd had them removed now, and her teeth were perfectly straight and white.

As a teenager she had been slow to develop, and had despaired about her boyish figure, but in the last year or so she had finally gained the womanly curves she had longed for. However, she still lacked self-confidence, and Dimitri's comment hurt. She tried to jerk away from him, but instead of releasing her arm he trailed his fingers very lightly up to the base of her throat and found the pulse that was beating frantically there.

'But now you have turned into a swan,' he said softly. '*Ise panemorfi*—you are very beautiful,' he translated, although he had no need. She spoke Greek fluently.

That had been the start of it, Louise thought, turning her head restlessly on the pillows. That moment when she had looked into Dimitri's olive-green eyes and made the startling discovery that he desired her. That had been the beginning of a golden few days when they had become friends, while the awareness between them had grown ever more intense.

When Dimitri had learned that she was spending her birthday alone he had insisted on taking her to dinner on the neighbouring island of Andros, which was a short boat ride away from Eirenne. It had been a magical evening, and at the end of it, when he had escorted her back to the Villa Aphrodite, he had kissed her. It had only been a brief kiss, no more than a gossamer-light brush of his lips on hers, but fireworks had exploded inside her and she had stared at him dazedly, her heart thumping, longing for him to kiss her again.

He hadn't, but had bade her goodnight rather abruptly, so that she had wondered if she had annoyed him in some way. Maybe he regretted kissing her because she was the daughter of his father's mistress? she had thought miserably. But the next morning he had arrived as she was sitting disconsolately by the pool, facing another day on her own. He had invited her to go to the beach with him, and the day that had seemed so bleak suddenly became wonderful.

They had swum and sunbathed and talked about every subject under the sun—apart from her mother's affair with his father. Dimitri never mentioned Tina.

Over the next few days Louise's faint wariness had faded and she'd grown more relaxed with him, so that when he'd kissed her again—properly this time—she had responded with an eagerness that had made him groan and accuse her of being a sorceress who had surely cast a spell on him.

It had seemed entirely natural for him to take her back to the house in the pine forest and make love to her one long, lazy afternoon, with the sun slanting through the blinds and gilding their naked bodies. He had been so skilled and so gentle that losing her virginity had been a painless experience.

Dimitri had been unaware that it was her first time, and she had been too shy to tell him. She had responded to the stroke of his hands and the exquisite sensation of his mouth on her breasts, teasing her nipples until they were as hard as pebbles, with a passion that had matched his. It had been perfect, their bodies moving in total accord, until simultaneously they had reached the zenith of sensual pleasure.

She had spent the whole of that night with him, and each time he'd made love to her she had fallen deeper in love with him.

The following morning he had walked her back to the Villa Aphrodite.

'Come and swim in the pool,' she had invited. 'No one is here.' By 'no one' she had meant her mother.

Dimitri hesitated. 'All right—but afterwards we'll go back to Iremia. I hate this place. I assume Tina chose the décor,' he said sardonically, glancing at the zebra-print sofas and the white marble pillars that were everywhere in the villa. 'It just goes to prove that no amount of money can buy good taste.'

His dislike of her mother was evident in his voice, and Louise felt uncomfortable, but then he smiled at her and the awkward moment passed. They swam for a while, and then he carried her out of the pool and laid her on a sunbed. She had wound her arms around his neck to pull him down on top of her—when a shrill voice made them spring apart.

'What do you think you're bloody well doing? Take your hands off my daughter!'

All these years later Louise could still hear Tina screaming at Dimitri as she tottered across the patio in her vertiginous heels, quivering with fury so that her platinum-blond beehive had seemed to wobble precariously on top of her head.

'It's bad enough that Kostas cut our trip short with some excuse about needing to be at a meeting in Athens. But to find *you* here, preying on Loulou, is the last straw. You have no right to be here. Your father banned you from the villa.'

'Don't you *dare* talk to me about rights.' Dimitri's anger had been explosive as he'd leapt to his feet and faced Tina.

The row that had followed had been a vicious exchange of words. Louise had said nothing, but her mother had said more than enough.

'Do you think I don't know what's in your nasty, vengeful mind?' Tina hissed to Dimitri. 'It's obvious you decided to try and seduce Loulou to get at me—out of some misplaced revenge for your mother.'

'*No!*' Louise interrupted desperately. 'This has nothing to do with you.'

'Doesn't it?' Tina laughed mockingly. 'So Dimitri has *told* you about his mother, has he? That she took an overdose and that he blames me for her death? Has he also told you that his father has disinherited him because of the way he has repeatedly insulted me?' Tina continued relentlessly. 'Or that now he is no longer in line to inherit a fortune the woman he hoped to marry has dumped him? This has *everything* to do with me—doesn't it, Dimitri? You hate my guts, and the only reason you've been sniffing around my daughter is because you want to cause trouble.'

Tina's accusations sent a cold chill down Louise's spine. Her mother had always been over-dramatic, she reminded herself. Dimitri couldn't have been pretending to be attracted to her. He had been so attentive, and the passion between them had been so intense that she had even begun to think—to hope—that he was falling in love with her.

'It's not true. *Is it?*' She turned to Dimitri, pleading for his reassurance, but inside her head doubts were already forming. She had not even known his mother had died, let alone the tragic circumstances of her death. Not once in the past few days had he mentioned it.

She had thought they were friends, and now they were lovers. But Dimitri had turned into a hard-faced stranger and the coldness in his eyes froze her blood.

'Yes, it's true.'

His harsh voice broke the silence, and like a pebble hitting the surface of a pool his words caused shockwaves to ripple through the tense atmosphere.

'My mother took her own life because she was heartbroken that my father had divorced her and thrown away the love they had shared for thirty years for a worthless whore.'

He stared contemptuously at Tina, and then turned and walked away without saying another word. He didn't even glance at Louise; it was as if she did not exist. And she watched him go, paralysed with shock and feeling sick with humiliation that she had been nothing more to him than a pawn in his battle with her mother.

'Don't tell me you were falling for him?' her mother said, when she caught sight of Louise's stricken face. 'For God's sake, Lou, until recently he was engaged to Rochelle Fitzpatrick—that stunning American model who is regularly on the covers of the top fashion magazines. He wasn't really interested in you. Like I said, he just wants to cause trouble. A while ago Dimitri overheard me telling Kostas how keen I am for you have a good career,' Tina continued. 'He knew I would be upset if you dropped out of university to have an affair with him. I imagine he thought that if you fell for his flattery he would be able to turn you against me. And of course his ultimate goal was to cause friction between me and his father.'

Tina prattled on relentlessly, unaware of the agonised

expression in Louise's eyes. 'It's lucky I came back before he persuaded you into bed. The villa staff told me he's only been hanging around for a couple of days. Go back to university and forget about Dimitri.' She gave Louise a sudden intent look. 'You're clever. You can make something of your life. You don't need to rely on any man. And if you take my advice you'll never fall in love like I did with your father. I swore after him that I'd never let myself care about any man ever again.'

Shaken by Tina's reference to her father, whom she had never known, and traumatised by the scene with Dimitri, Louise left Eirenne within the hour. She hadn't expected to see him again, but as she climbed into the motor launch that would take her to Athens she was shocked to see him striding along the jetty.

'*Loulou*…wait!'

Wearing bleached jeans and a black tee shirt that accentuated his incredible physique, he looked unbelievably gorgeous, and it struck her then that she'd been mad to believe he could have been attracted to her. He could have any woman he wanted, so why would he want an unsophisticated student whose looks could at best be described as passable?

Overwhelmed by self-doubt, she instructed the boatman to start the engine.

Dimitri broke into a run. '*Theos!* Don't go. I want to talk to you about what I said up at the villa.'

'But I don't want to talk to *you*,' she told him stonily. 'You made everything perfectly clear.'

She felt a fool, but she'd be damned if she would let him see that he had broken her heart. The boat engine roared, drowning out Dimitri's response. He looked furious as the boat shot away from the jetty, and shouted something after her. But she didn't hear his words over the rush of the wind, and told herself she did not care that she would never speak to him again.

She had been unaware when she had left Eirenne that a few weeks later she would urgently need to talk to Dimitri...

Louise tossed restlessly beneath the sheets. She sat up to thump her pillows and flopped back down again, wishing the bombardment of memories would stop. Tiredness swept over her, and her last conscious thought was that in a few short hours she had to get up for work.

She must have fallen into a deep sleep at first, but towards dawn the dream came. She was running down a long corridor. On either side were rooms like hospital rooms, and in each room was a baby lying in a cot. But it was never her baby. Every time she went into a room she felt hopeful that this was the right one—but it was always someone else's child looking up at her.

She ran into the next room, and the next, feeling ever more frantic as she searched for her baby. She was almost at the end of the corridor. There was only one room left. This had to be where her child was. But the cot was empty—and the terrible truth dawned that she would never find her baby. Her child was lost for ever.

Dear God. Louise jerked upright, breathing hard as if she had run a marathon. It was a long time since she had last had the dream, but it had been so real she was not surprised to find her face was wet and that she had been crying in her sleep. For months after the miscarriage that she'd suffered, three weeks after discovering she was expecting Dimitri's child, she had dreamed that she was looking for her baby. And each time she had woken, just as now, feeling a dull ache of grief for the new life she had carried so briefly inside her.

Seeing Dimitri again yesterday had triggered memories buried deep in her subconscious. She had never told anyone about the baby, and had struggled to deal with her sense of loss alone. Maybe if she had been able to confide in someone it would have helped, but her mother had been totally absorbed in her relationship with Kostas, and as for Dimitri—well, it was probably better that he had never known she had conceived his child.

No doubt he would have been horrified. But she would never know how he might have reacted, because he had refused to speak to her when she had plucked up the courage and phoned him to tell him she was pregnant. A week later, when he had finally returned her call, she had switched off her phone. There hadn't seemed any point in telling him she had lost his baby. At the time there hadn't seemed a lot of point in anything. The weeks and months following the miscarriage had been desperately bleak, and she had just wanted to stay in bed and hide from the world, she remembered.

She had told herself it would not have been ideal to bring a fatherless child into the world. She knew only too well what it was like to grow up with only one parent, to feel the nagging sense of failure that perhaps it was her fault her own father had rejected her. She had tried to convince herself it was for the best that her pregnancy had ended. Yet even now, whenever she saw a child of about six years old, she imagined what *her* child would have been like and wished she could have known him or her.

Tears filled her eyes and she blinked them away. There was no point in dwelling on the past. She stroked Madeleine's downy-soft, cream fur. 'At least I've got you,' she murmured to the cat. And Madeleine, who seemed to possess an intuition that was beyond human understanding, gently purred and rubbed her pointed chocolate-coloured ears against Louise's hand.

CHAPTER THREE

'ON THIS tour of the Louvre you will be able to admire some of the world's greatest masterpieces, including the *Wedding Feast at Cana*, the *Venus de Milo*, and of course, the *Mona Lisa*.'

Louise addressed the group of visitors who were assembled in the Hall Napoléon, beneath the spectacular glass pyramid. One of her duties as a visitors' assistant was to give tours in both French, which she spoke fluently, and English. Her group this afternoon seemed to be mainly American and Japanese tourists, who nodded and smiled to show that they had understood her.

'If you would like to follow me, we will go first to the Denon Wing.'

Out of the corner of her eye she caught sight of a figure striding across the hall and she waited, assuming the man wanted to join the tour. But as he drew closer her heart performed a somersault beneath her ribs.

What was Dimitri doing here? Yesterday had been the third day since she had visited him at his office in Athens. By midnight, when he hadn't contacted her, she had assumed he had decided not to buy Eirenne, and she had spent all night worrying about how she was going to raise the money for her mother's treatment.

The rest of her tour group were already climbing the

stairs when he halted in front of her. The glint of amusement in his olive-green eyes told her he knew she was shocked to see him, and to her irritation she felt herself blush as if she was still the schoolgirl who years ago had had a huge crush on him. She hated the effect he had on her, but good manners forced her to greet him with a cool smile.

'Did you want to see me? I'm just about to conduct a tour of the museum, so I'm afraid I can't talk to you right now, but if you give me your phone number I'll call you as soon as I'm free.'

'Don't let me interrupt you.' He indicated that she should follow her tour group, and fell into step beside her as she headed towards the stairs.

'So you realised your dream,' he murmured.

She gave him a startled glance—and immediately wished she hadn't made eye contact with him when her heart gave a jolt. He was even more gorgeous in real life than in the image of him that she had been unable to dismiss from her mind for the past three days. She was supremely conscious of his height and his toned, muscular body as he walked beside her. He was wearing a suit but no tie, and the top couple of his shirt buttons were undone to reveal the tanned column of his throat. The dark stubble shading his jaw added to his raffish sex appeal.

Louise choked back a slightly hysterical laugh as she imagined his reaction if she gave in to the crazy urge to reach up and press her lips to the sensual curve of mouth. She bit her lower lip and the sharp pain brought her to her senses. 'I don't understand what you mean,' she said shortly.

'I remember you studied the history of art at university, and you told me your ambition was to work at an art museum. I think you spent some time as volunteer at the National Gallery in London while you were a student.'

'I'm sure I bored you to death, talking about my career plans.'

She was embarrassed to remember how unsophisticated she had been at nineteen. No one had ever taken much interest in her before—her mother had always been too busy with her own life. She had been dazzled by Dimitri, and had lapped up his attention like a puppy desperate to please its master, she thought painfully. It was a surprise to hear that he had actually listened to her.

'I assure you—you never bored me, Loulou,' he said softly.

His use of her nickname took her back in time—to seven years ago when she had been young and heartbreakingly naïve. She remembered the old house among the pine trees on Eirenne, the feel of warm sunshine on her skin, and Dimitri whispering her name reassuringly as he drew her down onto a bed and slanted his lips over hers. *I want you, my lovely Loulou.*

She snapped back to the present. 'Please don't call me that. I prefer to use my proper name rather than a childish nickname.'

'Louise is certainly more elegant,' he agreed. 'It suits you.'

Dimitri turned his head and subjected her to an unhurried appraisal, taking in her honey-blond hair swept up into a chignon and the functional navy-blue uniform that all the Louvre's visitors' assistants wore. She looked neat, almost demure, with barely any make-up other than a slick of pale pink gloss on her lips. Unlike when she had visited him in Athens, she was not dressed as a *femme fatale* today, but her plain clothes could not disguise her innate sensuality. Desire uncoiled in Dimitri's gut and he had to fight the urge to pull her into his arms and kiss her temptingly soft mouth.

Flustered by the hard glitter in Dimitri's eyes, Louise tore her gaze from him and increased the speed she was walking at so that she could catch up with the group of visitors ahead of her.

'Well, anyway, after I gained my degree I did a post-grad in Museum Studies, which included a three month placement at the Louvre, and I was lucky enough to be offered a permanent position.' She frowned as a thought occurred to her. 'How did you know I work here? I'm sure I didn't mention it.'

'I had a private investigator check you out.'

'You did *what*?' She stopped dead and glared at him. *'How dare you?'*

'Quite easily,' he said with a shrug. 'I needed to be sure you are the legal owner of Eirenne and that you have the right to sell it.'

It was a reasonable explanation, Louise acknowledged grudgingly. But the idea that an investigator had been nosing around in her private life was horrible, and it made her feel like a criminal. Another thought struck her. What if his sleuth had found out about her mother's illness and learned that Tina's only chance of survival was to have expensive specialist treatment in America? Had Dimitri discovered why she needed a lot of money as quickly as she could lay her hands on it?

She focused on what he had said a moment ago and looked at him uncertainly. 'When I didn't hear from you yesterday I assumed you had decided not to buy Eirenne.'

'I haven't made a decision yet. I require a little more time to think about it.'

'Oh…' Louise's breath left her in a whoosh as relief flooded through her.

Dimitri was clearly interested in buying the island—otherwise he would have told her straight that they did not have a deal. The lifeline for her mother which last night had seemed out of reach was still a possibility. She sagged against the wall, struggling to regain her composure, and did not see the intent look he gave her.

'It infuriates me that the only way I can regain own-ership of my birthright, which should *never* have passed out of the Kalakos family's possession, is to buy it back,' he told her harshly. 'But my grandparents are buried on Eirenne, and my sister is distressed at the prospect of los-ing it for good. It is for Ianthe's sake more than anything else that I am still considering your offer, but I need more information regarding the sale. We'll discuss the details over dinner tonight.'

He hadn't lost any of his arrogance, Louise thought rue-fully. It clearly hadn't occurred to him that she might not be free tonight. But he was calling the shots. If he had asked her to meet him on the moon at midnight she would have done her best to get there, because he had given her hope that her mother might have a chance of beating the disease that was ravaging her body.

They had reached the Pre-Classical Greek Gallery, where ancient sculptures were displayed on marble plinths. At the far end of the gallery, at the top of a wide stair-case, stood the majestic *Winged Victory of Samothrace*. The group of visitors had paused and were waiting expec-tantly for Louise to begin the tour.

She glanced at Dimitri. 'I don't finish my shift until seven-thirty tonight.'

'I'll meet you at eight-fifteen at La Marianne on the Rue de Grenelle. Do you know it?'

Louise had heard of the exclusive restaurant, which had a reputation for serving the finest French cuisine and charg-ing exorbitant prices. It was not the sort of place her salary would stretch to, she thought ruefully.

'I'll be there,' she confirmed. 'Now, I'm afraid you'll have to excuse me.'

She turned and walked away from him, fighting an uncharacteristic urge to burst into tears. She rarely cried. Ever since the miscarriage few things had seemed important enough to cry about. But her emotions seemed to be all over the place. Meeting Dimitri again had brought back painful memories.

She wished she did not have to see him again. But perhaps tonight he would agree to buy Eirenne. The sale would be dealt with by their respective lawyers, Dimitri would return to Greece, and maybe, if she tried hard enough, she would forget him, she told herself. But the assurance rang as hollow as her footsteps on the floor of the gallery.

Pinning a smile on her face, she joined her group of visitors and began the guided tour, leading them first to view the paintings in the Grande Galerie. Usually she enjoyed giving tours, but to her dismay Dimitri had joined the group, instead of leaving the museum as she had expected him to do. He made no attempt to talk to her, and appeared to listen intently to the information she gave on various artworks. She tried to ignore him and concentrate on the tour, but she found his presence disconcerting—especially when she glanced at him a couple of times and discovered his olive-green eyes were focused on *her* rather than a Raphael or a Caravaggio hanging on the gallery walls.

From the Grande Galerie she led the group into the Salle des Etats, where the *Mona Lisa*'s enigmatic expression was protected behind bulletproof glass. The world's most famous portrait needed little introduction, and Louise stood back while the visitors crowded around the barrier.

'I have to say the most famous painting in the world is rather smaller than I'd imagined,' Dimitri murmured wryly.

She tensed when she found him standing next to her, but

she could not refrain from smiling. 'I can't tell you how many times I've been told that. I hope you're not disappointed. The *Mona Lisa* is exquisite. But personally I find the *Wedding Feast at Cana* more interesting.' She turned towards the immense painting on the opposite wall. 'The colours are so intense that the figures seem to almost leap from the canvas.'

'You love your work, don't you? I can hear the passion in your voice.'

Something in Dimitri's tone caused Louise's heart to skip a beat. Passion was such an evocative word. It brought back memories of the wildfire passion they had shared on Eirenne—memories she had never been able to forget and which now flooded her mind with such shocking clarity that once again she felt herself blush. She darted him a glance, startled to find that his eyes were focused on her, and she felt certain that he was also remembering the past.

'I feel very privileged to work at the Louvre,' she admitted, thankful that she sounded cool and composed even though she did not feel it. 'But I'm surprised you decided to join the tour. Are you interested in art?'

He shrugged. 'It's not a subject I have ever studied in great detail, but even for a layman it is impossible not to be awed by the beauty and the history of the masterpieces on display. I enjoyed the tour. You have a way of bringing the works of the Great Masters to life with your expertise and enthusiasm.'

Louise's melodious voice and her impressive knowledge of the historical artworks housed in the Louvre *had* made the tour fascinating, but if Dimitri was honest he had spent more time studying the attractive guide than the paintings. She was seriously beautiful, and he was slightly ashamed of his erotic fantasy in which he ripped off her prim skirt and blouse and had hot, hungry sex with her on one of the plush red velvet bench-seats that were dotted around the gallery.

He didn't even understand what he was doing here, he thought irritably. He was interested in buying the island, but in truth he was intrigued by Louise. Seeing her again had awoken memories of the brief time they had spent together, and he had come to Paris and spent the past hour looking at paintings of fat cherubs when he should be working on the Russian deal.

He hadn't been able to get her out of his thoughts since she had turned up at his office. He had never forgotten what had happened between them on Eirenne. But seven years was a long time. During those years he had been focused on establishing his own company and then proving that he was a worthy successor to his father at Kalakos Shipping, and his memories of the pretty nineteen-year-old girl he had known as Loulou had faded.

The grown-up Louise was an attractive woman no red-blooded male would forget in a hurry, Dimitri mused. But since he was a young man he'd had more beautiful mistresses than he cared to remember. He couldn't explain what it was about Louise. All he knew was that his trousers felt uncomfortably tight, and he did not dare to meet her cool gaze in case she guessed he was fantasising about making love to her right here in the most famous art gallery in the world.

He cleared his throat. 'I come to Paris frequently for business, but I've never had time to visit the Louvre.' He glanced at his watch and grimaced. 'Regrettably, my free time rarely lasts for long. I'm due to hold a conference call in half an hour, and I must to go back to my hotel.'

There was a hint of weariness in his voice, and the fine lines fanning around his eyes told of someone who worked long hours and no doubt spent too much time in front of a computer screen. Louise felt an unwanted tug of sympathy for him. But perhaps he was tired for a different reason, she reminded herself sharply. He had a reputation as a playboy, and his numerous affairs were discussed with frenzied interest in the gossip columns. She was ashamed of the little stab of jealousy she felt when she pictured him making love to one of the gorgeous, glossy-haired American supermodels he seemed to favour. How Dimitri lived his life was of no interest to her, she reminded herself. Yet something intrigued her...

'I heard that your father named you as his successor to run Kalakos Shipping, despite his threat to disinherit you,' she murmured.

She wanted to ask him if he and his father had resolved their differences, but she did not dare mention the bitter argument between the two men about Kostas's affair with her mother.

Dimitri nodded. 'It was a shock, frankly. I hadn't expected it. You know of the rift between me and my father. I was determined to make it in business without his help and I set up my own company, which became extremely successful. But I sold Fine Living a year ago so that I could concentrate on Kalakos Shipping. Running it is a huge responsibility—especially at the moment, when my country is experiencing financial problems. The company employs thousands of staff and I have a duty to protect their jobs. Hence the importance of the business deal I am currently negotiating.'

'As you're so busy, why don't we forget dinner?' Louise seized the opportunity to avoid seeing him again. 'You have my phone number, and you can call me once you've reached a decision. There's no need for us to meet tonight.'

Dimitri's sudden smile transformed his hard-boned face

from serious to seriously sexy, and Louise felt a tingling sensation run through her right down to her toes.

'I disagree,' he drawled, the gleam of amusement in his eyes warning her that he had seen through her ploy to avoid meeting him. 'We haven't seen each other for seven years, and I'm looking forward to catching up. *Au revoir*, Louise—until tonight,' he murmured, before he strode out of the gallery, leaving her staring after him thinking that his words had sounded more like a threat than a promise.

It took Louise ten minutes to walk back to her flat after she had finished work. Often in the summer she liked to stroll along by the Seine and browse among the booksellers' stalls, but this evening she was in a hurry.

As soon as she arrived home she fed Madeleine and called the hospital to check on her mother, explaining to the nurse that she would visit tomorrow. Then she showered, blow-dried her hair and applied make-up in record time, aware that she was due to meet Dimitri in twenty minutes.

At least choosing something to wear was not a problem. Her friend and neighbour Benoit was a fashion designer, who regularly gave her his stunning creations, and there were several dresses in her wardrobe that she'd never had an opportunity to wear before.

One cocktail dress in particular seemed suitable for dinner at an exclusive restaurant. The simple sheath of black silk skimmed her breasts and hips and flared slightly at the hemline, which was decorated with layers of tulle ruffles. It was a striking design, and as with all Benoit's clothes very feminine and very sexy. Louise almost lost her nerve as she studied her reflection and noted how the sheer material seemed to caress her curves. The black silk felt cool and sensual against her skin, and for the first time in years she felt intensely aware of her body.

She briefly debated whether to change into something less eye-catching, but time was racing—at least that was the excuse she made to herself. The truth was that ever since she had met Dimitri in Athens she'd felt quite unlike her usual sensible self. Every time she thought of him—and he seemed to dominate her thoughts—molten heat pooled low in her pelvis and she felt an ache of sexual longing that she hadn't experienced since she was nineteen. Perhaps it was because he had been her first lover—her *only* lover, she amended ruefully. She had dated a few other men since, but none of them had caused her heart to race like Dimitri did.

What was she trying to tell him tonight by wearing this dress? That she was fiercely aware of him, and that she had glimpsed the hungry gleam in his eyes when he had met her at the Louvre? She could not answer herself, or explain the hectic flush on her cheeks. It was easier to turn away from the mirror and slide her feet into the strappy black stiletto sandals that matched the dress. A silver purse and a dove-grey pashmina completed her outfit, and she hurried out of her flat, her heart thudding.

As she stepped out of the lift on the ground floor she cannoned into a man who had just entered the apartment block.

'Fais attention!' His frown cleared when he recognised Louise, and he caught hold of her shoulder and studied her intently. *'Chérie*, you look divine in that dress.'

Louise smiled at Benoit Besson. 'I'm glad you approve—seeing as it's one of your creations.'

A grin flashed on Benoit's thin face and he pushed his long black hair out of his eyes. 'I can see why I am called a genius,' he drawled, only half-jokingly. 'Where are you going? Don't tell me you have a date?' He looked surprised. 'It's about time. You are too beautiful to live your life alone. You need a lover, *chérie.*'

'I'll never *need* a man,' Louise said firmly. She had vowed years ago that she would never copy her mother. Tina had always needed a man in her life, and she had lurched from one disastrous affair to the next without ever pausing to consider whether she would be happier without the jerks she hooked up with.

Kostas Kalakos had been better than most, Louise remembered. He had seemed genuinely to care for Tina. And he had been kind to *her* when she had stayed on Eirenne in the school holidays. But she could not forget that he had left his wife to pursue his affair with her mother—a fact that Dimitri had certainly never forgotten either, she thought heavily.

Benoit gave her a speculative look. 'So—not a date, but in *that* dress you can only be meeting a man. I can't deny I am curious, *mon amie.*'

'I'm having dinner with a friend I used to know years ago…an acquaintance, really.' Louise felt herself blush. 'I must go or I'll be late.'

'Have fun.' Benoit's smile was decidedly smug. 'I'm flying to Sydney in the morning, but you can tell me all about this non-date when I come back.'

Her friendship with Benoit went back many years. Benoit's grandmother had been a close friend of her *grand-mère*, Céline, and Louise had known him when he was a student—before he had taken the fashion world by storm. He was the closest she had to a brother, and she treated his teasing with affection.

'There'll be nothing to tell,' she promised him, and hurried out before he could ask any more questions.

Dimitri had chosen a seat at the bar at La Marianne, which afforded him a clear view of the door. During the past ten minutes half a dozen blondes, wearing the ubiquitous little black dresses, had entered the restaurant, and all of them had sought to make eye-contact with him—even the ones who were hanging on to the arm of a husband or boyfriend, he noted sardonically. He considered it a matter of luck that he had been blessed with facial features that women found attractive, but cynically he suspected that his huge wealth meant he could have resembled the Hunchback of Notre Dame and still have had females flocking to his bed.

He ordered a drink and glanced towards the door again. This time his attention was riveted by the blonde in a black dress who had just walked in.

Hair the colour of honey was swept into a loose knot on top of her head, and a few stray curls framed a heart-shaped face dominated by eyes that even from a few feet away he could see were sapphire-blue. She looked as though she had been poured into the black silk dress which moulded her hourglass figure as faithfully as a lover's touch, and her long legs, sheathed in barely-there black silk hose, looked even sexier with the addition of four-inch stiletto heels.

Despite his intention not to allow Louise to affect him, Dimitri felt a sharp tug of desire jack-knife through him. He lifted his glass and drained his whisky sour, but his eyes seemed determined to stray towards her.

Most women would have teamed the striking diamond *fleur-de-lis* with matching earrings, and perhaps a diamond ring or bracelet, but Louise's decision to wear only the pendant and no other jewellery gave her an understated elegance. Her dress was almost starkly plain compared to some of the exotic outfits on display in the restaurant, but clearly she understood that the beauty of haute couture was the fact that it allowed a woman to wear the dress rather than the dress wear the woman.

Dimitri recognised the designer motif of two entwined letter Bs on Louise's purse. Benoit Besson had taken the fashion world by storm after revealing his first collection at Paris Fashion Week two years ago, and had quickly become the darling of Europe's social elite. But the price of Besson's clothes reflected his undoubted skill as a designer. Louise's dress might easily have cost upwards of five or six thousand pounds, yet he knew her job as a museum guide would not pay a high salary.

Dimitri ran his mind over the facts the private investigator had dug up about her. There wasn't much, and so far no evidence of a rich lover in Louise's life. She lived alone, worked, as he knew, at the Louvre, and socialised occasionally with colleagues from the museum. But if she was not the mistress of some rich guy how could she afford to wear Benoit Besson designs? And why did she suddenly need money so quickly that she was prepared to sell Eirenne for considerably less than the island was worth? The idea that she was in debt seemed a logical possibility. Her mother's track record with money was appalling, and it was conceivable that Louise had inherited Tina's inability to live within her means.

She had hesitated when she had entered the restaurant, but now she looked towards the bar and saw him. Even though Dimitri was a few feet away from her he noticed the sudden flush of colour that highlighted her high cheekbones, and he felt a fierce sense of male satisfaction that she could not hide her awareness of him. The evening promised to be interesting, he mused, feeling suddenly more alive than he had done in months as anticipation made his nerve-endings tingle.

He stood up from the bar stool and walked over to meet her.

'Louise, you look stunning.' He bit back the question— *How the hell can you afford to wear a dress that probably cost a chunk of your annual salary?*

The bar was crowded. Someone knocked into her and Dimitri caught hold of her arm to steady her as she swayed slightly on her high heels.

Her skin felt like satin beneath his fingertips and her perfume, a delicate floral fragrance, teased his senses. Without stopping to question what he was doing, he lifted her hand to his mouth and grazed his lips over her knuckles. He heard her faint gasp and smiled when she blushed. For a moment he was reminded of the innocent girl he had known seven years ago.

But she was no longer a gauche teenager. She was a beautiful woman, and undoubtedly sexually experienced. He pictured her naked in his bed, pictured himself sinking between her thighs...

Their eyes met, held, and he watched her pupils dilate so that they were deep, dark pools. He could almost taste the intense sexual awareness between them.

It was a relief when the *maître d'* appeared and informed him that their table was ready.

Get a grip, Dimitri ordered himself impatiently, irritated that he seemed to have no control over his hormones. Louise was stunning, but no more so than countless other women he had dated in the past. And he should not forget that he was here for one reason only. He had invited her to dinner to discuss a business deal—namely the possibility of him buying back his family's Greek island, which should never have been hers to sell.

He remembered how shocked he'd felt when he had learned that his father had left Eirenne to his mistress. Dimitri hated Tina Hobbs to the depths of his soul. But he had never had cause to hate Tina's daughter, he acknowledged. In fact, far from disliking her, he had found himself captivated by her seven years ago. They had been lovers, but they had shared more than just sex. There had been something between them—a degree of emotional involvement he had not wanted to define.

Those memories had always lingered in the back of his mind, and sometimes when he heard a song that had been popular at the time he felt a curious pang inside as he remembered Eirenne in springtime and a golden-haired girl whose gentle smile had briefly touched his soul.

Startled by thoughts that he had never cared to dwell on too deeply before now, he threw Louise a sideways glance as they followed the waiter to their table—and discovered that she was looking at him with an unguarded expression that made him want to forget dinner, forget everything but his burning desire to sweep her into his arms and carry her out of the restaurant and into the nearest hotel, where he would hire a room for as many nights as it took to sate himself on her gorgeous body.

CHAPTER FOUR

THERE was champagne chilling in an ice-bucket. The white damask cloth was pristine, and the silver cutlery gleamed in the flickering light of candles set amid a centrepiece of white roses and fragrant mauve freesias. Louise tried to focus on the beautiful table setting, but in her mind all she could see was the look of scorching desire in Dimitri's eyes as he had drawn out a chair for her to sit down.

She was shaken by the sexual hunger he had made no effort to disguise. It was all the more shocking because they hadn't seen each other for seven years and were little more than strangers. She tried to block out her memories of the one night they had spent together. It had been so long ago, and he must have slept with so many other women since then that it did not seem likely he would remember. But somehow she knew that he *did* remember, and heat surged through her veins, making her breasts ache and evoking a dragging sensation low in her pelvis.

'Champagne, *mademoiselle*?'

'Oh…*oui. Merci.*' She nodded distractedly to the waiter, who was hovering at her elbow, and watched him fill a tall flute with champagne. The waiter walked around the table to fill Dimitri's glass and then presented them both with a menu before he finally left them alone.

'I think a toast to old friends is appropriate,' Dimitri murmured, raising his glass.

Friends. Louise felt a sharp pang as she remembered laughter and lazy days on a paradise island. She had thought they were friends—until her mother had shattered her illusions about Dimitri's motives. None of it had been real. Not the companionship or the friendship—or the passion. Dimitri had deliberately set out to seduce her, knowing that his actions would anger her mother, and his aim had been to cause trouble between Tina and his father. How could he have the nerve to suggest a toast to their friendship when it had been a lie? Louise wondered bleakly.

But there was no point in dragging up the past when she would probably never see him again after tonight. Somehow she managed a cool smile and touched her glass to his. 'To friends.'

Her throat felt parched and the words emerged as a husky whisper. She sounded like a *femme fatale* from an old movie, she thought disgustedly, and took a long sip of champagne to ease the dryness. The bubbles fizzed on her tongue and it belatedly occurred to her that it was hours since she'd had lunch, and alcohol on an empty stomach was not a good idea.

Focus on the reason why you're here, she told herself as she forced herself to meet his brooding gaze across the table.

'You said you might be interested in buying Eirenne. Is there any information I can give you that might help with your decision?'

Dimitri took a sip of champagne before answering. 'I haven't been back to the island for seven years, but I have many memories of it. Has it changed much?' His jaw hardened. 'Surely even your mother can't have done too much damage to the place?'

'Of course she hasn't.' Louise instantly leapt to her mother's defence. 'What do you imagine she might have done?'

'When my father was alive she tried to persuade him to build a nightclub and casino, so that she could hold private parties rather than have to travel to one of the bigger islands for entertainment,' he told her dryly.

'Oh.' Louise grimaced. Owning a nightclub was just the sort of thing Tina would have loved, she acknowledged ruefully. Her mother would not have worried about spoiling the peace and tranquillity of Eirenne.

'Well, she hasn't done anything like that. In fact she hasn't been back to the island since Kostas died.' She hesitated, and then said huskily, 'I know you believe Tina was only interested in your father because he was wealthy, but I think she really loved him.'

Dimitri shot her a sardonic look. 'The only person Tina Hobbs has ever loved is herself. *Theos*, even you must admit she was not a great mother. I know you spent most of your childhood dumped in boarding schools while she lived the high life, flitting from one rich sucker to another. My father was the biggest sucker of all, and I blame him as much as Tina for breaking my mother's heart.'

Dimitri's voice had risen, attracting curious glances from people at a nearby table. He muttered something beneath his breath and snatched up his menu, and Louise did the same, holding it in front of her so that she did not have to meet his angry gaze. Tension simmered between them. She took another gulp of champagne and welcomed the slight feeling of light-headedness as the alcohol hit her bloodstream.

The evening was on course to be a disaster, and the only surprise was how much she cared. Maybe she should leave? It was doubtful she could say anything that would persuade Dimitri to buy Eirenne. He was arrogant and powerful and it was clear he made his own decisions. There seemed little point in her staying.

She put down her menu, and a tremor ran through her when she discovered he was watching her. He didn't look angry any more, but she could not define the expression in the green eyes that glittered beneath his heavy brows.

'Louise, I'm sorry,' he said roughly. 'The last thing I want to do is drag up past issues that have nothing to do with us. My father's relationship with your mother was never our concern.'

Taken aback by his apology, she gave him a startled glance. 'How can you say that? You blame Tina...'

'My feelings about her are irrelevant,' he insisted. 'Look...' He leaned across the table, his expression intent as he held her gaze. 'I don't want to fight with you, *pedhaki mou*.'

What he wanted to do was walk around the table and pull Louise into his arms; feel her soft, curvaceous body pressed up against him as he crushed her lips beneath his, Dimitri acknowledged silently. Would she respond to him? His gut instinct told him that she was as fiercely aware of him as he was of her, and he was sure that, like him, she remembered the passionate night they had spent together seven years ago.

But there was a correct order to seduction, which he intended to follow. His body might be acting as if he was a hormone-crazed adolescent, but first they would enjoy good food and conversation, and he would savour the anticipation of bedding her as he'd savour a fine wine.

'What I would like to do,' he said softly, 'is to forget the past and pretend that we've only just met. Let us imagine that we are strangers, having dinner in Paris and getting to know one another a little better. What do you say?'

'I...'

Louise could not tear her eyes from Dimitri's face. He was as beautiful as a Michelangelo sculpture. She studied the chiselled lines of his cheekbones and his square jaw and longed to run her fingers over his five o'clock stubble, trace the sensual curve of his mouth. That gentle endearment, '*pedhaki mou*', had weakened her defences. If she had any sense she would insist that she only wanted to discuss the sale of the island, keep their conversation strictly to business and leave as soon as they had finished dinner.

Instead she heard herself say huskily, 'All right. I guess it would be nice to enjoy dinner without tension and probably indigestion.'

Her stomach had felt as if it was tied in knots since she had left her flat, but Dimitri's smile—or maybe it was the champagne—had induced a relaxed, warm feeling inside her. What harm could come from spending a pleasant evening in the charming surroundings of La Marianne?

The answer was directly in front of her, his dark head bent so close to hers that she could feel the soft whisper of his breath on her cheek. Her instincts warned her that Dimitri posed a serious threat to her peace of mind. But she was no longer an innocent nineteen-year-old. She was twenty-six, a self-confident career woman, and she would never make the mistake of falling for a man just because he had the dark, devastating looks of a fallen angel and a glint in his eyes that promised heaven.

'Good.' Dimitri sat back and noted that the hunted look in Louise's eyes had faded. For a moment, when the subject of her damned mother had come up, he had been consumed with the usual bitterness he felt towards Tina. But when he'd noticed Louise's expression he had controlled his anger and regretted that he had upset her. That had certainly not been his intention when he had invited her to dinner. He wasn't actually sure why he had arranged to meet her.

It had been a spur-of-the-moment decision—which for a man who never did anything on impulse was highly unsettling, he thought wryly.

He glanced at the extensive menu written in French and decided he needed a translator. 'Would you mind helping me choose what to eat? I can speak French reasonably well, but I'm not so good at understanding the written word.'

'Yes, of course.' Louise's heart did a little skip at his rueful smile, that made him seem more human somehow. Perhaps he wasn't as arrogant as she had first thought. She studied the menu. 'You had better not have *moules à la crème* or *coquilles Saint-Jacques*. I assume you're still allergic to shellfish?'

'I am, but I'm impressed that you remembered.'

She flushed and silently cursed herself for letting slip that she hadn't forgotten anything about him during the past seven years. 'It's surprising how many random facts linger in our brains,' she murmured. 'I read a food critic's report which recommended La Marianne's speciality—roasted beef fillet served with horseradish sauce,' she added, quickly changing the subject.

'That sounds good. I'll come closer so that you can talk me through the other main courses.'

Before she could object Dimitri had moved his chair around the table and sat down beside her, so close that his thigh pressed against hers. She stared at the menu and tried to banish the thought that if she turned her head her lips would be mere centimetres from his.

The spicy scent of his aftershave tantalised her senses and intensified her awareness of his raw masculinity. The bare skin of her arm felt acutely sensitive when she brushed against the sleeve of his jacket and, glancing down, she was mortified to see that her nipples had hardened and were jutting provocatively beneath her silk dress.

She hurriedly began to explain the menu options, but her voice emerged as that embarrassing husky whisper again, and she quickly gulped down more champagne. It was a relief when the waiter came over to take their order and Dimitri moved to back to his side of the table.

'How long have you lived in Paris?' he asked as he re-filled her glass.

'Four years. But it has always seemed like home. My grandmother used to live close to Sacré-Coeur, and when I was a child I spent many school holidays with her.'

Dimitri looked puzzled. 'Was she your father's mother?'

'No, my *grand-mère*, Céline, married my grandfather, Charles Hobbs, and they lived in England, where my mother was born. But when my grandfather died she moved back to Paris.' Unconsciously, her hand strayed to the diamond *fleur-de-lis* as she thought of her beloved grandmother. In many ways Céline had been more of a mother to her than Tina, and Louise still missed her.

The first course arrived, and conversation halted while the waiters fussed around them. Glancing across the table, Dimitri frowned when he saw the faintly wistful expression on Louise's face as she touched the diamond pendant. Was she thinking of whoever had given it to her? A wealthy lover, perhaps?

He was surprised by the sudden violent urge to wrench the necklace from around her throat. Even worse was the re-alisation that even if she had a dozen lovers he still wanted her. Maybe it was a stupid male pride thing, but he was certain that if she spent a night with him the other man or men in her life would be history.

He ate automatically, without really being aware of what he was eating. He was sure the food was superb, but he could not concentrate on it when he was captivated by the woman sitting opposite him. Like him, Louise did not appear interested in the food, and only picked at her starter and main course. He glanced at her, and felt something coil deep in his gut when he found that she was watching him. Colour winged along her high cheekbones and she quickly dropped her gaze.

'You must know Paris well, as you've spent so much time here,' he murmured.

She nodded. 'It's a beautiful city. You said you often come here on business. Have you done much sightseeing?'

'Only of hotel conference facilities and company boardrooms,' he said wryly.

'That's a pity. You should take a coach tour, or a river cruise.'

'Maybe I'll do that. But I'd need a guide—someone who knows Paris well and is knowledgeable about its history.' He held her gaze. 'Are you interested?'

Maybe it was a trick of the candlelight, but there seemed to be a wicked glint in Dimitri's eyes, and Louise sensed that his question held a double meaning. Surely it was her over-active imagination after too much champagne? she told herself. But some invisible force seemed to have welded her gaze to his, and her heart was beating so hard that it felt as though it would burst through her ribcage.

'I expect you'll have to return to Greece soon,' she said abruptly.

'I leave Paris tomorrow. But we still have tonight,' Dimitri gave up on his *entrecôte hongroise* and reached across the table to capture her hand in his. He felt the tiny tremor that ran through her and tightened his grip a fraction to prevent her from snatching her fingers away. 'I understand the view from the top of the Eiffel Tower at night is spectacular.'

Louise was finding it hard to concentrate as Dimitri stroked his thumb over the pulse beating frantically in her wrist. 'You…you want to climb the Eiffel Tower?' she asked shakily.

Not particularly, he thought to himself, but he was reluctant for the evening to end. He had a feeling that Louise would refuse an invitation to go on to a nightclub. She seemed edgy again, although he wasn't sure why, and his instincts told him that once they had finished dinner she would bid him goodnight. He did not want to let her go. He wanted to spend more time with her, get to know her better. Okay, if he was honest he wanted to slide that tantalising slip of black silk from her body and kiss her naked breasts before trailing his lips over her stomach and lower…

He inhaled sharply and focused on persuading her to spend the remainder of the evening with him. 'I confess I was hoping to take the elevator to the top.'

Dimitri's sexy smile made Louise's pulse race. 'That would be sensible, as there are well over a thousand steps,' she said gravely. 'And actually the only way to reach the summit *is* by lift.'

'So, that's settled. But first would you like dessert—or more champagne?'

'No, thank you,' she assured him quickly. Her appetite had disappeared and she had struggled to eat the first two courses. As for champagne—she had already drunk way too much. That had to explain why she felt so peculiar. It was as if the bubbles had exploded inside her and filled her with a wild, reckless energy.

But deep down she knew it was Dimitri, not the champagne, that was making each of her nerve-endings feel ultra-sensitive. She felt fiercely alive, and was so intensely aware of him that throughout the meal she had kept darting little glances at him, drinking in his handsome features.

It was a relief when they left the restaurant and she took deep breaths of fresh air, grateful for the gentle breeze that cooled her hot face. The Eiffel Tower dominated the sky-line, its giant metal structure illuminated by light projectors so that it appeared to glow gold against the inky-black sky.

The famous landmark was a popular attraction, even late at night, and there was a short queue waiting for the elevator. The young couple standing in front of them had clearly been caught up in the romantic atmosphere of Paris and were wrapped in each other's arms.

It must be wonderful to be so in love, Louise thought wistfully. The couple's unrestrained passion reminded her of those few days on Eirenne years ago, when Dimitri had kissed her with fierce hunger and she had eagerly responded to him. Heat surged through her and she could not bring herself to look at him or at the kissing couple. In despera-tion she stared at the ground, as if she was utterly fasci-nated by the tarmac beneath her feet.

They rode the lift to the second level, and then another elevator whisked them to the top of the tower. Louise heard Dimitri catch his breath as they stepped out onto the walk-way.

'I hope you have a head for heights. We're over a thou-sand feet up.'

He laughed. 'It feels as though we are in the sky. The view is amazing.' He stood close beside her and stared through the wire cage that enclosed the walkway. 'Is that the Arc de Triomphe down there?'

Louise nodded. 'The lights of the city sparkle like jewels, don't they? I love the way they are reflected in the river.'

The night-time view over Paris was breathtaking. But there was another reason why she was finding it difficult to draw oxygen into her lungs. The few other visitors who had come up to the top level had walked around the other side of the tower, and it felt as though it was just her and Dimitri standing on the top of the world. She had never felt so aware of a man in her life. Her eyes were drawn to his sculpted profile and a tremor ran through her, making the tiny hairs all over her body stand on end.

The breeze was stronger this high up and the air cooler. She drew her pashmina round her shoulders and caught Dimitri's attention.

'Are you cold? Do you want my jacket?'

She shook her head. 'No, I'm fine.'

'Liar,' he said softly, 'you're shivering.'

His eyes were shadowed in the darkness, but Louise could feel his intent gaze. Far below the lights of Paris blazed, but for Louise nothing existed but the sultry heat in Dimitri's eyes. All evening she had been agonisingly aware of him, and now she could no longer fight the fire surging through her veins.

'Come here.'

His voice was suddenly rough and deep, caressing her senses like crushed velvet. Her breath caught in her throat and she could not move when he slid an arm around her shoulders and pulled her against his chest. The warmth of his body immediately enfolded her and the sensual musk of his aftershave swamped her senses. She could feel the thud of his heart beating at the same frantic pace as her own and she stared up at him, her eyes wide and unguarded.

Dimitri muttered something beneath his breath. He had wanted to kiss Louise all evening, and now the temptation of her moist, slightly parted lips was too strong for him to resist. He dipped his head and slanted his mouth over hers. He remained poised for timeless seconds while their breath mingled. Then he captured her lips in a feather-soft caress, slowly at first, gently. She tasted of champagne, and the feel of her soft mouth beneath his made his heart pound.

She made a little choked sound and stiffened, but he tightened his arms around her, drawing her inexorably closer to him. Wildfire excitement shot through him when she opened her mouth so that he was able to explore her with his tongue.

Molten heat was coursing through Louise, suffusing her entire body with delicious warmth. Her breasts felt swollen and heavy and her nipples tingled as they were crushed against Dimitri's chest. She was conscious of a throbbing sensation deep in her pelvis—a restless ache that drove her to press her hips against his rock-hard thighs.

He kept on kissing her and kissing her, his mouth moving hungrily over hers, demanding a response which she gave unresistingly. *Stupid*, taunted a voice in her head, *weak and pathetic. Where is your pride?* But she ignored the voice, pushed it to the back of her mind while her body capitulated to his exquisite seduction, and she slid her hands to his shoulders as he deepened the kiss to something so erotic that she trembled in the circle of his arms.

Voices shattered the magic and snapped Louise back to her senses. People were heading towards them along the walkway. She pulled out of Dimitri's arms, breathing hard. Her mouth felt bruised, and she lifted her fingers to her lips and felt their swollen softness.

Dear heaven, what had she been *thinking*? All evening she had been haunted by memories of their brief affair years ago, but that was no excuse for her to fall into his arms. Life had moved on—*she* had moved on—and the past was history.

'You shouldn't have done that,' she whispered, dismayed to realise she was shaking from the firestorm of passion he had evoked in her.

'But you didn't stop me.' His eyes glittered, and his smile was faintly mocking, but the hand that gently brushed a tendril of hair back from her cheek shook slightly, and Louise realised with a jolt that he was no more in control of his emotions that she was.

She shivered again—a combination of reaction to his kiss and being deprived of the warmth of his body. But this time he kept his arms by his sides.

'We should go.' His voice was suddenly terse.

They were both silent as the lift whisked them back down to the ground. It was nearly midnight, Louise saw when she glanced at her watch. She was glad when Dimitri hailed a taxi. She was still stunned by that kiss, mortified when she remembered how she had responded to him. She should have given him the big freeze, hung on to her dignity. But instead she had melted in his arms as if she had spent the past seven years missing him—which she certainly had *not*, she assured herself.

They had barely discussed the sale of Eirenne, she remembered as she stared out of the taxi window. *Why* hadn't she stuck to business over dinner? And what had induced her to agree to go to the top of the Eiffel Tower with him when she knew full well that it was one of the most iconic venues in Paris, the city of lovers? The romantic atmosphere was no excuse for the fact that she had practically eaten him. She felt hot with shame when she recalled how she had clung to him.

The taxi drew to a halt and she climbed out onto the pavement after Dimitri, frowning when she realised that they were not at her apartment—which was where she had assumed they had been heading. She glanced at the grand front entrance of a well-known hotel and then at him, her eyes questioning.

He gave her a level look. 'Do you want to join me for a drink? We can continue our discussion on the possibility of me buying Eirenne.'

Persuading him to buy the island was the only thing that

mattered—the only realistic chance of saving her mother. Yet Louise knew it would be the height of stupidity to accept his invitation when he was looking at her with an intent expression in his eyes that made her blood pound in her veins.

So why didn't she bid him goodnight and climb back into the taxi? Why did her mind keep replaying his kiss? She stared at him, knowing she should refuse to join him but unable to bear the thought of leaving him. After tonight she would probably never see him again.

She shivered—but not because she was cold.

Dimitri's eyes darkened. He caught hold of her hand and lifted it to his mouth, grazing his lips across her knuckles. 'Come with me?' he murmured, in a voice as rich and sensuous as molten chocolate.

She gave up the fight with herself and nodded her assent, feeling beyond words, beyond the boundaries of common sense. Dimitri paid the taxi driver and, still holding Louise's hand, led her into the hotel. She had a vague image of an opulent lobby: elegant pillars, ornately patterned marble floor and extravagant gold décor. They entered a lift. Moments later they arrived at the top floor and walked a short distance along a corridor until he stopped and ushered her into his suite.

'What a beautiful room,' she murmured, desperate to break the silence and bring an element of normality into an increasingly unreal situation.

The suite was a luxurious blend of pale grey velvet carpet and silk wallpaper, with cushion-filled sofas and soft furnishings in duck-egg-blue. Through an open door Louise saw that the colour scheme was repeated in the bedroom, but the sight of a vast four-poster bed made her quickly look away.

'I spend too much time in hotels to appreciate them.'

Dimitri shrugged out of his jacket and dropped it over the arm of a sofa before walking over to the bar. He took two glasses, filled them, and strolled back across the room to hand one to Louise. 'A nightcap—Cointreau,' he explained.

She really did not need any more alcohol, but it seemed safer to sip the drink than to make eye-contact with Dimitri. The orange-tasting liqueur was sweet, but with a subtle heat that elicited a delicious warm feeling inside her—yet she could not seem to control the tremors that were making her body shake.

'Please—have a seat.' He indicated the two-seater sofa.

Louise stared at it and froze as she pictured herself sinking against the cushions and Dimitri sitting down close beside her. She was desperately aware of his lean, hard body, and now that he had discarded his jacket she could see the shadow of dark chest hair beneath his white silk shirt.

She shouldn't have come here, she thought frantically. She felt helpless, like a fly trapped in a spider's web. But to be fair she was not afraid of Dimitri but of herself, her reaction to his brooding sensuality.

Her glass was still half full. Not wanting to appear rude, she swallowed the rest of her drink and felt it burn a fiery path down her throat.

'Look, it's getting late. I'm not sure there's much more I can tell you about Eirenne. I haven't been back there since we…' She faltered as memories of the passionate night they had spent together on the island flooded her mind. 'Since we were there seven years ago. Perhaps you would be good enough to phone me when you have made a decision?' Panic made her talk too fast. 'Thank you for dinner. You're leaving tomorrow, so I guess we won't have a chance to meet again,' she finished in a choked voice.

She did not notice the faint flare of impatience in

Dimitri's eyes—did not know that the betraying tremor of her lower lip had made his gut clench.

'You little idiot,' he said roughly. 'Do you really think I can let you walk away from me?'

Her eyes flew to his face and she caught her breath at the hard glitter in his olive-green gaze. Time stopped. Her heart was thundering so hard that her ribcage jerked erratically. He drained his glass and set it down on the table. She waited, barely able to breathe, as he walked towards her with determined intent.

'Louise,' he said, in a low, a sexy growl that made her skin prickle. 'Come to me, *pedhaki*.'

A warning voice clamoured inside her head. But she was deafened by the thunderous beat of her heart and with a little cry went into his arms. The world exploded.

CHAPTER FIVE

THE room tilted as Dimitri seized Louise in his arms and sank down on the sofa, pulling her onto his lap. His dark head swooped and he captured her mouth in a searing kiss that destroyed any idea she might have had of resisting him. This was what she had yearned for all evening, she admitted silently. No man had ever excited her in the way Dimitri did, and she had no self-protection against the sensual onslaught of his lips and the bold thrust of his tongue into her mouth as he explored her with hungry passion.

His hands roamed feverishly over her body and traced the length of her spine, before he cupped her nape and tugged her head back so that he could deepen the kiss. It became flagrantly erotic. He moved his other hand to her shoulder, slid a finger beneath the narrow strap of her dress and drew it down her arm, lower and lower, slowly exposing her breast.

The air felt cool on her naked flesh, but Dimitri's touch was warm as he curled his hand possessively around the soft mound. Sensation arrowed through Louise as he trailed his lips down her throat and found the pulse thudding frantically at its base. The brush of his thumb-pad across her sensitised nipple made her catch her breath.

She was on fire for him. Molten heat flooded between her legs and she gave a little desperate moan when he slipped his hand beneath the hem of her dress and stroked her taut, trembling thighs. Higher and higher his fingers crept, inching towards where she was frantic for him to touch her. She was lost in a swirling sea of sensation where nothing mattered but that she follow the dictates of her body, which was begging for sexual release. Her sensible self had deserted her, and she was gripped by an urgent need for Dimitri to relieve the pressure that was building inside her.

He discovered the strip of bare flesh above the lace band of her stocking-top and made a primitive growl deep in his throat. The sound was raw and it triggered a throb of white-hot desire in Louise. And then his hand was at the junction of her thighs, and he eased the edge of her French knickers aside so that he could run his fingertips up and down her moist opening.

He eased her back so that she was half lying across his knees, with her head resting against the cushions. Glancing down, she saw the whiteness of her bare breast above the crumpled black silk of her dress. Her nipple was taut and erect, and she shivered in anticipation as she watched him lower his dark head. The feel of his lips closing around the hard peak sent starbursts of sensation through her. Caught up in a maelstrom of pleasure, she squirmed in his lap and felt the solid ridge of his arousal beneath her bottom.

Without conscious thought she opened her legs a little, enabling him to slide his finger into her feminine heat. The feel of him inside her drove her instantly to the brink, and she arched her hips so that he could slide deeper, gasping when he rubbed his thumb-pad lightly back and forth across her clitoris.

This was what he had wanted to do ever since Louise had walked back into his life four days ago, Dimitri acknowledged. When she had faced him in his office in Athens—a gorgeous siren in her short scarlet skirt—he had fantasised about spreading her across his desk and making hot, urgent love to her. For the past seven years she had hovered on the periphery of his mind like a lingering melody. But the flesh-and-blood woman was a thousand times more beautiful than the image of her that had occasionally flitted into his thoughts.

Ideally he would like to carry her into the bedroom and undress her slowly, take his time to explore every inch of her delectable body before he indulged in a leisurely sex session. But there wasn't a chance in hell of that happening when he was more aroused than he could remember being for a long, long time, he thought derisively. Louise's little cries of delight as he pleasured her with his fingers were fast sending him out of control.

She was breathing heavily, twisting her hips restlessly so that her bottom ground against the hardened shaft that was throbbing unbearably beneath his trousers. He felt an unexpected tug of tenderness as he studied her flushed face and the tendrils of damp hair that clung to her cheek. He controlled his own hunger and concentrated on bringing her to orgasm, moving his fingers faster in and out of her slick wetness and at the same time capturing her pebble-hard nipple in his mouth, caressing it with his tongue.

She gave a keening cry and bucked convulsively as her internal muscles tightened and relaxed again and again, each spasm making her shudder. Her head was thrown back, her golden hair spilling over the cushions, and Dimitri could not resist claiming her parted lips in a fierce kiss. He remembered how wildly responsive she had been on Eirenne. Sex with her had been amazing. He had never known another woman to be as passionate or such a generous lover.

'Ise panemorfi,' he murmured huskily. She was so beau-

tiful. He was impatient to settle himself between her thighs and thrust his erection into her velvet softness.

He gripped the hem of her dress to push it up to her waist. But something was wrong. She was staring at him with an expression of horror in her eyes, and she caught hold of his wrist to prevent him from lifting her skirt.

'What is it, *glikia mou*?' he demanded raggedly, breathing hard as he struggled for control.

'Oh, God! What am I *doing*?' Louise choked, not realising that she had actually spoken the words out loud.

The sound of Dimitri's voice had shattered the sensual web he had wrapped around her and reality had reared its ugly head. She glanced down at herself, sprawled on Dimitri's knees with her legs open and the top of her dress pulled down, exposing her naked breast. Her jutting, reddened nipple seemed to taunt her, and self-disgust rolled over her with the force of a tidal wave.

Ise panemorfi...Dimitri had often murmured those words to her on Eirenne, and the memory of their brief affair and his lies made her feel sick with shame. 'Come to me,' he had said tonight—and she had immediately thrown herself at him, forgetting how he had hurt and humiliated her seven years ago.

His eyes narrowed, but his voice was carefully controlled. 'What *we're* doing hardly requires an explanation, surely?' he drawled. 'I want to make love to you, and I assume from your response to me that you want it too.'

Scorching colour tinged Louise's white face at his reminder of what a fool she had been. With trembling fingers she jerked the strap of her dress back into place and scrambled off his lap, swaying a little when she discovered that her legs felt like jelly.

'You invited me here to discuss Eirenne,' she reminded him shakily. She was horrified that for a few reckless minutes she had forgotten the reason why she had accepted his invitation to come up to his hotel suite. Without specialist treatment in America her mother would die. And if Dimitri did not buy back his family's island Louise feared she had little chance of raising the money to pay for Tina's medical costs before time ran out.

'Have you reached a decision?' she demanded.

'Not yet,' Dimitri replied curtly, struggling to hide his irritation that Louise had called a halt to their passion to talk about business. He ached low in his gut, and it was hard to think about anything other than his burning need for sexual release.

Doubts crept into his mind. Was she one of those women who liked to play games? He had met a few in his time—calculating women who used their sexual favours as a bartering tool in exchange for expensive jewellery or designer dresses.

He stared at her with mounting anger. 'You never did tell me why you're so anxious to sell the island—or why you are prepared to let it go at a knock-down price.' His eyes fell on the diamond pendant sparkling between her breasts and he could not prevent the ugly suspicions growing in his mind. 'Why do you need a large amount of money in a hurry? Are you in debt?' He ignored her sharp denial and continued relentlessly, 'I find it hard to believe that your job as a museum guide pays enough for you to be able buy valuable jewellery and designer clothes.'

'My dress was a present,' Louise told him coldly. 'I didn't pay for it. And I'm certainly not in debt.'

She was furious at his accusation, but the hard glint in his eyes warned her that he did not intend to drop the matter of why she needed to sell Eirenne. She was on dangerous ground, because she could not allow him to find out that she needed the money for her mother.

She stared at him, searching her mind frantically for a believable reason why she had offered to sell him the island. 'I admit there are a few things I need to pay for,' she muttered. 'I want to clear my student loan. And my car is ten years old and the garage has advised me that it won't cope with another winter.' Both of those statements were true, but she could not reveal to Dimitri that they were not her main priority right now.

Can't you persuade the lover who bought you your dress to buy you a new car? Dimitri thought grimly. Louise had confirmed his suspicions about her. Clearly she was the type of woman who was prepared to sell herself for personal gain—just has her mother had done. It was stupid to feel surprised or disappointed, he told himself. In many ways it made things easier, because even knowing what she was he still wanted her. And she wanted him to buy Eirenne. It felt good to know that he had the upper hand, that he was in control of the situation.

He got up from the sofa and smiled to himself when he saw a tremor run though her as he stood in front of her. 'So there *are* financial reasons why you're desperate to sell the island,' he murmured. 'Why didn't you say so from the start?'

'I'm not desperate,' Louise lied shakily, catching her bottom lip with her teeth as an image of Tina's painfully thin face flashed into her mind. She *was* desperate to help her mother, she acknowledged silently. She would do everything possible to raise the money for Tina's treatment.

'No?' Dimitri idly wound a honey-blond curl around his finger. 'So are you saying you *didn't* come up to my suite in the hope of persuading me to buy Eirenne?'

Louise stiffened. Dear God, what did he mean by *persuading*? Did he think she would…? The gleam in his olive-green eyes caused her heart to miss a beat.

'Because I *am* open to persuasion, *glikia mou*,' he drawled.

His voice lowered, and it was so deep and soft that it seemed to whisper across Louise's skin like a velvet cloak, enfolding her and drawing her to him. She could not look away from him, and her breath hitched in her throat when he lifted a hand and smoothed her hair back behind her ear. The feather-light brush of his fingertips on her neck sent a quiver through her, and she could feel the hard tips of her nipples straining beneath her silk dress, practically begging him to touch them.

From somewhere deep inside her a tiny voice of common sense pointed out that it would be madness to sink into the sensual web he was wrapping around her. Becoming involved with Dimitri would bring so many complications. But the sultry gleam in his eyes was mesmeric, inviting—inciting all sorts of exciting fantasies in her mind. Maybe she *could* persuade him to buy the island, whispered a voice in her head. Would it really be so wrong to do *anything* to save her mother's life?

She could not tear her eyes from his. He was standing so close that she could feel his breath on her cheek, and she ached for him to close the gap between them and slant his mouth over hers.

She swallowed. 'I should go.' Her voice emerged as a tremulous whisper.

'Why not stay?'

There must be a good reason. Probably dozens. But his sexy smile decimated her ability to think logically.

'I want to make love to you.' Dimitri's voice thickened with desire. He did not understand what it was about this woman that made his body ache, made him shake like a testosterone-fuelled youth anticipating his first sexual experience. All he knew was that Louise was like a fever in his blood, and the only cure was to possess her and find the sweet satiation his body craved.

He pulled her into his arms and his heart slammed against his ribs when he felt the tips of her nipples pressed against his chest. 'I want to take you to bed and undress you, slowly. I want to lay you down and kiss every inch of you—your mouth, your breasts, between your legs,' he whispered in her ear. 'And then I want to take you and make you mine, and give you more pleasure than you've ever had with any other man.'

His voice was like honey sliding over her, and his words made Louise melt. She was conscious of liquid warmth between her thighs, and the throbbing ache that had only been partially appeased when he had pleasured her with his hands now clamoured for his complete possession.

He cupped her chin and stared into her eyes. 'I've been honest with you. I'm not ashamed to admit how much I desire you. Now I'm asking you to be honest too.' There was no hint of softening on his arrogant features, and he spoke firmly, decisively. 'If you don't want to be with me tell me now and I'll take you home.'

No other man had ever made her weak with sexual longing, Louise thought. Yet the desire blazing in Dimitri's eyes also made her feel powerful. He had awoken feelings inside her that she hadn't felt since she was nineteen. It was as if her sensuality had been on hold for the intervening years, but with one kiss he had aroused a level of need in her that only he could assuage. It was her choice whether to stay with him or leave.

'Dimitri...'

He tightened his arms around her. 'You know you want me, and I am burning up for you.'

The raw urgency in his voice allayed her last lingering doubts. She wound her arms around his neck and tugged his head down. Words were beyond her. Seven years ago he had been her first lover, and there had never been anyone else. Undoubtedly she had lost her sanity, but she could not deny her body one more night of pleasure with him. However, a sense of self-preservation held her back from telling him that her need was as great as his, and instead she reached up on tiptoe and kissed him.

Dimitri muttered something against her lips, and then he was kissing her hungrily, fiercely, desperately.

Louise cupped his face in her hands. The stubble on his jaw felt abrasive against her palms. He pushed his tongue into her mouth and slid one hand to her nape to hold her tightly to him. His other hand cupped her bottom and jerked her hard against his thighs, so that she could feel the solid ridge of his arousal jabbing her stomach.

The evidence of his desire escalated her excitement to fever-pitch. There were too many barriers between them: her dress, his shirt. She tugged at the buttons and moaned softly as she pushed the material aside and skimmed her hands over his bare chest—an olive-gold satin covered with whirls of black hair.

'Patience, *pedhaki*,' he murmured. 'We're going to do this properly, on a bed.'

He fought the temptation to strip her and position her over one arm of the sofa and lifted her into his arms to carry her into the bedroom. He set her down at the foot of the bed and turned her round so that he could undo the zip that ran the length of her spine. His hands shook and he cursed as the material caught. *Theos*, he was acting like an inexperienced boy. He dragged air into his lungs and worked the zip down to reveal the semi-transparent French knickers that covered her *derrière*. The dress slithered to the floor and he hooked his fingers in the top of her panties and pulled them down to her knees. The sight of her rounded bottom,

as smooth and velvety as a ripe peach, caused his arousal
to strain painfully against the restriction of his trousers.
The knickers slipped to her ankles and she gave a faintly
embarrassed laugh as she stepped out of them and kicked
them and the black silk dress away.

Dimitri had never seen anything so erotic as Louise
wearing only black hold-up stockings and stilettos. He
turned her to face him and cupped her breasts in his hands,
heat surging through him as he watched her pupils dilate
when he rubbed his thumb-pads over her nipples.

Honey-blond curls framed her flushed face, and her
eyes were the intense blue of sapphires. She was so beautiful he could just stand there looking at her. The throb of
his arousal reminded him that looking wasn't enough. He
wanted her to touch him, wanted to feel her cool hands caress his hot flesh.

'Undress me,' he demanded raggedly.

He sensed her faint hesitation as she reached for his belt
buckle, and once she had unfastened it she hesitated again
before sliding the zip of his trousers down. It suddenly hit
him that she was shy, and he felt a tugging sensation in his
gut when she blushed. His instincts told him that it was
a while since she'd had sex. But that didn't make sense.
Maybe he had been wrong about her and there was no rich
lover in her life? He frowned, remembering that she had admitted her dress had been a gift. Surely only a lover would
buy her sexy designer wear?

But at that moment Dimitri didn't give a damn about the
dress or anything else. All he could think was that he had
never been so turned on in his life and that the chances of
him making love to her with any degree of finesse were
distinctly unlikely.

He remembered how he had told her he wanted to kiss
her everywhere, and he kept his promise—starting with her

mouth. With practised efficiency he slipped off his shoes, socks and trousers, and then drew her into his arms and claimed her lips. His excitement intensified when she responded instantly. She was an intriguing mix of diffidence and boldness, and when she tentatively pushed her tongue into his mouth he groaned and crushed her against him, the last vestiges of his restraint decimated by his savage need to possess her.

It was an amazing bed, Louise thought as Dimitri lifted her and laid her on the mattress. She looked up at the silvery-grey silk canopy above her head. The satin bedspread she was lying on felt decadently sensual against her skin, but the touch of Dimitri's naked body aroused her even more. She hadn't been aware of him stripping off his underwear, and as he knelt over her she could not help but stare at his massive erection.

She felt a faint flicker of trepidation when she imagined taking him inside her. She had done so once before, she reminded herself, albeit seven years ago. Giving her virginity to him had been a beautiful experience, and the quivering sensation in the pit of her stomach was a sign that her body was impatient for him to make love to her with unrestrained passion.

But first it seemed that he wanted to play—to tease and tantalise her. He slipped off her shoes and then peeled her stockings down her legs before he started to kiss her. Within minutes of him trailing his mouth over every dip and curve of her body she was breathing hard and trembling with anticipation.

'Please…' she whispered when he finally lifted his mouth from hers after a kiss that had plundered her soul. She was on fire, and molten heat flooded between her thighs in readiness for his possession.

'I intend to please you, *glikia*.'

The quiet intent in his voice escalated her excitement, and she caught her breath when he cradled her breasts in his big palms and bent his head to kiss one nipple and then the other, curling his tongue around each tight bud and lapping her, licking her, until the pleasure was almost too much to bear. She arched her hips in instinctive invitation. He accepted as he moved down her body and pushed her legs open so that he could bestow the most intimate kiss of all.

She bucked and shook, and he laughed softly and held her firmly while he dipped his tongue into her honeyed sweetness. He brought her to the edge, held her there, but when she pleaded for him never to stop he positioned himself over her, supporting his weight on his elbows.

'Touch me,' he bade her harshly, and groaned when she obeyed and circled him with her slender hands.

He loved the way she blushed—her pink cheeks and soft smile reminded him of the girl who had given herself to him so shyly and yet with gut-wrenching eagerness on Eirenne. Common sense told him that his instincts had to be wrong, and she must have had other lovers apart from him. But not many, he guessed, and perhaps not for a while. She was still a little hesitant, and seemed content for him to take the lead. That suited him fine, Dimitri thought, because he was too fired up to wait any longer.

There were condoms in the bedside drawer—thankfully he always carried them with him. Not that he had expected he would need them when he had come to Paris. He hadn't planned to take Louise to bed, but deep down he *had* hoped, he admitted to himself. There was something between them that defied explanation—a sense that she belonged to him, which was curious because he'd never felt possessive about other women he'd slept with.

The moment had come. Louise knew from the darkness of Dimitri's eyes that the time for foreplay was over. But she felt no fear or doubt, only a fierce joy as she stared at his face and saw the younger man she had known on Eirenne as well as the man he was now. They were one and the same—the Dimitri she had been falling in love with many years ago and the Dimitri who, if she was not on her guard, could easily threaten her heart now.

He kissed her lips softly, sweetly, so that tears filled her eyes. His hands were gentle as he spread her legs wider and slowly lowered himself onto her. She felt the tip of his penis push against her, and as he eased into her with exquisite care his eyes locked with hers and she felt that their souls as well as their bodies were joined.

'Are you all right? Is it hurting?' She was so hot and tight it was all he could do not to explode instantly, Dimitri acknowledged, gritting his teeth as he fought for control.

'No, it's fine…it's good.' *It's unbelievably wonderful,* Louise added silently. 'Really,' she assured him, and kissed away the slight frown between his brows. She lifted her hips. 'I want you to…'

Her words died away as he slid deeper, filling her, completing her. He seemed to know exactly what she wanted, and he withdrew and slid deep again, each thrust more intense than the last, driving her relentlessly on a heart-stopping journey towards a place that she sensed was there but remained frustratingly out of her reach.

'Dimitri…' She gripped his shoulders and felt the sheen of sweat on his skin. She arched up to meet the rhythmic strokes of his body and gasped as he held her hips and drove into her harder, faster, until the world spun out of control.

He claimed her mouth and her heart leapt when she sensed tenderness as well as passion in his kiss.

'Relax and let it happen,' he murmured.

And then it did happen, and the beauty of it took her breath away. He thrust powerfully, the deepest yet, and the hot, throbbing ache in her pelvis suddenly imploded, sending wave after tumultuous wave of pleasure through her. She sank into the exquisite ecstasy of her orgasm, drowned in its tidal force, and sobbed his name as the waves continued to pound her.

Her internal muscles convulsed around him, squeezed and released him in frantic spasms that blew Dimitri's mind. He paused, every sinew straining as he sought to prolong the journey and delay the pleasure he knew was ahead for just a few seconds longer. The anticipation of it clawed in his gut. He took a shuddering breath, and as he stared down at Louise's rose-flushed face he thought how lovely she was. No other woman had ever made him feel this way—as if he was a king and could conquer the world. He couldn't hold on, and he made a harsh, primitive sound in his throat at the moment of release before he sank into the haven of her arms and she cradled his head on her breasts.

CHAPTER SIX

LOUISE opened her eyes and stared at the grey silk drapes around the bed. She was instantly awake as memories of the previous night flooded her mind. She had never slept in a four-poster before, or in a bed of this size. Two people could sleep in a bed this big and never touch each other. But that hadn't happened with her and Dimitri.

They had touched and kissed and caressed each other and made love twice during the night—three times, actually. But the last time had been just before dawn, when the sky outside had lightened from indigo to purple but the stars had yet to go out.

Now the cool grey light of early morning was filtering through the half-open curtains, and the new day brought with it big doubts about whether it had been wise to spend the night with a man who was to all intents and purposes a stranger. She had thought she had known him seven years ago, but their brief relationship had been based on lies. The reality was that she did not know Dimitri Kalakos at all.

The feverish excitement that had overwhelmed her last night had faded and common sense had returned. Sleeping with him had not been wise at all, said a voice in her head. It had complicated everything.

She turned her head to study him. He was lying on his front, his head pillowed on his arms and his face turned towards her. His thick, dark eyelashes were fanned against his cheeks and Louise's gaze lingered on the sensual curve of his mouth. She felt a little tug of emotion as she watched him sleeping. He looked relaxed. The fine lines around his eyes had smoothed out and he looked more like the younger Dimitri she had met on Eirenne.

He must have been a beautiful child. Her heart ached as she wondered whether their child would have resembled him. If she had had a son, he would be six years old now. She pictured a wiry, olive-skinned little boy, with a mass of dark hair and olive-green eyes, a cheeky grin and a streak of daring that would inevitably get him into trouble from time to time.

Sadness hit her like a blow to her chest. It did not matter how many times she told herself it was stupid to grieve for a child who had never been born. The loss of her baby still hurt after all this time, and being with Dimitri again made the memories so much more intense.

She wondered what he would have been like as a father. *If he had stuck around*, pointed out the voice in her head. There was no guarantee he would have supported her. If her pregnancy had continued she would have contacted him and told him she was expecting his baby, but perhaps he would have rejected his child as her father had rejected her.

The box of condoms on the bedside table was a mocking reminder of their night of physical pleasure. She could only be thankful he had remembered to use protection. She felt ashamed that in the heat of the moment contraception hadn't crossed her mind. How awful was that? she berated herself. Hadn't one unplanned pregnancy been enough? It was true that even if she *had* had unprotected sex her chances of conceiving were slim after the problems she'd suffered with her first pregnancy. But there was no escaping the fact that last night she had behaved utterly irresponsibly.

She stared up at the canopy above the bed and chewed on her bottom lip. Dimitri had told her he was returning to Greece later today. He was a notorious playboy and in all likelihood regarded last night as a one-night stand. What was the protocol when you woke up in bed with a man you'd had casual sex with? she wondered. Would he offer her breakfast and ring Room Service? Or would he be impatient for her to leave and arrange a taxi to take her home?

She couldn't do it, she thought bleakly. She could not go through with the charade of acting as though spending the night in a guy's hotel bedroom was something she did regularly. It was not that she was ashamed of sleeping with him; she was a free and single female living in the twenty-first century and she would not judge any woman for enjoying sex without strings. It was just that it wasn't *her*. She had certain rules she lived by, and last night she had broken all of them.

Another thought struck her. Had she managed to *persuade* him to buy Eirenne? She paled. What had she been thinking last night? The truth was she had not been thinking at all, but had been swept away by passion tinged with evocative memories of their relationship years ago. Now, in the cold light of day, she could not bear for him to believe that she had followed in her mother's footsteps and become the type of woman who was prepared to sell herself for financial gain—even if it was not for her own gain.

It suddenly became imperative that she left before Dimitri woke up. She couldn't face him when her emotions were all over the place. Taking care not to disturb him, she slid out of bed and winced when she discovered muscles she had not known existed. The ache inside her was worse. She felt empty and a little bit sick as she gathered up her clothes from the floor and crept into the bathroom.

* * *

The clock on the bedside table flashed 9:13 a.m. As Dimitri stared at the red digits they changed to 9:14. *Theos!* He sat up and raked a hand through his hair. He had never stayed in bed until a quarter past nine in his life—or not to sleep, anyway. On rare occasions he invited a mistress to stay the night with him—the single benefit being that he could have sex the following morning. Last night had been one of those occasions, but it had backfired, because from the empty space in the bed beside him and the strangely muted silence of the hotel suite it appeared that Louise had already left.

Frowning, he flicked back the sheets and padded into the bathroom. The absence of the dress, shoes and underwear that last night had been strewn across the floor confirmed her disappearance. Maybe she'd gone to work, he mused as he stepped into the shower. He felt irritated that she had not woken him before she left. He was uncomfortable with the idea that she might have watched him sleeping, and that was crazy because he had never felt vulnerable in his life.

His bad mood was due to frustration that he hadn't stirred first and kissed her awake, he decided. He'd bet she looked gorgeous first thing: sleepily sexy, with her hair all mussed and her mouth all soft and moist and eager. He would have liked to trail his lips down to her breasts and tease her dusky pink nipples until she made that little whimpering moan she had made last night. Hell, he would have liked to roll her beneath him and ease his swollen shaft into her, taking them both on an early-morning ride and watching her come apart in his arms.

He felt himself harden and turned the shower's temperature setting to cold to cool his desire. There would be other mornings—and definitely other nights. He was not a fan of long-distance affairs, but the flight time between Athens and Paris was only three hours and it would be easy enough to meet up with Louise at weekends.

In many ways the fact that they did not live in the same city was good, he thought as he reached for a towel. There was less danger that their affair would slip into complacency and become boring. He could smell the lingering scent of her perfume when he walked back into the bedroom, and he kept picturing her lying naked on the satin sheets as he lowered himself onto her. The thought struck him as he donned chinos and a black polo shirt that he was disappointed that she had gone without saying goodbye or arranging when they would next meet.

Dimitri frowned again. The way she had sneaked out like that—it was as if she did not care if she ever saw him again. Maybe she didn't. He was conscious of a peculiar sinking feeling in his stomach, and felt irritated with himself. Hell, how many times had he spent the night with a woman and in the morning made vague assurances about calling her that he had no intention of keeping? The fact that Louise hadn't acted like a clinging vine should be cause for celebration, not regret.

He slipped on his jacket and checked his cell phone. There were no messages, but he had her number. He would give her a call later. Sure, he wanted to see her again, but he didn't want to appear too keen.

The humiliation of scurrying out of a five-star hotel at dawn, wearing a dress that she had clearly worn the previous evening, was something Louise doubted she would forget in a hurry. The doorman's face had been inscrutable, but she had been painfully aware that her wild hair, old make-up and bare legs—she hadn't wasted time pulling on her stockings—had all indicated that she had spent the night in bed with a lover, and the dark circles beneath her eyes were proof that she'd had very little sleep.

Madeleine stared at her reproachfully when she let herself into the apartment, and showed her disapproval by remaining regally on her cushion on the windowsill.

'I know, I know.' Louise groaned. 'I must have taken leave of my senses. But it won't happen again.'

Dimitri would be back in Athens in a few hours. If—as she hoped and prayed—he agreed to buy Eirenne, the sale would be dealt with by their respective lawyers and there was no reason why they should ever meet again.

She headed straight for the shower and stood beneath the spray for ages, as if she could wash the touch of his hands from her skin. Images kept pushing into her mind of the way he had made love to her—with the consummate skill of a renowned playboy but also with an unexpected gentleness. It made her heart ache when she recalled the soft endearments he had whispered in Greek as she had lain spent and utterly sated in his arms...

A message on her answer-machine drove Dimitri and every other thought from her head. The consultant in charge of her mother's care was voicing his concerns that Tina's condition had worsened, and he suggested that Louise should meet with him as soon as possible.

The hospital was in a suburb of Paris. She found her mother dozing when she slipped into her private room, and as she sat by the bed she noted with a pang of dread that Tina had lost more weight and her skin was ashen. The scarf tied around her head hid the fact that she had lost her hair after chemotherapy. Tears stung Louise's eyes as she remembered Tina's blond beehive hairstyle. How cruel was this disease that had robbed her mother of her looks and seemed intent on stealing her life.

'Loulou?' Tina's eyes fluttered open.

'I'm here.' She wished she could call her mother 'Mum', but Tina had always insisted that Louise should use her Christian name.

'It makes me seem old to have a teenager address me as Mum,' Tina had complained.

For years she had lied about her age and told her lovers that she was twenty-eight.

Louise sighed and curled her fingers around Tina's bony hand. 'I'm sorry I didn't visit yesterday. I worked until late, and then I...' She faltered when she thought of what she had done after work. 'I went out to dinner.'

A gleam of curiosity flickered in her mother's eyes. 'With a boyfriend?' She studied Louise. 'I'm glad you've started to make more effort with your appearance. The suit you're wearing is gorgeous. You've got a great figure and it's about time you started to show it off. That's the only way to attract a man.'

Louise gave a wry smile, but did not explain that she was wearing one of Benoit's designs because she knew her mother liked her to dress well. 'I'm not trying to attract a man,' she murmured. 'I'm too involved with my job. Did I tell you I've applied for a position as an assistant curator in the Department of Paintings at the Louvre?'

Tina had closed her eyes, but after a moment she opened them again. 'I'm pleased you've got a good career. I always hoped you would. Not like me—I never trained in anything.'

Talking seemed to tire her and she fell silent for a few minutes. Louise was just about to tiptoe from the room when Tina spoke again.

'Kostas was in love with me, and I cared about him. He was the only one. All the others just wanted me for one thing. It boosted their egos to have a mistress, but they never thought about me as a person and after a while I stopped hoping they would. I used them like they used me.'

Louise swallowed the lump in her throat. She had never realised before that her mother had been looking for love with all those different men. In the end she had found it with Kostas Kalakos, but their relationship had hurt so many other people—especially Kostas's wife and family. She understood why Dimitri despised Tina, she thought bleakly.

'The tumour is growing quicker than we had expected,' explained Alain Duval, the cancer specialist who was caring for Tina, after he'd invited Louise into his office. 'I can't guarantee that the pioneering treatment offered at our associate hospital in Massachusetts would be successful, but it *is* your mother's only chance. Soon the opportunity for that chance will be lost,' he added quietly.

'How long does she have before time runs out for her to have the treatment?' Louise asked tensely.

'A few weeks at most. Ideally she needs to start the newly developed form of radiation therapy immediately. I appreciate that medical costs in the United States are high, and that your mother does not have health insurance that would cover the costs. But if there is any way at all that you could raise the money I suggest you do so without delay.'

If *only* Dimitri would agree to buy Eirenne. She could not give him any more time to make up his mind, Louise thought frantically. She prayed he had not left Paris. As soon as she had finished at the hospital she would go back to his hotel and plead with him to give her an answer.

Her mind whirled. If he refused to buy the island she would instruct the estate agent to advertise for a buyer. In the meantime she would try to arrange a temporary loan. But she had already asked the bank once and her request had been refused. Panic churned in her stomach.

'I'm in the process of selling some assets to cover the medical expenses,' she explained to the consultant. 'The money should be available soon. But I want my mother to begin the treatment right away.'

'I can make arrangements for her to be transferred

to the U.S. But I have to advise you that the hospital in Massachusetts is unlikely to start Madame Hobbs's treatment until they have assurance that all her medical costs can be covered,' Alain Duval explained gently. 'You will also need to pay for your mother's flight on an air ambulance.' He checked his computer screen and scribbled down a figure. 'This is the amount you'll need to find initially.'

There was only one other way she could raise any kind of capital.

Louise nodded resolutely. 'I'll organise it now.'

Her grandmother Céline would have approved, she told herself a few hours later when she walked out of the jeweller's shop. The jeweller had honoured the price that he had originally valued the diamond *fleur-de-lis*, and had also bought the last few pieces of Tina's jewellery. Louise hoped her mother would forgive her. Tina adored her jewels, but life was more valuable than a few baubles.

Having delivered a cheque to Alain Duval, and learned that Tina would be flown to Massachusetts once the hospital had received assurance that her medical costs would be met, Louise felt as if her emotions had been put through a mangle. She had phoned Dimitri's hotel and learned that he had not yet checked out, but was unavailable to speak to her.

The prospect of meeting him again made her heart sink. But she *had* to get an answer from him. First, though, she decided to go back to her flat to feed Madeleine and try and drum up some courage before she paid him a visit.

The lift in the apartment block only went as far as the fifth floor. Louise trudged up the narrow flight of stairs leading to the eaves of the building, feeling utterly drained. Reaction to the events of the past twenty-four hours had set in. She was still trying to come to terms with the fact that she had slept with Dimitri, and she was desperately worried about her mother.

The sound of footsteps from above warned her that one of her neighbours was coming down the stairs, and she shrank against the wall to allow them to pass.

'Where in hell's name have you been all day?'

Dimitri came round the bend in the staircase and strode towards her, his face furious and beautiful, with his olive-gold skin stretched taut across his slashing cheekbones, his green eyes spitting fire.

The shock of his appearance was the last straw. Louise stared at him wordlessly.

'Why did you shoot off like that this morning?' The question had been bugging Dimitri all day. 'I tried ringing you a dozen times but you didn't answer.'

'I switched off my phone at the...' Just in time she stopped herself from saying *hospital*, and coloured guilt-ily. 'I went to see a...friend, and turned my phone off.'

'I assumed you had left early to go to the museum, but when I couldn't get hold of you I checked at the Louvre and was told that you weren't scheduled to work today.' Dimitri's eyes narrowed when Louise refused to meet his gaze. 'You ran, didn't you? What was it?' he queried sar-donically. 'Self-recrimination after the night before?'

She flushed. 'You told me you were returning to Athens today. It just seemed easier to avoid any awkwardness. I mean...' She bit her lip. 'We both know last night didn't mean anything.'

'Do we?' His face was unreadable.

What friend had she rushed off to visit? Dimitri won-dered. She seemed cagey. Had she gone to see a lover—perhaps to give an excuse for where she had spent the previous night? And how was it that she was wearing an-other Benoit Besson outfit?

He was annoyed that he had felt concerned when he'd been unable to contact her. She was not a child, and certainly not his responsibility, he reminded himself. His irritation increased when he felt his body's predictable reaction as he raked his eyes over her champagne-coloured pencil skirt and the matching jacket with its nipped-in waist that emphasised the firm swell of her breasts. Her hair was swept into a chignon and her face discreetly made-up. The combination of cool elegance and simmering sensuality that she projected heated his blood to boiling point. No woman had ever run out on him before, and if he was honest his ego had been dented by Louise's abrupt departure from his bed that morning, he acknowledged grimly.

Louise could not define Dimitri's expression and she was too weary to try. 'What are you doing here, anyway?' she muttered.

He looked dangerously seductive in casual clothes that bore the hallmarks of superb tailoring. His black polo shirt clung to the hard ridges of his abdominal muscles and his dark hair brushed the collar of his tan leather jacket. For a crazy moment she almost gave in to the temptation to fling herself against his broad chest and absorb some of his strength.

A thought hit her and she drew a sharp breath. 'Have you made a decision about the island?'

'I have, but a public stairway is not the place to discuss it. I believe your apartment is on the top floor?'

Her legs were shaking, Louise discovered as she led the way up the stairs and along the hallway to her flat. A sense of dread settled like a lead weight in her stomach. Dimitri did not know it, but he held her mother's life in his hands.

'Please—come in.' She opened the front door and ushered him into her home, hating her body's involuntary reaction when he brushed against her. Why *him*? she thought bitterly. Why was he the only man she had ever met who could turn her brain to mush and make her feel like a hormonal adolescent instead of the intelligent woman she knew was?

Entering Louise's flat was like stepping into a doll's house, Dimitri thought as he was forced to duck to avoid bumping his head on the doorframe. An estate agent would probably describe the apartment as a bijou residence, but that was a euphemism for small. It occurred to him that if Louise did live with some rich lover he must be a midget.

He followed her into the living room and saw no signs of a male influence in the pretty but decidedly feminine décor. A door led into what he could see was an equally tiny bedroom. The apartment was functional but hardly luxurious, and he felt certain that Louise lived alone.

Not completely alone, he amended as his eyes settled on the exotic-looking cat which was regarding him suspiciously from the windowsill.

'That's Madeleine,' Louise told him, following his gaze. 'I got her from the cat rescue centre and she's wary of strangers.'

He glanced around the room. The colour scheme of white and powder-blue was charming, but nothing could disguise the fact that the apartment was no bigger than a shoebox.

'It's not what I was expecting,' he said, frowning. When Louise had told him she lived in the centre of Paris he had envisaged a grand, opulent apartment. 'I thought you would live somewhere bigger and more expensive, frankly.'

'I can't afford the rent on a bigger place. This is fine for me and Madeleine.'

'Surely your mother could contribute towards the costs of renting or even buying a larger apartment? After all, she inherited a sizeable fortune from my father.'

'I have never touched a penny of Kostas's money,' Louise said sharply.

She had caught the note of bitterness in Dimitri's voice

and in all fairness could not blame him for it. Her mother's affair with his father hovered like a spectre between them. She dared not reveal that the reason she was so anxious for him to buy Eirenne was because Tina had frittered away the inheritance Kostas had left her.

She twisted her hands together, unaware that Dimitri had noticed the betraying gesture. 'You said you had made a decision,' she reminded him.

Why was she so tense? he wondered. It was obvious she was desperate for him to agree to a deal on Eirenne, but he still did not know *why* she needed the money so urgently. The explanation she'd given about wanting to pay off her student loan wasn't believable, and once again he came back to the idea that she was in debt. Her mother had been facing bankruptcy just before she had met his father, he remembered. Tina had not been a good role model when it came to financial matters—or personal integrity, he thought grimly. Was it any surprise that Louise seemed to be following in her mother's footsteps?

But what did it matter? Dimitri asked himself. He wanted Eirenne and he wanted Louise, and he was determined to have both. One night with her had not satisfied his desire and he had decided that the only way to get her out of his system was to make her his mistress until his fascination with her faded. He had a short attention span where women were concerned, and he was sure it would not take long before he was bored of her.

He glanced at her and felt a white-hot surge of lust as he imagined stripping off the elegant suit and the lace-edged camisole visible beneath her jacket. Was she wearing a bra? No matter—he would quickly remove it so that he could cup her voluptuous breasts in his hands. Then he would kiss her nipples, lick them and tease them with his tongue, until they hardened and she whimpered and begged him to make love to her as she had done last night...

His nostrils flared as he inhaled sharply. He turned towards the window and pretended to study the view of Paris rooftops while he endeavoured to bring his body under control.

'I am prepared to pay your asking price of one million pounds for Eirenne.'

'Thank God!'

She spoke the words beneath her breath but Dimitri heard her, heard the raw emotion in her voice, and he flicked his head round to see her sink down onto the sofa as if her legs would not support her.

'That's...great news.' Louise frantically fought for composure as relief flooded through her. The one thought pounding in her head was that now she could phone Alain Duval and tell him to arrange for her mother to be flown to America to begin the treatment immediately.

'There is a condition.'

Dimitri's clipped statement seemed to reverberate off the walls. Louise shot him a lightning glance, and something about his calculating expression unnerved her. She licked her dry lips.

'What...condition?'

'You will return to Athens with me.'

Why was her heart thudding so erratically beneath her ribs? she wondered. After all, Dimitri had not made an unreasonable request.

She stood up and faced him across her tiny sitting room. 'I suppose it will be necessary for me to sign a sales contract. Of course I will fly to Athens when the paperwork has been prepared,' she assured him. 'But I imagine it will take at least a few days before your lawyers are ready to finalise the deal.'

He shrugged. 'Probably. But that's not what I meant.' He walked towards her, his intent gaze holding her prisoner. 'I want *you*, Louise—to share my bed every night until I have sated my desire for you. Let's say for a couple of weeks.' His smile was deeply cynical. 'I have a low boredom threshold, and experience tells me that my interest will wane fairly quickly when you are available around the clock.'

'Available?' she choked furiously. His suggestion was so shockingly outrageous that she almost thought he was joking—but the hard gleam in his eyes warned her he was deadly serious. 'Do you really expect me to play the role of your...your *concubine*? Always on hand to serve you and satisfy your sexual demands?'

She paused to drag oxygen into her lungs, and opened her mouth to tell him in succinct terms just what she thought of his suggestion. He cut her off before she could speak.

'If you want me to buy Eirenne then, yes, that's exactly what I expect.'

Stunned by the finality of his words, she felt her defiance crumble. 'That's blackmail,' she whispered.

He gave her an impatient look. 'Oh, come on, *glikia*. It's a little too late to play the innocent. You were a wildcat last night and you know damn well you're as hungry as I am.'

Before she had time to guess his intention Dimitri shot out a hand and unfastened the single button on her jacket, before flicking the material aside to reveal the sheer camisole she was wearing beneath it.

'Even if you want to deny it, your body betrays you— see?' he taunted, a sardonic smile lifting the corners of his mouth as he deliberately trailed a finger down one breast and over the pebble-hard nipple jutting provocatively against its silk covering. 'Why do you wear a bra when your breasts are so firm? While you are my mistress I demand that you will go braless.'

'You can go to hell!' The soft mockery in Dimitri's voice released Louise from the sexual spell he had cast on her. She despised him, but she despised herself more for her shameful inability to resist him. 'I refuse to be any man's mistress, and I'd rather sell my soul to the devil than agree to your despicable suggestion.'

'Then the deal is off,' he said calmly, regarding her flushed face and anger-bright eyes with a detached air that caused Louise to clench her fists. 'I wish you well in finding another buyer for Eirenne.'

'You don't mean that. You're calling my bluff,' she blurted, panic rising inside her when he strolled towards the door. 'Dimitri...*please*! There has to be a way we can reach an agreement.'

She had no right to look hurt, Dimitri told himself, determined to ignore the tug on his insides when he glimpsed tears in her eyes. She had proved last night that she was a woman like her mother—willing to sell herself for the right price. He would not be taken in by the air of vulnerability that reminded him of the girl he had known years ago.

'I've explained my terms—it's up to you whether you agree them.' He glanced at his watch. 'My private jet is on standby at Orly airport and my chauffeur is waiting in the car. If you're coming with me, you have precisely ten minutes to pack.'

'For God's sake—I have a job. I can't just give it up.' Louise glared at him, her temper simmering at his sheer arrogance.

'You must be allowed to take annual leave?'

'It will be difficult at such short notice.' But not impossible, Louise acknowledged silently. A few weeks ago she had explained the situation with her mother to her manager and arranged to take time off if the need arose. There would not be a problem at work.

The problem was with herself, she admitted. She resented with every fibre of her being the idea of becoming Dimitri's mistress—but what choice did she have? she thought bleakly. To refuse him would be to sign her mother's death warrant. The only way to raise the money for Tina's cancer treatment quickly was to sell Dimitri the island. And maybe he had a point. Maybe being forced to spend time with him, to live with him and share his bed every night, would free her from his sensual spell.

She drew a shaky breath, hardly able to believe what she was about to do. The sight of him reaching for the door handle prompted her to speak.

'*All right*—I agree to your terms. But I want your signed confirmation that you will pay one million pounds for Eirenne, and that you will transfer the money to me as soon as possible.' She crossed to the bureau and took out a sheet of paper and a pen which she held out to him. 'Do it now—before we leave.'

He studied her speculatively for a moment, but made no comment as he strolled back into the room and took the blank paper from her. Resting it on the lid of the bureau, he scribbled a few lines, added his signature, and handed it back to her.

Louise scanned what he had written and nodded. She did not know how legally binding the agreement was, but she felt better for having something more than his spoken promise. Promises, as she knew too well, could be broken.

She lifted her head, and her heart thudded when she glimpsed the unguarded desire in his glinting gaze. It took every ounce of her will-power to say in a dignified tone, 'I'll go and pack.'

'In a minute.' His arm snaked around her waist and he jerked her towards him. 'First I'd also like confirmation of our agreement,' he drawled as he lowered his head.

His kiss was hard, hungry, demanding her response. He caught hold of her chin and pushed his tongue into her mouth to explore her with devastating eroticism until she was trembling and pliant in his arms. Louise hated herself for capitulating to him, but she could not deny him when molten heat was surging through her veins and she was aware of nothing but the feel of his hand on her bare breast as he slid it beneath her camisole and bra and rolled her nipple between his fingers.

Her mouth was swollen when he finally released her, and she dragged her clothes back into place with shaking hands while he watched with cool detachment.

'I think we understand one another,' he murmured. 'Hurry up and get your things together, I have a busy schedule and I should have left Paris hours ago. One other thing.' He halted her as she began to walk into her bedroom. 'The suit you are wearing—where did you buy it?'

'I didn't—it was given to me.' She gave him a puzzled look. 'Why do you ask?'

'I was merely curious.'

His tone was bland, yet Louise sensed that he was angry although she had no idea why. A movement from the windowsill caught her attention.

'Madeleine!' She was horrified that she had momentarily forgotten about the cat. 'What am I going to do about her?'

'Can you arrange for one of your friends to look after her while you're away?'

She ran a mental check-list of her closest friends and shook her head. Nicole had recently given birth to her first baby, Pascale was on her honeymoon, and Monique had just started a new job. Louise felt reluctant to bother her. Even Benoit was not around.

'The neighbour who sometimes feeds Madeleine for me is away.'

'Then you'll have to put her in a cattery.' Dimitri did not bother to disguise his growing impatience.

'Absolutely not,' Louise told him fiercely. 'Madeleine was abandoned by her previous owner and I'm not going to allow her to feel abandoned for a second time. She'll have to come with us. Her carrier is in the kitchen.'

Dimitri was tempted to remind her that she was not in a position to dictate terms, but the determined gleam in Louise's eyes told him she would fight to the death for the sake of her pet and he did not have time for any further delays. He caught hold of her arm as she walked past him.

'I'll see to the goddamned cat while you collect your things.'

'I doubt you'll manage. I told you—she doesn't like strangers.'

Louise watched him walk back to the windowsill and stretch out a hand towards Madeleine. *Bite him*, she willed. But, to her amazement, the cat arched her back and purred blissfully as Dimitri stroked her ears. Of course. She had underestimated his ability to charm all members of the female sex—human and animal, she thought bitterly. It was stupid, but Madeleine's acceptance of him felt like a betrayal, and tears stung Louise's eyes as she marched into her bedroom and dragged a suitcase from the wardrobe.

CHAPTER SEVEN

LOUISE had travelled by private jet on a few occasions when her mother had been Kostas Kalakos's mistress. As she glanced around the luxurious cabin of Dimitri's plane she was reminded of how much Tina had relished the glamorous lifestyle she had enjoyed with her billionaire lover. Her mother had sold herself to the highest bidder, she thought bleakly. Tina had insisted she'd loved Kostas, but there was no doubt she had also loved his money.

Was what she was doing any better? Louise asked herself. The stark truth was that she had agreed to sell her body to Dimitri for one million pounds. He did not know and must never discover that she intended to use the money to save the life of the woman he hated and blamed for destroying his family.

She glanced at him, sitting beside her on one of the plush white leather chairs, and felt the familiar lurch of her heart as she studied his sculpted features. Would she have agreed to be his mistress if she hadn't found him so attractive? The thought sat uncomfortably with her and she tried to blank it out and concentrate on the only reason why she was flying to Athens with him. Tina.

The journey had so far been effortless—Dimitri's chauffeur-driven limousine had whisked them to the airport, where they had boarded his jet, and two impossibly elegant stewardesses had served them champagne as soon as the plane had soared into the sky. The signature of extreme wealth was everywhere—not simply in his material possessions but in the deferential way people treated him, Louise mused. She did not belong in Dimitri's world, but for the next two weeks she would live with him and share his bed every night.

Nervous tension churned in her stomach. Part of her wanted to scream that she could not go through with it, that she was not a woman like her mother. But it was for her mother's sake that she had agreed to Dimitri's demands, and she would stick to her side of the deal because it was the only way she could give Tina a chance to beat the disease that threatened her life.

She tore her gaze from him to stare out of the window as the plane circled above Athens airport, unaware that her pensive expression was causing him to frown.

Despite her sophisticated clothes Louise looked young and curiously vulnerable, Dimitri brooded. He was reminded of the innocent girl Loulou, whom he had known years ago, and was momentarily assailed by doubts. Was she *really* a cynical gold-digger like her mother, or could he have misjudged her? Her agreement to be his mistress in return for a million pounds surely answered that question, he thought grimly.

'We should land in five minutes.'

She made no comment and his irritation grew. 'You're very quiet. In fact you've barely spoken a word since we left Paris. What's the matter?'

Louise refused to admit that she felt as nervous as hell. Through the window she could see the airport runway grow bigger as the plane descended. It was hard to believe that less than a week ago she had made this same trip to Athens—although on an economy flight. When she had left Dimitri's office she had felt optimistic that he would agree to buy Eirenne, but she could not have foreseen the condition he would impose.

She turned her head and met his hard gaze. If only she was immune to his sexy charm, but the acceleration of her heartbeat was a shameful reminder of how much he affected her. Bravado was her only defence against him.

'I didn't realise you expected me to entertain you outside of the bedroom.'

His smile faded and his jaw hardened. 'I don't. The knowledge that you will spend every night of the next two weeks naked and *willing* in my bed is all I want from you, *glikia.*'

She flushed at the predatory gleam in his eyes and tried not to feel hurt by his sarcasm. Years ago he had called her *glikia mou*—my darling—and meant it. At least she had believed he had. But her illusion that he cared about her had been shattered when she'd discovered he had only feigned interest in her to upset her mother.

The voice of the pilot asking them to fasten their seat-belts prior to landing was a welcome distraction, but as the plane touched down Louise could not shake off the feeling that she was trapped in a nightmare—destined to spend the coming weeks as the mistress of a man who clearly only regarded her as a sexual plaything.

Dimitri lived in an exclusive suburb to the north-east of Athens, where luxurious villas were surrounded by land-scaped gardens. Louise's tension had increased with every mile during the short journey from the airport, and as the car swept onto a gravel driveway and electric gates closed smoothly behind them she instantly felt as though she was a prisoner.

His house certainly did not resemble a prison, she acknowledged. It was dusk, but even though the light was fading she could not fail to appreciate the beauty of Dimitri's home. Built in a neoclassical style, it had graceful arches and elegant pillars. The tall windows must allow light to flood into the rooms, she thought as she climbed the sweeping stone staircase leading up to the front door. The light coral-coloured walls reminded Louise of the old villa on Eirenne where she and Dimitri had first become lovers, a lifetime ago it seemed, and she felt a sharp pang as memories flooded her mind.

The interior décor of the house reflected the timeless elegance of its exterior. The spacious high-ceilinged rooms were painted in neutral tones, and the plush sofas and pale oak furnishings were discreetly expensive. It was a home rather than a show house, she mused, as he gave her a tour of the ground-floor rooms.

'*Your* home is not what I had expected either,' she told him, recalling his surprise when he had looked around the tiny sitting room of her flat in Paris.

'What were you expecting it to be like?'

'I don't know—a typical bachelor pad, I suppose. Minimalist chic meets playboy mansion, with lots of seductive lighting and leopard-print throws.'

He threw back his head and laughed—a deep, mellow sound that eased the tension between them.

'*Thee mou*, I hope you will think my home more tasteful than that. I promise you won't find animal print of any description here. I grew up here,' he explained. 'This was the family home until my parents split up. My father gave my mother the house as part of the divorce settlement, and when she died she left it to me.'

He glanced around the room they were standing in, which was at the front of the house, overlooking the drive.

'This was the playroom when my sister and I were children. Every evening I used to kneel on the windowsill and watch for my father's car when he came home from work, and then I would rush out to meet him and beg him to play football with me.' Dimitri paused and stared out of the window. 'He always did. However tired he was after a long day at the office, he always had time for me.' He grimaced. 'I wish things hadn't changed.'

Louise knew he meant that he wished his father had not met her mother and felt guilty, even though she could not have prevented Tina's affair with Kostas. In her mind she pictured a little boy watching excitedly for his father to return home. But although the boy resembled Dimitri it was *their* child she imagined. If her pregnancy had been successful they might now have a son, she thought wistfully. Perhaps they would have lived here in this house as a family—maybe even had other children.

The familiar ache of grief swept through her and she bit her lip to stop herself from blurting out the truth to him. There was no point in telling him about the baby she had lost. It was stupid to keep thinking about it and tormenting herself with daydreams of what might have been. There was a good chance that Dimitri would not have wanted their child—as he had not wanted *her*—and she would have spent the past six years as a single mother with all the problems that entailed, she reminded herself.

Dimitri swung away from the window and frowned when he saw Louise's pale face. She looked fragile, with dark shadows under her eyes, and once again he felt a prickle of doubt about his decision to bring her to Athens. He had not forced her, he reminded himself. She was here of her own free will because she wanted something from him—namely for him to buy the island that should have been his.

'You look as though you could do with something to eat,' he said abruptly. 'Dinner should be ready.'

Louise's insides churned at the prospect of food, but she followed him across the hall and into the dining room, where the table had been set for them.

'This is my butler, Joseph.' Dimitri introduced the man who entered the room. 'His wife, Halia, works for me as cook and housekeeper. Please sit down.' He indicated that she should take a seat at the table. 'Would you like wine or a soft drink?'

'Water is fine, thank you.' The need for a clear head was imperative, but perhaps it would be better if she got blind drunk, Louise thought wildly. At least then she would have no recollection of the night with Dimitri that was to follow.

Joseph had disappeared, but returned almost immediately to serve dinner. The roast lamb cooked with herbs and served with potatoes and vegetables smelled tempting and she suddenly discovered that she was ravenous. Was it only the previous evening that she'd had dinner with Dimitri in Paris? She had been so intensely aware of him that she had only picked at her food. So much had happened in the space of twenty-four hours.

The memory of what had happened during some of those hours made her blush. Dimitri undressing her and laying her down on the huge four-poster bed, stripping off his own clothes and stretching out beside her on the satin sheets, bending his head to her breasts and teasing her nipples with his tongue...

She choked and quickly took a gulp of water.

'Are you all right?'

She could not bring herself to look at him. 'Fine, thank you. The food is wonderful.'

Against the odds she enjoyed the meal, but afterward her tension returned. Through the French windows she could see the moon gleaming silver against the black sky. It was late in the evening, and she assumed that soon Dimitri would want to take her to bed.

'Would you like dessert or coffee?'

Caffeine would not help the ache that was rapidly becoming a throbbing pain across her brow. She gave him a lightning glance, unaware of the faint desperation in her eyes. 'Actually, I wonder if you would show me to my room? I have some headache tablets in my case.'

'Of course.' Dimitri rose from the table and led her out of the room and up the sweeping staircase. He strode along the landing, halted to open a door and ushered her inside.

The suite of rooms comprised a sitting room which led through a big square arch into a bedroom. Like the rest of the house the rooms were luxuriously decorated, with champagne-coloured silk wallpaper, pale gold carpets and curtains, and sofas covered in a darker gold silk brocade that matched the bedspread.

Louise did not need to see the jacket slung over the arm of a chair, or the squash racket and sports bag on the floor, to tell her that this was the master suite. She stiffened when she noted her suitcase standing by the bed.

'This is *your* bedroom, isn't it? I know we have an…arrangement…' She flushed hotly as she thought of the terms of that arrangement. 'But I assumed I would at least have the privacy of my own room.'

'I didn't deem it necessary,' Dimitri said blandly. 'As you pointed out, we have an arrangement, the terms of which require you to share my bed every night. However, you do have your own bathroom.' He crossed the room and opened a door to reveal a shower room and walk-in wardrobe. 'This is for you, but there is a bath in my *en suite* bathroom which you are welcome to use.' He glanced at his watch. 'I have a couple of calls to make, so I'll leave you to settle in. But I won't be long.' His green eyes glinted with amusement at her rebellious expression. 'Make sure you wait up for me, *glikia*.'

Panic gripped her. Last night she had been swept away by passion, but tonight the idea of getting into bed with him, having sex with him, seemed so cold-blooded. 'Is it too much to ask that I be allowed to spend this one night alone? I have a headache,' she said tightly.

There was no hint of sympathy in his smile. 'Then you'd better hope that your painkillers work quickly. I'll be back in half an hour.'

How on earth had she fallen in love with him seven years ago? Right at this moment she could happily murder him. 'You bastard,' she said shakily.

For long moments after he had gone Louise continued to stare at the door he had closed behind him, desperately tempted to flee the room, the house, *him*. The feel of soft fur rubbing against her leg made her look down, and with a little cry she stooped and lifted Madeleine into her arms.

'I've made a pact with the devil,' she whispered, 'and I have no choice but to see it through.'

The cat purred softly and then sprang down and walked elegantly over to the windowsill where, Louise saw, a cushion had been placed for her.

She watched Madeleine leap onto it and sighed ruefully. 'I'm glad *you* feel at home, anyway.'

Fifteen minutes later she had scrubbed off her make-up, brushed her teeth and hair, and donned the tent-like nightshirt she had packed. Dimitri was in for a shock if he expected to find a glamorous sex-siren in his bed, she thought with grim satisfaction as she studied herself in the mirror. The nightshirt was old and comfortable and reached past her knees. She looked more like a maiden aunt than a temptress.

In fact she could not bring herself to get into the huge bed after she had drawn back the bedspread and discovered that he slept on silk sheets. Instead she stood by the window, staring out at the dark garden and listening to the seconds on the clock ticking past relentlessly.

'Your choice of nightwear is not quite what I had envisaged,' a voice drawled, making her start.

She swung round to discover that Dimitri had entered the suite and was strolling towards her, his footsteps muffled by the thick carpet. He moved with the silent grace of a panther and was far more threatening to her peace of mind. He had discarded his jacket and undone his shirt almost to the waist. The sight of his darkly tanned chest covered with a fine mat of dark hair set her pulse racing.

She despised herself for her weakness and said sharply, 'You might have forced me into your bed, but you can't dictate what I choose to sleep in.'

Dark brows winged upwards. '*Forced*, Louise? There is no lock on the door to keep you here, nor chains to bind you. You are free to leave whenever you like.' He studied her thoughtfully. 'To be honest, I'm growing tired of being made out to be some kind of villain. We are two consenting adults who made a deal.'

He pulled a sheet of paper from his trouser pocket and handed it to her. 'I spoke to my lawyer a short while ago, and he sent an e-mail to confirm that he has already begun proceedings to purchase Eirenne. The money should be in your bank account within a week.' He paused and speared her with a hard look. 'But I can easily stop the process if you have changed your mind?'

Tomorrow her mother would be on her way to the specialist cancer hospital in America. Changing her mind was not an option, Louise acknowledged. She drew a swift breath.

'I want the sale to go ahead.'

The moonlight slanted over Dimitri's face, highlighting his sharp cheekbones and resolute jaw. He was arrogant and uncompromising, but the predatory gleam in his eyes told her that his desire for her was something he could not control. She sensed that he resented it, just as she resented her fierce attraction to him. They were both trapped by sexual need, and she gave a little shiver as she remembered how Dimitri had stated his intention to slake his hunger by making love to her until his unwanted fascination with her had faded.

'In that case you won't need this.'

Before she could stop him he gripped the hem of her nightshirt and dragged it over her head. She knew she was blushing, but she refused to give in to the temptation to cover her breasts with her hands and instead lifted her head proudly.

'*Thee mou*, you are beautiful.'

As Dimitri studied her naked body his breath hissed between his teeth. Louise was startled to see streaks of colour flare on his cheekbones.

'You were lovely seven years ago, but now you are beyond compare,' he said thickly.

Don't, she wanted to cry out. She did not want to be reminded of the most incredible night of her life and have those memories sullied by the soulless coupling they were about to perform.

Dimitri captured her chin and stilled when he felt the betraying moisture on her skin. Irritation flared inside him. Did she really think he would hurt her or take her by force? Or was she playing mind-games? Trying to make him feel bad for wanting what she had given willingly enough last night?

'Why the tears, *pedhaki*? Am I really such an ogre?'

She could not have heard a faint note of hurt in his voice—not from a man who was as hard as nails and immune to emotions. And yet... Louise lifted her eyes to his face and for a second she glimpsed the younger Dimitri, who had made love to her with such tenderness seven years ago that she had wept with the beauty of it.

He traced his thumb over her lower lip. 'Are you afraid of me?'

'No,' she admitted honestly. At least she did not fear he would ever cause her physical harm. But she *was* scared of the way he made her feel—out of control and a slave to her fierce desire for him.

He did not seem convinced. 'I have never taken a woman by force—I find the very idea abhorrent. You chose to come to Athens with me,' he reminded her.

'I know.' Her tongue darted out to moisten her dry lips. 'I will abide by the terms of our arrangement.'

Louise tried to ignore a flicker of panic when he cupped her shoulders and drew her inexorably towards him. She had never noticed before that his olive-green eyes were flecked with gold. Like tiny flames, she thought, blazing with an intensity of need that lit the fire inside her. He lowered his head and brushed his mouth over hers, lightly at first, as if he was giving her the chance to pull back. But she sensed his hunger, felt it in his hands that shook slightly, and as he deepened the kiss and it became an erotic exploration of her mouth he demolished all her carefully erected barricades.

He moved a hand down to her breast and teased her nipple with his fingers until it felt tight and tingling. Sensation arrowed down to her pelvis, evoking molten heat between her legs, and with a low groan she parted her lips beneath his and kissed him back. Without taking his mouth from hers he lifted her and strode through to the bedroom, where he placed her on the bed.

She was exquisite, Dimitri thought as he knelt over her and ran his fingers through her hair so that her curls were spread across the pillow like a golden halo. The bedside lamps were turned low and bathed her nakedness in a soft glow that made her creamy skin gleam. Her limbs felt like satin beneath his fingertips as he explored every inch of her, like a blind man reliant on touch, determined to imprint the shape of her on his brain.

Her breasts were rounded, delightfully soft and voluptuous, and when he pressed his face into the valley between them he inhaled the delicate fragrance of lilies. He raised himself up so that he could kiss her mouth again. Desire was pounding a pagan drumbeat through his veins and he wanted her with an urgency he had never experienced with any other woman. But he glimpsed the faint wariness in her eyes, and the memory of what she had said a few moments ago taunted him.

'I will abide by our agreement,' she had told him dully, as if she had resigned herself to a terrible fate. *Gamoto!* His male pride was stung. He did not want a sacrificial lamb. He wanted the eager sex-kitten she had been at his hotel in Paris and he *would* have her, he vowed. He would tease and tantalise her with his hands and mouth until she begged for his possession.

With deft movements he shrugged out of his clothes and lowered himself onto her so that their naked bodies touched from head to toe. His rock-hard arousal jabbed against her belly and he heard her catch her breath when she realised the size of him. He slanted his mouth over hers and kissed her, slow and deep, drawing a response from her that fanned the flames of his desire.

His body was impatient for sexual release, but he forced

himself to slow the pace while he trailed his mouth down to her breast and captured the dusky pink nipple between his lips, caressing her until she cried his name. She arched her hips in instinctive invitation and he laughed triumphantly, transferring his mouth to the other breast, lapping her eager flesh with his tongue.

'Dimitri...please...' she whispered tremulously.

He liked the fact that she could not deny her need for him. He slid his hand between her thighs, and when he discovered the proof of her arousal his restraint cracked. Pausing only to don protection, he positioned himself over her.

'Ise panemorfi.' The words were torn from him as he stared into her sapphire-blue gaze. 'I have to have you now, *glikia mou.'* He discarded his pride and did not care that he had revealed the intensity of his need for her.

'I want you too,' she admitted, and the unguarded honesty in her eyes made Dimitri's gut clench. She was no longer playing games. Maybe she never had been, he thought. Maybe she had never stopped being the lovely girl Loulou, who had once given herself so sweetly to him.

And then his thought process was obliterated as he thrust into her and felt her muscles stretch to accommodate him, to draw him deeper into her velvet softness.

Something curled around his heart—a feeling of possessiveness that would have bothered him if he'd had time to dwell on it. But his blood was pounding in his ears as she matched his rhythm and moved with him, accepting every hard stroke that drove them both higher. She sobbed his name and lifted her hips, her body as taut as an overstrung bow, before he tipped her over the edge. She shook with the force of her orgasm, twisting her head on the pillows, and raked her nails over his shoulders.

Dimitri's control shattered spectacularly. 'Wildcat,' he groaned raggedly, and tumbled with her into ecstasy.

CHAPTER EIGHT

A LONG time later Dimitri eased himself from Louise, surprised by his reluctance to break the physical connection between them. Sex with her had been as amazing as it had the previous night, and he felt a surge of male satisfaction as he propped himself up on an elbow and idly wound a honey-gold curl around his finger.

'That was incredible, *glikia*. I'm beginning to wish I'd stipulated that you should stay with me for longer than a couple of weeks.'

He frowned when he realised he was actually serious. Not that he was contemplating anything long-term, of course, he reassured himself. He was happy with his life the way it was—uncluttered by the emotional dramas that women seemed so fond of. But he could not deny it would be easy to become addicted to Louise's potent sensuality.

He studied her face, still rose-flushed from the passion they had just shared, and once again he was struck by her beauty, and the curiously innocent air that evoked a primitive urge to claim his woman and protect her from harm.

'Perhaps we will have to renegotiate the terms of our deal,' he murmured.

Dimitri's words dragged Louise from the blissfully relaxed state that followed intense physical pleasure, and dumped her back into the harsh world of reality. A deal—

that was all sex with him had been. Yet foolishly she had allowed herself to feel that it had been a complete union—not only of their bodies, but of their souls. Clearly that had not been the case for him. She swallowed the lump in her throat and clung to her pride.

'We agreed on the length of time I would be your mistress,' she reminded him coolly. 'I trust you won't go back on your word and try and force me to remain here for a day longer?'

'So we're back to accusations of force, are we?'

His tone was soft, his anger controlled, but the warmth in his eyes had died and Louise felt the sensation of an ice-cube slithering down her spine.

'I didn't see any sign of your supposed reluctance to have sex with me. In fact I gained the impression that you rather enjoyed it—and I have the marks to prove it.'

He sat up so that she could see his back, and she gasped at the sight of several red weals on his shoulders, where she had raked her nails across his skin in the throes of feverish passion.

Her face burned with mortification. 'I'm sorry. I didn't realise I had marked you.'

'I'm flattered you found me so exciting, *glikia*,' he drawled as he lay back down and folded his arms behind his head in a position of indolent relaxation.

He looked like a sultan who had just been pleasured by his favourite whore, Louise thought bitterly. Her long and traumatic day had caught up with her and she ached with tiredness, but the prospect of sharing Dimitri's bed for the rest of the night was too much to bear. In a strange way sleeping with him seemed even more intimate that having sex with him. If they were proper lovers she would snuggle up to him and rest her head on his chest, and he would cuddle her as they drifted off to sleep.

Memories of the night they had spent together on Eirenne made her heart ache. They had fallen asleep in each other's arms that night, and had woken at dawn to make love again. But the situation between them now was very different from seven years ago. She was only with him because they had made a deal, and surely she had fulfilled her side of it adequately tonight.

She slid her legs over the side of the bed and remembered that her nightshirt was in the sitting room. During their wild lovemaking Dimitri had flung the silk top sheet to the floor, and she quickly snatched it up and wrapped it around her to cover her nakedness.

He frowned as she backed away from the bed. 'Where are you going?'

'If you have finished with me, I would like to sleep alone in my own room. I don't think it is an unreasonable request.'

Dimitri made no attempt to hide his impatience. He was tempted to pull her down onto the mattress and show her that he was far from finished with her. Her tangible tension and his sudden realisation that her composure was close to snapping prevented him.

'None of the guest bedrooms are prepared, and I'm sure you'd agree it would be unreasonable to expect Halia to make up a bed for you at midnight.'

'Well…then I'll sleep on the sofa.'

Louise flushed beneath his speculative look. She expected him to insist that she join him back in the bed, but after a few seconds of silence, he shrugged.

'Please yourself. I have an important business meeting in the morning and I need some sleep.'

And with that he settled back against the pillows and shut his eyes, as if he was supremely indifferent to where she decided to spend the rest of the night.

Half an hour later Louise shifted position yet again on

the sofa, trying to get comfortable. She had demonstrated to Dimitri that she was not his puppet, but for some reason her victory seemed hollow. The sofa's cushions were much firmer than a mattress, and her neck already ached from where she was using the armrest as a pillow. With a sigh she pulled the sheet tighter around her, wishing that the air-conditioning did not work so well. She was cold and tired and felt stupidly close to tears.

Something soft brushed against her hand as Madeleine sprang up onto the sofa and settled in the crook of her knees.

'In two weeks' time Tina will be responding to the treatment, Dimitri will own Eirenne and our agreement will be finished. I'll never have to see him again,' she told the cat, and wondered why that last statement did not fill her with satisfaction as it surely should.

Sunlight dancing across her eyelids roused Louise from the restless sleep that had finally claimed her just before dawn. She stretched, and winced as her aching neck and shoulders reminded her of the uncomfortable night she had spent.

'I trust you slept well?' Dimitri strolled out of his bathroom, dressed in a dark suit and white shirt accessorised with a navy silk tie. He looked impossibly gorgeous and energised to face the day ahead—in contrast to Louise, who felt as if she had been flattened by a truck.

'Fine, thank you,' she muttered, gritting her teeth as his amused smile told her he knew she was lying. She felt tired and irritable, and his arrogance riled her. 'I would like some measure of privacy while I am here. I'll ask Halia for some sheets so I can make up a bed in one of the guest rooms.'

'No, you won't,' he said implacably. 'Our deal was for you to spend every night in my bed. And I would appreciate it if you could start acting like an adult rather than a petulant child.'

Louise's temper simmered. The temptation to throw the marble paperweight on the coffee table at his head was so strong that she clenched her fists to stop herself from grabbing it. Instead she verbalised her frustration. 'You can go to hell.'

'And *you* can go back to Paris and find yourself another buyer for Eirenne. Because frankly, *glikia*, I'm getting tired of your martyr act.' Dimitri strode towards the door, anger evident in every taut line of his body. 'If you don't want to be here you are free to leave.'

He did not add that if she returned home he would not continue with the purchase of the island, but the unspoken threat hung in the air.

Louise bit her lip, panic surging through her as she realised she had pushed him too far. Why *had* she so deliberately antagonised him? she wondered. The truth, she acknowledged painfully, was that she wished he would take her in his arms and kiss her into submission. She wanted him to make love to her but her pride would not let her admit it.

'I *do* want to be here.' She pushed the sheet away and stood up from the sofa to face him, thankful that she had put her nightshirt back on after she had left his bed. 'It's just that I'm finding this hard,' she admitted. 'I've never stayed with a guy before. I live alone, with just Madeleine for company, and I'm not used to this level of intimacy or to sharing my personal space with someone else.'

'Are you saying you haven't had many other lovers?'

Dimitri was surprised by his curiosity. He never asked about his mistresses' past history—partly because he considered it bad manners, and partly because he wasn't interested. But he was intrigued by Louise. She responded to him so passionately during sex that he had assumed she was experienced—which was why her air of innocence at other times puzzled him so much. And then there was the question of her designer clothes and the diamond pendant that she had told him had been given to her as presents. He believed they had been gifts from a lover, but perhaps he was wrong.

'Not many, no.' Once again Louise's pride asserted itself and prevented her from admitting that he was her only lover.

'Why not? You're a very attractive woman, and I can't believe you haven't had offers of relationships.'

She shrugged. 'I'm not interested in having a relationship.' She sensed he was waiting for her to explain her comment, and after a moment she continued quietly, 'Throughout my childhood I watched my mother lurch from one affair to another. I was sent to boarding school at the age of eight, and I never knew at the end of term where I would be spending the holidays. Often I visited my grandmother, but after she died there was no alternative but for me to stay with Tina and her current lover. My mother usually lived in a luxurious apartment when she was some rich guy's mistress, but inevitably after a few weeks or months he would tire of her and end the affair. Then she would have nowhere to live, and we would have to stay in hotels or she would rent a cheap place—until she found another man to keep her.'

She gave Dimitri a fierce look. 'I vowed when I saw how my mother was treated by her lovers—like she was an object rather than a person—that I would never have casual affairs or be reliant on anyone.'

Tina Hobbs had no one to blame but herself, Dimitri thought grimly. He felt no sympathy for his father's mistress who, in his opinion, had been no better than a prostitute. But for the first time he appreciated how Louise's upbringing must have affected her.

Children were far more perceptive than most adults gave them credit for, he mused. From an early age Louise's views about men had been formed from witnessing Tina's experiences, and he could not blame her for being wary and mistrusting of all men—including him.

His anger lessened and he walked back across the room to her. 'And yet you were happy to have a relationship with me seven years ago,' he said softly.

Louise stiffened, not wanting to be reminded of how stupid she had been. 'I was young and gullible back then.'

He frowned. 'What do you mean by gullible? I have good memories of the time we spent together on the island.'

Presumably he meant that he had enjoyed making a fool of her and breaking her heart. Memories of how he had hurt her, and the river of tears she had shed over him, evoked a dull pain in Louise's heart. She wished she could leave and never set eyes on him again, but for her mother's sake she had to stay and somehow survive the next two weeks with her emotions intact.

'What happened between us was over long ago,' she said tersely. 'I'm not the naïve girl I was then. I agreed to be your mistress in return for you buying Eirenne, and I am prepared to do whatever you ask of me.'

Something about their past brief relationship clearly troubled her, Dimitri mused. It was true they had parted abruptly, and events immediately after Louise had left Eirenne had meant he'd been unable to contact her for months. When he had eventually tried she had not answered his calls and at last he had given up.

He wanted to get to the bottom of the mystery, but a glance at his watch told him he did not have time before his meeting with the CEO of a Russian export company, with whom he hoped to finalise a deal. Further discussion with Louise would have to wait until tonight. It seemed that she was still desperate for him to buy the island and had decided to stay and stick to the terms of their agreement.

'In that case, my first request is that you bin the granny gown,' he murmured.

Her nightshirt had a row of tiny, fiddly buttons down the front that would take far too long to undo. Instead he gripped the two edges of the shirt and yanked them apart, sending buttons pinging in all directions and evoking a startled cry from Louise.

'You...*Neanderthal*!' Her voice shook with fury. 'Now I have nothing to sleep in.'

He looked unconcerned. 'Request number two—no, let's make that a demand: you sleep naked. Your body is far too beautiful to keep covered up.'

Dimitri trailed his eyes slowly over her and lingered on her breasts. The heat in his gaze made Louise's skin prickle and to her shame her nipples jerked to attention and stood proudly taut, demanding his attention.

'I see that the air-conditioning is set a little too cool,' he drawled.

She flushed. 'I hate you.'

'Really?' He gave her a sardonic look. 'I don't think it's me you hate, *glikia*, but you resent the way I make you feel.' He cupped her breasts in his palms and smiled when he felt the tremor that ran through her. 'Sexual desire between two consenting adults is nothing to feel ashamed of.' He lowered his head until his breath whispered across her lips. 'You want me. And I sure as hell want you.'

She wanted to deny it, and hated herself for the heated desire that licked through her veins. Her heart thudded as she waited for him to close the tiny gap that separated his mouth from hers. She longed for him to kiss her, and he must have sensed her impatience because he gave a low, triumphant laugh before he claimed her lips with fierce possession.

The effect was electric. Passion instantly flared between them, white-hot and simmering with potent urgency. She might resent him, but Louise could not resist him, and she gave up the fight that she had never stood a chance of winning and sank against him as he deepened the kiss and it became intensely erotic.

He skimmed his hands over her body and caressed her breasts, then moved down to probe his fingers between her thighs and discover her slick wetness.

Everything faded from Louise's consciousness but her need for Dimitri to make love to her. She slid his jacket over his shoulders and ran her hands over his torso, tugged at his shirt buttons and pushed the material aside so that she could feel his satiny skin and wiry chest hairs beneath her fingertips. Her body trembled with a primitive need to take him inside her and she boldly traced the hard ridge of his erection straining beneath his trousers.

Dimitri muttered a harsh imprecation as he swept her into his arms and strode into the bedroom. He dropped her onto the bed and knelt over her, caught her wrists and held them above her head while he captured one dusky pink nipple in his mouth. He lashed the taut peak with his tongue and then transferred his lips to her other breast and sucked hard, until she gasped and arched her hips in mute invitation.

Louise was all he could think of—his hunger for her. She aroused a level of desire in him that he had never felt with any other woman and his body shook with the intensity of his need.

Yet something hovered on the periphery of Dimitri's mind. The Russian deal. The ten o'clock meeting that, if it went well, would mean job security for hundreds of his employees at Kalakos Shipping—that would enable him to offer employment to hundreds more people who were without work at this time of economic hardship that Greece was currently experiencing.

Duty. He could not ignore its demands, even though his body was craving sexual release.

Louise must have sensed his hesitation. She stared at him, her expression unguarded and increasingly wary, as if she thought he was rejecting her. The shimmer of tears in her eyes made Dimitri's gut clench.

'Dimitri, what's wrong?'

'Nothing, *pedhaki.*' He quickly sought to reassure her. He groaned. 'But my timing is atrocious. I'm due at a meeting this morning to finalise a deal which is worth millions of pounds to the company and, more importantly, which will secure jobs for thousands of my employees.'

Louise released a shaky breath. For a moment she'd been afraid that he was playing a cruel game intended to prove his dominance over her. She traced the deep groove of his frown with her fingertips. She had read the news reports about Greece's financial problems, and how successful companies like Kalakos Shipping were vital to the country's economic recovery. Dimitri carried a huge weight of responsibility on his shoulders. He had been groomed from a young age to take over Kalakos Shipping from his father. After they had rowed Kostas had threatened to disinherit his only son, but presumably he had later realised that Dimitri was the best person to head the company.

She gave him a rueful smile and tried to ignore the restless ache of unfulfilled desire that throbbed deep inside her. 'Then you should go,' she said softly. 'People are relying on you and you can't let them down.'

Dimitri drew a ragged breath and rested his brow on hers

while his body reluctantly accepted that it was not going to be granted the release it craved. Another woman might have sulked and accused him of putting business before her. He'd had mistresses who had not understood that running the company his grandfather had begun sixty years ago was more than just a job.

But never before had he resented the commitment Kalakos Shipping demanded of him, and never before had he been tempted to ignore his duty. It took all his willpower to get up from the bed, and he felt a sharp pang of regret when Louise sat up and tugged the sheet across her.

'I'm sorry,' he said roughly. 'I promise I'll make it up to you tonight.'

Her eyes met his. 'I'll hold you to that.'

She was so lovely. Her shy smile tugged on his heart, and he ignored the fact that he was running late and leaned over her to give her one last, lingering kiss.

'Last night you were crying in your sleep.'

He ran a finger lightly over the smudges beneath her eyes, remembering how he had been woken by a sound some time around dawn and had gone to investigate why Louise had made that harrowing cry. She had been curled up on the sofa, fast asleep, but tears had slipped from beneath her lashes and he had been sorely tempted to wake her and try to comfort her.

'You seemed to be having a dream that upset you. Do you want to tell me about it?'

Louise shook her head. She hadn't been aware that she had been crying, but now she recalled fragments of the dream in which she had been searching for her baby. It must be seeing Dimitri again and being reminded of their past relationship that had brought back memories of the miscarriage, she thought unhappily.

She looked into Dimitri's eyes and felt a little pang inside when she glimpsed a gentle expression in his olive-green eyes that she had never seen before. For a moment she debated telling him about the miscarriage. But she had never spoken about it to anyone, and it hurt—even after all this time it still hurt so much to know that she had lost his baby. Her greatest fear was that he would not care, that he would shrug his shoulders and say it had been for the best because he hadn't wanted a child. She could not bear to hear him say that, when she had wanted their baby so very much.

'I…don't remember what I dreamed about,' she told him huskily. 'It was probably about a film I watched recently. Sad endings tend to make me embarrassingly emotional.'

Dimitri studied her speculatively, not wholly convinced by her explanation. 'If you have a problem that's bothering you I would be happy to try to help.'

'I don't—but you'll have a problem if you're late for your meeting.'

He still felt reluctant to leave her. As he walked into the sitting room to retrieve his jacket another thought suddenly struck him.

'*Theos!* It's the fifteenth today. I'm supposed to be holding a dinner party tonight, and my sister is bringing her new baby,' he explained to Louise, who had wrapped the bedspread around her and followed him. He raked a hand through his hair. 'I'll cancel.'

'No, you can't do that.' Louise bit her lip. 'I didn't know Ianthe had had a baby.'

She thought of Dimitri's younger sister, whom she had met a few times when Ianthe had visited her father on Eirenne. The visits had been awkward occasions, during which her mother had monopolised Kostas's attention and Ianthe had clearly been upset by the break-up of her parents' marriage. But despite that a tentative friendship had started between Louise and the Greek girl, who was a similar age to her.

'Her daughter is six weeks old,' Dimitri told her. 'Are you sure you don't mind about dinner? You might like to see the baby—Ana's a cute little thing.'

Louise felt a sensation as if a lead weight had dropped in her stomach. The subject of babies was always painful—especially so when her emotions were still raw after the dream. But she could not explain her fear that seeing Dimitri's sister's baby would open a deep wound in her heart and intensify her grief for the child she had lost.

She realised that Dimitri was waiting for her to reply. 'I'm sure the baby is lovely. And I'd like to meet Ianthe again.'

'Okay, that's settled.' He snatched up his briefcase, dropped a disappointingly brief kiss on her lips, and headed for the door.

'Will the dinner party be a formal affair?' Louise ran a mental check-list of the clothes she had brought with her to Athens and concluded that she had nothing suitable to wear. 'I didn't pack anything that could remotely be called evening wear. It's a pity, because I have several dresses at home that would have been ideal.'

Dimitri paused on his way out of the door. 'Like the dress you wore to dinner in Paris?'

His jaw hardened as he recalled the black Benoit Besson dress, and the elegant suit by the same designer that Louise had worn the previous day. He still hadn't discovered who had paid for her clothes. He told himself it did not matter. He did not want to believe that she was a gold-digger like her mother. But his curiosity about the mysterious benefactor who bought her haute couture continued to bug him.

Louise frowned, wondering if she had imagined the sudden curtness in his voice. He was probably thinking about his business meeting and did not want to be delayed by a discussion about clothes, she told herself.

'The suit I wore yesterday will be okay, won't it?' She'd suddenly remembered it was hanging in the wardrobe.

'It'll be fine.'

Dimitri strode out of the room without glancing at her again, leaving Louise to wonder what on earth she was going to do all day when she did not have her job to occupy her.

CHAPTER NINE

AFTER breakfast, which Joseph the butler served on the terrace, Louise spent some time exploring Dimitri's well-stocked library, and was pleased to find the latest thriller from an author she enjoyed. But although the plot was intriguing her day passed slowly. She was not used to having spare time. Her job at the Louvre was absorbing, and for the past few months she had gone straight from work to the hospital, to visit her mother.

Later that afternoon she phoned the hospital in Massachusetts and was reassured to hear that Tina had arrived and was comfortable. The specialist hoped to start the treatment the following day, and seemed optimistic about her mother's prognosis. Louise knew that Tina's chance of making a full recovery was not a certainty, but at least now she had a chance.

Even though she resented the condition Dimitri had imposed, she was grateful to him for agreeing to buy Eirenne. It was highly unlikely that she would have found another buyer who could have raised one million pounds so quickly. Being his mistress for two weeks was a price she was willing to pay for her mother's life, and as long as she remembered that he only wanted her body there was no danger that he would be a threat to her heart.

'Kyria Frobisher?' Joseph walked across the terrace to

where Louise was sitting in the shade of a parasol. 'Kyrie Kalakos has left a message to say that if you wish to swim in the pool there is a selection of swimwear in the summerhouse,' he said in Greek.

'*Efkharistó.*' She smiled at the elderly butler. The late afternoon sun was scorching and the idea of a swim to cool off was tempting.

Following the path that Joseph showed her, Louise discovered a huge pool surrounded by white marble tiles that gleamed in the bright sunlight. The air temperature felt even hotter here, and the tall pine trees that circled the pool area prevented the breeze from rippling the surface of the turquoise water.

The summerhouse was unlocked, and after a few minutes of searching she found a storage box containing several bikinis. Who had they belonged to? she wondered. She hated the idea that Dimitri had invited other women to his house. From the skimpy cut of some of the swimwear she guessed that his girlfriends were happy to show off much more of their bodies than she was.

She chose a plain black bikini which was more substantial than a couple of triangles held together with string, and once she had changed went back outside to dive into the pool. The feel of the cool water on her heated skin was bliss, and she swam for a while and then climbed out and lay on a sunbed, telling herself that she would only close her eyes for a minute…

'I hope you used sunscreen.'

Dimitri's voice dragged her from sleep and she lifted her eyelids to see him striding towards her. Her heart gave a familiar lurch when he sat down on the edge of the sunbed. He had changed out of his business suit into black shorts and a sleeveless tee shirt and looked unbelievably gorgeous. Louise knew there was a gym and squash court in the basement of the house, and guessed from his toned physique that he worked out regularly.

'You didn't, did you? You idiot—don't you realise how quickly your fair skin will burn in this heat?'

Gorgeous, but as bossy as hell, she thought ruefully.

'I'm not a child,' she reminded him. 'I've only been lying here for a minute.'

'Sometimes you act like one.' Dimitri skimmed his eyes over her slim body and thought how unbelievably sexy she looked in the halterneck bikini.

His frown faded and was replaced by a wicked glint that set Louise's pulse racing.

'But you certainly don't look like a child, *glikia*. You are a beautiful, sensual woman,' he murmured against her lips, before he slid his tongue between them and explored the moist interior of her mouth.

She responded to him with an eagerness that made him instantly harden. *His* woman—Dimitri frowned again as he felt a surge of possessiveness that was unexpected and unwanted. She *had* been on his mind all day, he admitted. Even during the meeting with the Russians he'd had to force himself to concentrate, and when he had taken his team of executives for a celebratory lunch he'd been impatient to race home and take Louise to bed.

He trailed his lips over her shoulder. 'You've caught the sun. I love your freckles.'

'No, really? Do I have freckles?'

Her horrified expression made him smile.

'Uh-huh. There's one here.' He kissed her cheek. 'And here.' He kissed the tip of her nose. 'And here...' He trailed his mouth lower.

'I don't believe you,' Louise said breathlessly, when Dimitri finally lifted his lips from hers after a sensual kiss that left her aching for more. 'I haven't got freckles on my mouth.'

He laughed. Their eyes met—and time seemed to stand still. She remembered how they had been on Eirenne, the way he had teased her and made her laugh, the way he had kissed her until they were both shaking with need and he had carried her into the house in the pine forest and made love to her.

Desire unfurled inside her—a molten heat low in her pelvis. Memories of how they had almost had sex that morning flooded her mind and she leaned back on the lounger.

'You're back earlier than I expected,' she murmured. 'How was your meeting?'

'Successful—we finalised the deal.' Dimitri stroked his hand over her thigh and halted at the edge of her bikini pants. The tightening sensation in his groin was almost painful. Sexual awareness fizzed in the air. It was hot out here in the garden, and the temperature between them was rapidly rising to combustion point. The way she was looking at him made his heart slam against his ribs. There was plenty of time to make love to her before tonight's dinner party, he convinced himself.

He suddenly remembered that he had interrupted his journey home from the office to visit an exclusive boutique.

'I bought you this,' he said, handing her the box he had carried down to the pool. 'It's for you to wear tonight,' he explained as she sat upright and stared warily at the box, as if she feared it might contain a bomb.

Louise read the name of a famous Italian fashion house emblazoned in gold lettering on the lid. A sense of foreboding gripped her and despite the heat of the sun she shivered. 'I don't think…' she began.

'You won't know if you like what's inside unless you open it.'

Without another word she lifted off the lid, parted the tissue paper and took out a sapphire-blue silk cocktail dress.

The silence quivered with tension. If he was honest, Dimitri was disappointed by her unenthusiastic response. 'Do you like it?'

'It's exquisite.' Louise recognised that the dress was a masterpiece of brilliant design, and she had a fair idea of its price. 'It must have cost a fortune.' She carefully folded the dress and placed it back among the tissue paper, replaced the lid and held out the box to him. 'I can't afford a dress like this.'

'I don't expect you to pay for it.' His eyes narrowed when he realised she was serious about returning it to him. 'The dress is a present.'

'No, thank you.' Her refusal was instant and instinctive.

Memories from her childhood surfaced in Louise's mind. She pictured her mother, gleefully opening a box that had been delivered to a penthouse apartment in Rome owned by an Italian count. Alfredo Moretti had been short and balding, but he had also been immensely rich and Tina had become his mistress.

'Oh, my gosh! Black mink,' Tina had murmured reverently as she had lifted the fur coat from the box. 'Do you have any idea how much this must have cost?'

'It's not your birthday, so why did Alfredo buy it for you?' the ten-year-old Louise had asked.

Her mother had shrugged and continued to admire the coat in the mirror. 'I keep Fredo happy,' she'd said airily, 'and in return he gives me presents.'

Feeling slightly sick, Louise pushed the memory away. Dimitri looked surprised and annoyed by her violent rejection of his gift, but she could not help it.

'You don't have to buy me presents—and certainly not

expensive designer clothes. I'm sorry, but I can't accept the dress.'

He glanced at the box she was holding out to him but did not take it.

'But you accept expensive clothes from someone else,' he said, in a soft voice that for some reason made her shiver. 'You told me the Benoit Besson outfits I've seen you wearing were given to you as presents—I assume by a rich lover. Why won't you accept a gift from me?'

'That was different. Benoit gave me the dresses.'

'You mean you are *Besson's* mistress?'

Louise could not define the expression in Dimitri's eyes; it was somewhere between speculative and contemptuous. Her temper flared.

'Benoit is a friend,' she said tersely. 'I've known him for most of my life. When he was a fashion student I was his muse, and he designed all sorts of weird and wonderful creations. Then he became a successful designer, and sometimes he still likes to try out his ideas on me rather than at his studio. The clothes he gives me are those that he's made specifically for me—prototypes, if you like, for designs that are later modelled on the catwalk.'

'I see.' Dimitri relaxed a little, finally able to dismiss the ugly suspicions about her that had persisted in the back of his mind. But his satisfaction did not last long.

'*What* do you see?' Louise said sharply. She could see all too clearly what he had been thinking, and anger and hurt surged up inside her as the horrible truth dawned. 'You thought I had been given those dresses by wealthy men, didn't you? You thought—' She broke off, so furious that she could barely speak. 'You thought I was like my mother—that I was prepared to be some rich guy's mistress in return for material possessions. Is that why you thought I slept with you in Paris?' Her voice rose and she jumped up from the sunbed. 'Did you think that because you had paid for an expensive dinner you had *bought* me?'

Dimitri shrugged. 'You slept with me because you hoped to persuade me to buy Eirenne.'

Louise paled. His words hung in the air between them and she could not look at him.

'You wanted a million pounds as quickly as you could lay your hands on it. Isn't that right?' he continued remorselessly. 'But you've never explained why you need the money.'

'I don't owe you an explanation.' She stared at his hard face. The warmth she had seen in his eyes when he had teased her about her freckles had disappeared and she sensed that a chasm had opened up between them. 'I am *not* like Tina,' she said fiercely. 'She is my mother, and I love her, but I hate how she lived her life.'

She did not understand why she cared so much about Dimitri's opinion of her, but she desperately wanted to convince him that she was not like his father's mistress, whom he had so despised.

'The money is not for me. It's to help…someone I care about.' When he made no response she continued huskily, 'It was not the reason I slept with you in Paris. I did that because…because I—' She broke off and stared at him miserably, knowing she would be a fool to reveal the truth— that she had yearned to recreate the special night they had shared on Eirenne seven years before.

'Because what?' Dimitri demanded. He got up from the sunbed and walked towards her, his jaw hardening when she backed away from him.

'If it wasn't to persuade me to buy the island, why *did* you make love with me? Was it because you couldn't help yourself? Because you wanted me so badly that you couldn't resist me or deny your desire for me?'

Louise wished she could sink through the floor. She was utterly mortified that he had been aware of his effect on her. 'You arrogant bastard,' she choked. 'What do you want from me—blood or just my total humiliation?'

'I don't want either.' He gripped her shoulders to prevent her from fleeing from him. 'I'm telling you how it was for *me*. I was listing the reasons why I made love to you, *glikia mou*.'

She was too hurt to believe him. 'Don't call me that. You thought I was like my mother—and you once referred to her as a whore.'

Dimitri felt as if his heart was being squeezed in a vice when he glimpsed tears in her eyes.

'I was jealous,' he said harshly. 'When you told me your clothes had been gifts it seemed reasonable to assume they were from a man—and I was jealous. I *hate* the thought of you having other lovers—even though I know you must have done so in the seven years since you were mine.'

'You were *jealous*?' Louise gave a bitter laugh. 'What gives you the right, when you have a reputation as a playboy and your numerous affairs are plastered over the tabloids?' Her temper fizzed. 'Your attitude is *so* chauvinistic.'

'I'm not proud of the way I feel,' he admitted grimly. 'It has never happened to me before—this feeling that I'd like to kill any guy who comes near you.'

He was serious, Louise realised with a jolt. Dimitri looked as stunned as she felt by his admission. Her anger drained away and she shrugged wearily.

'I was never yours seven years ago. We spent a couple of nice days on Eirenne and slept together one night. We both know you only made love to me to get at my mother.'

Dimitri looked genuinely taken aback. 'Where did you get that crazy idea from?'

She ignored him as seven years of pent-up hurt burst from her like a torrent from a dam.

'I didn't stand a chance, did I?' she said bitterly. 'I admit I was painfully naïve for a nineteen-year-old—but, Goddammit, you took advantage of my innocence. You took my virginity without a second thought.'

Dimitri tensed at her accusation. Shock and another emotion he did not want to define but which felt disturbingly like possessiveness surged through him. He speared her with an intent look.

'You're saying I was your first lover? You told me at the time that you'd had other boyfriends.'

Louise flushed guiltily, knowing that she had not been entirely truthful with him. 'I'd been on a couple of dates with guys I met at university. But I'd never had a…a sexual relationship. I spent most of my teenage years at an all-girls boarding school and I hardly had an opportunity.' She sighed. 'Tina might not have been the most maternal mother, but she was very protective of me—especially with regard to boyfriends. I must have made it so easy for you.'

She cringed when she remembered how years ago she had fallen into Dimitri's hands like a ripe fruit ready for picking. In Paris, and again last night, she had fallen into his bed with embarrassing eagerness. Had she learned nothing? Where was her self-respect? she asked herself furiously.

Dimitri shook his head. 'The relationship we had on Eirenne had nothing to do with your mother. I don't know why Tina came out with all that rubbish about my motives, but I suspect it was because she disliked me as much as I disliked her and she was determined to turn you against me.'

'You can't deny you blamed her for your mother's death,' Louise said fiercely. 'Or that you held her responsible for your estrangement from your father. When Tina accused you of coming on to me because you wanted to get at her you admitted it. You said it was true. And then you...' Her voice fractured. The agony she had felt seven years ago was as acute now as it had been then. 'You walked away without speaking to me. You didn't even look at me. But why would you? I had served my purpose. You had riled my mother, and that was all you cared about—you certainly never cared about me.'

'I walked out because if I hadn't there was a strong possibility that I would have done something I would later regret,' Dimitri told her explosively. He took a deep breath. 'Look at me,' he commanded in a calmer tone.

When Louise refused, he slid one hand beneath her chin and forced her head up to meet his gaze.

'I swear the only reason I made love to you on Eirenne was because I couldn't help myself. I didn't go there with the intention of seducing you. *Theos*—' he made a harsh sound '—I went to the island to collect some of my mother's things that were still at the old house. She died two months before, but whether she meant to take an overdose of her sleeping pills or it was an accident we will never know. Certainly she was devastated when my father divorced her, but she did not write a note, and I can't believe she would have chosen to leave me and my sister.'

He lifted his other hand and brushed a stray curl back from Louise's face. 'When I saw you on the island my only thought was that you had transformed from a skinny kid into a gorgeous woman, and to be brutally honest I quickly became obsessed by my desire to take you to bed. The fact that you were the daughter of my father's mistress was irrelevant, and when we spent time together and I got to know you better I realised that you were nothing like Tina.'

Louise stared at him in shocked silence.

'After I stormed out of the Villa Aphrodite and my temper had cooled it occurred to me that you might have misunderstood what I had said,' he continued. 'I went back to talk to you—only to find that you had gone. I tore down to the jetty to catch you, but you were already on the boat and you refused to wait and listen to me.'

Dimitri's explanation of the events all those years ago sounded so reasonable, so believable, Louise thought shakily. Could she have been wrong and misjudged him? It was almost impossible to accept when she had spent so long thinking that he had cruelly used her. But he was staring at her now with a burning intensity in his eyes, as if he was determined to make her believe him—as if it mattered to him that she did.

She had been so young and unsure of herself, she remembered. At nineteen she'd had no experience of men, and until she'd started university she had led a sheltered life at a convent school buried deep in the English countryside.

She had been overawed by Dimitri's stunning looks and easy charm, and amazed when he had shown an interest in her. Her lack of self-confidence had meant that it had been easy for her to believe her mother, and she had felt stupid for imagining that a gorgeous, sexy playboy could have desired *her*.

She was finding it hard to think straight when he was standing so close to her that she could feel the warmth of his body. The spicy scent of his aftershave teased her senses, and when she looked into his eyes and saw his gentle expression her heart ached. She longed to sink against him and have him wrap his strong arms around her.

'How can I believe that what you've told me is the truth? That you didn't con me into sleeping with you? I saw you on the jetty as I was leaving the island, but I was hurt and confused and I couldn't bear to talk to you then. If I had mattered to you at all you could have contacted me. I'd told you I was studying at Sheffield University, and you had my phone number. But when I phoned you a few weeks later you refused to take my call. Your secretary said you were unavailable. You must have instructed her to tell me that,' she said accusingly.

Dimitri ran a hand through his dark hair. 'My PA told you the truth. I *was* unavailable. I was in South America with my sister—who was fighting for her life in an intensive care unit.'

Louise caught her breath. 'What happened?'

'Ianthe had gone on an adventure holiday in Peru and had been thrown from her horse on a mountain path, miles from civilisation. It took three days to transport her to the nearest city, and by then she had slipped into a coma. She had multiple injuries, including a broken neck.'

'Oh, Dimitri! Is she okay now?'

'Thankfully she made a full recovery, but it took a long time, and for a while the doctors feared she would not walk again. I lived at the hospital for weeks, sitting by her bed and talking to her. They said the sound of my voice might rouse her.'

Dimitri's expression became shuttered as he recalled the agonising wait and his desperate prayers that Ianthe would wake up and be well again. It had seemed unbearable that his beautiful, sport-mad sister might be confined to a wheelchair, and he was not ashamed to admit he had wept when she had eventually emerged from the coma and the doctors had confirmed that her spinal cord had not been damaged.

'I put my life on hold during that time. Your name was on the list of people my PA said had called me, and I did try to phone you from Peru, but to be honest all I could think about was my sister. My relationship with my father was still strained, but I spoke to him to update him on Ianthe.

He mentioned that you were doing well at university and I thought...' He shrugged. 'You were obviously getting on with your life. It seemed fairer to leave you alone—especially when I didn't know how long I would have to stay in South America.'

Louise cast her mind back to those dark days after she had lost the baby. Dimitri *had* called her and left a brief message with the number of his cell phone, but she had not tried to contact him again. In retrospect it was probably for the best that she hadn't, she thought heavily. He'd had enough to worry about with his sister. The news that she had miscarried his child would have been a shock when he had not even known that she was pregnant.

She ran her mind over everything he had told her. According to him he hadn't had an ulterior motive seven years ago but had genuinely been attracted to her. The tight knot of tension inside her loosened a little. If he hadn't played her for a fool, as she had thought all this time, was it possible that their brief affair had meant something to him after all?

'Louise, it was never my intention to hurt you. I can't pretend that I will ever feel anything but contempt for Tina,' Dimitri said harshly. 'I saw from the start of her affair with my father what kind of woman she is. But you are not responsible for her actions. I blamed her for breaking my mother's heart, but I blamed my father equally.' He sighed. 'We were both caught up in our parents' relationship and the fall-out from it, but it had no bearing on how I felt about you seven years ago.'

Louise's heart missed a beat. 'How *did* you feel about me?'

He gave her a rueful smile. 'That you were very lovely, and probably too young for me. After you left the island I couldn't get you out of my mind. But then Ianthe was injured and my place was with her. She needed me, and I was prepared to take care of her for the rest of her life if necessary. Seven years ago the time wasn't right for us to have a relationship. But now fate has conspired to make us meet again,' he murmured.

He was curious about the identity of this person Louise had told him she cared about. Evidently he or she meant a lot to her if she was prepared to go to the lengths she had to raise money for them. But was this person her lover? He couldn't believe it, Dimitri brooded. The way she responded to him made him certain that he was the only male in her life.

He wished she trusted him—but it was hardly surprising that she didn't after the lies her damned mother had told about him years ago. Trust was something that grew slowly as a relationship developed. But did he want a relationship with Louise that was based on any more than simply great sex?

'When you walked into my office a week ago I felt like I'd been poleaxed,' he told her roughly. 'You looked stunning, and if I'd followed my first instinct I'd have made love to you there and then on my desk. I couldn't forget you, and I used my interest in buying the island as an excuse to find you in Paris.'

Louise could not drag her eyes from Dimitri's face. His voice was so soft that it seemed to whisper across her skin like a velvet cloak, enfolding her and drawing her to him. Her heart thudded as his head slowly lowered.

'I'm glad you're here with me,' he said, and kissed her.

It was a slow, drugging kiss that stirred her soul. She could not resist him and parted her lips so that he could slide his tongue between them and explore the interior of her mouth until she trembled with need for him.

'I'm glad too.' The words slipped out before she could

stop them. But it was the truth, Louise acknowledged as Dimitri scooped her into his arms and laid her on the sun-lounger.

He knelt over her and she wound her arms around his neck to pull his mouth down to hers. This was the only place she wanted to be, and he was the only man she had ever wanted to be with.

The kiss became fierce and hungry as passion quickly took control. His hands shook as he untied the straps of her bikini top and pulled it down to bare her breasts.

'I want you, *glikia mou*,' he said thickly. 'I don't think I'll ever have enough of you.'

She watched him pull off his shirt and shorts and her mouth went dry as she stared at his naked bronzed body. He was a work of art—as perfect as a Michelangelo sculpture. Her eyes traced the dark hair that arrowed down over his powerful abdominal muscles and grew thickly at the base of his manhood. The size of his arousal made her catch her breath, and molten heat flooded between her legs when she saw the fierce intent in his eyes as he straddled her.

Soon he would be inside her. She arched her hips, impatient for his possession, but he smiled and shook his head.

'Not yet. Not until you are ready.'

He could arouse her simply with a look, with one of his sexy smiles, but the feel of his lips closing around one nipple and then its twin was so exquisite that she gave herself up to the mindless pleasure he was eliciting with his hands and mouth. Her heart thundered when he trailed kisses down her body. What he was doing seemed shockingly decadent when they were out in the open, with the hot sun beating down on them. But he slipped his hand between her thighs and gently parted her to explore her with his fingers and then his tongue, and the world disappeared as she became a slave to sensation.

'Louise…' Dimitri groaned when she reached for him and stroked the swollen length of his erection. 'It has to be now.'

Sweat glistened on the bunched muscles of his shoulders as he positioned himself over her. He had never felt like this before—so out of control. He wasn't sure he liked the feeling. He was used to being in command of himself and everyone around him. But when Louise smiled at him as she was doing now, with her eyes as well as her mouth, he felt—he felt that nothing in the world was more important than making her happy.

'Dimitri…' His name left her lips on a soft sigh and she looked into his eyes and saw the tiny gold specks dancing like flames. And then he thrust into her so powerfully that she gasped. But it was pleasure not pain that made her cry out, and as he withdrew almost fully and then thrust again she arched her back and welcomed each forceful stroke that took her higher and higher.

His woman… *His* woman. The drumbeat thundered in Dimitri's head and matched the rhythm of his movements as he quickened his pace. He was out of control, driven by a primitive need for this woman and only her.

Faster, harder…with each thrust Dimitri filled her—and Louise loved the way he moved inside her, making their two bodies one. She belonged to him—heart and soul. The thought floated into her mind as unobtrusive yet as tangible as a feather carried on a breeze.

And then he thrust the deepest yet and she stopped thinking, her entire being focused on the explosion of pleasure that detonated within her and sent shockwaves of sensation hurtling to every nerve-ending in a mind-blowing orgasm.

He came almost simultaneously. For a few seconds he fought it, but the intensity of pleasure caused by her internal muscles convulsing around him could not be borne for long, and he gave a savage groan as the tidal wave crashed over him and he felt the sweet flood of release pump from his body.

For a long time afterwards Dimitri could not move. He felt utterly relaxed, with his head pillowed on Louise's breasts, and he was reluctant to withdraw from her and break the bond between them. He hadn't had sex that good since—well, he couldn't remember when. *Maybe never,* whispered the little voice inside him. But it was still just good sex. There was no reason to think that the wildfire passion he had just experienced with Louise was anything more profound.

No reason at all, he reminded himself as he lifted his head from her neck and saw the sparkle of tears on her lashes.

'*Pedhaki*, are you all right? Why are you crying?'

Louise swallowed the tears that clogged her throat. She felt stupidly emotional and utterly overwhelmed. 'It's just… it was beautiful.'

Dimitri nodded. Beautiful was a perfect description. He couldn't have put it better.

CHAPTER TEN

'You look incredible,' Dimitri murmured later that evening, when he strolled out of his bathroom and caught sight of Louise wearing the blue silk cocktail dress.

'It's a beautiful dress.' Louise studied her reflection in the mirror and felt a little thrill of feminine pleasure as she acknowledged that she did look good. 'Thank you for buying it for me.'

She had agreed to wear the dress on the understanding that he would not give her any more presents. She believed him when he insisted he did not think she was like her mother, but the memory of Tina wearing expensive clothes and jewellery that had been gifts from her lovers strengthened Louise's determination not to accept anything from Dimitri. That way there could be no misunderstandings.

'My grandmother's diamond *fleur-de-lis* would have been the perfect accessory.' She voiced her thoughts unthinkingly.

Dimitri frowned. 'The pendant belonged to your grandmother?'

'Yes. My grandfather gave it to her as a wedding present. When she died she left it to me. I loved it because it reminded me of her.'

He had misjudged Louise badly, Dimitri thought guiltily. He had been quick to label her a gold-digger, but the truth was that she was nothing like her mother.

'You speak as if you no longer have it.'

There was a brief, awkward silence before Louise said quickly, 'It's at the jeweller's. The clasp was loose. Actually, that's where I went after I left your hotel in Paris.'

It was not a lie. The jeweller *had* told her that the clasp which secured the pendant to the gold chain was faulty and that he would have to repair it before he could sell the necklace.

Dimitri studied her intently, as if he guessed she was keeping something from him. 'It doesn't matter,' he said finally. 'You don't need any adornment. The colour of the dress matches the blue of your eyes just as I thought it would. If you would allow me to I would love to fill your wardrobe with beautiful clothes.'

'You said you like me best wearing nothing at all,' she reminded him with a wicked smile that set his pulse racing.

'That is true, and I will demonstrate my appreciation for your naked body later, *glikia mou.*' He laughed softly when she blushed. 'Anyone would think you were an innocent virgin,' he murmured, running his finger lightly down her pink cheek. 'But we both know that's not true.'

His kiss held tenderness as well as desire, and Louise melted into it, parting her lips beneath his so that his tongue could probe the moist interior or her mouth.

'I knew I should have cancelled dinner,' Dimitri growled, wondering how the hell he was going to get through the evening with a rock-solid erection straining against his zip.

Dimitri's dinner guests were personal friends rather than business associates. Louise sensed their surprise when they learned that she was staying with him, and was puzzled because she'd assumed that she often invited his mistresses to his home.

She did not like to think of herself as his mistress. Having seen her mother flit from one affair to the next, she had vowed that she would never give up her career and her independence for any man. Tina had treated the men she'd had affairs with like gods—but when they had tired of her they had treated her like dirt.

When her affair with Dimitri was over she would go back to Paris and the job she loved, and she would do her best to forget about him, Louise told herself, trying to ignore the way her heart lurched when he strode across the room towards her.

'My sister has just phoned to say she's running a little late,' he explained. Dimitri introduced the man with him. 'Louise, this is a good friend of mine—Takis Varsos. Takis is a curator at the National Art Gallery in Athens.'

'It is a pleasure to meet you,' Takis murmured.

He was a few years old than Dimitri, Louise guessed, pleasant-faced, with greying hair and brilliant black eyes behind heavy spectacles.

'I understand you work at the Louvre? I have many questions I'd like to ask you—and perhaps I can tell you about Greece's national art collection?'

Dimitri laughed. 'I'll leave the two of you to talk while I go and check that Halia is okay to delay dinner until Ianthe arrives.'

Fifteen minutes later Louise had finished a fascinating conversation with Takis when Dimitri rejoined her, accompanied by a dark-haired woman whose facial features bore a striking resemblance to his. She felt suddenly nervous, wondering if his sister resented her because of her mother's affair with Kostas Kalakos, but Ianthe greeted her warmly.

'Louise, I'm so pleased to meet you again. It's many years since we met on Eirenne, and there wasn't time for us to get to know one another,' she said without a hint of bitterness. 'How amazing that you and Dimitri met by chance in Paris.'

Louise flushed as she caught Dimitri's eye. 'Yes, it's a small world,' she murmured dryly.

'I'll get you some champagne, *agapiti*,' he told his sister, and strolled away.

'He's wonderful, isn't he?' Ianthe glanced after him. 'I was badly injured a few years ago, and he looked after me for months after I left hospital.' She looked curiously at Louise. 'I understand you are selling Eirenne to Dimitri? It will be nice to go back to the island. We loved it when we were children, and I would like to take Ana there for holidays when she's older.'

She turned towards the man who had come to stand beside her. 'This is my husband, Lykaios.'

Louise returned Lykaios's greeting, but her eyes were drawn to the tiny bundle wrapped in a shawl that Ianthe now carefully lifted out of her husband's arms.

'And this is our daughter,' Ianthe announced with fierce maternal pride. 'Ana Maria—which was my mother's name. I fed her before we left, so hopefully she'll stay settled during dinner. Would you like to hold her?'

She could hardly refuse. Louise hoped that if anyone noticed her sudden tension they would think she was simply nervous about holding a newborn baby.

Ianthe placed the precious bundle in her arms and she stared in wonder at the little face peeping from the folds of the shawl. Ana was beautiful, with a mass of black hair and petal-soft pink cheeks, her long eyelashes fringing huge dark eyes.

The pain in Louise's chest was so intense that she drew a sharp breath. It shouldn't hurt so much after all this time, she thought bleakly, but the loss of her baby was something she would never forget. A lump formed in her throat. If things had been different years ago she would have held her own baby in her arms, breathed in the evocative scent of her own newborn son or daughter. Dimitri would have been a father. But he was not even aware that she had conceived his child.

She wished now that she had told him—wished they could have shared the pain of losing their child. But perhaps he would not have cared. Perhaps he would have been relieved that her unplanned pregnancy had ended in a miscarriage.

The other guests had crowded round to admire Ianthe's baby and there was some good-natured teasing going on among the men about who was next in line for fatherhood.

'Dimitri's way behind,' Lykaios commented. 'He's not even married yet. You'll have to get a move on,' he told his brother-in-law. 'It's up to you to produce an heir to take over running Kalakos Shipping.'

'I don't think a child should be brought into the world to fill a pre-determined role.' Dimitri's tone became serious as lifted his niece from Louise's arms. 'A baby should be conceived from love, and if I ever have children I would encourage them to follow their dreams and live their life how they choose.'

Louise shot him a startled look. It was a bittersweet irony that his views on parenthood were exactly the same as hers. She'd felt instinctively that he would be a good father, and the tender expression on his face as he cradled Ana against his chest intensified the ache inside her.

She would *love* to have his child.

The thought stole into her head and refused to leave. It was stupid to think things like that, she reminded herself. After her first pregnancy had failed she had been warned that she might have difficulty conceiving again. And more pertinently, she must not forget that Dimitri had brought her to Athens so that she could fulfil her side of the deal they had made. She was his temporary mistress, and two weeks from now she would return to Paris and never see him again.

The guests had departed and the staff had returned to their own homes for the night. As Dimitri walked through the ground-floor rooms switching off the lights his thoughts were focused on Louise. She had seemed to enjoy the dinner with his friends, but beneath her smile he had sensed an air of sadness about her. He had even leaned close to her at the dinner table and asked if anything was wrong, and although she had assured him she was fine he had glimpsed a haunted expression in her eyes that bothered him.

The patio doors in the sitting room were open, the voile curtains billowing in the soft breeze. Louise was standing on the terrace and appeared to be absorbed in her own thoughts. She glanced up as Dimitri reached her and dashed her hand across her face—but not before he caught the glimmer of tears on her cheeks.

'*Glikia*, what's wrong?'

Louise shook her head, unable to explain the ache in her heart. If only she could turn back time…if only she hadn't listened to her mother and believed the worst of Dimitri… if only she hadn't lost their baby…

Regrets were pointless, but knowing it did not stop her wishing that things had been different.

Dimitri caught a tear clinging to her lashes on his thumbpad and felt a strange sensation, as if a hand was squeezing his heart. '*Pedhaki?*'

'I was just looking at the stars and thinking how small and insignificant we are.' She laughed self-consciously. 'I think I must have had too much champagne.'

He knew she had only had one glass, but he said nothing and stared up at the black sky, pinpricked with millions of tiny diamonds.

'You see that bright star up there?' He pointed. 'That's the North Star.'

Louise stared at the heavens. 'Have you studied astronomy?'

'Not in great detail, but I used to go sailing with my father when I was a boy and he taught me a little of how to navigate using the stars. Of course GPS systems mean there's no need to look at the night sky now, but it was fun.' He sighed. 'I often wish I could turn the clock back.'

It was uncanny that they had both been thinking the same thing—almost as if their minds were connected, Louise thought.

'Why do you wish that?' she whispered.

'I regret that I was never reconciled with my father. Both of us said things that would have been better left unsaid, and I never got the chance to tell him that I was sorry, that I loved him. No one could have predicted his heart attack,' Dimitri said heavily. 'I was on the other side of the world when it happened and by the time I arrived back in Athens I was too late. He died an hour before I reached the hospital.'

'I'm sorry.'

Louise heard the raw pain in his voice and her heart ached for him. Dimitri had been estranged from his father because of Kostas's relationship with her mother, and although he did not mention it the spectre of the affair that had ripped his family apart hovered between them.

'It's not your fault,' he said gently, as if he had read her mind. 'None of it was your fault. I blame myself and my pigheadedness. I was young and arrogant. I saw everything in terms of black and white and forgot that life doesn't last for ever.'

Louise stared up at the stars. Sometimes life was over before it had even begun, she thought painfully.

'Dimitri—if what we had on Eirenne meant something to you, why didn't you try to contact me again later?' She tilted her head and studied his handsome face, felt the familiar dip of her stomach. His eyes were shadowed and she had no idea what he was thinking, but she had to ask the question that had been eating away at her. 'I know you couldn't at first, while Ianthe was in hospital, but after she had recovered why didn't you call?'

'I didn't for several reasons,' he said after a long silence. 'My damnable pride was one of them.' Louise had rejected him and it had hurt—although he had refused to admit it. He raked a hand through his hair. 'I wasn't in a position to contemplate any sort of relationship with you. My father had disinherited me and I thought—what the hell? I was angry and determined to prove to him that I didn't need him. I established my company, Fine Living, and worked obsessively to make it a success. I guess I needed to prove to myself as well as my father that I could make it on my own. My social life took second place to my ambition, and the women I dated were…'

'Were what?' Louise queried when he hesitated.

He shrugged. 'Women who knew how to play the game—who understood that all I wanted was an affair without emotional attachment. When my father died and I discovered that he had named me as his successor to head Kalakos Shipping after all I felt I needed to prove that I was worthy of the role.'

The long hours he'd put in at the office had left him with little time for anything else, Dimitri brooded. He had focused on work as a way of dealing with his grief at the death of his father. He stared at Louise. The moonlight had turned her to silver, and she looked ethereal and so very lovely that his heart clenched.

'My life was organised and under control until you stormed back into it.' He sounded almost angry. 'I thought I knew what you were—a common gold-digger who would sell your body for hard cash. I couldn't even blame you. How could you know any different when your mother had behaved that way? I told myself.'

He lifted his hand and wound a honey-blond curl around his finger. 'But you have proved my opinion of you to be wrong. *Thee mou*, we practically had a fight when I tried to give you this dress,' he muttered as he slid one strap down her arm and brushed his lips over her bare shoulder.

Louise could not restrain the little tremor that ran through her when he trailed a line of kisses along her collarbone. 'I'm sorry I reacted badly about the dress,' she whispered. 'And I'm sorry if I've disrupted your life.'

'I'm not.' Dimitri's voice deepened as he pulled her into his arms. 'I want to make love to you, but—' He broke off, thinking about the deal he'd made with her. He'd thought he could control her, like he controlled everything, but his plan had backfired.

'But what?' she said in a puzzled voice.

'But it has to be what you want too, *glikia mou*, and if it's not then you can sleep in your own room. I won't bother you or make any demands on you.'

Louise stared at him uncertainly. 'We have an arrangement…'

'I had no right to impose that condition on you. I'm *glad* to have the opportunity to buy Eirenne, and I will go ahead with the purchase whatever you decide about our sleeping arrangements.'

Her heart was beating so fast that Louise found it hard to breathe. She was still struggling to comprehend that

Dimitri had changed his mind and no longer expected her to be his mistress. He had given her a choice—and she already knew her answer.

'I want to share your room, your bed.' *Your life for ever,* she thought. For ever wasn't on Dimitri's agenda, but she would have tonight with him, and all the nights for the next two weeks. It would have to be enough.

He cupped her face in his hands and kissed her—a long, sweet kiss that sought a response she gave willingly. When he lifted her she wound her arms around his neck and rested her head on his shoulder as he carried her through the dark house and up to his bedroom, where moonbeams slanted through the blinds.

The sapphire-blue dress fluttered to the floor, followed by the wisps of her lacy underwear. Dimitri kissed her mouth, her breasts, and then knelt and trailed his lips over her stomach and the cluster of dark gold curls between her legs. He bestowed the most intimate kiss of all and dipped his tongue into her moist feminine heart until she cried out his name. And then he drew her down onto the bed and made love to her with fierce passion and an unexpected tenderness that brought tears to Louise's eyes.

'We really should get up.' Louise glanced at the clock the following Sunday morning and discovered that it was nearly afternoon.

'Why?' Dimitri murmured lazily as he pulled her closer to him and hooked his thigh over her leg. 'I'm quite happy here.'

'You said you needed to do some work today,' she reminded him. 'I feel I've already disrupted your schedule more than enough. You only went to the office two days last week. I don't want you to think you have to entertain me.'

He lowered his head and kissed the dusky pink nipple jutting provocatively above the sheet. To keep things fair he did the same to its twin, laughing softly when she caught her breath.

'I haven't noticed you complaining, *glikia mou.*'

'You've been a very attentive host,' she assured him gravely, and then giggled when he tickled her. 'Seriously, though, aren't you bored of staying at home? Joseph told me he's never known you to spend so much time at the house.'

'I haven't before,' Dimitri admitted. He rolled onto his back and drew her down on top of him. 'But I like being here with you.' His eyes gleamed wickedly. 'And I especially enjoy entertaining you.'

Louise gave up. She certainly wasn't going to complain about the attention he'd lavished on her. They rose late each morning and ate a leisurely breakfast-cum-lunch on the terrace. Dimitri usually disappeared into his study for an hour to catch up on e-mails, and then they would spend the afternoon by the pool—swimming, reading, and inevitably making love in the hot sun.

She loved simply being with him—just as she had all those years ago on Eirenne. The friendship they had shared then had been rekindled, as well as their passion for each other. She felt as though they were in a bubble, distanced from the rest of the world. But everyone knew that bubbles eventually burst, and she was aware that reality would soon intrude on their dream existence.

'I've just remembered I was going to take you to lunch at a great little restaurant I know in Rafina. It overlooks the marina, and I thought that afterwards I would take you out on my boat.' Dimitri kissed her lingeringly and groaned when she parted her lips beneath his. He rolled her beneath him. 'On the other hand, we could always go there for dinner this evening…'

* * *

The days sped past. Dimitri took her to the Acropolis and the Parthenon, and wandered patiently around with her when they spent a whole day at the National Gallery. Louise fell in love with Athens—especially at night, when it was cooler, and they browsed the shops that stayed open until late and visited lively tavernas.

Dimitri had given Joseph and Halia paid leave and arranged for them to visit their son, who lived on one of the islands. The couple deserved a break, he reasoned, and he had to admit that he liked being alone in the house with Louise. They could make love when they liked, where they liked. It occurred to him after a particularly erotic sex session on the sitting room carpet that he was fast becoming addicted to her.

Towards the end of the first week his lawyer had phoned to say that the sale of Eirenne was nearing completion.

'Once we have both signed the contract the money will be paid into your bank account,' Dimitri explained to Louise as he drove them to his lawyer's office. He was puzzled by her lack of enthusiasm. 'I expected you to look more pleased,' he murmured as they stepped out of the car.

'I *am* pleased,' she mumbled, unable to meet his gaze.

She knew Dimitri was happy to own the island, but she was sure he would be a lot less happy if she revealed that the money would pay for her mother's cancer treatment. He had every reason to hate Tina, she acknowledged miserably. She felt torn, her loyalties divided between two people she loved.

The thought was so shocking that she barely registered walking into the lawyer's office. *Love?* Where had that sprung from? She wasn't in love with Dimitri.

Her heart did that strange little lurch it always did as she studied his sculpted profile. She loved the sharp angles of his cheekbones and the sensual curve of his mouth, loved his unusual olive-green eyes with their fiery golden flecks—loved *him*, whispered that voice inside her.

He was everything, she admitted, and the realisation was terrifying—because she had vowed that she would never make a man the centre of her universe as her mother had so often done. She had promised herself that she would never fall desperately, madly, deeply in love—and she had broken that promise. She felt a sharp pain in her chest, as if an arrow had pierced her heart. Soon she was going home, and Dimitri had given no hint that he wanted to continue with their relationship.

He arranged to take her back to Paris on his private jet, and on her last evening in Athens they had dinner at a charming little taverna, where they lingered over wonderful food and drank retsina before strolling home hand in hand.

He made love to her with fierce passion and exquisite tenderness, and although Louise told herself she had imagined it she sensed a faint air of desperation in his lovemaking that made her wonder if he regretted that she was leaving as much as she did. She felt that they had become close in recent days. But right at the start he had warned her he did not have a long attention span where women were concerned. Perhaps he had grown tired of her but was too polite to say so…

Unusually for midsummer, it was raining in Paris. The grey sky echoed Louise's mood, but Madeleine seemed pleased to be home, and when she was freed from the carrier she leapt up onto her usual windowsill, gave an elegant stretch, and then curled up and fell asleep.

'Your apartment was not designed for a person of my height,' Dimitri muttered as he forgot to duck and hit his head on the doorframe. 'Leave unpacking for now. I've got something I want to show you.'

She gave him a puzzled look. 'What is it?'

'You'll see. It's a surprise—one that I think you'll like.'

Mystified, she followed him back down to the car. 'Do you want another tour of the Louvre?' she asked a few minutes later, when the chauffeur parked opposite the Jardin des Tuileries.

'Come with me,' was all Dimitri would say, and he ushered her through the front door of a graceful old building that overlooked the famous gardens.

'Will you tell me what's going on?' Louise demanded as the lift took them upwards.

He grinned. 'Patience, *pedhaki*.'

They stepped out of the lift on the top floor. There was only one door on the landing, and Dimitri took a key from his pocket and opened it before standing back to allow her to precede him inside.

'What do you think?'

She looked around a huge, high-ceilinged sitting room which was beautifully decorated and luxuriously furnished.

'It's a fantastic apartment—especially with the view over the Tuileries. But why have you brought me here? Who lives here?'

'You do.' He laughed softly at her stunned expression. 'The agent left the key with the porter so that I could show you the place. If you like it I'll sign the lease and you can move in immediately.'

Louise stared at him, her mind whirling. 'I like the apartment I'm living in,' she said at last. 'I can't afford to move here. The rent must be astronomical.'

'Don't worry about that. I'll pay for all your living costs.' He ignored her frown. 'You must agree that your current apartment is too small for both of us.'

She caught her breath. 'Do you mean you want us to live

here together?' Her heart was beating a wild tattoo in her chest. 'Are you going to move to Paris?'

She watched him stiffen, watched his dark brows draw together, and her excitement trickled away.

'No,' he said slowly. 'You know I have to be in Athens to run Kalakos Shipping. But I'll visit you as often as I can. Why are you looking at me like that, *glikia mou*?'

Dimitri stared at Louise's wintry expression and felt a flare of irritation. What had she expected? He couldn't disrupt his life for her any more that he had already. He could not simply up sticks and move to France, and he did not expect her to leave her job and move to Greece. This was the best compromise he could think of.

'If you don't like this apartment there are plenty of others on the agent's books.'

'It's not the apartment. I mean, it *is*—but not in the way you think.' Louise felt sick with disappointment.

If she had any sense she would say nothing more and retain her dignity. Instead she discarded her pride.

'I thought when you said the apartment was for us that you were making some sort of commitment to me,' she whispered. 'I thought you wanted us to be together.' For a few heart-shaking seconds she had believed he cared about her.

He walked towards her, his frown deepening when she backed away from him. Women—he would never understand them, Dimitri thought grimly. He had thought he understood Louise, but now she was being irrational.

'Leasing an apartment for you—for us so that we can spend time together—is a kind of commitment.'

'No, it's not.' Memories of visiting her mother at the Italian Count's penthouse in Rome, or an apartment in Monaco paid for by a television celebrity who wanted to keep his affair with Tina secret from his wife flooded

Louise's mind. She would never give up her independence and allow a man to keep her.

'I refuse to be your mistress.'

'*Gamoto!* What have you been these past two weeks if not my mistress?' Dimitri demanded furiously.

He was tempted to shake her, but felt an even stronger desire to pull her into his arms and kiss her until she melted against him and they could end this crazy argument.

'I thought that we'd had fun these last two weeks. I thought you had enjoyed being with me just as I enjoyed being with you. Not just the sex.' He ignored her when she opened her mouth to speak. 'Everything—the companionship, the friendship we shared. What more do you want from me?'

His eyes narrowed as he realised that this was a familiar argument. He'd had it with several of his ex-mistresses. And it had always been a prelude to the end of an affair. Once a woman started talking about commitment it was time to head out of the door. So why wasn't he walking? Why did the idea of ending his relationship with Louise turn his mood as dull and grey as the sky outside the window?

'What were you hoping for when you said you thought I was making a commitment?' He gave a harsh laugh. 'Did you think I was going to *propose* to you?'

'No, of course not,' Louise denied quickly, her face flaming.

She hadn't expected that, but she *had* wanted some sign that she was more important to him than her mother had been to all those men who had used her and then discarded her when they'd grown tired of her. Dimitri setting her up as his mistress in an expensive apartment fell far short of the relationship she longed for. Maybe he had mistresses dotted around various European cities, she thought bleakly. No way was she going to join their ranks.

The sound of her cell phone made her jump. She quickly searched through her handbag, intending to cut the call, but the name of the hospital in Massachusetts on the caller display sent a chill of foreboding through her. The phone stopped ringing before she could answer it.

She glanced at Dimitri and bit her lip at his grim expression. He looked angry—and perhaps with good reason, she acknowledged painfully. Perhaps she had misjudged him and his motives for wanting to lease the apartment. She was just so scared of ending up like Tina that she was afraid to trust him.

'I need to return that call,' she told him flatly.

'Sure,' Dimitri spun round from the window and strode across the room. 'The driver is waiting downstairs and will take you home. I'll take the key back to the agent and tell him I don't want the apartment.'

He stared at her and felt a surge of frustration when he saw the undisguised misery in her eyes. To say that events were not turning out as he'd planned was a laughable understatement, but at this moment he had never felt less like laughing.

'I have to fly straight to Norway for a meeting I postponed last week.' It wasn't absolutely true. He had planned to spend the night with her here at the new place before leaving for his business trip in the morning. But he could do with some space, he thought grimly. He was angry that she had thrown the apartment back in his face.

He had enjoyed a lot more than simply physical gratification with Louise during the past two weeks, he admitted. But he had still regarded her as a mistress. He didn't want anything else. What was the point in commitment anyway? His parents had been married for thirty years, but their relationship had been blown apart by his father's affair and his mother had died heartbroken. Life was a lot simpler without emotions to screw it up, he thought sardonically.

Louise had followed him down the hallway to the front door. As he wrenched it open he glanced at her, and felt his heart clench when he saw the shimmer of tears in her eyes. So this was the end. He was shocked by how strongly he did not want it to be.

'Dimitri...' Her voice was choked, as if it hurt her throat to speak. 'I'm sorry.'

'So am I.' He wanted to kiss her, but knew that if he did he might make promises he did not know if he could keep. 'I'll call you.' It was what he always said when he ended an affair, but he knew damned well he wouldn't phone her. There was no point. They had reached a stalemate.

She moved past him. He watched her walk away from him down the hall. She did not look round as she entered the lift. The doors closed—and only then Dimitri realised that he was not ready to let her go.

CHAPTER ELEVEN

LOUISE's first priority when she arrived back in Paris from Massachusetts was to collect Madeleine from her neighbour.

'Chérie,' Benoit said gently as he studied her white face and hollow eyes. 'I'm so sorry about your mother. Is there anything I can do?'

She shook her head. 'Everything has been taken care of. I just need some time.'

She craved solitude. Her tiny apartment was a sanctuary and Madeleine a faithful companion who did not leave her side in the following days while she grieved.

At his office in Athens, Dimitri stared at the cheque for one million pounds that had arrived in the post and was now burning a hole on his desk.

During the past three weeks he had run through a whole host of emotions—ranging from anger when Louise had turned down the apartment he'd found for her in Paris to confusion, frustration and increasing fury when she had not answered any of his calls. In the last few days a feeling of dull despair had settled over him—a sense that all the joy had disappeared from the world.

That had changed when he had opened the letter addressed for his personal attention in Louise's handwriting and skimmed the brief note attached to the cheque. It explained that she was returning the full amount he had paid for Eirenne. There was nothing else—no explanation of her reasons, or indeed why she apparently wanted nothing more to do with him.

The lethargy that was so alien to him had been replaced once more by blazing anger. He deserved more than a pithy two-line note, he thought savagely. After three weeks of ignoring him, was that all Louise deigned to send him? No woman had ever ignored him before—and if they had he wouldn't have cared, he admitted. But Louise was different—or maybe it was he who was different? He had never felt like this before—as if his heart had been ripped out.

One thing was for sure: he was not going to allow her to ignore him any more.

He hit the intercom on his desk and growled like an angry bear at his PA. 'Arrange for the jet to fly me to Paris immediately. And cancel all my appointments—indefinitely. Please,' he added. Because in all fairness the mess he seemed to be making of his life wasn't Aletha's fault, and he felt guilty that she had been tiptoeing around him as if she feared his temper might explode.

Later that same day Dimitri stood in the hallway outside Louise's apartment and felt an uncomfortable cramping sensation in his gut. He couldn't wait to see her. Hell, he had missed her—he had refused to admit how much until now. But her note had given no indication that she missed him. There was every chance she would slam the door in his face when she saw him. He rang the bell and moved his foot forward, ready to jam it in the doorway.

He heard footsteps from the other side of the door and remembered her apartment had bare polished floorboards. The security chain was drawn back and then the door opened.

'Thee mou!' He could not restrain his shocked reaction. Her face was paper-white and there were purple shadows beneath her eyes. She looked at him dully, and her air of fragility tugged on his insides.

'Dimitri!'

She blinked, as if her brain had only just registered him.

'Glikia mou, what has happened?'

Louise drew a shuddering breath. 'My mother died.'

Dimitri felt a jolt of shock. It was hard to take in. Tina Hobbs—his father's mistress, the woman he had blamed for breaking his mother's heart—was dead. Seven years ago he had despised her, but now he felt nothing but pity for Tina. And for her daughter.

He stepped into the flat, remembering just in time to duck his head and avoid the low doorframe.

'Pedhaki,' he murmured gently, and drew her into his arms. She made no attempt to pull away, and as he stroked her honey-gold curls everything fell into place in his mind.

'When did it happen?'

'Two weeks ago.' Her voice was muffled against his chest.

He tightened his arm around her. 'Why didn't you call me? I would have come to you.'

The tenderness in Dimitri's voice brought tears to Louise's eyes. Her emotions were still raw, but she felt embarrassed that she had literally thrown herself at him. She eased out of his arms and led the way into the sitting room.

He looked gorgeous, she noted. Despite everything that had happened—especially her mother's death—she was blown away by the sight of him in beige jeans and a black silk shirt. The dark stubble on his jaw added to his dangerous sex appeal and her heart gave a familiar lurch.

'I tried to phone you many times but got no reply,' he said quietly.

'I was in America, and for some reason my phone didn't work there. I didn't contact you because...' Her voice faltered. She moved away from him and stood by the windowsill, absently stroking Madeleine. 'I couldn't after what happened the last time you were in Paris—those horrible things I said. You had found that lovely apartment for us, but I...I was too scared to accept what you were offering,' she said with painful honesty.

'It doesn't matter,' Dimitri assured her. 'I understand.' She'd needed to feel secure in their relationship, and at the time he hadn't appreciated how deeply her childhood experiences had affected her.

Louise bit her lip. 'There was another reason. I had done something awful.' Her voice shook. 'Dimitri, I sold you Eirenne so that I could use the money to pay for my mother's medical treatment. She had cancer, and her only chance was to have treatment in America. I didn't tell you because I knew you hated her and I was afraid you would pull out of the deal. You were my only hope—*her* only hope. Tina needed to start treatment immediately, and I knew you were keen to own the island and would push the sale through quickly.'

She paused, and then continued in a choked voice, 'In the end the money wasn't necessary. She wasn't strong enough for the doctors to try the treatment and she died in the hospital in Massachusetts. I was with her at...the end... and the funeral was held over there. I've always believed that your father should have left Eirenne to you, so when I came back to Paris I returned the money to you.'

'I received your cheque this morning.'

Louise's eyes flew to his face. His expression was unreadable, but she was certain he must be furious at her confession. Legally she had done nothing wrong, but morally—morally she had been torn between him and Tina, she thought bleakly.

She stared at the floor, tension spiralling inside her when she sensed him cross the small sitting room to stand in front of her.

'I knew while you were in Athens why you needed the money.'

He didn't look angry. He looked… She was afraid to try and define his expression. She shook her head, utterly confused. 'You can't have. How *could* you have known?'

He sighed. 'I was curious about why you were prepared to sell Eirenne for a lot less than it was worth. When you said you needed money quickly I wondered if you had debts, if maybe a loan-shark was hounding you for repayment. I didn't know what else to think,' he murmured when she gave a horrified gasp. 'I asked a private investigator to find out what he could. I wanted to protect you if necessary. But the investigator discovered that your mother was seriously ill and had been transferred to a specialist cancer clinic in the U.S. soon after I had agreed to buy the island. It wasn't hard to work out why you were so desperate for money.'

The room swam. 'Why did you go ahead with the deal once you knew the money was for my mother?' Louise said faintly. 'You hated her…'

'But *you* loved her.' He gave her a gentle smile. 'Faced with the same situation I would have done the same for someone I loved. I hoped you would trust me enough to tell me about Tina's illness, and when you didn't I felt that I couldn't mention it.'

He pulled her into his arms and Louise sagged against him, feeing too drained to understand anything any more except that Dimitri was here, holding her.

'I find it hard to trust,' she admitted thickly. 'I never

wanted to end up like Tina. She wanted to be loved, but when she was rejected by my father, and then by her lovers, she grew hard and used them like they used her.'

Louise's upbringing had left her with a ton of emotional baggage, and as a man who disliked emotions and kept his own under tight control Dimitri would ordinarily have run a hundred miles rather than get involved. But his life had been turned inside out from the moment she had walked into his office looking like a sex goddess in her short red skirt, he thought ruefully.

'Do you trust me, *glikia mou*?' He was conscious of the painful thud of his heart as he waited for her answer.

'Yes.' Simple, unequivocal. Louise knew she would trust him with her life.

'Then bring Madeleine and come with me.'

She did not even ask where he was taking her. It was enough to be with him.

Louise fell asleep on the plane. Dimitri carried her to the bedroom at the rear of the jet, laid her on the bed and tucked a blanket around her before he settled down with his laptop and fired off a few e-mails to his top executives. Kalakos Shipping was important, but Louise was more so, and he decided that it was about time he learned the art of delegation.

It was a short journey from Athens airport to the port of Rafina, where his boat was moored.

'Are we going to Eirenne?' she asked him as they sped out of the harbour and headed in a direction she remembered from years ago.

'Back to where it all began,' he said softly. There was a little more colour in her cheeks after her sleep, but the breeze blowing her clothes revealed she had lost weight, and she looked so fragile that his heart clenched.

The sun was low in the sky when they reached the island, a fiery orange ball that streaked the few wispy clouds to gold and bathed the path leading from the jetty in mellow light.

'Nothing has changed,' Louise murmured as they followed the path into the pine forest. She had mixed feelings about coming back to this place that held special memories but also regrets.

'I was surprised by how well Eirenne had been maintained,' Dimitri told her. 'It was only when I came here two weeks ago that I discovered your mother had employed staff to take care of the island and the two houses.'

The old house that had been built by Dimitri's grandfather was just as Louise remembered it. Half hidden among the pine trees, its many windows looked out over the sea that sparkled like a precious jewel in the evening sunshine.

Joseph and Halia greeted them at the front door. The couple were delighted with the staff cottage and happy to come to the island whenever they were needed, Dimitri explained as he led the way into the dining room. Louise couldn't remember the last time she had eaten a proper meal; her appetite had been non-existent lately. But the baked sea bass served with a colourful salad was delicious, and the crisp Chardonnay Dimitri served with the meal was a perfect accompaniment.

After dinner they sat on the terrace and finished the wine while the sun sank below the horizon and the air became filled with the song of the cicadas. For the first time in weeks Louise felt some of her tension leave her. She turned her head to study Dimitri's handsome profile and tried to ignore the ache in her heart. Nothing had been resolved regarding their relationship, but here on Eirenne she could pretend for a little while that everything was perfect.

'Thank you for bringing me here. I'd almost forgotten how beautiful the island is.'

'I haven't forgotten anything about this place.' He met her gaze, and in the shadows of dusk she saw the golden flecks in his eyes burning brightly. 'I remember bringing you to this house for the first time. I looked at you and thought you were more beautiful than any woman I'd ever seen.'

She gave a faint smile. 'That can't be true. You had been engaged to that stunning American model, Rochelle Fitzpatrick, but she had broken off the relationship. Perhaps you would have been attracted to *any* woman when you were on the rebound?' She voiced the doubt that still lingered.

Dimitri threw back his head and laughed. 'I wasn't on the rebound from Rochelle. If anything I was glad I'd had a lucky escape. Your mother was right about one thing—Rochelle did dump me when she learned that I'd fallen out with my father and I was no longer his heir. I realised that she was in love with the fortune she'd expected me to inherit rather than with me. I admit my ego was bruised, and I was disappointed with myself that I hadn't spotted her for a gold-digger, but I certainly wasn't heartbroken.'

'I see.' Another ghost had been laid to rest, and Louise's heart leapt when he stood up and stretched out his hand to her.

'Somehow I doubt that you do,' he said obliquely, but then he lowered his head and captured her mouth, and she was instantly lost in the beauty of his kiss.

The scent of the pine trees was evocative. Memories swirled in Louise's mind as Dimitri swept her up and carried her into the house. He set her down in the bedroom they had shared one night long ago, and undressed her and then himself. Pale fingers of moonlight gilded them, following the path of their hands as they explored each other's bodies. He kissed her breasts and her stomach, then knelt to bestow the most intimate caress of all, gently parting her thighs to dip his tongue into her honeyed sweetness.

When he laid her on the bed she reached for him and stroked his already hard arousal until he groaned and positioned himself over her. Their eyes met and held as he slid deep inside her, and when he began to move Louise thought that her heart would burst.

Four days later Dimitri woke at dawn and found that he was alone. Pausing only long enough to pull on a pair of denim cut-offs and slip something into his pocket, he walked quickly through the quiet house. The front door was open and he felt a flare of relief when he looked across the garden and spied Louise on the beach.

'That's the second time you've disappeared from my bed,' he murmured, remembering how she had left him sleeping at his hotel in Paris. He slid his arms around her waist. 'I don't like it, *glikia mou*. I've become addicted to waking and seeing your face on the pillow beside me.'

She gave him a faintly wistful smile. 'I was thinking that I need to go home. I've had almost a month of compassionate leave from work, but it's time to pick up the threads of my life again. My mother would want me to.' Her voice caught. 'She was proud of my career.'

Dimitri was conscious of a peculiar sensation in the pit of his stomach. Ever since they had arrived on the island he had been waiting for the right moment. And this moment, with the sun just rising above the pine trees and the sky streaked with pink and gold clouds that were reflected in the waves curling onto the shore, was the perfect moment.

'There is a job vacancy at the National Gallery in Athens

which Takis Varsos is very keen for you to accept,' he murmured.

Louise looked puzzled. 'At best it's a three-hour commute from Paris to Athens.'

'But if you lived in Athens…' He threaded his fingers through her hair and looked into eyes that were the colour of the sapphire hidden in his pocket.

If he asked her to be his mistress would she have the strength to refuse? Louise wondered. Should she throw away a chance of happiness because she was afraid of how she would feel when their relationship ended?

She was not her mother, she reminded herself. She was strong and independent and she was brave enough to live for the present rather than worry about the future.

'Commitment was something I had no interest in,' Dimitri admitted. 'I never understood how two people could know for certain that they wanted to spend their lives together. But then I met a golden girl who crept into my heart—and she stayed there, even though I didn't see her again for many years. Without realising it I compared every woman I met to her, but at last I understood and I knew that I wanted to be with her for ever.'

'Dimitri…?' Louise whispered. She had told him she trusted him. But she was afraid to trust the expression in his eyes, afraid to believe he could be saying what he seemed to be saying.

'I love you, Louise. You are my golden girl, the love of my life.'

Dimitri's hand was shaking as he felt in the pocket of his cut-offs and withdrew a ring—an oval sapphire surrounded by diamonds that sparkled in the brilliant light of the new day. He heard Louise catch her breath, and he captured her hand and lifted it to his lips.

'Will you marry me and spend the rest of your life

with me? Will you be the mother of my children? When I watched you holding my sister's baby something clicked inside me, and l imagined us having a child together—Sweetheart, what's wrong?'

Shock jolted through him as Louise snatched her hand out of his. She looked devastated. That was the only way he could describe her expression. And she was backing away from him, shaking her head.

'I can't,' she said in an anguished voice. 'I can't marry you. It wouldn't be fair.'

'*Theos!* I thought it was what you wanted—I thought, hoped…'

He must have been mistaken to think she cared about him. The realisation was gutting. For the first time in his life Dimitri was utterly floored. He couldn't think straight, and he felt a pain in his chest as though a knife had been plunged through his heart. *This* was why he had turned his back on emotions, he thought savagely. He had been perfectly content with his uneventful personal life that was never troubled by trauma and drama. But then Louise had gatecrashed his life and changed everything—changed him. She had made him love her and now he couldn't stop.

She had run down to the sea. For a moment he thought she was going to keep on running until the waves dragged her under, but she turned slowly to face him and he saw his pain reflected in her eyes.

'There's something I haven't told you. Something I should have told you.'

Fear made his voice harsh. 'Then for pity's sake tell me now.'

Louise drew a ragged breath. 'Seven years ago I fell pregnant with your baby. I was back at university when I found out, and I was shocked and scared, but…' She bit her lip, as if she could somehow hold back the emotions surging inside her. 'But I was excited too. I knew it would be difficult—I mean, it was totally the wrong time for me to have a child—but I wanted the baby...*our* baby. I loved it from the moment I knew it was growing inside me. I phoned you to tell you. I know now, of course, that you were in South America with Ianthe, but I assumed that you didn't want to have anything more to do with me.'

'*Thee mou,*' Dimitri said in a raw tone. 'I had no idea. I used protection—but nothing is one hundred percent effective. I should have checked you were okay after you went back to Sheffield, but I was angry that you had left me. And then Ianthe was injured and I was focused on her. But I did return your call eventually. Why didn't you tell me then? And the child...' The enormity of what she had revealed was only slowly sinking in. 'What happened about the baby?'

He watched her wipe her hand across her eyes.

'I miscarried in the seventh week of my pregnancy. Everything seemed fine, but then I woke up one day in agony. I was bleeding, and I guessed I was losing the baby.' Louise's voice shook as memories of that terrible day overwhelmed her. 'One of my housemates was a medical student. She suspected something was seriously wrong and insisted on driving me to A&E. I owe her my life. I was discovered to have an ectopic pregnancy, where the baby develops in the fallopian tube rather than the womb. The tube had ruptured, causing internal bleeding. Not only did I lose the baby, but the doctors had to remove my damaged tube.'

Intent on telling Dimitri everything, Louise hadn't noticed him move until she suddenly found him beside her. His expression was tortured and her heart turned over when she was that his eyes were wet.

'Louise, *pedhaki*—' His voice cracked. 'The thought of you going through all that alone, without my support, rips me apart. If I had known I would have come to you—even if it had meant leaving my sister. You needed me, and I will never forgive myself for not being there, not helping you through the grief of losing our child.'

'It happened so quickly. I was rushed into surgery and there wasn't time to contact you. Afterwards I didn't answer your call. I couldn't. I was so unhappy I couldn't bear to speak of what had happened, and it seemed pointless to tell you about a baby that I was no longer carrying.'

She touched his damp face and felt tears slip down her own cheeks.

'I love you,' she whispered. 'I always have. Through all the years that we were apart you lived in my heart and you always will.' She pressed a finger against his lips when he made to speak. 'I saw the tender look on your face when you held Ana. You would be a wonderful father, Dimitri. But I might never be able to give you a child. Even if I did fall pregnant there is a strong risk that I could have another ectopic.'

Dimitri brushed away her tears and cupped her face in his hands.

'I love you,' he told her fiercely. 'I will love you if we have children and I will love you if we don't. No one can predict what the future holds. Perhaps we will be blessed with a family, but if we're not we'll deal with it together. What matters is that you love me, my golden girl. And I adore you, *kardia mou.*'

He slanted his lips over hers and kissed her, and it was the sweetest, gentlest, most beautiful kiss because it was given with love.

'I want to fall asleep with you in my arms every night and see your face on the pillow next to mine every morning,' he said deeply. 'I want you to be my friend and my lover and my one true love. Will you be my wife, Louise, and stay with me for ever?'

'Yes,' she said simply—because no other words were necessary when her love for him blazed in her eyes. And her tears were tears of joy as he slid the sapphire engagement ring onto her finger.

EPILOGUE

A YEAR later, Louise sat with her sister-in-law on the terrace of the old house on Eirenne and watched Dimitri playing with his niece on the beach.

'I can't believe Ana is walking already. She's growing up so quickly.' Ianthe sighed.

'In a few months she'll have a little brother or sister and you'll be glad she's walking.' Louise studied Ianthe's bump with interest. 'I wonder if this baby is a boy or girl.'

'Lykaios and I don't mind. But it would be nice for Theo to have a boy cousin—they could play football together.'

Louise laughed and looked down at her son, who was sleeping peacefully in her arms. 'It's hard to imagine Theo running around—he's only eight weeks old.'

She stroked her baby's downy soft cheek and his shock of dark hair. 'I can't get over how perfect he is.'

'Or how tiny!' Dimitri had joined them, and crouched down beside his wife and baby boy. 'Look how small his fingers are. He's amazing,' he murmured, still awed by the fact that he was a father.

'He's our little miracle,' Louise said softly. 'Although he didn't seem that little when I gave birth to him. The midwife said he was a good weight for a first baby.'

She met her husband's gaze and her heart gave a familiar flip at his sexy smile. They had married a month after

Dimitri had taken her to Eirenne. The wedding in Athens had been the quiet event they had both wanted, attended only by close family and friends. Benoit Besson had made the bride's dress and had given her away in a simple but emotional church ceremony. Louise had carried a bouquet of fragrant lilies and had worn her grandmother's diamond *fleur-de-lis* pendant, which had been a wedding gift from Dimitri.

'When I realised you had sold it to raise money for your mother's treatment I scoured every jeweller's shop in Paris and eventually found it,' he had explained, when she'd stared tearfully at the necklace sparkling in a black velvet case.

Louise had been delighted to have the memento of her grandmother once more, but something that had made her even happier was Dimitri's decision to donate the one million pounds she had returned to him to the cancer research project at the Paris hospital where her mother had been a patient. She loved him more and more with each passing day, and knew that he loved her just as deeply.

She turned her head from him to watch Ianthe, who was lifting her daughter into the pushchair.

'I'll take Ana back to the villa for her nap. You two must come and see her nursery and the rest of the Villa Aphrodite now that the decorators have finished.'

'We'll be over later,' her brother promised.

When Ianthe had gone, Dimitri took Theo from Louise and settled him in his pram. 'He should sleep for a while yet, don't you think?'

'Probably—he had a good feed. Why? What do you want to do?' Louise's pulse-rate quickened when Dimitri swept her up in his arms and laid her on a sun-lounger.

'What I always want to do and will never tire of doing,'

he murmured as he unclipped her bikini top. 'I want to love you—with all my heart and soul.'

'And your body, I hope,' she whispered against his lips.

The golden flecks in his eyes blazed with love and passion and teasing amusement. 'If you insist, *glikia mou*.'

* * * * *

LET'S TALK
Romance

For exclusive extracts, competitions and special offers, find us online:

f facebook.com/millsandboon

🐦 @MillsandBoon

📷 @MillsandBoonUK

Get in touch on 01413 063232

For all the latest titles coming soon, visit
millsandboon.co.uk/nextmonth

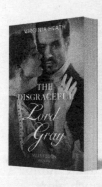

MILLS & BOON

THE HEART OF ROMANCE

A ROMANCE FOR EVERY KIND OF READER

MODERN

Prepare to be swept off your feet by sophisticated, sexy and seductive heroes, in some of the world's most glamourous and romantic locations, where power and passion collide.
8 stories per month.

HISTORICAL

Escape with historical heroes from time gone by. Whether your passion is for wicked Regency Rakes, muscled Vikings or rugged Highlanders, awaken the romance of the past.
6 stories per month.

MEDICAL

Set your pulse racing with dedicated, delectable doctors in the high-pressure world of medicine, where emotions run high and passion, comfort and love are the best medicine.
6 stories per month.

True Love

Celebrate true love with tender stories of heartfelt romance, from the rush of falling in love to the joy a new baby can bring, and a focus on the emotional heart of a relationship.
8 stories per month.

Desire

Indulge in secrets and scandal, intense drama and plenty of sizzling hot action with powerful and passionate heroes who have it all: wealth, status, good looks…everything but the right woman.
6 stories per month.

HEROES

Experience all the excitement of a gripping thriller, with an intense romance at its heart. Resourceful, true-to-life women and strong, fearless men face danger and desire - a killer combination!
8 stories per month.

DARE

Sensual love stories featuring smart, sassy heroines you'd want as a best friend, and compelling intense heroes who are worthy of them.
4 stories per month.

To see which titles are coming soon, please visit
millsandboon.co.uk/nextmonth

JOIN US ON SOCIAL MEDIA!

Stay up to date with our latest releases, author
news and gossip, special offers and discounts, and
all the behind-the-scenes action
from Mills & Boon...

 millsandboon

 millsandboonuk

 millsandboon

It might just be true love...

MILLS & BOON
True Love

Romance from the Heart

Celebrate true love with tender stories of
heartfelt romance, from the rush of falling
in love to the joy a new baby can bring,
and a focus on the emotional
heart of a relationship.

MILLS & BOON

MODERN

Power and Passion

Prepare to be swept off your feet by sophisticated, sexy and seductive heroes, in some of the world's most glamourous and romantic locations, where power and passion collide.